Robert Davies

The Life of Marmaduke Rawdon of York, or, Marmaduke Rawdon

The Second of that Name.

Robert Davies

The Life of Marmaduke Rawdon of York, or, Marmaduke Rawdon
The Second of that Name.

ISBN/EAN: 9783744778541

Printed in Europe, USA, Canada, Australia, Japan

Cover: Foto ©Raphael Reischuk / pixelio.de

More available books at **www.hansebooks.com**

THE LIFE

OF

MARMADUKE RAWDON OF YORK,

OR,

MARMADUKE RAWDON

THE SECOND OF THAT NAME.

NOW FIRST PRINTED FROM THE ORIGINAL MS. IN THE POSSESSION OF
ROBERT COOKE, ESQ. F.R.G.S.

EDITED BY

ROBERT DAVIES, ESQ. F.S.A.

PRINTED FOR THE CAMDEN SOCIETY.

M.DCCC.LXIII.

WESTMINSTER :
PRINTED BY JOHN BOWYER NICHOLS AND SONS,
25, PARLIAMENT STREET.

[NO. LXXXV.]

CONTENTS.

viii CONTENTS.

INTRODUCTION.

MARMADUKE RAWDON, whose biography, printed for the first time from the original MS., forms the volume now offered to the Camden Society, sprang from a younger branch of the ancient family of Rawdon or Rawden, which was seated for many centuries at a place of that name, situate in the parish of Guiseley in the West Riding of Yorkshire. "Near unto New-Lathes Bridge (Thoresby tells us in his quaint manner) the parish of Leedes is bounded with Rawden, which place gave name to a race of gentlemen, among whom Sir George Rawden was so deservedly famous for repulsing the Irish in the year 1641."[*] If reliance may be placed upon the authenticity of the pedigree printed by the Leeds historian, which, he says, he received from Madam Priscilla Rawden, the surviving sister of Sir George, there were twelve or thirteen generations of the lords of Rawden, commencing at the Norman Conquest, and coming down in an unbroken line to John Rawden, Esquire, who lived at Rawden in the reign of King Henry VIII., and had two sons named John and Ralph. JOHN, the elder son, succeeded to the family estate, and was the ancestor of Sir George Rawdon of whom Thoresby speaks—who was created a Baronet in 1665— and whose great-grandson, Sir John Rawdon, was the first

[*] Ducatus Leodiensis, or the Topography of the Town and Parish of Leedes in the West Riding of the County of York. By Ralph Thoresby, F.R.S. Folio. London, 1715, p. 868.

Earl of Moira. RALPH, the younger son, migrated from his paternal home in the West Riding, and settled at a place called Kepwick in the North Riding. He was the father of a second Ralph Rawdon, who, towards the close of the sixteenth century, was a country gentleman living at Stearsby, one of a number of small villages that lie nestled among the picturesque hills which form the north-eastern border of the great central plain of Yorkshire. Stearsby is not very far distant from Kepwick, which is situated near the southern extremity of the adjacent vale of Cleveland.

The second RALPH RAWDON had several sons. The eldest was Laurence Rawdon of York, who flourished in that city as a respectable merchant in the reigns of Queen Elizabeth and King James I. One of the younger sons was Sir Marmaduke Rawdon, the brave and zealous royalist of the time of King Charles I., who became as "deservedly famous" as the Leeds historian represents his kinsman Sir George Rawdon to have been at the same period.

Ralph Rawdon, of Stearsby, belonged to a numerous class of Yorkshire gentlemen of good family and small estate—the *gentes minores* of the county—who in the sixteenth and seventeenth centuries thought it no degradation to bring up their sons to the trade or commerce of the city. He bound his eldest son apprentice to a mercer or merchant at York; and in the year 1593 LAURENCE RAWDON was admitted to the city franchise and became a member of the Company of Merchant-Adventurers. A few years afterwards we find him married, and established in business.[a] His wife's name

---

[a] Laurence Rawdon ranked as a merchant, but his special business or trade was that which would now be called a wholesale grocer. Sugar, a costly luxury in those days, was one of the articles in which he dealt. Here is one of his bills for sugar-loaves supplied to the corporation to form part of a complimentary offering presented by the Lady

was Margery, daughter of William Barton esquire, the head of a
family which had long been seated at the village of Cawton, not far
distant from Stearsby. The Bartons of Cawton and Whenby were
of old gentilitial blood, and connected with the Danbys, the Picker-
ings, the Lascelleses, the Nortons, and others of the best families of
the North Riding.

Laurence Rawdon lived at York in the palmy days of that
" ancient and famous city,"[a] which, during the long and for the most
part peaceful reign of Elizabeth, had gradually attained a high
degree of material prosperity and social refinement. At the close
of the sixteenth century the commerce of the city was widely extended—her merchants were enterprising and affluent—her tradesmen numerous and thriving. The great Court of the Presidency
of the North had long been stationed at York. For nearly a
quarter of a century Henry Hastings, Earl of Huntingdon, a
learned and pious nobleman, had administered the affairs of the
vice-regal government. He and his countess, a sister of Queen
Elizabeth's former favourite Robert Dudley, Earl of Leicester,
passed great part of every year at the royal palace, called " the
King's Manor," which stood in close proximity to the city. They
drew around them a polished and brilliant society. The Court of

Mayoress of York, and the aldermen's ladies, to Lady Sheffield, the wife of the Lord
President of the North, upon her first coming to the Royal Manor at York in the year
1603.
    Bought of Laurance Rawdon,
        ij loves of superfine sewgar weinge xij[li]. xiiij[oz]., at xxiij[d]. per [li].   xxiiij[s]. ix[d].
    The following payment is entered in the account of the city chamberlains for the year
1606:
    To Lawrence Rawdon for xxviij[li]. v[oz]. of sugor, bestowed of Mrs. Mathew, my lord
archbusshop's wife, at her first coming to York, by my lady Mares & ladies, xlij[s]. iij[d].
    [a] See Memoir, p. 1, post.

the Lord President was composed of his executive council and a numerous staff of legal functionaries, many of whom were distinguished by rank and position in the county, or eminent for literary and professional acquirements. The accomplished and hospitable Archbishop Matthew Hutton was at the head of the church of York during part of this period, and he was succeeded by the witty and eloquent prelate, Tobie Mathew. The Deanery of York was held by Dr. John Thorneborough, who was at the same time Bishop of Limerick.[a] Among the dignitaries and ecclesiastical officers of the cathedral were many persons whose names are not unknown to fame—men celebrated as able theologians or skilful lawyers. Possessing social attractions and advantages unattainable by any mere provincial town, York was the constant resort of most of the principal families of the surrounding counties, and fully maintained her claim to be the Metropolis of the North.

The progress of the mercantile community of York in intelligence and respectability had kept pace with that of the higher classes, and the leading citizens were freely admitted into the social circle of their aristocratic neighbours. Many of the contemporaries of Laurence Rawdon, merchants and tradesmen who filled the more important municipal offices, acquired wealth by commercial enterprise, and became founders of families which subsequently rose to rank and distinction.[b] Laurence Rawdon's course of worldly prosperity

---

[a] Afterwards translated to the see of Bristol, and finally Bishop of Worcester.

[b] A single example may suffice. The late Thomas Philip Weddell Robinson, Earl de Grey, K.G. and his brother the late Frederick John Robinson, Earl of Ripon, were of the seventh generation in lineal male descent from William Robinson, a merchant and alderman of York, who died in the year 1616. His great-grandson Sir Metcalfe Robinson was created a Baronet in 1660. A century later, Thomas Robinson, the grandson of Sir Metcalfe, was advanced to the dignity of the peerage as Lord Grantham, and

was interrupted by his premature death. He was one of the sheriffs of the city in 1615, and was elected an alderman and took his seat on the magisterial bench in 1624. Within two years afterwards, before it came to his turn to occupy the civic chair, he died at the comparatively early age of 58.[a] His wife survived him, with four children, of whom, Marmaduke, the subject of the following memoir, was the youngest.

Young MARMADUKE RAWDON, his biographer tells us, "was brought up with all manner of learning that the City of York could afford." This, doubtless, means that he was a pupil in the grammar school of St. Peter of York, which was then, as it is now, one of the most celebrated places of education in the North of England. It had been established under the patronage of the Dean and Chapter of York at the time of the Reformation, and by a royal grant, made in the reign of Philip and Mary, was endowed with the house and possessions of the dissolved hospital of Saint Mary that stood near a place called the Horse-fair in the suburbs of the city. Fuller in his "Worthies of England,"[b] and Strype in his "Life of Sir John Cheke,"[c] have perpetuated the fame of the York school by particularising some of the eminent persons who were pupils there in the latter half of the sixteenth century, when Mr. John Pulleyn, B.A. was the master.[d] Mr. Pulleyn died in the year

afterwards succeeded to the baronetcy. The present Earl de Grey and Ripon, the great-grandson of the first Lord Grantham, enjoys the peerages of his father and uncle and the baronetcy of his more remote ancestor. Alderman William Robinson was a near neighbour of Laurence Rawdon. They lived and died in the same parish and were buried in the same church.

[a] He was buried in the parish church of Saint Crux at York on the 6th July, 1626.

[b] Ed. 1811, vol. ii. p. 540.   [c] Ed. 1705, p. 190.

[d] Thomas Morton, the eminent Bishop of Durham, whose father was a York merchant,

1590, and was succeeded in the office of " *ludimagister* of the free
school in the Horse-fayre," by the Reverend John Bayles, M.A.
The biographer of Marmaduke Rawdon, with a spice of pardonable
vanity, has recorded the names of such of his *condiscipuli* as he considered to be persons of consequence. The list includes several
youths who were connected with principal families of the city and
county.

Upon the death of his father, Marmaduke Rawdon, who had then
attained his sixteenth year, was suddenly removed from the quiet
routine of scholastic discipline in his native city to the activity of
mercantile life in the heart of what was even then the great metropolis. His uncle Marmaduke, afterwards Sir Marmaduke Rawdon,
who had risen to eminence as a London merchant, requested that
the boy might be committed to his parental care. Sir Marmaduke
gratefully remembered, that, when he was of the same age, his
elder brother Laurence had taken him to London, had placed
him in business there, and had thus laid the foundation of his fortunes.
He at once adopted his orphan nephew, and received him into his
family as one of his own children.

When the younger Marmaduke became a member of his uncle's
household, the London merchant was in the prime of life,
and at the height of prosperity. He had married a wealthy heiress,

was educated at York under Mr. Pulleyn. In a memoir of the bishop, published at York
in 1669, the author of which was his secretary and chaplain, we have this passage :—
" He was put to schoole to learne the English elements in the same city, where, as I have
heard him say, were his school-fellows Mr. Thomas Cheeke (after knighted by King
James) grandchild to that famous scholler Sir John Cheeke, and Guy Faux, who afterwards proved that famous and fatall incendiary in that never to be forgotten gunpowder
treason, which God Almighty, through King James his singular and divine wisdome, most
happily prevented and subverted."—The Life of Dr. Thomas Morton, Bishop of Duresme.
12mo. York, 1669, p. 4.

and was the father of a numerous family. He enjoyed the reputation of being one of the most enterprising and successful of
the English mercantile adventurers of his day. His transactions
extended to almost all parts of the known world. He traded largely
in the wines, both of France and the Peninsula, through agencies or
factories established at Bordeaux and Oporto. From the merchants
of Holland and the Netherlands he purchased the produce of the
vintages which flourished on the banks of the Rhine and its tribu-
taries. To encourage the introduction into this country of the wine
recently produced in the Canary Islands, he joined in forming an important factory at Teneriffe. He was among the earliest of the adventurers who invested capital in the cultivation of the sugar planta-
tions of the Island of Barbadoes.[a] It is said that he was one of the
first who rigged out a ship for the discovery of the North-West
Passage. He was a member of the Company of Turkey Merchants;
and he possessed the confidence of the French merchants who traded
with England, and acted as their friendly advocate when negotia-
tions with our government took them before the council-table. We

---

[a] Barbadoes was first settled under the authority of letters patent granted by James I.
A subsequent grant was made by Charles I. (See Verney Papers, ed. Camden Soc. p.
193, note.) We learn from the Calendar of State Papers, 1628-29, that Mr. Marmaduke
Rawdon was either sole or part owner of the following ships in the years 1626 and
1627:—

	Owners.	Names.	Tonnage.	Captains or Masters.
1626, Sept. 15.	Marmaduke Roydon, Rowland Wilson, and others.	Transport of London	200	Henry West.
1627, Jan. 30.	Marmaduke Roydon	Patience of London, George	300 80	Christopher Mitchell.
Feb. 21.	Marmaduke Roydon and others	Vintage of London	140	Richard West.

arc not surprised to be told that he was much esteemed by the royal favourite Buckingham, and that he received marked attention from both the great Duke's masters, King James I. and King Charles I.

That Mr. Rawdon was upon terms of friendly and familiar intercourse with the latter monarch is apparent from a letter addressed by him to the Secretary of State, Sir John Coke, which happens to be preserved among the State Papers of the year 1627.

Right Honorabl'.

After his maiestie had read that p't of the Spanish letter that is hear translated, his maiestie saide it was of great importance, and comaunded me and Capt. Marsh to deliver both the oregenall with the p't translaited, and this letter from the fathers at Rome, unto your honneur, till his further pleasure was known. Thes letters I had, wth a number of others, in a shipp wch we tooke at sea, with sugars newly comed from Brasill, and fynding it of consequenc I thought it my dewty to present it to his maiestie; thus humbly kissing your honeurs hands, I wish all health and good fortunes may attende you.

Your honeurs sarvantt to dispose of,

MARMADUKE RAWDON.

Tottnam, this 7th September, 1627.

(Addressed)

To the Right Honorabl'. Sir John Cooke, Knight, one of his maiesties secretary, att Tottnham, thes.

We gather from this letter that Mr. Rawdon and the captain of one of his merchant-ships had called at the palace and been admitted to an interview with the King. A Spanish vessel freighted with sugars from Brazil had been captured by the Englishman, and her papers seized. Among them were letters which the merchant thought of sufficient importance to be presented to the notice of his sovereign. The King was of the same opinion, and in the usual manner commanded them to be laid before his Secretary of State.

In the year 1628 Mr. Rawdon sat in the House of Commons as one of the representatives of the commercial and ship-building town of Aldborough in the county of Suffolk, but it does not appear that he was returned to any subsequent parliament. At an early period of his career he was made a member of the municipal corporation of the city of London, but upon being afterwards elected an alderman he refused to accept the office. As soon as he perceived that the citizens were "inclined to the parliament," he resigned his commission as one of the lieutenant-colonels of the city militia. Of his loyalty to the King, and his military services and bravery in the Civil War, I shall afterwards speak.

To enter into active life under the auspices of a relative who had attained so distinguished a position was an advantage of which the youth from Yorkshire was not slow to avail himself. By intelligence and aptitude for business he soon acquired the confidence of his uncle. In the spring of 1627, the year after his arrival in London, he was sent to Holland as supercargo of a small merchant-vessel, and during great part of that and the two following years was stationed at Bordeaux, where he transacted the commercial business of his relative and other English wine-merchants, under difficult circumstances, in a highly creditable manner. He had scarcely completed his twenty-first year when his uncle determined to intrust him with the management of his affairs in the island of Teneriffe. He embarked for the Canaries in April 1631, and it was not until he had been absent nearly seven years that he was recalled from his responsible post. Arriving in England in the early part of 1638, within a twelvemonth the urgency of his uncle's affairs again required his presence at Teneriffe, and he embarked on his second voyage to the Canaries in the spring of the following year. The memoir shows us the extent of the commercial relations that subsisted between this country and the Canaries during the long period of his second residence at Teneriffe. It seems to have been his principal occupation to superintend the business of the factory which had been established there by the English merchants for the general purposes of trade, and more especially for the manufacture and exportation of the wine produced upon the islands. This engagement did not, however, preclude him from entering into mercantile undertakings on his own account.

The importation of the wine of the Canary Islands into England was a branch of commerce that had risen into importance since the commencement of the seventeenth century. A grape, said to have been originally brought from Bacarach on the Rhine, was successfully cultivated upon the sunny slopes of Teneriffe, and one or two others of this group of volcanic islands, and was found to yield a potent and highly-flavoured wine peculiarly adapted to the English taste. Under the name of Canaries, or Canary Sack, or Malmsey, it soon obtained a large share of popular favour, and superseded to a great extent the thinner sacks imported from Spain and Portugal.[a] Howell, in his well-known letter upon wines addressed to Lord Clifford in the year 1634, says, " I think there's more Canary brought into England than into all the world besides. When Sacks and Canaries were brought in first among us, they were us'd to be drunk in *aqua-vitæ* measures, and 'twas held fit only for those to drink of them who us'd to carry their leggs in their hands, their eyes upon their noses, and an almanack in their bones: but now they go down every one's throat, both young and old, like milk."[b]

[a] " Your best sack is of *Zeres* in Spain—your smaller, of Galicia and Portugal—your strong sackes are of the islands of the Canaries and Malligo." Gervase Markham's English Housewife, 1st ed. 1631.

[b] Epistolæ Ho elianæ, ed. 1655, vol. ii. p. 71.

I do not find any notice of the use by the citizens of York of a wine under the denomination of Sekk or Seck earlier than about the middle of the sixteenth century.[a] On the festival of Corpus Christi in the year 1554, the Lady Mayoress and her sisters the wives of the aldermen, who were assembled to see the pageantry of the day, were treated at the expense of the city with a slight collation, or perhaps I ought rather to term it potation, consisting of $3\frac{1}{2}$ dozen gallons of ale, 6 gallons of clary wine, and 1 pottell of sekk. That sekk was then a rare luxury appears from the quantity introduced and its high price. The cost of the ale was threepence a gallon, and of the clary wine eightpence a gallon, but for the solitary " pottell of sekk" sixpence was paid, which was after the rate of two shillings a gallon. Upon a similar occasion thirty years later, the proportion of sekke allowed to the ladies was increased to a gallon, but there was no alteration of the price. In the following year a single pottel of "seck" cost one shilling and four pence. This was probably an exceptional case, for, although the price gradually advanced, it did not at the close of the century exceed three shillings a gallon. In the year 1596 the Lord Mayor and Corporation of York presented to Archbishop Matthew Hutton a "butt of seck," for which they paid to Mr. George Watkinson, one of the city sheriffs who was a

[a] The Spaniard made
  A shrugg and said,
After my pipe, come follow me ;
  Canary sack
  Did go to wrack ;
Some marchants went to Malago,
Some drown'd in good old Charnico ;
  A joyful sight to see.
     Shirley's Poems, ed. 1646, p. 28.

———— ———— thy iles shall lack
Grapes, before Herrick leaves Canarie sack.
     Hesperides, 1648.

,wine-merchant, the sum of 11*l*. 10*s*. The price of course varied according to the quality of the wine. In 1599, when Thomas Cecil, Lord Burghley, first came to York as Lord President of the Council of the North, the corporation propitiated him with a present of a " butt of seck " which cost 16*l*. 10*s*. At that time a pipe of ordinary Gascony wine cost no more than 10*l*. If it were of the finest vintage the price was 13*l*. 10*s*.

There can be little doubt that the wine here spoken of as " secke " was the produce of the vineyards of Spain and Portugal. The generous beverage that was so freely quaffed by Falstaff and his boon-companions under the name of sack was of this description. The few allusions made by Shakespeare to Canary wine are found only in his later plays; and these show that it was then used rather as a stimulating cordial or dram, than for ordinary refreshment. When Sir Toby taunts Sir Andrew Aguecheek with his timidity— " O knight, thou lack'st a cup of Canary: when did I see thee so put down?" he answers, " Never in your life, I think, unless you see Canary put me down." The Hostess says to Doll, " But, i'faith, you have drunk too much Canaries, and that's a marvellous searching wine, and it perfumes the blood ere one can say What's this ?" Canary sack was obviously used at first only in small quantities, or, as Howell describes it, " in *aqua-vitæ* measures."[a] But, after the accession of that certainly not abstemious monarch King James I., the wines of the Canaries were largely imported, and in the succeeding reign the rage for them became so universal as to occasion Howell to observe, that " there was a hundred times more drunk under the name of Canary than there was brought in."

[a] " The best attendance, the best drink, sometimes
Two glasses of Canary, and pay nothing."
Alchemist, act iii. sc. 4. 1610.

Mr. Rawdon's biography contains many proofs of the prosperous state of the trade up to the time of his quitting the islands. After the Restoration, when our commercial intercourse with the Spanish colonies was renewed, the English wine-merchants became desirous of reviving their trade with the Canaries. In 1664 Mr. Rawdon joined a Company which was established for that purpose, and subscribed 1500*l.* towards their capital. With some difficulty a royal charter of incorporation was obtained. But in the year 1666 the monopoly of the Canary Company was the subject of debate in the House of Commons, and they "voted it down." One of the charges against Lord Clarendon was that he took 4000*l.* for the Canary patent.

The sixteen years of Mr. Rawdon's second residence in Teneriffe were eventful years in England. When he left his native country in 1639 the clouds of political discontent had begun to gather. Soon the storm burst and carried away in its violence many of his friends and kindred. Among them was his uncle and benefactor the great and prosperous London merchant, who had never wavered in his attachment to the cause of his royal master. In 1643 he had hastened to the King at Oxford, and was made colonel of a regiment raised at his own cost. He took a gallant part in the defence of Basing House, and was rewarded for his services with the empty honour of knighthood. In 1645 he was made governor of the little town of Faringdon in Berkshire, which he held for the King with distinguished bravery and success. But he sank under the fatigues of a military life, was stricken with sickness at Faringdon, and died at his post in the month of April, 1646.

Thomas Rawdon, the eldest son of Sir Marmaduke, was no whit behind his gallant parent in loyalty and devotion to his sovereign. He held the rank of colonel in the royal army—fought in both the

fights of Newbury, and accepted many dangerous commissions for
the service of the King. Having thus become a marked man, he fled
from the persecution of the ruling powers, and took refuge with
his kinsman, and younger brother, in the Canaries. By them he
was cordially received, and entertained for a considerable time with
princely hospitality.[a]

The example of their relatives in England does not appear
to have excited any emulation on the part of the absentees at
Teneriffe. We do not learn from Mr. Rawdon's biography
that during all the troubles of the Civil War it ever entered
into his contemplation that loyalty to his sovereign or affection for
his kindred had any claim upon his help or active sympathy. He
must have been well informed of all that happened whilst he was
absent, yet he betrays no inclination to quit his luxurious abode
among the Fortunate Islands of the Atlantic, or to take a share in
the dangers and conflicts at home. It was a solitary instance of his
having manifested any kindly feeling or remembrance when he
dispatched his kinsman to England as the bearer of a present to
Sir Marmaduke Rawdon. The brave old merchant received his
son at Basing House, where he was stationed as one of the com-
manders of the garrison. The chain of gold his nephew had sent to
him he readily accepted, but with noble independence and touching
loyalty he rejected the heap of glittering coins that his son poured
out upon the table before him,—all, save a few of the best of
them, which he desired to keep that he might convert them into a

---

[a] In the "Catalogue of Lords, Knights, and Gentlemen who have compounded for
their estates" (London, 1655) are these names :—

Rawdon, Thomas, of London, merchant	£400 0 0
Royden, Marmaduke, Del. (per Edmund Hardman and William Green)	£559 3 2

medal of the King's portrait to be worn as a pendant from the chain.[a]

Mr. Rawdon's indifference did not escape the notice of his friends at home. His continued absence was felt, and perhaps resented, as something like a desertion. One or two hints to that effect are given in the poetical tribute sent to him by his former pastor, the honest vicar of Broxbourne, which was written soon after the battle of Marston Moor, when the fatal result of "Charles's struggle for the crown" had become but too apparent.

The couplets,

> Duke! thou art safe in the Canaries,
> Whilst England's vexèd with contràries,

and

> Thou hast left us in the lurch,
> I am no vicar of a church;

imply a reproach of the person to whom the lines are addressed, and show that the poet himself had not escaped the sad effects of the times.[b]

It must be acknowledged that Mr. Rawdon's was an enviable lot. Whilst his friends in England were steeped to the lips in misery, he was passing his time at Teneriffe in the peaceful enjoyment of all the luxuries that a delicious climate, a beautiful country, a princely residence, and an ample income could impart. By his talents for business, his active habits, and his courageous bearing, he had gained a high reputation in the islands, and had acquired great ascendancy over all classes of the inhabitants, whether native Canarians or English colonists. To his desire to promote the welfare of the people around him we may trace the chief source

---

[a] Memoir, p. 33 post. [b] Memoir, p. 33 post.

of his influence. Among other benefits conferred upon them by his exertions and liberality, the appointment of an English clergyman as chaplain to his own countrymen, and the introduction of an English physician for the advantage of the whole community, must have been felt as boons of inestimable value.

Mr. Rawdon's biographer gives us a relation of numerous " actions done by him " during his residence at Laguna.[a] One of his boldest exploits was his ascent of the Peak of Teneriffe. The route he took to the summit of the volcano was the same as that followed by Glas a century later, and by Humboldt and other travellers of modern times. In the account of Mr. Rawdon's ascent we cannot expect to meet with scientific observations or precise descriptions of natural objects; but, on comparing his slight notices of what he saw with the more exact and extended narrative of either Glas or Humboldt, we discover very few, if any, points of substantial variance. The desire of the ambitious Englishman to, become the highest man in the world by mounting upon the shoulders of the tallest of his party when they had arrived at the summit of the Peak, is an amusing trait of character.

At length Mr. Rawdon was compelled to take his departure from the Canaries. Our quarrel with Spain left him no choice but to relinquish his appointments, and to bid farewell to the delightful spot where he had so long dwelt, and to the people who had so long looked up to him as a benefactor. In the year 1656 Mr. Rawdon, accompanied by his kinsman and namesake Marmaduke, arrived once more in his native country. Open political strife had for the time subsided under the strong government of Cromwell. The widow of the brave royalist Sir Marmaduke Rawdon was still alive and residing

[a] Memoir, p. 42 post.

in her husband's old mansion at Hoddesdon, in the possession of which she had not been disturbed. There she received the long absent travellers with a noble welcome.

Mr. Rawdon lived thirteen years after his last return to England. Being unmarried he formed no domestic establishment of his own, but took up his abode chiefly with his kinsman Marmaduke, who after his marriage built a house at Hoddesdon for his own residence. Here the elder Marmaduke spent his time in the quiet enjoyment of the leisure and fortune which his previous labours had secured. He took great delight in travelling. The extracts given by his biographer from the journals of his various tours contain much interesting information. We might have excused him had he introduced more sparingly the knowledge he derived from books only, but he describes the objects he saw simply and clearly, and expresses his opinions in a lively and interesting manner. His name will take a respectable place in the scanty list of early British tourists who have left any record of their travels.

Although the party feeling occasionally displayed in the memoir is that of a decided royalist, all allusions to events or circumstances which are not of a strictly personal or local character are studiously avoided. With subjects religious or political, except in a very few instances, neither Mr. Rawdon nor his biographer presumes to meddle. The memoir is chiefly to be prized for presenting a series of vivid and truthful sketches of social and domestic life and manners, both in town and country, during a considerable part of the seventeenth century. These sketches would have been more acceptable had the details been given with greater exactness, and had the colouring been somewhat hieghtened. But we must be

grateful for them as valuable contributions to a department of litera-
ture every day becoming more sought for and appreciated.

The biographer informs us that when Mr. Rawdon was at home
he spent the most part of his time in his closet reading or writing,
"being naturally inclined to study," and that he had compiled
several books of his own collections. The memoir now printed is
obviously a compilation from materials furnished by the MS. collections and memoranda here referred to, which were probably put
together in his lifetime, and perhaps under his own eye. From one
or two passages it may be inferred that the writer had been one of
Mr. Rawdon's companions at Teneriffe, and a witness of some of the
scenes he describes. This would lead to a conjecture that the
biography was from the pen either of his kinsman Marmaduke
Rawdon the younger, or his friend Marmaduke Harrison, the
Yorkshire gentleman with whom he had been acquainted in his
youth, and who held a confidential appointment in his household
during his second residence at Teneriffe. The writer makes frequent
allusions to Mr. Rawdon's journals and collections, and speaks of a
"brief history of cathedrals" which he had compiled. From
another source we learn that besides these works Mr. Rawdon was
the author of a "genealogical memoir of the family of Rawdon,"
which he had intended for the press, if not for publication. It was
to have been illustrated with portraits of himself and of other
members of the family, of which several had already been engraved
by the well-known artist Robert White.[a]

[a] The following is a list of the Rawdon portraits which were once brought together at
Sledmere, in the marvellous collection of engravings formed by the late Sir Mark Master-
man Sykes :—

1. Lawrence Rawdon, Alderman of York. Died at York 25th July, 1626. By
A. Hertocks.

Nearly half a century after the death of Mr. Rawdon, his MSS. were in the possession of Samuel Bagnall, esquire, a gentleman residing in London, whose wife was the granddaughter of Colonel

2. Marmaduke Rawdon, son of that worthy gentleman Laurence Rawdon, late of the cittie of Yorke, alderman. By R. White.

3. Robert Rawdon, governor of Saint Thomas's Hospital. Died 15th Sept. 1644. *A. Hertocks fec.*

4. The true and lively portraiture of the most virtuous Lady Elizabeth Rawdon, wife to that most valliant collonel and worthy knight Sir Marmaduke Rawdon of Hodsden in Hartfordshire. Ætatis suæ 76. *R. White sculp.*

5. Collonel Thomas Rawdon, eldest son of that worthy knight Sir Marmaduke Rawdon. He died at Hodsden 30th July, 1666. Ætat. 54. By R. White.

6. Marmaduke Rawdon of Hodesdon, esquire, second son to that valiant colonel and worthy knight Sir Marmaduke Rawdon, born in London 16th August, 1621. By R. White.

7. Katharine Bowyer, one of the daughters of Sir Marmaduke Rawdon, knight, and wife to William Bowyer of Laytonstone in Essex, esquire. *R. White sculp.*

8. Martha Williams, one of the daughters of Sir Marmaduke Rawdon, knight, and wife to Thomas Williams, gentleman, the fourth son of Sir Henry Williams of Gwernent in Brecknockshire, knight and baronet. *R. White sculp.*

9. Elizabeth Rawdon, wife to Mr. William Rawdon of Bermondsey. *R. White delin. and sculp.*

10. Sara Rawdon, wife to Marmaduke Rawdon of Hodsden, esquire. *R. White sculp.*

Such was the rarity of these engravings that, when the Sledmere collection was dispersed by auction in March 1824, they were sold for five guineas each. The only Rawdon portrait I have found in the print-room of the British Museum is a small one of Sir George Rawdon :—" The true and lively pourtraiture of that valliant and worthy patriot and captaine Sr George Rawdon, knight and barronet. Ætatis suæ 63." *R. White delin. et sculp.* The armorial bearings used by the elder branch of the family are placed within an oval beneath the portrait: Quarterly, 1. Argent, a fess between three pheons sable, *Rawdon;* 2. Argent, a fess between two lions passant regardant sable, *Folifoot;* 3. Argent, a chevron between three hind's heads erased gules, *Beckwith;* 4. On a fess three escallops, a canton ermine. On an inescutcheon the badge of a baronet of England. Crest, a pheon. Motto, " Nisi Dominus frustra."

Thomas Rawdon, the eldest son of Sir Marmaduke. In August, 1712, Ralph Thoresby, the Leeds historian, was permitted by Mr. Bagnall to inspect the collection,[a] and his extracts from some of the MSS. are made use of both in his own great work, Ducatus Leodiensis, and in the notices of Sir George Rawdon, which Bishop Gibson introduced into his edition of Camden's Britannia. When the editor of Wotton's Baronetage, which was published in 1741, was collecting materials for that useful work, the Rawdon MSS. appear to have been still in the possession of Mr. Bagnall. With their subsequent history the owner of the work now printed is unacquainted. By what fortunate accident this one manuscript emerged from its hiding place, and escaped the destruction which too probably was the fate of the rest, we have no means of discovering.

The brief account, with which the memoir concludes, of the circumstances attending the last illness of Mr. Rawdon, and of the particulars of his will, is written by a different hand, and seems to have been added a short time after his death. The will itself is an interesting document, abounding in genealogical evidences, and in curious illustrations of the manners of the time. It is worthy of being printed at length:—

In the name of God, almighty and all merciful. I, Marmaduke Rawdon, of London, merchant, sonne of Laurence Rawdon, late of the city of York,

[a] "August 7th, 1712. Evening at Mr. Bagnal's, who obliged me with the sight of some curious manuscripts relating to the Rawdons, his wife's family."

"August 8. Evening a little at the Grecian coffee-house with Dr. Sloane; was pleased in reading manuscript memoirs of the ancient family of the Rawdens, of Rawden in Yorkshire, of which Sir George, Sir Marmaduke, Colonel Rawden, and Mr. Marmaduke Rawden, the benefactor at York, were particularly memorable." Diary of Ralph Thoresby, vol. ii. p. 154.

alderman, being at present, blessed bee God, in perfect health both of body and mind, yet mindful of my own mortalitie, doe by this my last will and testament thus dispose of my selfe and the poore things I shall leave behind mee. First, my soule I bequenth to the imortal God my Maker, Father of our Lord Jesus Christ, my Blessed Redeemer and Mediator, through his all sole sufficient satisfaction for the sinns of the whole world and efficient for his elect, in the number of whome I am one by his mercy and grace, and thereof most unremoveably assured by his Holy Spiritt the One Eternal Comforter. My body I bequeath to the earth, and, if I shall end my transitory days at or neare York, I desire to be buried in Crux Church in the chancell, in the same grave where my deare father and mother and most of my family have been buried, or as nigh them as conveniently may bee, expecting a joyful resurrection with them in the day of Christ. But if I should die at Hodsden Town I shall desire to bee buried in the chancell of Broxbourne church, as neare my cossen Bowyer as conveniently may bee. Item, I give and bequeath to the sonnes and daughter of Sir Roger Jaques, vizt. Roger, Henry, William, Robert, and Grace, twenty shillings a peece to buy them a gold ringe in full of what they may expect from mee either of goods or lands: Item, I give unto my aunt, Lady Rawdon, tenn pounds for mourning: Item, I give unto Collonell Thomas Rawdon, to his son Marmaduke, his daughter Elizabeth, and to his wife thirty pounds for mourning, and to his sonne Marmaduke my emerald ringe with the Rawdon's arms, which I desire may goe to his eldest sonne, and soe successively to the heirs of the family: Item, I give unto my cossen Bevill Rawdon my great ringe of diamonds with the King's picture in it, my silver cuppes with salt cellar and candle sticke in them, and pepper box, one of my Spanish rapiers and dagger, and my leather boracha.[a] Item, I give unto my cossen Mrs. Katherine Bowyer my drinking cup of pure gold and my great cupp of mother of pearle set in silver and guilt, and tenn pounds for mourninge: Item, I give unto Mrs. Elizabeth Forster tenn pounds for mourninge: Item, I give unto Mrs. Jane Crew and her husband twenty pounds for mourning, and I forgive them

---

[a] Borrácha (Span.), a leathern bag or vessel used for holding wine in travelling.

what they owe mee upon bond; also I give unto my said cossen Jane Crow my great gold tooth picker, or three pounds in gold for default of it: Item, I give unto Mrs. Martha Williams fifty pounds, and tenn pounds for mourninge, and my gold hatbande of small links to make her braceletts, and for default of it tenn pounds: Item, I give unto her sonne Mr. David Williams tenn pounds: Item, I give unto my cossen Allington and his wife tenn pounds for mourning: Item, I give unto my cossen Mr. William Bowyer five pounds for mourning, and to his sister Kate, and the rest of his brothers, five pounds a peece: Item, I give unto Mr. Thomas Boycott, and Mr. Nathaniel Fen his brother, five pounds a peece: Item, I give unto my cossen William Rawdon and to his wife twenty pounds for mourning; more I give unto his said wife one hundred pounds, and to each of his sons living at my death fifty pounds; only to my godson Laurence I give one hundred pounds, and to each of his daughters twenty pounds a peece, the interest of the money to be paid them yearly towards their maintenance by my executors, and the principal to be given them when the sonns come of age, and the daughters theirs when they come at age or marry: Item, I give unto my cossen Raphe Trattle and his wife, if living at my death, ten pounds a peece for mourning: Item, I give unto my cossen Mrs. Mary Fellows five pounds for mourning: Item, I give unto my cossen Mrs. Jane Tice [a] five pounds: Item, I give unto my cossens Christopher Hebden, William Hebden, and Thomas White, a silver tankard of five pounds a piece, to each, and that my arms bee engraven on them before they bee given them by order of my executors, and to every one of their children twenty shillings a peece: Item, I give unto my cossen Mrs. Anne Brice, wife to Mr. Francis Brice, my ring with five faucett diamonds, and for the defect thereof ten pounds to buy another: Item, I give unto the eldest sonne, or daughter if no sonne, of Mr. John Harrison of Bransbie five pounds, for the great love I have for their uncle my stuart Marmaduke Harrison: Item, I give unto my cossen Mrs. Elizabeth Templer my orientall emerall ringe, and in default of it five pounds: Item, I give unto my Lady Hewley, wife unto Sir John Hewley,[b] my great jewill of gold

---

[a] Probably Brice.

[b] Sir John Hewley, knight, a Puritan lawyer, who settled in York some years prior to

with King David his picture offeringe his heart to God, as a token of the great love and service I have had always towards her: Item, I give to the parish of Crux in the citty of York, where I was borne, one hundreth pounds to be imployed in land, and the rent thereof to be equally divided for serving every Sunday, to bee imployed in penny loaves of bread and given every Sunday in the forenoone in the church after sermon or service by the churchwardens, or whome they shall appoint, amongst the poore of the parish, and this to be soe ordered that it may bee a perpetual rent for ever: Item, I give sixty pounds to the cittie of York to be imployed in a gold chaine to be worne by the Lady Maioresse successively: Item, I give to the said cittie four hundred pounds for the buying those houses which belonged to Mr. Scott next Allhallowes, for them all to be puld downe to enlarge the Pavement, and what the materials of the old houses may come to, be toward making a Crosse or shelter for the markett people that sell meale and corne: Item, I give unto the said cittie one drinking cup of pure gold of the vallew of one hundred pounds, which I desire my executor to have handsomely made, and the cittie armes and my armes graven upon it, " This is the guift of Marmaduke Rawdon, sonne of Laurence Rawdon, late of this cittie, alderman;" alsoe, I give unto the said cittie a silver chamber pott of the value of tenn pounds, booth which are to goe from Lord Maior to Lord Maior, and if these two bee converted to any other use the

the Restoration, was the son of a country gentleman seated at Wistow in the West Riding. He was nearly related to the Hewleys of York, who were drapers or cloth merchants residing in Mr. Rawdon's native parish of St. Crux. Sir John was made a freeman of York in 1659 that he might be qualified for the appointment of city-counsel, which the corporation conferred upon him at that time. He represented the city in the parliaments of 1678, 1679, and 1681. He was also recorder of Doncaster. His wife, Dame Sarah Hewley, of whom Mr. Rawdon speaks with so much affection, was a wealthy heiress, the only child of Robert Wolryche, esquire, of Gray's Inn. The noble manner in which, after the death of her husband, she devoted her large estates to pious and charitable uses, became well known a few years ago by the protracted litigation of which they were the subject. Sir John Hewley died at Bell Hall, a country house he had built a few miles from York, on the 24th August, 1697, at the age of 78. Lady Hewley died at York on the 23rd August 1710. My friend the Reverend James Raine in his " Memoir of Mr. Justice Rokeby " (Surtees Society Publications, vol. 37) has printed several letters addressed by Lady Hewley to Sir Thomas and Lady Rokeby, which show the deep piety of her life and character.

vallew thereof to return to my executor or his heirs: Item, I give to the
poore of Bransbie and Stearsbie, where my dear father was borne, and to
the parish of Cawton, where my good mother was borne, five pounds a
peece to be disposed of as my cossens Hebdens of Stersbie, and cosen
Barton of Cawton, shall think fitt: Item, I give unto Mary Low, once servant to my sister the Lady Jaques, five pounds for the great care shee had
of me when I was sicke at Yorke: Item, I give towards the repairing of
the chappel in the towne of Hodsden tenn pounds: Item, I give unto my
godsonne, Marmaduke Rawdon, sonne of Robert Rawdon of Yorke, pinner,
tenn pounds to bind him aprentice, or towards his learning if hee intend
to be a schollar, and fifty pounds when he is out of his tyme to sett upp
with, or at [one] and twenty years of age if hee bee a scholler: Item, I
give unto my nephew Mr. William Jaques, and to Mrs. Margarett Browne,
tenn pounds a peece for mourning. Also it is to bee understood that if
any of the persons concerned in these legacies die before mee, it is not to
goe to their heires, but to my executors; only the silver tankard, if cosen
Hebdens and cosen White bee dead, I desire they may be given to their
wives: Item, I give unto my cosen Raphe Trattle the elder, if living at my
death, besides the mourning, my furr coate with the fower dozen of pure
gold buttons uppon it: also I desire my executor to bestowe one hundred
[pounds] or thereabouts upon a monument in Broxborne church, in that
east windowe where Mr. Baily lieth buried, which may correspond with
the monument of Sir Robert Cock on the other side, which I give in
memory of my ever honoured uncle Sir Marmaduke Rawdon, where I
would fane Sir Marmaduke's pictures and my ladies cutt at length in
marble, with their sonne and daughters, as the stone cutter and my executor shall best advise: alsoe, hard by the great windowe in the chancell,
to correspond with my cossen Bowyer's monument, I desire there may bee
imployed twentie or thirty pounds in a small monument, about the bigness
of my cossen Bowyer's, in memory of me, with my picture halfe body, or
without it, as may be thought most convenient, given therein a relation
whose sonne I was, and something of my travells abroad in Holland,
Flanders, France, and the dominions of Spain:[a] Item, I give unto Mrs.

---

[a] It may be doubted whether any of the sepulchral monuments which the testator

Martha Williams more than is already given her my silver sugar box which was her owne, and the sugar spoone in it. All the rest of my lands, goods, debts, monies, plate, jewells, and household stuffe unbequeathed, I give and bequeath, my debts if any appeare and my legacies being first paid, unto my loveing cossen Marmaduke Rawdon, second son of Sir Marmaduke Rawdon of Hodsden, knight, to him and his heirs for ever, for the great love and affection [which] hath been always betwixt us, and for other good causes mee thereunto moveing, whome I make the sole executor of this my last will and testament, whome I desire to bee carefull to see all my will performed; and I do revoke and annul all former wills by me made, and this only to stand good. Witness my hand and seale in London the nineteenth June 1665.—MARMADUKE RAWDON—and signed, sealed, published, and declared as my last will and testament in the presence of Tho. Savage, Thomas Boycott. I give unto Mr. Hugh Hassall my plaine gold ring with the King's picture and five pounds for mourning.

MARMADUKE RAWDON.

Proved in the Prerogative Court of Canterbury, 19th February, 1668, by Marmaduke Rawdon the executor.

The will of Mr. Rawdon is singularly characteristic. It displays his pious and benevolent disposition, his unbounded affection for his kindred, and his deep reverence for the memory of his father. Whilst his various bequests to the city of York manifest his strong attachment to the place of his birth, we may trace in them that gallantry to the softer sex, and that love of personal display, of which the memoir affords numerous examples. His taste for the convivialities of social life is evinced by his desire to add to the state and splendour of those civic feasts for which York was distinguished, and at which he had been a frequent guest.

The gold chain, purchased with the legacy he bequeathed for that

wished to be placed in Broxbourne church, were ever executed. None such are now to be found there.

purpose, is yet carefully preserved, and adorns the person of every Lady Mayoress of York in succession, upon all occasions of ceremony. The drinking-cup of pure gold, which he desired his executor to provide, bearing the arms and inscription he directed to be engraved upon it, continues to be one of the most valued objects in the handsome collection of plate belonging to the city. It has been constantly used by the corporation for nearly two centuries as their *poculum caritatis*, or loving-cup.

The market-cross upon the Pavement, which Mr. Rawdon probably intended to be the most enduring memorial of himself, was built in accordance with his wish, but has since been wholly removed.

An intention to benefit the inhabitants of his native city by increasing the accommodation of their market-place had been expressed some years earlier by a greater man than Mr. Rawdon. In Sir Thomas Widdrington's MS. history of York the following passage occurs:—"The Pavement, which is the chief market-place, is not very large. The learned Dr. Thomas Morton, Bishop of Durham,[a] who was born in this city, did purpose to have bestowed some considerable cost in the enlarging of it, but one who was the owner of a house which he intended to have bought and pulled down for that purpose, stood upon so high terms in the sale of it, that this good purpose was frustrated."[b] The circumstance here alluded to happened a short time previous to the commencement of the civil war.

[a] Thomas Morton, bishop of Coventry and Lichfield, translated to the see of Durham in 1632, died 22 September, 1659, ætat. 95. Le Neve's Fasti Eccles. Angl. ed. Hardy, vol. iii. p. 296.

[b] Sir Thomas Widdrington, the well-known Speaker of the House of Commons, and Lord Keeper of the great Seal in the time of the Commonwealth, was recorder of York from 1638 to 1658. His valuable work entitled "Analecta Eboracensia, or some Remains of the antient City of York" has never been printed, although several MS. copies are still in existence. Mr. Drake borrowed largely from his predecessor.

In September 1640 the corporation at the request of Bishop Morton made an attempt to purchase the house on the Pavement on the bishop's behalf, but were unsuccessful. Thirty years later, by the liberality of Mr. Rawdon, they were enabled to accomplish that object which the good bishop probably lost sight of when evil days arrived, and his attention was directed to more momentous concerns. In February 1671, having received Mr. Rawdon's legacy, the corporation appropriated the greater part of the money to the purchase of several houses which stood at the east end of the church of All Saints Pavement, and were then the property of Lady Scott, the widow of Alderman Scott, and her son Mr. Joseph Scott. A few months afterwards the site was cleared, and the building of a new market-cross commenced "according to a draught shewn thereof by Mr. Thomas Mann." In the following year the cross was completed. A curious description of this useful structure, probably written by the architect himself, is preserved in a nearly contemporary manuscript [a] belonging to the Dean and Chapter of York:—

The Description of ye Cross in ye Pavement of Yorke.

It's a commendable piece of architecture; the ichnography or ground plan is a quadrate or right angled square, to which you ascend by two stepps: upon the area (or the flower) of the uppermost is erected 12 columes or pillars crowned with architrave, freese, and cornise; upon the cornise is erected a tarrase or battlement, not with ballisters or indented, as has formerly been used, but with a pedistall or foot of a pillar perpendicular over every collume, whose breadth agrees with the naked of the colume above, open'd before into a pannell and with sollid pannells betwixt, only the pedestalls breake before the pannells, as also the coronett or small cornice which covers it; upon every breake or pedestall stands the forme of an urne (or flower pot rather) for finishing: the rafters of the roofe

[a] MS. $\frac{XVI}{I}$ in the Minster library, described as "Drake's History of York." See Eboracum, p. 189, note, where Mr. Drake acknowledges his obligations to this manuscript, which was then in his hands, the collector, he says, unknown.

make a semicircle from the one side to the other (like unto a cupolo) or round loover, on each side or face of which is a lucia window finished with pedamett or cornice; and on the side next the markett stands the head or effigie of Mr. Rawdon the donor, with an inscription showing the same, in the centre of which roofe rises a turret octa-angular, finished on each angle with pillasters which revolves into scrowles, on which is 4 quadrans or sun dyalls, lanskipt with several inscriptions; (*i.e.*) on the east quadran EHEU FUGACES, on the south quadran DUM SPECTUS FUGIO, on the west quadran FUGIT HORA ORA, on the north quadran TEMPUS EDAX RERUM. On his pedestalls below and above is finished with architrave, freese, and cornice, with breaks about the head of each pillaster, and is rooft with a cupullo of the same angles, upon which is a flower pott, in the centre of which is fixed the standard for the ffaine, on each side of which is sett of with scrowl'd worke of iron E. W. N. S. signifying or showing the 4 cardinall winds or quarters of the horrizon; above is the ffaine, upon which is depicted 1672, being the year in which it was built. Upon the pavement below, and equa-distant from each side, is erected 5 or 6 stepps of stone quaderanguler in the center of the area; above is erected a newell octa-angular, about which rises a pair of winding staires of the same angles and finisht with rayles and ballisters on the outside, by which you ascend into the roofe or chamber above.

Half a century ago, by an order of the corporation, Pavement Cross was taken down and the materials sold. A single vestige of it that escaped from the spoiler, is a portion of the stone architrave thus inscribed:[a]—

MARMADUKE RAWDON, DECEASED, SONNE OF
LAURENCE RAWDON, LATE ALDERMAN OF
THIS CITTY, WAS FOUNDER OF THIS CROSS.
ERECTED IN Y° MAIIORALTY OF WILLIAM RICHARDSON IN Y° YEAR 1671,
FINISHED IN Y° MAIIORALTY OF S[r] HENRY THOMSON, JUNIOR, KT. IN Y° YEAR
1672.

[a] William Frederick Rawdon esquire, of York, the present representative of one of the numerous branches of the family of Rawdon, preserved this relic from destruction and judiciously consigned it to the care of the Yorkshire Philosophical Society, in whose collection of antiquities it is now placed.

The only sepulchral memorial of Mr. Rawdon, now known to exist, is the marble slab which covers his grave in the chancel of the church of Broxbourne, bearing this inscription:—

GLORIOSÆ RESURRECTIONIS FIDUCIÂ HAC IN URNÂ SE REPOSUIT
MARMADUKE RAWDON, FILIUS LAURENTII RAWDON CIVIT. EBORACI ARM.
VIR TAM GENERE QUAM INGENIO CLARUS,
IN DEUM PIUS, IN PROXIMUM CHARUS,
IN AFFINES COMIS, IN EGENOS LIBERALIS,
TAM EXTERIS QUAM SUIS NOTUS, ET AB UTRISQUE DILECTUS.
QUI ULTRA 58 ÆTATIS SUÆ ANNUM EXPIRANS CÆLEBS
HINC MIGRAVIT AD CÆLUM, FEB. 7, 1668.

However imperfectly my editorial task may have been performed, I have had much pleasure in assisting to present to the members of the Camden Society THE LIFE OF MARMADUKE RAWDON OF YORK. By committing it to the press the Society has conferred an honour upon the city from whence he sprang, and has used the most effectual means of perpetuating the memory of one of her most generous benefactors.

I desire gratefully to record my obligations to my friends, John Bruce, esquire, the Director of the Camden Society, Professor Phillips of Oxford, the Rev. James Raine of York, and John Gough Nichols, esquire, for information kindly afforded to me during the progress of my work; and also to the Reverend George H. Dashwood of Stow Bardolph, for having allowed me the use of the illuminated Roll of the pedigree of Rawdon, exemplified by Sir John Borough, Garter, which was exhibited at the Society of Antiquaries in 1862. ROBERT DAVIES.

The Mount, York, 30th April, 1863.

PEDIGREE OF RAWDON.

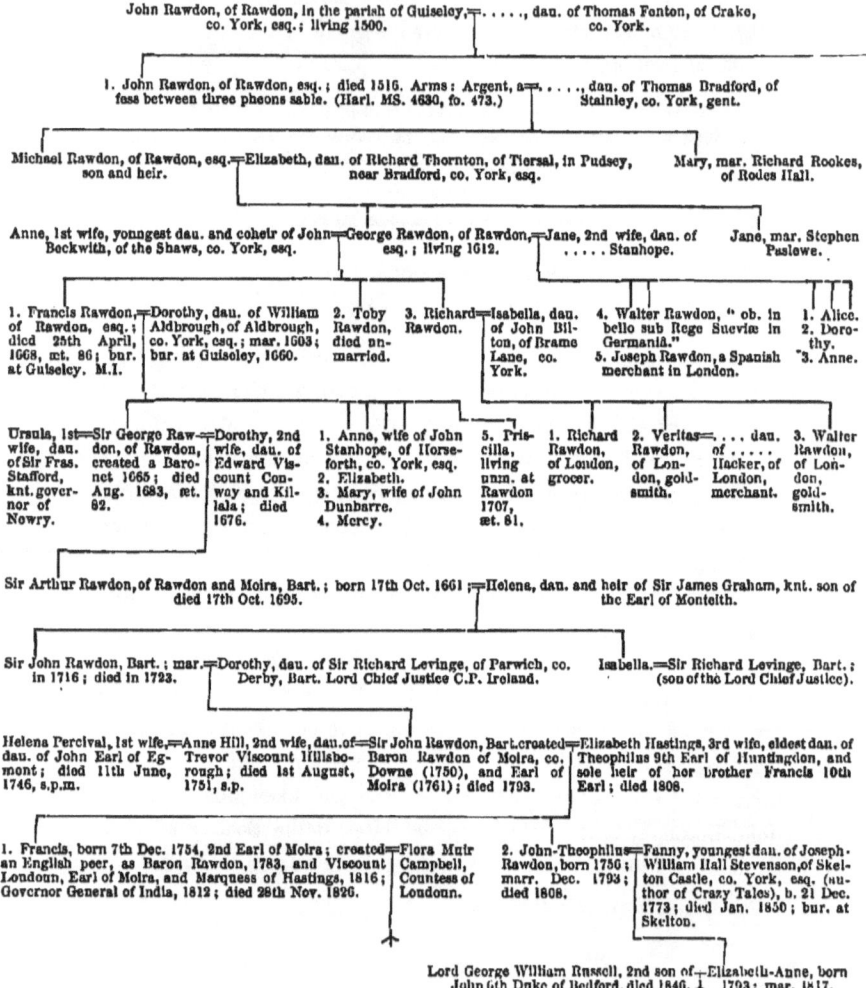

John Rawdon, of Rawdon, in the parish of Guiseley,═ . . . . ., dau. of Thomas Fenton, of Crake, co. York, esq.; living 1500. || co. York.

1. John Rawdon, of Rawdon, esq.; died 1515. Arms : Argent, a═ . . . . ., dau. of Thomas Bradford, of fess between three pheons sable. (Harl. MS. 4630, fo. 473.) || Stainley, co. York, gent.

Michael Rawdon, of Rawdon, esq.═Elizabeth, dau. of Richard Thornton, of Tiersal, in Pudsey, son and heir. || near Bradford, co. York, esq. || Mary, mar. Richard Rookes, of Rodes Hall.

Anne, 1st wife, youngest dau. and coheir of John═George Rawdon, of Rawdon,═Jane, 2nd wife, dau. of Beckwith, of the Shaws, co. York, esq. || esq.; living 1612. || . . . . . Stanhope. || Jane, mar. Stephen Paslewe.

1. Francis Rawdon,═Dorothy, dau. of William of Rawdon, esq.; || Aldbrough, of Aldbrough, died 25th April, || co. York, esq.; mar. 1603; 1668, æt. 86; bur. || bur. at Guiseley, 1660. at Guiseley, M.I. || 2. Toby Rawdon, died un-married. || 3. Richard═Isabella, dau. Rawdon. || of John Bil-ton, of Brame Lane, co. York. || 4. Walter Rawdon, " ob. in bello sub Rege Sueviæ in Germaniâ." || 5. Joseph Rawdon, a Spanish merchant in London. || 1. Alice. 2. Doro-thy. 3. Anne.

Ursula, 1st═Sir George Raw-═Dorothy, 2nd wife, dau. || don, of Rawdon, || wife, dau. of Sir Fras. || created a Baro- || of Edward Vis-Stafford, || net 1665; died || count Con-knt. gover- || Aug. 1683, æt. || way and Kil-nor of || 82. || lala; died Newry. || || 1676. || 1. Anne, wife of John Stanhope, of Horse-forth, co. York, esq. 2. Elizabeth. 3. Mary, wife of John Dunbarre. 4. Mercy. || 5. Pris-cilla, living unm. at Rawdon 1707, æt. 81. || 1. Richard Rawdon, of London, grocer. || 2. Veritas═ . . . . dau. Rawdon, || of . . . . of Lon- || Hacker, of don, gold- || London, smith. || merchant. || 3. Walter Rawdon, of Lon-don, gold-smith.

Sir Arthur Rawdon, of Rawdon and Moira, Bart.; born 17th Oct. 1661 ;═Helena, dau. and heir of Sir James Graham, knt. son of died 17th Oct. 1695. || the Earl of Monteith.

Sir John Rawdon, Bart.; mar.═Dorothy, dau. of Sir Richard Levinge, of Parwich, co. in 1716; died in 1723. || Derby, Bart. Lord Chief Justice C.P. Ireland. || Isabella.═Sir Richard Levinge, Bart.; (son of the Lord Chief Justice).

Helena Percival, 1st wife,═Anne Hill, 2nd wife, dau. of═Sir John Rawdon, Bart. created═Elizabeth Hastings, 3rd wife, eldest dau. of dau. of John Earl of Eg- || Trevor Viscount Hillsbo- || Baron Rawdon of Moira, co. || Theophilus 9th Earl of Huntingdon, and mont; died 11th June, || rough; died 1st August, || Downe (1750), and Earl of || sole heir of her brother Francis 10th 1746, s.p.m. || 1751, s.p. || Moira (1761); died 1793. || Earl; died 1808.

1. Francis, born 7th Dec. 1754, 2nd Earl of Moira; created═Flora Muir an English peer, as Baron Rawdon, 1783, and Viscount || Campbell, Loudoun, Earl of Moira, and Marquess of Hastings, 1816; || Countess of Governor General of India, 1812; died 28th Nov. 1826. || Loudoun. || 2. John-Theophilus═Fanny, youngest dau. of Joseph Rawdon, born 1756; || William Hall Stevenson, of Skel-marr. Dec. 1793; || ton Castle, co. York, esq. (au-died 1808. || thor of Crazy Tales), b. 21 Dec. 1773; died Jan. 1850; bur. at Skelton.

Lord George William Russell, 2nd son of═Elizabeth-Anne, born John 6th Duke of Bedford, died 1846. || 1793; mar. 1817.

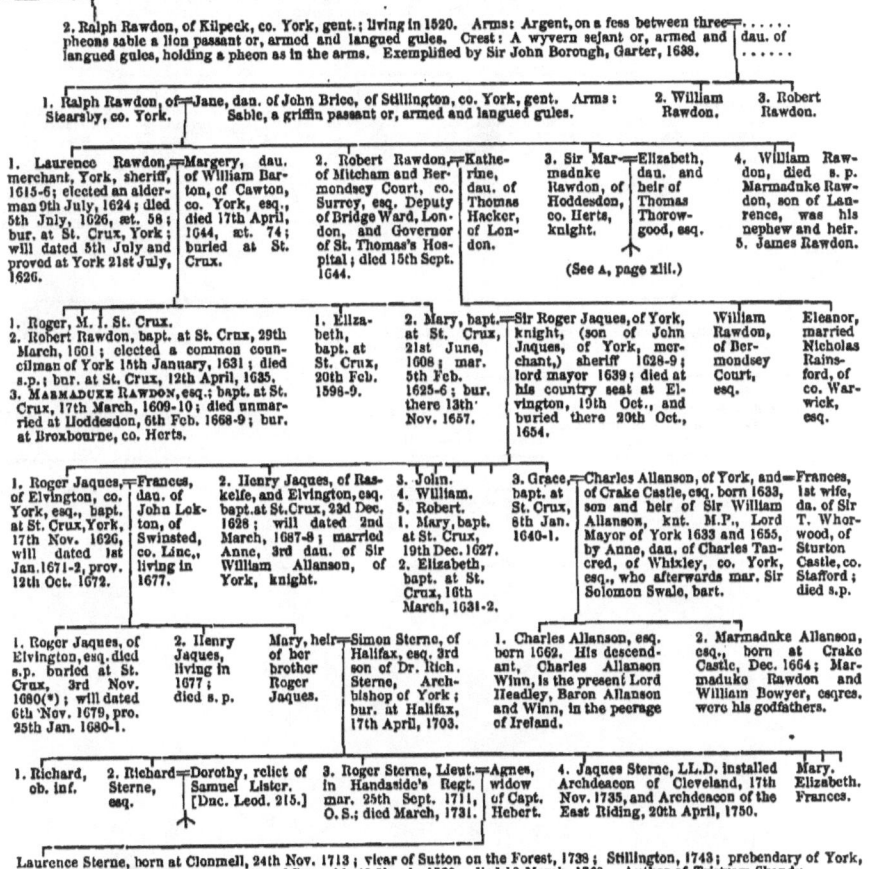

2. Ralph Rawdon, of Kilpeck, co. York, gent.; living in 1520. Arms: Argent, on a fess between three⹀...... pheons sable a lion passant or, armed and langued gules. Crest: A wyvern sejant or, armed and ⹀dau. of langued gules, holding a pheon as in the arms. Exemplified by Sir John Borough, Garter, 1638. ......

1. Ralph Rawdon, of⹀Jane, dau. of John Brice, of Stillington, co. York, gent. Arms: | 2. William | 3. Robert
Stearsby, co. York. | Sable, a griffin passant or, armed and langued gules. | Rawdon. | Rawdon.

1. Laurence Rawdon, ⹀Margery, dau. | 2. Robert Rawdon,⹀Kathe- | 3. Sir Mar-⹀Elizabeth, | 4. William Raw-
merchant, York, sheriff, | of William Bar- | of Mitcham and Ber- | rine, | madnke | dau. and | don, died s. p.
1615-6; elected an alder- | ton, of Cawton, | mondsey Court, co. | dau. of | Rawdon, of | heir of | Marmaduke Raw-
man 9th July, 1624; died | co. York, esq., | Surrey, esq. Deputy | Thomas | Hoddesdon, | Thomas | don, son of Lau-
5th July, 1626, æt. 58; | died 17th April, | of Bridge Ward, Lon- | Hacker, | co. Herts, | Thorow- | rence, was his
bur. at St. Crux, York; | 1644, æt. 74; | don, and Governor | of Lon- | knight. | good, esq. | nephew and heir.
will dated 5th July and | buried at St. | of St. Thomas's Hos- | don. | | | 5. James Rawdon.
proved at York 21st July, | Crux. | pital; died 15th Sept. | | (See A, page xliii.) |
1626. | | 1644. | | |

1. Roger, M. I. St. Crux. | 1. Eliza- | 2. Mary, bapt.⹀Sir Roger Jaques, of York, | William | Eleanor,
2. Robert Rawdon, bapt. at St. Crux, 29th | beth, | at St. Crux, | knight, (son of John | Rawdon, | married
March, 1611; elected a common coun- | bapt. at | 21st June, | Jaques, of York, mer- | of Ber- | Nicholas
cilman of York 15th January, 1631; died | St. Crux, | 1608; mar. | chant,) sheriff 1628-9; | mondsey | Rains-
s.p.; bur. at St. Crux, 12th April, 1635. | 20th Feb. | 5th Feb. | lord mayor 1639; died at | Court, | ford, of
3. MARMADUKE RAWDON, esq.; bapt. at St. | 1598-9. | 1625-6; bur. | his country seat at El- | esq. | co. War-
Crux, 17th March, 1609-10; died unmar- | | there 13th | vington, 15th Oct., and | | wick,
ried at Hoddesdon, 6th Feb. 1668-9; bur. | | Nov. 1657. | buried there 20th Oct., | | esq.
at Broxbourne, co. Herts. | | | 1654. | |

1. Roger Jaques,⹀Frances, | 2. Henry Jaques, of Ras- | 3. John. | 3. Grace,⹀Charles Allanson, of York, and⹀Frances,
of Elvington, co. | dau. of | kelfe, and Elvington, esq. | 4. William. | bapt. at | son and heir of Sir William | 1st wife,
York, esq., bapt. | John Lok- | bapt. at St. Crux, 23d Dec. | 5. Robert. | St. Crux, | Allanson, knt. M.P., Lord | da. of Sir
at St. Crux, York, | ton, of | 1628; will dated 2nd | 1. Mary, bapt. | 8th Jan. | Mayor of York 1633 and 1655, | T. Whor-
17th Nov. 1626, | Swinsted, | March, 1687-8; married | at St. Crux, | 1640-1. | by Anne, dau. of Charles Tan- | wood, of
will dated 1st | co. Linc., | Anne, 3rd dau. of Sir | 19th Dec. 1627. | | cred, of Whixley, co. York, | Sturton
Jan. 1671-2, prov. | living in | William Allanson, of | 2. Elizabeth, | | esq., who afterwards mar. Sir | Castle, co.
12th Oct. 1672. | 1677. | York, knight. | bapt. at St. | | Solomon Swale, bart. | Stafford; s.p.
| | | Crux, 16th | | | died s.p.
| | | March, 1631-2. | | |

1. Roger Jaques, of | 2. Henry | Mary, heir⹀Simon Sterne, of | 1. Charles Allanson, esq. | 2. Marmaduke Allanson,
Elvington, esq. died | Jaques, | of her | Halifax, esq. 3rd | born 1662. His descend- | esq., born at Crake
s.p. buried at St. | living in | brother | son of Dr. Rich. | ant, Charles Allanson | Castle, Dec. 1664; Mar-
Crux, 3rd Nov. | 1677; | Roger | Sterne, Arch- | Winn, is the present Lord | maduke Rawdon and
1680(*); will dated | died s. p. | Jaques. | bishop of York; | Headley, Baron Allanson | William Bowyer, esqres.
6th Nov. 1679, pro. | | | bur. at Halifax, | and Winn, in the peerage | were his godfathers.
25th Jan. 1680-1. | | | 17th April, 1703. | of Ireland. |

1. Richard, | 2. Richard⹀Dorothy, relict of | 3. Roger Sterne, Lieut.⹀Agnes, | 4. Jaques Sterne, LL.D. installed | Mary.
ob. inf. | Sterne, | Samuel Lister. | in Handaside's Regt. | widow | Archdeacon of Cleveland, 17th | Elizabeth.
| esq. | [Dnc. Leod. 215.] | mar. 25th Sept. 1711, | of Capt. | Nov. 1735, and Archdeacon of the | Frances.
| | | O. S.; died March, 1731. | Hebert. | East Riding, 20th April, 1750. |

Laurence Sterne, born at Clonmell, 24th Nov. 1713; vicar of Sutton on the Forest, 1738; Stillington, 1743; prebendary of York,
5 Jan. 1741; perpetual curate of Coxwold, 29 March, 1760; died 18 March, 1768. Author of Tristram Shandy.

* Buried in the church of St. Crux, 30th Dec. 1683, Mrs. Eliz. Dawson, "neare Mr. Roger Jaques whom she lov'd."
Par. Reg.

A

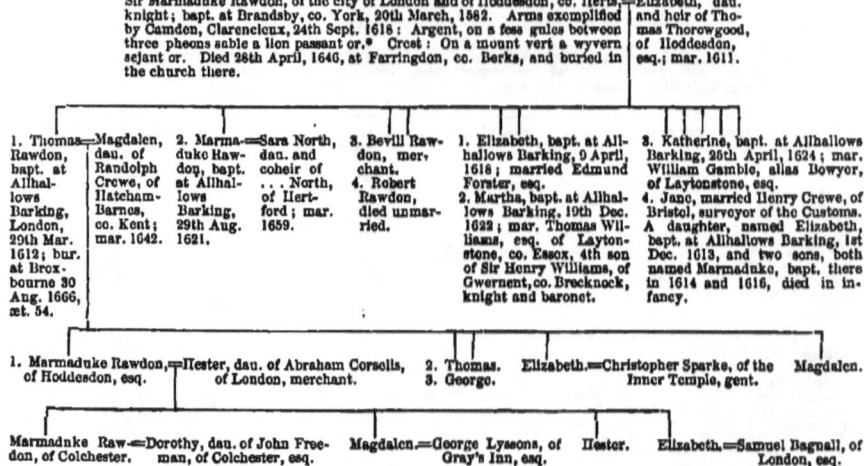

Sir Marmaduke Rawdon, of the city of London and of Hoddesdon, co. Herts,══Elizabeth, dau.
knight; bapt. at Brandsby, co. York, 20th March, 1582. Arms exemplified   and heir of Tho-
by Camden, Clarencieux, 24th Sept. 1618: Argent, on a fess gules between   mas Thorowgood,
three pheons sable a lion passant or.* Crest: On a mount vert a wyvern   of Hoddesdon,
sejant or. Died 28th April, 1646, at Farringdon, co. Berks, and buried in   esq.; mar. 1611.
the church there.

1. Thomas══Magdalen,	2. Marma-══Sara North,	3. Bevill Raw-	1. Elizabeth, bapt. at All-	3. Katherine, bapt. at Allhallows
Rawdon, dau. of	duke Haw- dau. and	don, mer-	hallows Barking, 9 April,	Barking, 28th April, 1624; mar.
bapt. at Randolph	don, bapt. coheir of	chant.	1618; married Edmund	William Gamble, alias Bowyer,
Allhal- Crewe, of	at Allhal- . . . North,	4. Robert	Forster, esq.	of Laytonstone, esq.
lows Hatcham-	lows of Hert-	Rawdon,	2. Martha, bapt. at Allhal-	4. Jane, married Henry Crewe, of
Barking, Barnes,	Barking, ford; mar.	died unmar-	lows Barking, 19th Dec.	Bristol, surveyor of the Customs.
London, co. Kent;	29th Aug. 1659.	ried.	1622; mar. Thomas Wil-	A daughter, named Elizabeth,
29th Mar. mar. 1642.	1621.		liams, esq. of Layton-	bapt. at Allhallows Barking, 1st
1612; bur.			stone, co. Essex, 4th son	Dec. 1613, and two sons, both
at Brox-			of Sir Henry Williams, of	named Marmaduke, bapt. there
bourne 30			Gwernent, co. Brecknock,	in 1614 and 1616, died in in-
Aug. 1666,			knight and baronet.	fancy.
æt. 54.				

1. Marmaduke Rawdon,══Hester, dau. of Abraham Corsellis,	2. Thomas.	Elizabeth,══Christopher Sparke, of the	Magdalen.
of Hoddesdon, esq. of London, merchant.	3. George.	Inner Temple, gent.	

Marmaduke Raw-══Dorothy, dau. of John Free-	Magdalen,══George Lyssons, of	Hester.	Elizabeth,══Samuel Bagnall, of
don, of Colchester. man, of Colchester, esq.	Gray's Inn, esq.		London, esq.

* An honourable augmentation was granted to him by King Charles I. upon his being knighted for his loyal services in the
civil war, viz. A canton of England, gules a lion passant guardant or.

THE LIFE

OF

MARMADUKE RAWDON OF YORKE,

OR

MARMADUKE RAWDON THE 2D OF THAT NAME.

MARMADUKE RAWDON, the only son now livinge of Lawrence 1600. Rawdon and Margery his wife, was borne in that antient and famous cittie of Yorke, and was baptised in‚ the church of the Crosse, commonly called Crux Church, the 18th day of March, 160$\frac{9}{10}$. He was brought up in his father's howse with all manner of learninge that cittie of Yorke could afford. He was in his childhood very active and full of life, and very wittie in his answers: a gentlewoman comminge to his father's howse askt him before much company why he did nott come to thir howse to play with hir little boy; he answerd hir he did not use to goe to anie place unbidden. His father one time askinge att the table amongst company what trade he would chuse to be of, he said a preacher; his father askt him why a preacher, he answerd, to teach them the worde of God that did nott know itt; and severall others, answers of this nature.

His father had once thoughts to have made him a scholler, and had a livinge promisd him of 200 pound a yeare, nere Barton, in Linconshir, which was in the guift of Squier Barton,[a] his mother's brother; but he was, beinge a child, soo extreame studious, readinge

[a] Robert Barton, Esquire, of Cawton, in the county of York, a descendant of Christopher Barton of Whenby in the same county, and his wife Margaret, daughter of Sir Robert Danby, Knight, of Farnley, near Leeds.

night and day, and best pleasd when he was pouringe uppon a booke, which was very prejudiciall to his eiesight, which his father percievinge did alter his resolution, fearinge if he should follow that callinge he might come to be blinde before he came to be aged.

1618.   Beinge about nine yeares of age, playinge amongst other boyes in a yarde amongst the timbers of an old howse, a pece of timber fell uppon him and broke his left arme above the elboe, but havinge expert surgeons his arme was well sett, and he in three weekes time was perfectly recovered.

1621.   Beinge about 12 yeares of age, before he knew what love was, he fell in love with a yonge gentlewoman, the daughter of one Mr. Michael Stanhop,* who was much about his owne yeares; he courted hir highly after his childish way, and did much delight in her company and she in his. Hir brother, Mr. George Stanhop, beinge his schoolfellow, he had the opertunitie to see hir often, and to play with hir brother in the gardens and orchards, and she would come and be amongst them; and uppon a time he had a minde to show Mrs. Susan, for soe the yonge gentlewoman was called, what fine crackinge squibs he could make; so he and 3 and 4 boyes more of his consorts had gott some quantitie of powder, and putt itt in one of the boyes hatts; Mr. Rawdon goinge to give fire to the crackinge squib, itt would not att first goe of; soe Mr. Rawdon fell a blowinge of itt, and the boy with the hatt of powder came nere Mr. Rawdon to see what was the matter that itt would not goe of, when of a sudden itt went of, and some sparks flew into the hatt of powder and blew up the fore part of Mr. Rawdon's clooths, burnt his band, and his face, and his clooths still burninge about him, which one Marabel, a maid of the howse, seeinge, took a kittle full of water, which she had now hunge on the fire, and was yett cold, and soe quencht the fire of his clooths, which other wayes would have gone nere to have spoyld him; some of the other boyes had some little

<hr>

* A physician then living at York. He was a brother of Sir Edward Stanhope, Knight, of Grimstone near Tadcaster, and of Dr. George Stanhope, a prebendary of York, rector of Wheldrake near York, and one of the chaplains of King Charles I.

hurt, and some cornes of powder in thir faces, and all of them left
Mr. Rawdon and run away, publishinge in severall parts of the
cittic this accidentall mischance, which quickly arived att his
father's howse, soe a servant was sent away presently to Mr. Stanhop's to see what the matter was, who finding him in that sad condition took him in his armes, wrapt his clooke over him, and carried
him home; when he came home, he was laid uppon a pallet-bed,
his heade sweld as big as tow heades, and his ciclids seemingly burnt
up, to the greate griefe of his parents, who presently sent for the
most eminent docters and surgeons of the cittic, who consultinge
togeather, did apply thosse things that were most convenient for
him. His mouthe was soe burnt up that his mother was in greate
care how to feede him, but he hearinge hir in that perplexitie, made
signes for a sukingbottle with which he was nurisht till his mouthe
grew better. He lay nine dayes blinde without anic sight att all,
and then began to see a little, and in a monthe's time a fresh skin
came over his face, the swellinge downe, and he as well as if he had
had noe hurt att all.

Whilst he staid att Yorke his recreations allowed him on play dayes
was bow and arrowes and bowlinge, in booth which he was reasonable expert; his recreations, by the by unknowne to his parents, was
ridinge of horses and swimminge, in booth which he many times
past noe small dangers.

His contemporary schoole fellowes and chief play fellowes was
Sir Watkinson Pailer,[a] Sir Henry Franklin[b] and his brothers, Sir

---

[a] Watkinson Payler was the only son of Sir Edward Payler, Baronet, of Thoraldby, in
the parish of Bugthorpe, in the East Riding of Yorkshire, by Anne daughter and heir of
William Watkinson, Esquire, of York. He died *in vitâ patris*, having married a daughter
of Thomas first Viscount Fairfax of Emley; she was afterwards the second wife of the
younger Sir John Hotham of civil war notoriety. Their son, Sir Watkinson Payler, was
the last baronet of that name. The Watkinsons and Paylers were York families, who
acquired wealth by their official connection with the great Council of the North and the
Church of York. Thoraldby Hall, prettily situated at the western foot of the Yorkshire
Wolds, is now a farm-house, the property of Sir Charles Wood, Baronet.

[b] Sir Henry Frankland, Knight, of Thirkleby in the North Riding of Yorkshire, was

Sollomon Swale,[a] Sir William Herbert,[b] Sir John Gibson,[c] Mr.
John Stapleton,[d] Mr. George Stanhop,[e] and Mr. Robart Scott,[f] all
which, except tow, are yett alive, and they have to this day a greate
respect one for another.

1626.   In this manner, att schoole and att his recreations, he spent his
time till the yeare 1626, att which time he was about 16 yeares of
age, and in July the said yeare itt pleased God to taike to his mercie
his indulgent father,[g] to the greate losse of his children, to the
greate griefe of his wife, and of all that knew him.

born in the same year as Marmaduke Rawdon. He had several brothers. .His son, Sir
William Frankland, was the first baronet of this family.

    [a] Sir Solomon Swale, of Swale Hall and South Stainley near Ripon, was born in 1610,
and created a baronet at the Restoration. The Swales were a Yorkshire family of great
antiquity. Three of the brothers of Sir Solomon were distinguished royalists in the civil
war.

    [b] The biographer undoubtedly means Sir Thomas Herbert, Baronet, the well known
oriental traveller, and the devoted servant of King Charles I. in his latest years. Sir
Thomas was the eldest son of Christopher Herbert, a York merchant, and grandson
of Alderman Thomas Herbert who was Lord Mayor of York in 1604. Sir Thomas received
his education at Saint Peter's School, but he was so many years the senior of Marmaduke
Rawdon that he could scarcely have been his contemporary there. He was made a
baronet soon after the Restoration.

    [c] The eldest son of Sir John Gibson of Welborne near Kirby-Moorside, Knight, LL.D.
High Sheriff of Yorkshire in 1630, and a member of the Great Council of the North. Sir
John Gibson, the son, died in 1665.

    [d] Probably the son of Sir Philip Stapleton, Knight, of Warter, in the East Riding of
Yorkshire, whose name was conspicuous in the disputes between King Charles I. and the
Parliament.

    [e] Son of Dr. Michael Stanhope. He probably died young, as his name does not appear
in the pedigrees of the family.

    [f] Perhaps a son of John Scott, D.D. who was made Dean of York in 1624.

    [g] The will of "Lawrence Rawden, alderman, dwelling in Crux parish in the city of
York," is dated the 6th of July, 1626. He desires to be buried in Saint Crux church
in the quire there. He gives all his lands, &c. in the lordships of Bransby and Stearsby,
which he purchased of Mr. Richard Cholmley and Mr. Thomas Cholmley, unto his son
Marmaduke Rawden his heirs and assigns for ever. He bequeaths the following legacies :
to his brother Robert Rawdon 33s. in gold—to his brother Marmaduke Rawdon 34s. in
gold—to his brothers William and James Rawdon each 33s. in gold—to Jane Rawdon of
Bransby, widow, 10s.—to the poor of every ward in the city of York 40s.—to Leonard

His father beinge dead, he remaind with his mother, followinge his studies, till September followinge, att which time his unckle, Sir Marmaduke Rawdon, wrote to his mother desieringe hir to send him up to London, and that he would have a care of him; soe he had a hansome geldinge bought for him, and in the same monthe of September he was sent up; his gardians uppon the roode, to whosse care he was recomended by his mother, were Mr. Violet Diamond,[a] a gentleman and a great travelour, and one Mr. Sutton, a draper of Yorke; this tow had a greate care of him uppon the roode all the journie, and brought him to Hodsden to his unckle's howse; his unckle beinge then att London, they delivered him to his aunt, and thir tooke thir leaves of him with much love and respect.

Here he staid some time, beinge very kindly entertained booth by Sir Marmaduke and his Lady;[b] but winter comminge on, about the beginninge of November the family removed from Hodsden to London and he with them, where he staid till February followinge, 1627. att which time his unckle, having discovered a ripnesse of wit and a good ingenuitie in him, was desierous to prefer him in the world, fraighted a ship called the Lambe of Flushinge, a ship of about 100 tuns, of which was maister one Giles Biscop, and with a small cargason [c] of goodes, sent him first for Flushinge in Zeeland; and from thence he was to goe to the cittie of Bourdeaux in France.

A longe time, nere 3 monthes, he lay wind-bounde att Flushinge, where he placed himselfe in a Dutch howse, and with the helpe of

Weddell 3s.—to Mr. Roger Bellwood 3s.—to Mr. Nicholas Fewster 3s.—to John Myers, in respect of his pains, 5s.—to his son-in-law Mr. Roger Jaques in gold 20s. and to Marie his wife 20s. He makes his well-beloved wife Margerie and his son Robert Rawden residuary legatees and executors. The will was provd at York, 21st July, 1626.

[a] Of this "great traveller," with the curious combination of names, I am unable to find any notice.

[b] The wife of Sir Marmaduke was sole daughter and heir of Thomas Thorowgood, Esq. of Hoddesdon, in the county of Hertford, a lady who brought him a fortune of 10,000l. (Wotton's Baronetage, vol. iii. p. 479.) Sir Marmaduke rebuilt the house at Hoddesdon, which had probably been the residence of his father-in-law.

[c] Cargo. Cargaison, Fr.; Cargaçon, Span. This now obsolete word was commonly used in the seventeenth century.

some bookes he bought att Midleborow, a cittie three miles from thence, he gott part of the language. In this entervall of time the warrs brooke out twixt England and France, of which his unckle gave him notice, and withall writ him; however, he left itt to his owne choyce, whether he would goe for France or returne for England, but he, whosse soule was boylinge for imployments and was begun to step forward in the world, was looth to goe backwards; soe he writ his unckle, that he gave him many thankes for his goodnesse towards him in advizinge him of the danger that might ensue by the warrs with France, but he thought that he, beinge an inconciderable boy, might passe well enough amongst them; and beinge that he was pleased to putt itt in his choyce to returne or goe forwards, being looth to returne for England till he was able in the French tongue to returne him thankes for his favours and the greate care he had of him.

This answer did noe wayes displease his unckle, who was no freind to people that were faint-hearted, for he usd to say he would nott have men when they went uppon great designes to be affraid of bugbeares, but to goe on with a resolution; as his nephew did in this, for, without expectinge aney further answer from Sir Marmaduke, he imbarkt himselfe about the middle of May for Bourdeaux, where ·he arrived about the end of the monthe; thir he fownd Captain James Holdip, his unckle's factor, who recieved him very civilly, disposed of his goods, and provided him a French tutor, in whosse howse he lived, and learnt to write and cypher after the French manner; and, to better his language, he went up the river to a towne cald Prigniac; thir he staid till February fol-

1628. lowinge, at which time the aforesaid Mr. Holdip sent for him to Bourdeaux, desieringe him to goe marchant of a ship, a Dutchman of 300 tons, laden with wines for Flushinge, thir to be reladen in English vessells for London, the laders havinge, by reason of the warrs, given in securitie that thosse wines should goe directly for. Holland or Zeeland.ᵃ He accepted of this imployment beinge a

ᵃ Several months before war between England and France was formally proclaimed,

greate part of those wines were for his unckle's accounte; soe he
sett saile out of the river of Bourdeaux in company of 70 more
marchant ships and three men of warr thir convoys. Comminge
nere the Land's-end of England they mett with a greate storme
which seperated them all one from the other; this ship with some
few more gott into Plimouth, where they staid 3 or 4 dayes
to refresh themselves, and, the wind beinge faire, away they went on
thir voyage, and, beinge on the coast of Zeeland, another greate
storme arose, which cast away some of thir company, but they,
with the lose of thir bolsprit, and some other small damage, gott
into Flushinge on a Sunday morninge, wher he was noe soner
arived but he (while others that came in with them thought only of
refreshinge and feastinge themselves) went to see what English
ships were thir to be fraighted for London; he found only tow, and
thosse he fraighted presently, and then he went to refresh himselfe,
and to be merry with his accquentance. Thesse ships he fraighted
att a cheape rate, beinge uppon thir returne emptie for England.

The next day, Munday morninge, he began to unlade his ship
and to lade thesse tow vessells, booth which he dispatcht that
weeke, and sent them away for London, consigninge every man's
wines to whom they did belonge, according to Captain Holdip's
directions. Thes ships had a good passage, and were the first ships
that arived att London; soe they were very welcome to thir
owners. Other marchants, havinge noe wines, enquiered what dili-
gent person sent thesse, where after enquiery they found itt to be a
yonge unknowne youthe that belonged to Sir Marmaduke Rawdon,
which madded them the more to thinke that thir factors should be
asleepe whilst this boy had done his busnesse; which busnesse made
Mr. Rawdon better knowne afterwards, and gott him much reputa-

Louis XIII. had laid an embargo on all English ships in French harbours. "At
Bourdeaux the crafty malicious French suffered our merchants to lade the wines, but
no sooner had they paid for the same but the French arrested ships, wines, and all,
and told the English in scorn that they should be permitted to be transported so it were
in French bottoms."—Pory to Mead, Nov. 26th, 1626. Court and Times of Charles I.
vol. i, p. 174.

tion, soe that severall of thesse marchants to whome he had sent
thesse wines gave him imployment, and made him thir factor att
Bourdeaux for some yeares afterwards as longe as he staid in France.

Thesse ships beinge dispatched, and all charges paid to people he
imployed in the lodinge his wines, he resolved to travaile and see
part of thosse countries; soe, havinge scene thosse places of importance in Zeeland, he saild over into Holland, see Amsterdam, and
the most of thir emenent citties, and the universitie of Leyden,
wher, to better his experience, he spent a good part of his comissions, and soe, returninge backe for Zeeland, he imbarkt himselfe att
Flushinge for England, wher he arived in Aprill, 1628, where he
was very well recieved by his unckle and severall others, who gave
him thankes for his care in thir businesse.

1629.   This yeare, and part of 1629, he spent in London, was his
unckle's cash keeper, and did dispatch most of his unckle's affaires,
till October, 1629, att which time his unckle was resolved to send
him againe for France; soe he deliverd up his cash to Captaine
Edmund Forster, then his unckle's partner, but fell short in his cash
about three pownds. He told him he was looth to pay itt, beinge
he was certaine he had nott spent itt, and that he would find itt in
one mistake or other, and, if he did not, if he soe thought fittinge,
he would then satisfie itt; he tooke his word, and after he had bene
a while in France Captaine Forster writt him that he had fownd
three peces of gold in the crevises of the cash-box.

About the middle of October he imbarkt att Rie, and soe for
Deepe, and soe to the cittie of Roan and Parris, and from Parris he
went away in company of the messenger for Bourdeaux, beinge
about 300 miles. To this mesinger givinge a certaine summe of
mony you are furnisht with a very good horse and exclent diet all
the way, havinge noe care of anie thinge more then to risse when
the mesinger calls you. In this journie Mr. Rawdon took accquentance with a yonge French gentleman much about his age, and,
ridinge alonge betwixt Blois and Potiers, they fell uppon a discourse of the goodnesse of swords. Mr. Rawdon told him he

thought he wore as good a blade by his side as most was in France; the French gentleman desird to see, soe Mr. Rawdon drew itt and showed him itt, which, havinge lookt uppon itt, in contempt he spitt uppon itt, which Mr. Rawdon taikinge as an affront, he gave him with the flatt of itt tow or three raps over the pate, and then lighted of his horse. The French gentleman did the like, but, before they came to engage, the relations of the French gentleman stept betwene to know what the matter was, which when they heard, they blamed the French gentleman very much, and commended Mr. Rawdon that, though he was in a strange place, he scornd to recieve an affront, and had him in great respect all the journie after.

He arived saifly att Bourdeaux, and remained thir factor for his unckle and severall other marchants that vintage, and in the springe about the beginninge of Aprill, 1630, he went to see the ruines of Rochell, whosse walls and fortifications tow yeares before were the best in France; but, uppon thir rebellion, Kinge Lewis the 13th, havinge taiken the towne, demolisht all save the walls towards the seaside, which he left standinge.[*] From thence he went through Britanie, beinge desierous to see that country, and in his way tooke Nantes and St. Malos, tow of the principall citties of that country, wher he was nobly entertained as he past, by the marchants thir resident. From St. Malos, after he had taiken a view of the country and had bene att Renes, where the Court of Parlement or Chiefe Court of Justice for that province is kept, he imbarkt for England and landed in the Ile of Waight. Here he staid about 3 dayes to taike a view of the Iland, went to Newport the chiefe towne, and, havinge satisfied himselfe thir, he tooke passage for Southampton, where by Mr. Prescod, Mr. Priaulx, Mr. Hilliard, and Mr. Chambers, merchants of the towne, he was highly feasted.

1630.

· [*] Howel, writing from London in September 1628, says : " Since I began this letter ther is news brought that Rochel hath yeelded, and that the King hath dismantled the town, and raz'd all the fortifications landwards, but leaves those standing which were toward the sea. It is a mighty exploit the French King hath don, for Rochel was the chiefest propugnacle of the Protestants there."—Familiar Letters, p. 188, ed. 1678.

In this journie he staid soo longe out, his letters from Brittany,
which should have given notice where he was, miscarynge, they
thought att his unckle's howse that some mischance had befalne him,
but he arived thir saifly about the begininge of June, where he
staid att London in his unckle's howse most part of that summer till
the begininge of September, att which time he was sent over againe
into France; soe, meetinge with one Monsieur David Battalier of
Bourdeaux, he imbarkt att Rie, and soe saild over to Diep, from
thence to Roan, and soe to Parris, where they tooke post, and in a
short time arived att Bourdeaux. They rid in one night from Parris
to Orleance, which was 15 stages.

Beinge at Bourdeaux, he laded that vintage a quantitie of wines
for his unckle and severall other marchants of London. About this
1631. time thir was peace proclamed betwixt England and Spaine,[a] soe
in January his unckle writ for him to come home, uppon which he
setled his businesse, leaving itt accordinge to the orders of them
that imployd him; soe he imbarkt abord the Elizabeth of Alborow,
a ship of about 200 ton, of which was commander Captaine Robart
Rippon, which ship was laden with wines by himselfe.

The ship beinge gon downe the river, and ridinge att anchor att
Pulliacke, a towne about 20 miles below Bourdeaux, going ashore
one afternone with the captaine to recreate themselves, thir came a
gentleman, well acoutred, and told him there was a lady att such an
inne desiered much to speake with him; soe he beinge allwayes a
greate courtier, he told the gentleman that he would by and by
waite uppon hir; soe he told the captaine of itt, desieringe him to
goe and drinke a glasse of wine att such a taverne, and that so soone
as he had spooke with this gentlewoman he would be with him;
soe the gentleman stayinge for him, he went alonge with him, wher
comminge to the inne he carried him up into a chamber where he
see a most beautifull yonge lady, about 18 yeares of age, very richly
clad, havinge a waitinge gentlewoman and hir foote-boy standinge
by hir; soe he went towards hir, saluted hir, and askt hir if she had

[a] Peace with France was concluded in April, and with Spain in November, 1630.

sent for him, and desird to know what service she would please to command him; she told him she had made bold to send for him, and desird to know if he were marchant of the greate ship that rid over against the towne; he told her, yes, he was; Then sir, saith she, I shall request you that I may have passage for my selfe and thosse three that did waite uppon hir, for England; he told hir that as he was marchant of the ship, the greate cabbin and the cabins thirin did belong to him, which should be att hir service; but for recievinge of passingers, itt did properly belonge to the captaine of the ship, as beinge his benefitt, and now he was ashore in the towne, and that, if she pleased, he would goe unto him and bringe him to hir, and did nott doubt but to give hir ladiship a good account of the busnesse; which she tooke very kindly, and desired him soe to doe. Soe he went to the taverne where the captaine was, and told him what had past, and what a gallant companion they were like to have for passinger, and that he should use hir kindly for hir passage, and that she should have one of the cabins of the greate cabin with him. The captaine was as much pleasd as the marchant, and said, that for hir passage she should make hir owne conditions. Soe they went to the inne where she was, and the busnesse was as sone agreed as comunicated; soe they askt her when she would please to goe abord, or, if she would stay ashore till the winde was faire, they would send for hir then. She said, no, she desird to goe abord soe sone as they could; soe the captaine sent to his men to goe abord for a Turkie carpett, which was spread in the boote, and then they carried hir, hir gentleman usher, hir waitinge maid, and foote boy abord. When she came abord she was by Mr. Rawdon led into the greate cabin, where she had the fairest cabin, which was raild about wher she lay in the cabin, hir maid within the railes in a bed uppon the flower by hir; Mr. Rawdon taikinge another cabin right against hir, which was lesse, but sufficiently convenient for one person. There they lay wind-bound about 3 weekes, a fortnight of which time they spent with much jollitie and mirth in good discourse and att cardes, in which time the gentleman usher and the foot-boy had a quarell,

soe that the gentleman beate him, which he tooke so much to heart,
that the next day beinge ashore, remembringe his callinge, made
use of his legs, and run away.

About tow dayes after, thir fresh provisions beinge well nere
spent, and Mr. Rawdon knowinge that thir was noe market att sea,
and nott knowinge how sone the wind might come faire, he desird
the captaine to lend him the boote to goe to Bloye, a market towne
about 3 miles up the river, to fitt himselfe with new provisions for
the voyage. Soe the boote was made reddie, and Mr. Rawdon went
in hir, when he was no soner landed, but he espies the ladies foote
boy; soe he cald him to him and carried him to an inne with him,
where he gave him a glasse or tow of wine, and enterd into discourse
with him, why he went away from his lady, and who his lady was.
He told him that she was such an earle's daughter of Province, whom
hir father had resolved to marry to a Barron of Gascoinie, a lord of a
greate estate, but very deformed, much against hir likinge; who
seeing she could not perswade hir father to alter his resolution, she
gott all hir rich apparell, jewels, and what mony and gold she could
gett of hir owne and hir father's, and taikinge advantage of hir
father's absence from home, with him, the gentleman usher, and the
waitinge woman, stoole away. Hir father, and hir entended husband
the Barron, comminge home after some few dayes and missinge of
hir, pursued hir with all posible dilligence to the cittie of Bourdeaux, which way they heard she had taiken, and procured the
gates of the cittie to be shutt up and garded, till they had made
scarch in all inns and other likely places for hir; but she, fearinge to
be discovered att Bourdeaux, left itt on hir right hand, and went
directly downe for Pulliack; where she imbarkt as aforesaid. They
seeinge they could not find hir, petitioned the high court of justice,
called thir the parlement, to issue out a proclamation, that none
uppon greate penalties should entertaine hir, and a greate reward to
anie that should give notice where she was, and that noe maister of
ship or boote should transporte hir out of the kingdom, or from the
place she was, uppon paine of imprisonment and confiscation of his

vessell. Soe, after all this discourse, he gave the foote-boy some monie to drinke, and disird him, though the gentleman usher and he was falne out, yet he ought to have soe much faith and love to his lady, who had trusted him, as not to discover to aney body where she was, which he promised very faithfully that he would nott discover itt to none; soe partinge with him he enquired further in the towne about the busnesse, and found what the footeboy had told him to be true. Att this discourse Mr. Rawdon was much trobled, not for himselfe, for he knew that he was to returne thir no more, beinge sent for to be sent for Spaine, but for his friend captaine Rippen, whosse only imployment and livelyhood was in thosse voyages; soe, havinge brought his provisions away, he went in the boote downe to the ship. In the way he had a greate conflict within himselfe whether his kindness to his freind or his amours with the lady should most prevaile; att last, before he gott abord, he resolved that the captaine's freindship should be more prevalent then the ladies bewtie. Withall he thought in doinge otherwayes he should doe a greate pece of injustice for the familliartie of a strange lady to venter the undoinge and ruin of the captaine and his famcley.

Soe after he was gott abord the ship he went into the round howse, which was the captaine's lodgings, and told him like a true freind all that had past, which the captaine tooke very kindly frome him, and gave him many thankes. About which time, the supper beinge redie, and carried into the greate cabbin, they went downe to the ladie to supper, to whome they were very civill, but nott with that alacritie and cherfullnesse as formerly, which she, beinge sufficiently quicke sighted, lett nott but to taike notice of.

Havinge supt, after some small discourse Mr. Rawdon and the captaine tooke thir leaves of hir, and went to walke uppon the dekes, leavinge hir with hir maide or woman in the greate cabin, where after some small time she went to bed. Beinge abed, she sent hir woman to Mr. Rawdon to tell him she desird him to come speake with hir; soe, goinge in and sittinge downe by hir bed side,

she askt him how he did? He answerd hir, "Very well." She
said she could nott believe soe, for that she had observed in his face
att supper some discomposure or indisposition of minde or body, and
desird him that he would ingeniously answer hir one question. He
told hir if he could he would; soe she desird he would only tell hir
whether he see hir foot-boy att Bloy or noe? He answered her he
had. "Well then," saith she, "I am undone. He haith told you
my hard fate and unhappie fortune. I pray you what doe you
intend to doe with me? for, rather then turne me ashore, I shall
desire you to give me a glasse of poyson, which I shall receive and
drinke with much more pleasure," and soe fell a weepinge. He
desird hir to raise up hir speritts, and to be confident she had to doe
with a gentleman who did scorne to exposse anie lady to such an
extremitie, and that, rather then she should receive aney prejudice,
he would venter his owne life to secure hirs, of which she might
be assured, and soe that she would rest in peace, and that in the
morninge he would give hir further satisfaction about itt. Soe, she
seeminge to be indifferently well satisfied, he left hir to hir reposse.
The next morninge Mr. Rawdon and the captaine were with some
care how to disposse of hir, soe he bethought him of a Hollander
laden with wines that rid hard by them, with whom he had some
small accquentance. Soe the captaine he went aborde him; she
beinge a faire big ship, thought itt might be a very convenient passage for the lady; soe when they came abord the Hollander they
told him they were come to breake thir fast with him: he caried
them into the greate cabbin and made them very welcome. While
they were att brakefast they told him they had a hansome lady
abord, who they thought would have made them happie in hir
company for England, but hir mind was altered, and she was
resolved to goe for Holland, and that they thought none would
entertaine hir and use hir more civilly then him selfe, and that if he
pleas'd, when the wind was faire (for they were looth to be deprived
of hir good company till then) that then they would bringe her
and hir retinew abord. The Hollander, beinge a lustie yonge fel-

low, was very much pleas'd with the motion, givinge them many
thankes for thir kindnesse to him, and promis'd them she should
have the best accomodation the ship could afford hir, and that he
would taike a time to come abord and to certifie as much to the
lady himselfe; which they desired him to doe, and that he should be
very welcome; and soe they for that time parted. They were no
soner come abord but the lady sends for Mr. Rawdon, desiringe to
know what he and the captaine did resolve concerninge hir. He
told her he did conceive that, by reason of the proclamation made
at Bourdeaux, itt would nott be saife for the captaine to transport
hir, but desir'd to know of hir if she would please to goe for Holland ? She said, as to that itt was indifferent to hir; that she was
a stranger to booth places, and itt would be all alike to hir, soe she
gott but out of the Kinge of France his dominions; though she was
very sorry it fell out soe that she could nott goe alonge with them,
where she had bene soe civilly treated. Mr. Rawdon did comple-
ment hir as to that, and told hir that the captaine and he went that
morninge abord the greate Hollander, whosse captaine, nott know-
ing aney thinge of hir busnesse, had promis'd them to give hir the
best accomodation the ship could afford, and that he would come,
they thought, the next day to certifie as much unto hirselfe; with
which she remained very well satisfied. Soe within four or five
dayes, the wind comminge faire, they carried hir with what belong'd
unto hir, abord the Hollander, givinge hir some peces of ordnance
att partinge, and the Hollander the like for hir welcome abord.
Soe, after they bene treated a while by the Hollander in the greate
cabin, where they see where hir accomodation should be, they tooke
thir last farewell of hir, they never after hearinge what became of
hir; and thus much, if nott to much, for the French lady.

The wind beinge faire, they sett saile, had a good passage, and in
few dayes gott the Ile of Wight, and from thence to London, where
they arived about the begininge of March, where he staid with his
unckle till Aprill, att which time his unckle ordered him to goe

into the west country to Bastable[a] to fraight a ship, and to goe to
the Canaries, which he accordingly did, laden hir with packe goods
and pipe staves. Whilst he was here he was very nobly treated by
Alderman Palmer and Alderman Page, Captain Nicholas Norris,
and a gentleman who was then chiefe çoustomer[b] of that towne.
The tow aldermen sent an adventure of goods with him, which
came to a very good market. He set saile from Bastable about the
1631. end of Aprill 1631; in the way he tucht at the Iland of the
Maderas, sold part of his goods thir for redie mony which he carried
with him to the Canary Ilands,[c] beinge a pretious commoditie in
thosse parts. Towards the latter end of May he arived in Santa
Crux, a port towne of the Iland of Tenerife, one of the chiefest
ilands of the Canaria, from whence the best Canary wine comes.
After he had bene thir some small time he setled himselfe in Lalaguna,[d] the chiefe cittie of that iland, where he hir'd a faire howse

---

[a] Barnstaple.   [b] Coustomer, Coutumier, Fr., farmer or receiver of the customs.

[c] The Canary Islands since the commencement of the fifteenth century have belonged to
the Crown of Spain. They are seven in number, Teneriffe and Canaria being the largest
and most important. They were first remarkable for the production of sugar. The cultivation of the sugar-cane, probably towards the close of the fifteenth century, had passed from
Sicily and the eastern shores of the Mediterranean to Madeira, and thence to the Canaries,
and, at a later period, from the Canaries to the Brazils. The merchants of Bristol are said to
have sent factors from Spain to the Canaries as early as in the reign of King Henry VII. In
1555 Robert Thomson, an Englishman, sailed from Cadiz to the Canaries, and at La Laguna
found an establishment consisting of the servants of Anthony Hickman and Edward Cas-
telyn, who were eminent London merchants in the earlier part of the reign of Queen
Elizabeth. (Hakluyt's Voyages, new ed. vol. iii. p. 531; Cal. State Papers temp. Eliz.
pp. 142, 143.) "So come our sugars from Canary Iles," is a line in Sylvester's version
of Du Bartas, which was published in 1613. In the "History of the Canary Islands"
by George Glas (London, 4to. 1764), it is stated that Teneriffe was the centre of the trade
between Europe and the British colonies in America, and that in the seventeenth century
that trade was engrossed by a company of Protestant English merchants who resided at
Teneriffe. The memoir of Mr. Rawdon contains much information relating to the factory
at Teneriffe and the trade carried on there in the seventeenth century which is not to be
found in any historical account of the islands hitherto published.

[d] Santa Cruz is now the chief port and real capital of the island of Teneriffe. In Mr.
Rawdon's time Laguna or La Laguna was the principal town of the island, and he showed

in which he lived nere scaven yeares, in which time he had large cargasons of goods sent him booth from his unckle Sir Marmaduke and other marchants of London, from other parts of England, France, and Ireland, his comissions beinge worth then above a thousand pownds per anum, with which he lived very nobly, in greate creditt, and gott a good estate.

About the yeare 1637, his unckle havinge sent one Marmaduke 1637. Squier,ᵃ the son of a Yorkshire gentleman, to be Mr. Rawdon's assistant, desired him to leave his busnesse with the said Squier, and to come home to see his freinds, and to caven some longe accounts which could nott well be done att soe greate a distance, and to leave what goods and debts he had of Sir Marmaduke's with the said Mr. Squier, who was then his unkle's sarvant. Mr. Rawdon beinge then in the hight of his imployments, and gettinge of mony, was looth to goe for England, but he had such a tender respect to his unckle, under whom he had bene soe carefully breed, that his will was allwayes with him a command. Soe, wavinge all inconveniences, he resolved to goe for England; soe, endeavoringe to settle his busnesse in the best manner he could, in Aprill, 1638, he 1638. resolved to goe home in an English ship of London, of which one Augustin Bright · was commander. Soe beinge accompanied with severall English marchants, severall Spanish captaines and collonells, with other grave Dons, to the number of about 40, most of them with thir gold chaines about thir neckes, he tooke horse att his owne howse in the cittie of Lalaguna, where they went in much order through the cittie, Mr. Rawdon ridinge the last, except sarvants, in the middle betwixt a Spanish collonell and Captaine Henry

---

his taste and discernment in choosing it for his residence. " The perpetual coolness which is found at Laguna is the reason why in the Canaries it is considered as a delightful abode. Situate in a small plain, surrounded by gardens, protected by a hill which is crowned by a wood of laurels, myrtles, and arbutus, the capital of Teneriffe is very beautifully placed." See Humboldt's Personal Narrative of Travels in 1799-1804.

ᵃ Probably a member of the gentilitial family of Squire, which at this period was seated at Ulleskelf, a village on the banks of the Wharfe near Tadcaster in Yorkshire.

Isham,[a] then chiefe of the English nation thir, and the first gentleman that ever made use of a coach in thosse ilands. Thosse
gentlemen accompanied him to the port of Orotava,[b] beinge fifteene
miles. By the way Mr. Rawdon had order'd a treatment to be provided of rosted hens, cold Portugall gamons of bacon, English neats
tongues, and other provisions, with exclent wines, with which they
did refresh themselves. The apparell he rid in, with his chaine of
gold and hattband, was vallued in a thousand Spanish duccatts,
beinge tow hundreth and seventie and five pounds sterlin. His
hatband was of esmeralds set in gold; his suite was of fine cloth
trimd with a small silke and gold fringe; the buttons of the suite
were of fine gold, goldsmith worke; his raper and dagger richly
hatcht with gold. In this manner he came to the port of Orotava,
where he rested that night. The next morninge the captaine of
the ship came ashore with his boote, to know when he would please
to goe abord, which was apoynted after dinner, att which time
came the alcalde or maior of the port, with some other Spanish gentlemen, to wish him a good voyage, and to accompany him downe
to the water side; where, taikinge leave of all thosse gentlemen, he
imbarkt with the captaine, his cash-keeper, and his blacamore footboy,
and went abord of ship, where he was welcom'd with a brave peale
of ordnance which the captaine had commanded to be redie against
thir comminge abord. Havinge bene abord about halfe an houre,
they waied anchor. As the seamen went about with the capstan
waighin the anchor, Mr. Rawdon bid them be coragious; that every
step they made then was a step towards England, with which they
run about very merrely. The anchor beinge wayed, they presently
sett saile, givinge three pece of ordnance as a farewell to the port of

---

[a] A younger son of Gregory Isham, esquire, of Barby in Northamptonshire, and a kinsman of Sir John Isham, baronet, of Lamport in that county. Captain Henry Isham was
living at Laguna in the Canaries in 1624. (Wotton's Baronetage, ii. 36.) He is frequently named in Pepys's Diary. One of his sisters was the second wife of Sir Sidney
Montagu, father of the first Earl of Sandwich.

[b] Oratava and Garrachica were then the principal ports of the island of Teneriffe.

Oratava, salutinge every towne as they sail'd downe the iland,
which was done by Mr. Rawdon's order, and uppon his cost, which
did move the inhabitants, who knew who was abord, to pray for
thir good voyage. The reason I say they knew who was abord is
this: itt hapned not longe before, some English marchants had taiken
up some quantitie of goodes to the vallew of six or seaven thousand
powndes, and had gon, or rather run away, in the Spaniards' debts
without leavinge them ancy order of satisfaction, much to the dis-
repute and scandall of the English nation. To repaire in some part
that discreditt, Mr. Rawdon did by order of justice cause a proclamation to be made by the common crier in all the port townes of
the iland, and in the cittic of Lalaguna, that within twentie dayes
he was to imbarke for England; soe that if ancy had aniething dew
to them from him, his factors, or sarvants that he did imploy, that
they should repaire to his howse in Lalaguna and recieve satisfaction; and whosoever did not come within that time, thir pretences
should be held as frivolous and unjust. This faire proceedinge got
Mr. Rawdon much creditt amongst the ilanders, and made them
believe, though one or tow had plaid them a slippery tricke, yet that
itt was nott a generall distemper of the nation, and that they might
expect more honourable proceedings from the rest that remaind.

But to come againe to our voyage. They steard that night for
the iland of the Gomera,* where they were to taike in some West
India comodities, and gott thir the next day. Here they staid
three dayes, in which time he was hansomly feasted by the governour,
and the governour by him abord the ship. Att his comminge
away the governour and the chiefe gentlemen thir accompaned him
to the sea side, where, taiking his leave of them, he imbarkt. Now
by the way I will give you notice of the provisions Mr. Rawdon
had for his voyage abord the ship, most of which was presented
unto him by Spaniards:

Two pipes of Canary wine.

---

* Gomera is one of the smaller of the Canary Islands. A century later Gomera and
Ferro were so poor that no ships went to them from Europe or America.—Glas.

Two dozen of gammons of bacon and neats' tongues.

Two firkins of severall sorts of fresh fish boild and sousd or pickled after a most exelent way.

Fowerteene live sheepe.

Thirtie turkies.

One hundreth and twentie hens.

Two live hoggs.

Fortie small jarrs of olives and capers of severall sortes.

Six smale barills of fine white bisket.

Fower smale barills full of boxes of mermelade of severall sorts.

Severall sorts of dried sweetmeates.

His provisions were soe greate that the ilanders reported he went for England to be made a bishop, thinkinge thosse provisions could belonge only to some greate churchman.

Abord the ship he was served all in silver plates and platters of his owne which he brought abord with him, and to his table he admitted only the captaine of the ship and a Spanish gentleman, one Don Gaspar de Osorio, who was recomended to his care by his freinds. Notwithstandinge his large provisions, they had soe longe a passage by reason of calme weather that they were seaven weekes att sea without puttinge into aney harbour; soe that, when they came uppon the coast of England, the most of thir provisions were spent. The people of the ship were very carelesse, and noe very good seamen, for they did nott know, for all itt was summer time, whether they were uppon the coast of England or France, or well where they were; which Mr. Rawdon percievinge by thir various opinions, he caused a pece of gold to be nailed to the maine mast, promisinge itt to him that should first discover land. A good pollicy in suche a casse to escape shipwracke, for by this meanes thir was allwayes one idle fellow or other, night and day, on the top mast's heades lookinge out for land; and, after tow or three dayes, itt was the fortune of the maister's mate of the ship to discover the iland of Silly, and soe had the gold. After this they had a fresh gale which carried them up the channell as high as Portsmouth, where he, his sarvant, and his blacamore landed. Att that time was Deputie Governour of Portsmouth, under my Lord of Linsey,[a] Captaine Hyams, a nere relation of his aunt the Lady Rawdon, who, hearinge of him, came to give him a vizitt, att which time he found the drumes and trumpets of the towne with their loud musicke proclaminge his welcome into England. After some complements, and drinkinge tow or three glasses of wine, Mr. Rawdon requested the Deputie Governour to come and sup with him, and to bringe with him halfe a dozen of his accquentance, men or women, which he pleasd, which he very kindly accepted of; and in the interim Mr. Rawdon desiered him to give him leave to see the fortifications. He told him he could nott waite uppon him himselfe, which he would willingly have done, but that he had some busnesse of importance in towne that afternone, soe he would send a soldier with him that should shew him all that was to be seene, and that, soe sone as he could, he would waite uppon him himselfe. Soe they parted, and he went alonge with the soldier to see the fortifications, which as he was viewinge he was mett by an officer which came up to him some-thinge angerly, sayinge, " Sir, I hope you are nott what your out-ward habit speakes you;" to which Mr. Rawdon answerd, " No, Sir; my outward habitt is accordinge to the coustome of the country from whence I come, but they have English linings and an English heart within them;" with which he was very well satisfied. Also the soldier told him he came by order of the Deputie Governour, soe he very civilly tooke his leave and went away, leavinge Mr. Rawdon to satisfie his curiositie in vewinge the workes.

Att supper time the Deputie Governour came, brought a cupple of gentlemen and three or four well-bred gentlewomen, in whosse exclent company they past the supper-time and part of the night, and att a convenient time parted. That eavninge Mr. Rawdon had ordered his blacamore boy that he should drinke noe wine for feare he should be drunke, but, goinge to bed, the boy came to him say-

* Robert Bertie, Earl of Lindsey, constituted Lord High Admiral of England in 1635; slain at the battle of Edge Hill in 1642.

inge, " Sir, may nott I drinke a small sorte of wine which is like
watter?" by which he percievd the boy had bene drinkinge of
French wine, which, in comparison of Canary sacke, he thought
was like water; but his maister told him that small wine would
make him drunke as well as Canary wine, and that he was only to
drinke small English beere, which afterwards he observed.   Att the
same time his maister askt him how he likt England; he said itt was
a plentifull country of victualls, for he had hardly seene soe much
victuals att a supper in all his life.

The next morninge he and his sarvants tooke horse for London.
They left thir horses with the fellow that came alonge with them,
and tooke boot at Putney for London, and landed att the Old Swan.[a]
When they came ashore, the blacamore boy after his ridinge, sitting
soe longe in the boote, was soe stiffe that he could niether goe nor
scarce stand, soe his maister calld a porter to cary him uppon his
shoulders after him to Sir Marmaduke Rawdon's howse in Water
Lane,[b] where he came on a Saturday morninge about ten of the
clocke.   The first man that came to the gate after he knockt was
John the Frenchman, Sir Marmaduke's caterer, who he left in the
howse when he went for the Canaries, who, after he had lett him
in, knowinge of him, kneld downe uppon the grownd to embrasse
his legs, and bid him in French welcome to England.   In a parler
in the courtyard he found Captane Edmund Forster [c] and Mr.
Swinarton, tow of Sir Marmaduke's former sarvants, and then had
a small part of stocke with him; also he thir found with them his
cossen Marmaduke, his unkle's seacond son, who was lately come

_____

[a] " The Old Swan, Upper Thames Street. A celebrated landing-place on the Middlesex
side of the river Thames, a little ' above bridge,' where people used to land and walk to
the other side of old London Bridge, rather than run the risk of what was called shooting
the bridge."—Cunningham's Handbook, vol. ii. p. 794.

[b] Sir Marmaduke's town residence was in Water Lane, between Tower Street and
Lower Thames Street, where the old Trinity House formerly stood.—Ibid. vol. ii.
pp. 848, 872.

[c] Captain Edmund Forster was both the partner and the son-in-law of Sir Marmaduke
Rawdon.

out of France; and, inquieringe for his unckle, who he presently
see through the glasse comminge out of his closett on the other side
of the courtyard, soe he imediatly left thosse gentlemen, and went
and mett his unckle in the middle of the court, payinge thosse
respects that was dew unto him. His unckle tooke him by the
hand, bid him welcome, and walkt into the parlor with him, where
the rest of the gentlemen were. After some discourse he understood
that his cossen Mr. Thomas Rawdon,[a] the eldest son of Sir Marmaduke, was the day before arived from Portugall, and was above in
his chamber ill disposd in bed; soe, they havinge bene allwayes
greate corespondents, and lovinge freinds att home and abrode, he
desird he might goe up to see him; soe, accompanied with his unckle
and thosse gentlemen, he went up to see him. The tow cossens
havinge complemented one the other, they sitt downe talkinge of
severall thinges, and, a little while after, they all went to the
Exchange togeather; which beinge done they came home to dinner.
Att dinner Sir Marmaduke told him he would have him goe downe
with him to Hodsden. He answered he was very redy to obey his
commands; soe Sir Marmaduke, his cossen Marmaduke, and he
went downe that afternone to Hodsden, where they spent some part
of the ensuinge weeke, and then wente to London, where he staid till
he had given up his accompts, in which busnesse Captaine Forster
was his greate oposer; but he did convince him with soe much reason, that all thinges was fairely concluded amongst them; which
beinge done Captaine Forster came to him sayinge, "Well, our busnesse now is done, our accounts beinge ended, and wee are to have
noe further disputes, and to be freindes togeather; but I will lett you

---

[a] Sir Marmaduke and Lady Rawdon had issue ten sons and six daughters. Thomas,
the eldest son, was born in 1612 and died in 1666. In 1630 his father sent him to
Oporto, where and at Lisbon he inspected his father's factorship, and was held in great
respect of that nation. In 1638 he returned through Spain to England, and attended on
his way the Duchess of Chevreuse, then intending a visit to Queen Henrietta Maria. The
Duchess was one of the ladies who accompanied the young Queen on her first coming to
England in 1625.

alone to make your partie good with anie man in England;" and
soe in token of kindnesse presented him with a curious silke strait
purse, which he kept a longe time after for his sake.

These thinges beinge thus concluded, thir was nothinge treated of
but mirth and feastinge; and Sir Marmaduke, for the joy of the
arivall of his tow sons and his nephew, made att his howse att
Hodsden a greate feast, to which was invited the Earle of Salisbury [a]
and his Countesse, the Lord Cranborne his son, with the rest of his
sons and daughters, the Lord Norris,[b] and severall other persons of
honor, where thir was all the varieties that England could afford,
for viands and severall sorts of wines, and cost, as I was informed,
one hundreth and fortie pownds.   When Mr. Rawdon went up first
from Hodsden to London he was to be new clothed after the English fashion, which was then blacke cloothes lind with plush for
black suites, and for collord clooths a tabie-dublett, cloth breches,
and the clooke lind with the same tabbie of the dublett.   Itt
hapned one Mr. Flower, his unckle's taylor, had taiken measure of
him for his cloothes, but had forgot to aske what price he would
have his cloth plush and tabbie of; soe he chanced to come to his
unckle's howse in Water Lane when his unckle, Captaine Forster,
Mr. Swinarton, Mr. Thomas Rawdon, and he were at dinner; soe his
unckle, hearinge he was in the yarde, orderd him to be brought in
to know what he would.   He said he only came to speake with Mr.
Duke Rawdon, for soe he cald him, to know of what price he would
have his plush-clothe and tabbie a yarde.   They told him he was
thir to answer for himselfe; soe he answerd Mr. Flower that he was
a stranger in England to the prises of thosse comodities, but that he
should buy for him the best of each sorte that he could get for

---

[a] William Cecil, second Earl of Salisbury, succeeded to the title in 1612, and died in
1668.   His countess was Catherine youngest daughter of Thomas Howard, Earl of
Suffolk.   Their eldest son, James Viscount Cranbourne, was born in 1616.   Hatfield,
Lord Salisbury's seat, is but a few miles distant from Hoddesdon.

[b] Probably James Bertie, in right of his mother Lord Norreys of Rycot, created Earl of
Abingdon by King Charles II.

mony, att which his unckle smilinge said, " I commend you, nephew; winn gold and weare gold."

About this time came out of Yorkshire to London the Lady Jaques his sister and Sir Roger hir husband[a] to see him, who were lodged at thir unckle's, Mr. Robart Rawdon's,[b] howse in Bermondsie Court, and from thence were daily invited by thir relations and accquentance, which were then many in London. Att other times they spent thir time in seeinge thosse rairities that were to be seen about London. They went to Greenwich, where the Court then was, where, uppon Sir Marmaduke Rawdon's accquentance, who went with them, they were highly favour by my Lord Chamberlane,[c] kist the Kinge and Queen's hand, see the lodgins, and what els that place afforded, and after dinner the gentlemen went to bowles att Blacke Heath. This afternoone Mr. Rawdon managd one of the King's horses before his unkle and sister and severall others of his relations with much dexteritie.

Amongst other sights that they see, it was none of the worst, the Royall Soverainge, who was then newly finisht, and rid att Erisfe; soe, hiringe a barge, thir went Sir Marmaduke Rawdon, Sir Roger Jaques, and thir ladies, Mr. Robart Rawdon and his lady, and some of thir sons, daughters, and relations, of which Mr. Rawdon, of whom we now treate, was one. The commander of hir then was Captaine Rainsbery,[d] an accquentance of Sir Marmaduke's, who

---

[a] Roger Jaques, a merchant and alderman of York, was married to Mary youngest daughter of Lawrence Rawdon, at the parish church of Saint Crux in York, on the 5th February, 162⅜. Roger Jaques was Lord Mayor of York in the year 1639, and was knighted by King Charles I. when that monarch visited the city on his way to Scotland. Sir Roger was the founder of the family of Jaques of Elvington near York. He was a staunch royalist, and was displaced from the office of alderman of York by order of the Parliament in 1645. In Dugdale's Visitation of Yorkshire (Surtees Soc. p. 162), Lady Jaques is erroneously stated to be the daughter of Sir Marmaduke Rawdon.

[b] Robert Rawdon, esquire, of Mitcham and Bermondsey Court in the county of Surrey, an elder brother of Sir Marmaduke Rawdon. He was a member of the Corporation of London, and Deputy of Bridge Ward.

[c] Philip Herbert, Earl of Pembroke and Montgomery, was then Lord Chamberlain.

[d] The commander of the Royal Sovereign was most probably Captain Rainsborough, who was one of the Lords of the Admiralty, as appears by an order of the Board dated April 21,

entertaind them with the best thinges he had abord. I have heard
them say they were eleven of them all togeather in the greate lanthorne of the said ship.[a]

Sir Roger and his lady havinge bene here a monthe, almost tyrd
out with feastinge, did desire to goe home into Yorkshire. Soe
they were accompanied by thir brother and relations downe to
Hodsdon, where they staid some little time; and, a day or tow after,
thir friends went with them as far as Ware, and thir they parted.
After this Mr. Rawdon spent the latter part of the summer in
country recreations, and buckhuntinge, sometimes in Hodsden woods
with my Lord of Salisbury, and other. places thirabouts. My Lord
of Salisbury told Sir Marmaduke that he thought his nephew would
have kild the stagg or rid him to death with his horse, he followed

1632 (Cal. State Papers, 1631-33), and the father of General Rainsborough who met
with an untimely fate at Doncaster in 1648. Clarendon says of the latter that "he was
the son of an eminent commander at sea lately dead." (Hist. of the Rebellion, vol. iii. p. 199.)

[a] In one of Howel's letters we have an interesting description of this "Great Eastern"
of the 17th century :

"I have other news also to tell you. We have a brave new ship, a royal galeon, the
like they say did never spread sail upon salt water, take her true and well compacted sym-
metry with all dimensions together. For her burden she hath as many tuns as there
were years since the Incarnation, when she was built, which are sixteen hundred thirty
and six. She is in length one hundred twenty and seven feet; her greatest breadth within
the planks is fourty-six foot and six inches; her depth from the breadth is nineteen foot
and four inches. She carrieth a hundred peeces of ordnance wanting four, whereof she
hath three tyre [tiers]. *Half a score men may stand in her lanthorn.* The charges his
Majesty hath been at in the building of her are computed to be four-score thousand
pounds, one whole year's ship-money. Sir Robert Mansel launchd her, and, by his Majesties command, calld her *The Soverain of the Sea.*"—To Simon Digby, Esq. at Moscow,
Familiar Letters, ed. 1678, p. 256.

A scarce tract by Thomas Heywood, entitled "A True Description of His Majesties
Royall Ship built this yeare, 1637, at Wooll-witch in Kent. To the great glory of our
English Nation, and not paraleled in the whole Christian World." (London, 1637),
informs us that the "prime workmen employed in this inimitable fabricke" were
Captain Phines Pett, overseer of the work, his son young M. Peter Pett, the master
builder, Master Francis Shelton, clerk of the check, and John and Mathias Christmas,
master-carvers. In 1641 Evelyn went to Chatham to see "the Royal Sovereign, a glorious vessel of burden lately built there, being for defence and ornament the richest that
ever spread cloth before the wind." (Diary, vol. i. p. 17, new ed.) The ship is said to
have been accidentally burnt at Chatham in 1696.

him so closse. After all thosse pastimes, about the latter end of September, he went downe into Yorkshire to pay his dewtie to his beloved mother,[a] and to give a vizitt to the rest of his relations in that country, where he was very kindly recieved, and spent the most of that winter amongst them till January, att which time his unckle had letters from the Canaries, how that Marmaduke Squier did behave himselfe very extravagantly, spendinge and consuminge his estate without controule, and, not only that, but that he did bringe his son Marmaduke,[b] who was then thir, into engagements of debts with him, which did very much troble Sir Marmaduke, who presently writ to Yorke to his nephew Marmaduke to come up, which he accordingly did, and, beinge come up, he gave him the sad relation of all Squier's miscariages accordinge to the advice he had from his son, and told him thir was a nescessitie to put a sudden remedie to thosse thinges, which he did nott know how to doe except he would goe over and call him to account. Mr. Rawdon answerd he was willinge to obey his comands in all thinges, and to doe him the best service he could, soe imediatly a gallant ship was fraighted, of which was commander Captain John Daniel, which, beinge laden with goods, was dispatcht downe into the Downes. Whilst this ship was a dispachinge Mr. Rawdon had a desier to see some of his old accquentance in the West country; soe, accompanied with his sarvant, he went first to Southampton, where he was very nobly feasted by Mr. Peter Priaux, but especially by Mr. Nicholas

---

[a] Mr. Rawdon had been absent twelve years when he revisited his native city in 1638, and this was the last opportunity he enjoyed of paying his duty to his mother. The widow of Lawrence Rawdon died at York on the 17th of April, 1644, at the age of 74, and was buried near her husband in the church of St. Crux. The nuncupative will of " Mrs. Margerie Rawdon of the city of York, widow," was made a little before her death. She gave all her household goods to her three daughters, and her best clothes to her daughter Lady Jaques, and the worst of her clothes to be at the disposal of her daughters. She made her two sons, Roger [Jaques] and Marmaduke, residuary legatees, " and said further that she ought [owed] not anything to any man." Proved at York, 24th Sept. 1646.

[b] The second son of Sir Marmaduke Rawdon.

Pescod, one of the greatest marchants, nott only of Hampton, but of the West country, who was very earnest with him to have married his eldest daughter Mrs. Katherin, with whome he offred him three thousand powndes in redie mony, tellinge him he had severall gentlemen of good estates suitors for hir, but that he had rather marrye hir to a marchant of good fame, that knew how to gett his livinge and preserve the portion he gave with his daughter, then to marrie hir to one that only knew how to spend itt; and withall shewed him his eldest son, sayinge, " Doe you see yon pulinge boy with the white cap on? If he die she will be a brave fortune to you indeed;" and in order to this did invite him to his howse; and one night the yonge gentlewoman and he were left after supper alone togeather, where they were allmost till midnight, he likinge hir company well enough (beinge a very accomplisht yonge lady), but nott as to marriage; soe thinges havinge gon soe far as civilly they might, he gave Mr. Pescod many thankes for his civill treatmente, a more especially for the good oppinion he had of him to thinke him worthy of his daughter and soe good a fortune with hir, but, to deale ingeniously with him, he could nott marry hir, for he was engaged to his unckle Sir Marmaduke Rawdon to make another voyage for the Canaries, to call an idle factor of his, who went consuminge his estate, to account, and how longe he should stay thir about that busnesse he could nott tell; which he tooke as an ingenious honest answer, and soe they parted very freindly. This gentlewoman, after hir father's death, was married into Normandie to a French marques. From thence he went to Poole, where he was kindly treated by the Scotts, greate marchants of that towne, whom he had formerly knowne in the Canaries. From thence he went to Weymouth, where he was entertained by a French gentleman called Captaine Piera de Salanueva, who was a famous surgeon, and a greate soldier under the Duke de Subiz, in the Protestant warr in France. To this captaine Mr. Rawdon had shewd much favour in the Canary Ilands, and thir lent him a good percell of mony which he could nott recover of him, but in token of his gratitude he told him, " Sir, here is like

now to be warrs in England; I have an armour of proffe which I
know will fitt you, and is one of the best that ever was made in
France, for I have seene the tryall of itt. Beinge I can give you
noe mony I will present itt to you, beinge the best jewell I have;
and, if itt be your fortune to goe into the warrs, you will esteem itt
soe;" which armour he did accept of, and was all he had for his
mony att that time.

From Weymouth he returned backe, and in his way to London
went to vizitt his former acequentance Mrs. Alis Randall, a little
gentlewoman, but estemed one of the greate beawties of England,
and much admired by the Kinge, beinge one very like the Queene
and much of hir hight. She had bene formerly his fellow sarvant
att his unckle's, by the name of Mrs. Alis Alsop,* and did waite
uppon the Lady Rawdon, whom he found att home; staid some
few houres thir, and that night went to London.

Beinge come to London he found the ship reddie, soe about the 1639.
middel of March, havinge dispatchd his busnesse in London, he
tooke his journie; his unckle Sir Marmaduke went with him into
Southwarke to Berdmondsie Court, where his other unckle Mr.
Robart Rawdon had a howse, where they brooke thir fasts, and here
he tooke his last farewell of booth his deere unckles, for he never
saw them more. Here he took horse for the Downes, where the
ship did stay for him, beinge accompanied by his tow cossen-germans,
Collonel Thomas Rawdon and Mr. Ralph Trattle,[b] as also by Liue-
tennant-collonel Forster,[c] Captaine John Smart, Mr. Robart Swinarton, Mr. Nicholas Rainsford,[d] and other freinds. Thir first dayes

---

* Mrs. Alice Alsop, the little gentlewoman and great beauty, had probably married one
of the family of Randall of Buckinghamshire, of which in the early part of the seventeenth
century Sir Edward Randall, knight, was the head. See The Verney Papers, p. 277.

[b] The Trattles were a Yorkshire family. "My cossen Ralph Trattle and his wife" are
named in Mr. Rawdon's will.

[c] The Captain Edmund Forster previously named.

[d] Ellinor, daughter of Robert Rawdon of Bermondsey Court, married Nicholas Rainsford
of Warwickshire. (Visit. of Lond. 1633, Harl. MS. No. 1476.) The Rainsfords were seated
at Clifford near Stratford-upon-Avon, a house at which the poet Drayton was accustomed

journie was to Rochester, thir next to Dover; a merry journie they
had of itt, and, havinge staid thir tow or three dayes rejoycinge
themselves, the wind came faire, soe they went to Deale, where they
lodgd one night; the next day they went with Mr. Rawdon to the
water side, and thir tooke thir leaves of him.   He then imbarkinge
himselfe with his fower sarvants, vizt. Mr. Marmaduke Harrison,[a]
a Yorkshire gentleman with whom he was accquented in his youth,
who was stuard of his provisions abord the ship, and afterwards
stuard of his howse in the Canarys; the seacond was Thomas Gill,
his cash keeper, whom he brought with him from the Canaries; the
third was John Wade, a youth of Dover, who beinge a good ac-
countant and writinge a good hand, he thir tooke to be his sarvant;
the fowerth was his trumpeter, whom he had hired for that voyage,
whosse dewtie was to sound when his dinner and supper was brought
up, att aney time when he was disposd to be merry or drinke healths
abord,[b] also when he understood he was arisinge or goinge to bed,
also when soever he went ashore or came abord duringe that voyage.
For this voyage he was as well stord with provisions as could well
be had, but what they wanted in meate, as the old proverb saith,
they might taike in drinke, for he had aborde the ship three hundreth bottles of wine, French and Spanish; soe when one of Sir
Marmaduke's sarvants went to the Coustome howse for a bill of
store for them, Sir Paul Pindar[c] merrily askt if Mr. Rawdon was
goinge to the East Indias.

to spend part of every summer, and which, Mr. Hunter thinks, must have been open to
Shakespeare. New Illustrations, vol. i. p. 84.

[a] Mr. Marmaduke Harrison was a native of Bransby, the parish in which Sir Marmaduke Rawdon and his brothers were born.

[b]   And, as he drains his draughts of Rhenish down,
            The kettledrum and trumpet thus bray out
            The triumph of his pledge.
The poet was probably satirising a vice of his own countrymen and his own age when he
condemned this custom as "more honoured in the breach than the observance."

[c] Sir Paul Pindar was a farmer or lessee of the customs. He was one of the great
merchants of the days of James I. and Charles I. who amassed immense wealth by the

He was noe soner abord but presently they sett saile in sight of 1639. his freinds with a faire winde, and a merry voyage they had, the wind continuinge constantly faire, soe that in 17 dayes they arived saifly att the iland of the Grand Canaries, where he solde a greate part of his cargason for reddic mony; and after eight or ten dayes stay he imbarkt himselfe and his mony for the iland of Teneriffe, wher in tow dayes he saifly arived att the port of Orotava, wher his cossen Marmaduke Rawdon mett him, and was glad to see him, thinkinge himselfe then stronge enough to make his partie good with Mr. Squier, and gave him a full account of all the said Mr. Squier's vaine proseedings, and how farr he was forced to be engaged with him; soe he cheerd him up, and told him he did nott doubt but he should doe well enough with him. The next day Mr. Squier came to see Mr. Rawdon, which day was only past in complements and enquieries after newes; soe they went to the cittie of Lalaguna, where they had thir howses; soe thir they began to speake of busnesse, Mr. Rawdon tellinge him what he came about, and that he had order from his unckle to taike an account of him, as he might percieve by thosse letters he brought him, and withall desird that itt might be done with freindship, and as sone as he conveniently could. Mr. Squier seemed willinge to give an account, but was led away by some wicked Englishmen of the iland who had gott into his debt; and to support thir owne decayd conditions did not care though they ruind his, soe that noe accompt of anie thinge could be gott, soe that Mr. Rawdon was forced to doe itt by order of justice. Att last he gave an account, but a most basse one, bringinge Sir Marmaduke ten thousand pownds in his debt. Mr. Rawdon tooke time to pose itt, and made his objections against all the unjust artickles he found in itt, which

contracts and patents for monopolies which were obtained from the crown in that corrupt age. He was remarkable for being the possessor of a large diamond worth 35,000*l*. See Cal. State Papers, 1619-1631, where his name frequently occurs. The house he lived in is now the "Sir Paul Pindar's Head," a publichouse in Bishopsgate Street Without. Cunningham's H. B. vol. i. p. 92.

amounted to fifteene thousand powndes, so as Squier came to be five
thousand powndes in Sir Marmaduke's debt, as in trueth he was;
soo att last itt was by a generall consent referd to arbitration, and
Squier only condemd to pay fifteen hundred powndes, though in
justice he ought thrice the mony. The ilanders to whom Mr.
Squier was indebted stood all att gaze to see the conclusion of this
busnesse; Squier makinge them believe that Rawdon would owe a
greate summe of mony, sufficient to pay them and more; but, the
busnesse ended, and Squier in Rawdon's debt, Squier's creditors
went about about to siez on what goods of Squier's they could find;
but Rawdon, havinge made the greate lords of the High Court of
Justice his frindes, gott orders first to siez uppon him and his sur-
ties which he had given to pay what should be awarded, siezd
uppon what goods was left, freed his cozen Marmaduke from his
engagements, and sent him home for England to give an account to
his father Sir Marmaduke of what had past.

    Mr. Rawdon still remained uppon the iland followinge his imploy-
ments; and, about a yeare after, Sir Marmaduke sent his son Marmaduke backe againe for the Canaries with a good cargason of goods,
recomendinge him to the assistance of his cossen Marmaduke; soe
they lived togeather till the latter end of 1643, att which time Mr.
Rawdon, of whome wee now treate, sent his cossen home with a
cargason of wines for booth thir accounts, desiringe him when he
was in England to goe and see his father, who was then Governour
of Basinge Castle,[*] and to present him from him, as a token of his
love and dewtie, with a curious gold hat-band of goldsmith worke
and a gold chaine; and that, of five hundred pownds he carried
with him in Barbary gold, he should show itt to his father to taike
itt all, or part, as he should best please. He arived saifely att Mount's
Bay in Devonshire, I would say Cornewell, and, according to his
cossen's request, went straite to his father att Basinge, havinge a
convoy from my Lord Hopton. When he came to his father, his
father askt him how he left his nephew. He told him very well, in

1640.
1641.
1642.
1643.

----

    * The siege of Basing House began in August, 1643.

good health, and that he had sent him a small present of a gold hat-
band and a gold chaine, with order likewisse that of 500 pounds he
had thir of Barbery gold he might taike part of itt or all if he had
occasion for itt.   He saied, "Lett me see your gold;" soe his son
pourd itt out of a greate silke nettworke purse uppon the table,
which lookinge uppon, he bid his son picke him out halfe a score of
the best duccatts and the finest gold, and told him, "This I taike to
make the King's picture to weare with the chaine of gold your
cossen haith sent me; for the rest, put them up and carry them
with you; itt may be my nephew and you may have more occasion
of them then I shall."

Here he staid some few dayes with his father, and then went for
Oxford, where he coynd some of his gold,[a] and from thence went to
London to meete the ship, where he disposed of his wines and gold
in comodities proper for the maine of Spaine, and soe tooke fraight
in a ship and went for Sevill, where he sold his goods very well,
imployed them in oyles and other goods proper for the Canary
Ilands, and, in the yeare 1644, about the monthe of June, he returnd   1644.
to the Iland of Teneriffe, to his cossen Marmaduke, who was very
glad of his arivall, and thir goods came to a very good market.

About this time Mr. Rawdon, of whome we now treate, receved
a letter in verse from Mr. Edmund Parlett, the honest vicar of
Broxborne and Hodsden,[b] beinge booth one parish; which, beinge
thir is somethinge of varietie in itt, I shall here insert:

To his honoured friend, Mr. Marmaduke Rawdon,
in the Canaries.

Duke! thou art saife in the Canaries
Whilst England's vexèd with contràries.
Here Protestant and Papist joynd
Fight against all thesse combin'd:

---

[a] King Charles I. had his mint at Oxford for several years during the Civil War.

[b] Edmund Parlett was at this time the incumbent of the vicarage of Broxbourne with
the chapel of Hoddesdon annexed.   Newcourt's Repertorium, vol. i. p. 813.

Brownists, Anabaptists, Famelists,
The Antinomians, Sepratists,
And thosse that make the greatest share
Of all, the Independents are.
Thir tailes, like Samson's foxes tide,
Thir heades, thir minds, are distant wide;
Yett all together doe conspire
To sett this wofull land on fire;
Thir union's only in this thinge,
Against a Bishop and the Kinge.
Thou hast left us in the lurch,
I am no vicar of a church;
The world's a sea with tempests oft
Tost, now under, now aloft.
Thir dangerous rocks, devowringe sande,
Shipwrakes various; thus is our land,
The ship of Church and State in floode
Orewhelm'd, not water, but of blood.
Nott only eies in salt teares steepes,
But blood in all hir members weepes. .
Curs'd be the hand, and curst the heade
That acted and this mischiefe breed.
England's in soe woefull casse,
Thou would'st nott know hir by hir face.
By raginge seas which cannot rest
Our kingdome may be well exprest;
Or like the standinge corne in fields,
Now this way blowne, now that way yields;
Now prettie even, now up, now downe,
Thus Charles doth strugle for his crowne.
But Bishops' seas and Bishops' name
Must post to Rome from whence they came
(The frontlesse say), when as the lie
Is given by all antiquitie.
England's church which haith made heade
Against the beast, and florished
In learninge, knowledge, more then all
Reformed churches, now must fall.
Which like a pleasant buildinge stood
Stronge, cemented with martirs' blood.

God's sacred worship, holy liturgie,
All must vaile to rude Prisbetery.
Send sighs sometimes from your hearts,
Pittie learning's fall, and arts.
Perticulers I dare nott tell,
And soe, my noble Duke, farewell!![a]

y[r] truly lo: freind,
E. P.

But now to come to our former discourse. Mr. Rawdon haveinge disposd of the cargason of goods he brought from Spaine, he staid with his cossen till the yeare 1648, att which time his cossen, out of the greate love he bore him, made him joynt partner with him in eaquall shares of all proffits whatsoever, and desired him to goe over againe to the maine of Spaine, and to goe and live att Madrid, the courte of Spaine, to see what good might be don thir; which he accordingly did, and his cossen, of whom we now treate, remained in the Ilands. He had nott bene longe thir in Madrid, but his cossen writt him to procure, if he could, the pattent of the tabbacco of all the Canary Ilands, that none should buy or sell anie tobacco thir but themselves or thir deputies; which he effected, payinge thirteene thousand duccatts a yeare rent; and, in the yeare 1649, 1649. sent over the King's letters pattents[b] to his cossen for the free administration of itt, with order that the Generall of the Ilands should be his judge conservator to defend him in itt, and to be the judge of all differences that might arise betwixt him and anie man concerninge tobacco. He was also alowed to have his sarjant peculiar to himselfe, which was calld El Alguazil del Tobacco, the Sarjant of the Tobacco, which went with his whitt rod, which thir they use insteade of a mace, before him, when he pleasd, in anie towne were he came to make search or aprehend anie man that had

[a] The verses of the "honest vicar" of Broxbourne are not of a high class, but they are quite equal to some other productions of the clerical muse of that period which have appeared in print. See Fairfax Correspondence, vol. i. p. lxxxi. &c.

[b] In England, ten years earlier, King Charles I. had made a vigorous attempt to abolish the oppressive system of monopolies, which seems still to have existed in full force under the government of Spain. See Rushworth, vol. ii. p. 917.

brought ancy tobacco into the iland privatly, without manifestinge
itt to the Arendador Maior, the chiefe renter or farmer, as he was
called.   This busnesse he governed with much quietnesse and indifferent good successe, but, thinkinge itt nott employment enough,
he writ his kinsman to Madrid to see if he could rent a principallitie
which did belonge to the Prince of Asculi,[a] whose predisessors were
conquerours of the Iland of Teneriffe, where he lived.   This with
good successe he effected, and sent presently orders for his cossen to
taike possession of the place and goverment thirof, which was a
place of much pleasure and delight, the chiefe seate of all the
ilands; a place likewise of greate proffitt, yielddinge six and seaven
hundred pipes of Canary wine per anum, besides severall tributes of
water, with which that howse was well stord; a pretious comoditie
in that country, soe that for lettinge thir water run one day in thir
nicbour's viniards they could have a pipe of Canary for every dayes
water.[b]   Itt had also severall tributes of corne, fruites, hens, sugar,

[a] The Prince of Asculi was the Adelantado or Lord-Lieutenant of Canaria.   "His
place by office is valued at 4000 ducats a year."   The present Estate of Spayne, by James
Wadsworth, p. 31.   London, 1630.

[b] Some of the towns of Teneriffe were well supplied with water by means of open
wooden spouts or troughs, which conveyed it from rivulets at a distance.   Near the city of
La Laguna "are many pleasant romantic little valleys and hollows, well watered, and abounding with shady groves." (Glas's History of the Canary Islands, p. 251.)   But in the whole
island of Férro or Hierro there were only three fountains.   On account of the scarcity of
water, the sheep, goats, and swine were not allowed to drink in the summer, but were
taught to dig up the roots of fern and chew them to quench their thirst; and the great
cattle were watered at the fountains and at a place where water distilled from the leaves
of a tree.   This precious water-yielding tree is described by Pliny in his account of the
Fortunate Islands, and is alluded to by many later naturalists and travellers.   It has not
escaped the notice of the poet :

> " In th'*Ile of Iron* (one of those same seav'n
> Whereto our elders *Happy* name had giv'n),
> The savage people never drink the streams
> Of wells and rivers (as in other realms):
> Their drink is in the aire; their gushing spring
> A weeping tree out of itself doth wring :
> A tree, whose tender-bearded root being spred
> In dryest sand, his sweating leafe doth shed

and monies; besids they had a thousand pownds a yeare out of the coustome howse, with other perquisetts; and for all this they paid but tow thousand pownds a yeare. Itt was likewisse a place of much honor, for the chiefe farmer had allowed him the tittle of Governour, and thir was many places belonginge to itt in the guift of the said governour, which made the ilanders to have him allwayes in greate respect; the governour of the whole iland,[a] his goverment, for matter of proffitt, is but a toy in comparison of this. Itt is a howse also uppon the matter previledged, for when thir was a presse for soldiers, and the maior of the towne searchinge all men's howses for soldiers, yet, though they partly knew that ther were some retird to this howse, they would nott offer to come in to search, nor to violate the antient respect that had bene allwayes given to itt.

> A most sweet liquor; and (like as the vine
> Untimely cut weeps at her wound) her wine
> In pearlèd tears incessantly distills
> A crystall stream, which all their cisterns fills
> Through all the Iland; for all hither hy,
> And all their vessells cannot draw it dry."
>
> > Du Bartas his Devine Weekes and Workes. Translated by
> > Joshua Sylvester, p. 66. London 1613.

Andrew Marvell, in his poem " On the Victory obtained by Blake over the Spaniards in the Bay of Santa Cruse, in the Island of Tenorif, 1657," thus alludes to the wonders of the Canaries:

> " ———— ———— and fortune smiles,
> For they behold the sweet Canary Isles,
> One of which doubtless is by nature blest
> Above both worlds, since 'tis above the rest.
> For, lest some gloomyness might stain her sky,
> Trees there the duty of the clouds supply.
> O noble trust which heaven on this isle pours,
> Fertile to be, yet never need her show'rs!
> A happy people which at once do gain
> The benefit, without the ills, of rain ! "

[a] The Governor-general of the whole of the Canary Islands commonly resided at Toneriffe, but the government of each island was invested in an Alcalde-Major and a Sargento-Major, otherwise called Governador de las Armas—the first being the head of the civil and the other of the military government. Glas, p. 218.

Itt is a coustome in that country, beinge thir is scarsitie of victualls, that, when anie flesh, fish, or foule is to be sold, that the maior be sent for to have the disposinge of itt; and so he would first serve himselfe, then the principall gentlemen of the towne, and then other people of meaner quallitie, in thir dew proportions as itt would hold out. But in this towne the Maior would allwayes send to Mr. Rawdon's stuart to know what he would please to have of what was thir, before he would taike aney for himselfe or give to aneybody, soe, he havinge taiken what he thought fitt, he would devide the rest amongst the niebours; and comonly the governour of the principalitie did indeavour to have the maior of the towne his owne creature, which was a thinge Mr. Rawdon, with the favour he had with the greate men, could easely doe, and was very good att things of that nature.

This place he and his cossen Marmaduke Rawdon the yonger governed five yeares with much noblenesse and greate applause, keepinge open howse for all thir countrymen that would come thir to recreate themselves; itt beinge, I thinke, one of the healthfullest places in the world, niether to hott nor to cold, winter or summer, and is in a manner blest with a perpetuall springe. Here they had a bowlinge alley and a billiard or   table to divert themselves and thir freinds. Thir expence of wines in thir howse did amount some yeares to eighteen pipes of Canary wines, besides French wine, Renish wine, and beere that they had brought them from England. They did soe order itt with thir tennants that they had tow fatt sheep brought home every weeke, most exclent meate; thay had of tribute hens that severall howses in the towne paid them, above three hundred, which did allmost serve the howse. As to hens, ducks, gheese, and turkies, they had good storre, havinge a ponde and a rivulett of water runninge through the yards of the howse, where they did breed thir ducks and geesse. This revolett of water they could carry where they pleasd into thir gardins and orchards, and many times, when they did feast thir friends, did cause some Spanish tables to be carried into the orchard under some orange trees, and thir have the water run rownd about them, and thir dine, and with canes have the watter into a tub or cisterne sett nere the table to wash thir glasses, and to coule thir wine att pleasure. I have sene about thir howse att one time fower score turkies which haith bene brought from severall parts of the iland for the provision thirof. Here the generall, who is thir in the quallitie of a viz-roy, chiefe commander booth by land and sea under his maister the Kinge of Spaine, would come here with his lady, and stay sometimes ten dayes togeather. The howse stood about a mile and a halfe from the sea, and about the same distance from the mountaines, and they had soe many tennants about them—some fishers, some fowlers—that uppon aney occasion they would order thir baily to send such men downe to the sea that were expert in fishinge, or such up to the mountaines and plaines that were expert in fowlinge, accordinge as the season requierd, and in a very short time be furnisht with fish or fowle, as the day requird.

But thir is nothinge permement nor certaine in this world; the pleasure thirof beinge much like unto a bird chirpinge uppon a tree, where, havinge made a little musicke, presently flyes away; aud soe itt hapned to thesse gentlemen concerninge the pleasure and the proffit they enjoyed in the goverment of that principal-litie. The unluckie warrs twixt Cromewell and Spaine expeld 1655. them from thence, which otherwayes they might have enjoyed for many yeares, and by that same warr were loosers of what they might have gott uppon certaine grownds above fiftie thousand pownds. Soe with the warrs thir comes an order from the Court of Spaine to imbargo all English ships, and to siez uppon all English-men's estates whatsoever, which was accordingly done, and thir estates siezd on; amongst the rest, severall Englishmen, for feare of beinge imprisond, imbarkt themselves in English ships that rid out of command for England; but he and his cossen Marmaduke Raw-don the yonger, havinge lived thir soe honorably, were looth to goe of privately, soe they went to visit the generall, and told him that they were desicrous to goe for England, but looth to goe without

recievinge his lordship's commands, and his licence to depart. To
which he answered, "Gentlemen, if you please to stay here, whilst
I am generall of the ilands none shall dare to offer you or aney
that belongs to you the least affront; but I dare nott give you a
licence to be gon, for the Kinge my maister would thinke me very
unworthy of the place he haith bestowed uppon me if I, knowinge
that your fleete of ships is, with an armie of men, gone to Hispaniola,[a]
and may probably taike some gentlemen of our nation prisners
(whome you may serve to ransome), that I should lett gentlemen of
your ranke and quallitie depart with my licence; but, if you are
resolved to goe, and will nott stay, for the freindship and familli-
aritie we have had togeather I will write a private letter to the
chiefe officers of that port where you are to imbarke, that they may
winke and conive att your imbarkinge, and att what you shall please
to imbarke, as well the maior of the towne as the officers of warr;"
which he accordingly did.   Soe within few dayes, havinge fitted
themselves, they went to a port towne calld Orotava in order to
imbarke themselves; and, havinge nere a dozen trunkes, chests, and
cabinetts of thir owne, thir nephew's, and retinew, uppon the sea
shore, which a Spaniard, thir baily, was about to imbark, the chiefe
customer of that port askt him where the keyes were, to see what
was in them.   He answerd he had them nott; but if he pleasd he
would goe and tell his maisters what he said.   He bid him goe,
and the keys were given him, with order to tell the chiefe coustomer that they did present thir respects to him, and that thir
was nothinge in thosse trunkes and cabinets but apparell and
conveniences for thir voyage and persons; soe he tooke the keys,
made as if he had kist them, and said to the baily, "Taike your
keyes, and returne them with my respeckts to your maisters; and
tell them if thir trunkes and cabinetts were full of gold I would nott

---

[a] War against Spain was not formally declared until October, 1655, but news arrived
in Europe several months earlier of the attack made by the English fleet under Penn and
Venables on the great Spanish settlement of Hispaniola. See Dixon's Life of Admiral
Blake, p. 296.

open one of them;" soe gave order presently that they might be
imbarkt. Another passage of this nature likewisse hapned: they
had halfe a dozen of birdinge and fowlinge peces of much curiositie
which they were looth to leave behind them, soe they lay by the
water side redie to imbarke. By chance an officer of the millitary
goverment came by and askt whosse guns thosse were. Thir bayly
answerd they were Mr. Rawdon's. The officer answered, "Though
we have a greate respect for thosse gentlemen, yet wee are now in
warrs with thosse gentlemen—I meane with thir nation—and we
must nott suffer them to cary armes from hence to beate us withall;"
and would have tane them away, butt thir bayly, and other sarvants
that were ther present, would nott permitt him; soe, while thesse
thinges were a disputinge, the collonell of the place, comminge
downe to the sea-side, and seinge one of his officers in much choller,
askt what was the matter; soe, understandinge the businesse, he
answered, "Thosse guns are guns that thosse gentlemen use only
for their recreations, and nott att all to hurt thir freinds;" soe gave
order to lett them be imbarkt.

All thesse thinges beinge done, the tow kinsmen with thir docter
of physicke, who uppon thir intreatie came to the Canarys, honest
Dr. Evan Picugh, a Welshman, and had lived nere twentie yeares
with them, and was looth (though he had very greate practice
amongst the Spaniards, which was very beneficiall unto him) to stay
behind his old freinds; soe he, with tow of thir relations and sarvants, imbarkt the latter end of November, 1655, abord the Elizabeth of London, Captaine John Salmon, a stout ship of twentie
pece of ordnance, and well mand, where we will leave them a while
to follow thir voyage, and give you an account of some actions and
accidents done by and hapned to Marmaduke Rawdon the elder, of
whom we now chiefly treate on, whilst he lived on the Canary
Ilands.

Actions done by him.

We will begin with a greate kindnesse he did for a greate prelate
of the church of Spaine, called Don Francisco Sanches de Villanueva,
Archbishop formerly of Taranta in Itally, which, beinge but a pore
archbishoprick, he left itt, and came to be Bishop of the Canary
Ilands.[a]   When he came thir first with his retinew he was very
barre of monies, and did want in particuler six thousand duccatts to
send to Spaine to have order to recieve his rents; soe he hoped his
clergie would have furnished him with soe much mony, who were
rich and able enough to doe itt, but they denied him; soe, beinge
in a greate straite, he sent for Mr. Rawdon and comunicated the
busnesse with him, tellinge him how unkindly his clergie had delt
with him, and desird to know if he could furnish him with the
mony.   He told him uppon such and such tearmes he would give
him bills of exchange to have his mony paid in Spaine where he
pleasd.   He told Mr. Rawdon he did nott only yielde to the conditions, but, if his bills were punctually paide, that his dispatches
might come that he might recieve his rents, he would taike itt as a
very greate favour, and be his freind as longe as he lived in the
ilands; soe he gave him his bills of exchange, with which he dispatcht
one of his gentlemen for Spaine.   When he came thir the bills were
punctually paid, and the gentleman in a short time returned with
the Bishop's dispatches, with which he was soe much pleasd and
oblidgd that he was Mr. Rawdon's greate freind ever after; and, if
the priests had committed aney miscariages, or had aney pretences
for benifices, they would request Mr. Rawdon to interceede with the
Bishop in thir behalfs; and the Bishop would seldome refusse to doe
aney thinge he requested of him, which made a grave Spaniard,

---

[a]   "The bishoprick of Canaria was worth in estate 12,000 ducats a-year." Wadsworth's
Present State of Spain, p. 34.

"The Bishop of the Canary Islands is a suffragan to the Archbishop of Seville, and has a
revenue of 6,000*l.* sterling per annum. He resides in the city of Palmas in Canaria, where
he is treated with all the respect and homage due to a prince." Glas, p. 353.

who see the greate friendship that was amongst them, say the world was come to a good passe that the bishopricke of the Canary Ilands must be governd by an English heriticke, for soe in thir fashion they call all people that are nott Roman Catholicks. He had likewisse a greate strooke with all that came to be generalls, governours, and judges, and had an exclent way of oblidginge them, from whom he could allwayes obtaine ancy resonable cortosie either for him selfe or freinds, in soe much that a Spanish gentleman told him one day he governd booth church and state in thosse ilands, and, if he could but obtaine heaven with soe much happinesse, thir was noe more to be desiered.

He thinkinge once to have gone over for the maine of Spaine, and for his better experience to have traveld thosse countrys, the then generall of the ilands, beinge Don Luis Fernandes de Cordova y Arce, Lorde of Arce, Governour and Captaine Generall of all the ilands by land and sea, and President of the Court of Parlement or High Council thirof, did give him a very honorable letter of saife conduct, the substance whereof I shall here briefly sett downe:

First: that he was a gentlemen of a very antient howse, which he did attest as havinge bene in England and knowne his relations, and had bene very nobly entertaind by them; that he had lived in the Canary Ilands much like a gentleman, keepinge in his stable horses for warr and other horses for his ordnary service, and a retinew of sarvants of all sortes; and that he had done booth thir and in England severall cortosies to the Kinge of Spain's subjects; and that he and his famely were greate affectors of the Spanish monarchy; for the which, and other thinges to large here to relate, he thought him worthy to enjoy in Spaine all the previlidges that Spaniards nobly borne did enjoy; and requested all governours of cities and townes, all captaines of castells and stronge holds, to be carefull to accomodate him and his sarvants with lodgings and all other thinges that were requisite for gentlemen of ranke and quallitie; and that att all publicke playes and pastimes he should be seated in a place convenient to behold them, as was fitt for a gentleman of birth and desert. Also he requested the Kinge, if he should have aney pretences in court, that he would be pleased to looke uppon him as a noble Englishman, and as one that had deserved very well for severall services done to his Majesties subjects booth in the ilands and in England; with many other thinges to this purpose.

He lent one Mr. Gilbert Lambell, a yonge merchant, tow hundreth powndes to begin the world with, gratis; which mony was paid him, when he came into England, in soe many peces of new coynd gold which he gott on purpose out of the Mint: and the said Mr. Lambell was very thankfull and serviceable to him soe longe as he lived.

He gave constantly every Sunday, ten, sometimes fifteene, sometimes twentie shillings, to severall pore antient people that were nott common beggers. He did much good to many Spaniards that he had a kindnesse for, or that had in the least anie wayes obligd him, makinge some of them, by the acquentance he had with greate men, alcades or small governours of townes; to others he gave viniards to make att halves, they to have the one halfe of the wine for thir paines, and he the other halfe; to others he gave licences that none should sell tabacco in such and such a towne but they, by which thinges they gott themselves a good livelihood to maintaine them and thir famelies; also to some preists that had made much of him att their howses when he was in the country uppon his recreations a hunttinge, also some pore preists that had a mother and sisters to maintaine, he did procure them of the bishop good benifices and other cortosies and dignities. He was very lovinge and liberall to all royalists that came thether, and entertaind them with much civillitie; and, when he herd our good Kinge of blessed memory was murderd, he putt himselfe and all his famely in mourninge, and was a greate occasion that the rest of the nation did the like.

His kinsman, Collonell Thomas Rawdon, havinge bene very much perceeuted by Cromewell and his soldiers for his loyaltie to the Kinge, wher Mr. Rawdon and his cossen Marmaduke receved him with all the love that posibly could be imagined, and entertained him with the greatest splendour that thir lordship or principallitie could afford, where he was nere tow yeares, where they would nott suffer him to be att the expence of one farthinge for himselfe, man, horse, nor anie thinge that did belonge unto him ; and, beinge desierous to goe to the Barbados to recover a plantation belonginge to his father Sir Marmaduke, which was allmost lost, they lent him seaven hundreth and fiftie pownds starlinge, with which he recoverd the plantation, which was of a conciderable vallew, and injoyed this 750*l.* ten yeares togeather without payinge a penny interest.

To severall Spaniards that were oprest by the higher powers with sentences of penalties that they were nott able to endure nor satisfie, if they came to him for refuge he would keepe them privatly in his howse till he could imbarke them for the maine of Spaine, where they would appeale to the supreame powers thir and find redresse.

He was the first that perswaded Dr. Piew, the English physitian, to come and live att the Canaries, and lent him monies to provide thosse nescessaries that were convenient for him to bringe with him.

He was the first that motiond the bringginge in of a devine to live amongst them in the ilands, and did contribute largely to the same, upon which one Dr. Burch, one of the Bishop of Armagh's chaplaines, came over amongst them, a greate schollar and a very able devine.[*]

He also gave tow hundreth duccatts towards the sendinge over an English agent for Madrid, to defend the English nation in all law suites against some pressinge judges that would encroach uppon thir privilidges, and to procure from the Kinge of Spaine what imunities he could gett for the English that did live uppon the Canary Ilands.

He contributed largely to the repairinge of severall high wayes in the iland where he lived, and to divers other thinges of this nature as they were desiered of him or propounded to him.

Whilst he lived upon the iland he had a greate desire to see the

---

[*] Dr. James Usher, the celebrated divine and historian, was at that time Archbishop of Armagh.

religious orders and goverment of the nunns,[a] whiche is a thinge
nott easely to be obtained by either stranger or naturall, beinge none
goes in thir except some few churchmen which are governours of
that order, and that uppon sett times and uppon greate occasions,
also docters of physicke and surgeons as occasion requiers; but he
brought his desires about as followeth: Docter Piew, whom we have
allredie mentiond, beinge growne famous amongst the Spaniards for
his greate cures, Mr. Rawdon understood that a nun, a person of
quallitie, was sicke, and that hir freinds would come to Docter Piew
to desire him to give hir a vizitt; so he presently went to Docter
Piew, and told him that such and such gentlemen would come and
desire him to goe and see a nun, and that he should tell them that
he would goe, but, beinge that he was nott very currant in the
language of the country, he should desire them that he might have
an interpreter with him, and if they offerd him the ordnary interpreter
of the place he should refuse him, and accept of none but himselfe;
soe, not longe after Mr. Rawdon was gone from the Docter, the
relations of the nun came to desiere he would doe them the favour
as to goe and vizitt thir kinswoman, a nun in such a covent; he
told them, Yes, he woulde waite uppon them, but beinge he was
nott very currant in the language, he desird to have an interpreter
alonge with him that understood the language better then himselfe,
to interpret what she might declare concerninge hir distemper, to
which they presently agreed, and would have sent for the common
interpreter which use to interpret for maisters of ships and the like,
to which the docter, accordinge to his instructions, told them, Noe,
that he desird to have some person of more satisfaction and knowledge, for that not only his creditt but the life of the yonge gentlewoman did partly depend uppon itt, and much inconvenience might
happen by the misinterpretation of one worde; soe they askt him

[b] The city of La Laguna contained two parish churches, three convents of friars, two
of nuns, and three hospitals. The convents of friars were of three different orders, viz.:
the Augustine, the Dominican, and the Franciscan; and those of the nuns, Dominicans
of St. Catharine and Franciscans of St. Clara. Glas, p. 248.

who he would please to have; he told them he should be very much
satisfied if they could procure Mr. Rawdon; they told him he was
a person of greate busnesse, and they could not presume soe much
favour from him as to leave his occasions to goe with him; the
docter told them itt was true, but that they should speake to him,
and that he was a very civill gentleman, and itt may be would nott
denie them, and if he did that then he would thinke of some body
els; soe they came to Mr. Rawdon's howse, and sent word that such
gentlemen did desire to speake with him, and, though he knew very
well what they came about, yett he went to them and very sollemely
desird to know what was thir pleasure; they told him they had a
very greate suite to him, and they hopd he would nott denie them,
and in doinge of itt he would putt a greate obligation uppon thir
fameley. He, beinge scarce able to hold for smiling, desird them to
speake what itt was. They told him itt was to preserve the life of
a bewtifull nun, Saint such a one, a relation of thirs who was very
ill, and that they had spooke with Docter Piew to goe and see hir,
who was willinge to goe if he would dispence with soe much time
as to goe alonge with him to be his interpreter. He answerd them,
that to serve them in soe good a worke he would leave all busnesse;
soe presently callinge for his cloake and rapier, went imediatly with
them to the docter's, and from thence to the nunnery. When they
came, notice was given att the turne wheele of thir comminge; soe
presently thir came fower nuns, neatly drest in thir habitts, and
opened the doore, tow standinge on one side of the dore and tow on
the other; here the gentlemen took leave of the docter and his
interpreter, who, beinge enterd, the dores were bolted, and another
nun stood thir who was reddie to conduct them where they were to
goe, she goinge before them, ringinge in hir hand a little bell to
give notice that thir was strangers thir, that if anie nun should
chance to be undrest she might retire out of the way. By this nun
they were brought to the infirmaria, or the chamber where they kept
the nuns that were sicke, where this nun lay; soe the docter ex-
amined hir condition, and gave order by his interpreter to tell them

that they should apply such and such thinges that were nescessary
for hir.   After which the lady abbesse came out and complemented
them, and treated them with wine and severall sortes of sweetmeates,
and sent for some of hir choyce nuns to play and singe to them and
to discourse with them; thus they past the afternone with much
content, as they did many more afterwards, for uppon this score they
could goe in when they pleasd without scandall, and the nuns were
very much pleasd with thir companies, and thir accquentance began
to be soe greate amongst the nuns that thir was scarce a nun's finger
akt but they were sent for, much oftner then they had liesure or
would goe.[a] By this goinge they see most of thir coustoms. They
see them in thir refetoria att dinner and supper; they see them in
prosession goinge about thir cloyster with thir images of saints caried
on thir shoulders, and they singinge before them; they likewise see
thir dormitoria or place of sleepinge, beinge a longe gallery with about
100 beds of a side, all done about with white lininge courtaines
very neatcly.   Thesse nuns were of the order of St. Dominick; thir
under garment was of a whitt sarge or say, with a blacke sarge
or say clooke or large mantle over itt, a very comely habit; thir
lininge about thir heads white.

Also by this meanes he see another order of nuns called the nuns
of Santa Clara, which is one of the orders of Saint Francis and
governed by the provinciall of the Franciscan Fryers; thir order of
habitt is a gray or blacke and white mixt sarge, that lininge about
thir heade starcht yellow.

He had likewisse a desire, whilst he staid on that iland, to. goe
uppon a high mountaine called the Pike of Teneriffe, which haith
snow and ice uppon itt all the yeare longe. Itt is by Sir Walter
Raighley and other learned men[b] held to be the highest land in the

---

[a] This was a hazardous adventure of the inquisitive little Englishman. It is a proof of
the respect in which he was held by the people of Teneriffe that he was not punished for
his curiosity by being lodged in the dungeons of the Inquisition. "In each of the islands
there is a house belonging to the holy office." Glas.

[b] Probably the "other learned men," referred to in the text, included Sir Thomas
Herbert, who has been previously named as one of Mr. Rawdon's schoolfellows at York

world; soe in company of severall English, Dutch, and Germaine
gentlemen, to the number of sixteene, besides sarvants, about the
middle of August,[a] haveinge horses and mules laden with wine and
provisions, they sett forward from the towne of Orotava,[b] and tra-
veled all that day on horsebacke till they came to the bottome of the
mountaine,[c] where they remained that night, where thir came a most

(ante p. 4). In 1634, Sir Thomas published "A Relation of some yeares' Travaile,
begunne Anno 1626, into Afrique and the greater Asia," in which he thus speaks of the
Canaries: "The sixt of April we discried the Canary Islands, in former years called Fortunate. Grand Canarie at this day precedes the rest in greatnesse and excellencie, for
thither all the other iles repaire for trial and justice. Howbeit, Teneriffe is thought to
equal it in wealth and circuit; in height I am sure it doth, and not it only, but any other
land in the world, allowing its immediate ascent from the ocean. The high peak is by
most geographers reputed the highest in the world; by some said to be fifteene miles high,
though a third part may well suffice to beget credulity and wonder. It is seen by seamen,
in a serene sky, a hundred and twentie miles, and serves as an apt sea-mark unto passengers." In the latest edition of his travels, Sir Thomas thus amplifies his former de-
cription of the Peak of Teneriffe: "Her high peak, touring so loftily into the air, as seems
not only to penetrate the middle region, but to peep into heaven, for 'tis by most accounted
15 miles in height; 60 says Scaliger, 70 Patricius, yea, one Nichols our countryman, who
lived here some time, affirms that it is 47."—Ed. 1677, p. 3.

   [a] The ascent of the Peak of Teneriffe was performed by Glas in September 1761, and
by Humboldt in June 1799. The most recent, as well as the most complete and scientific
exploration of the whole volcanic range, was made in the summer of 1856 by Mr. Piazzi
Smith, the Astronomer Royal for Scotland, whose excellent description of the results is
contained in his work entitled "Teneriffe: an Astronomer's Experiment, or Specialities of
a Residence above the Clouds. London, 1858."

   [b] Port Orotava is a place of considerable trade, lying close in to the sea-shore on the
western side of the island of Teneriffe. Above it, about a league inland, is another town
somewhat larger called Villa de Orotava. It appears that Mr. Rawdon went from his
residence at La Laguna to the town of Orotava that he might from thence commence his
ascent of the Peak. Humboldt travelled from Santa Cruz to Laguna, and from thence to
Orotava. "For the ascent of the Peak," Mr. Piazzi Smith tells us, "they could give no
better advice than that we should betake ourselves to the town of Orotava, close under the
highest part of the volcano, and from thence arrange our mountain operations."

   [c] That which is here spoken of as the bottom of the mountain was doubtless the place
described by Glas and Humboldt as "Estancia de los Ingleses," which Mr. Piazzi Smith
states to be at an altitude of 9,700 feet. Glas and his party started from Orotava at four
o'clock P.M. and, not having the day before them, were climbing the mountain during the
greater part of the night. Mr. Rawdon more judiciously left Orotava early in the day,

bitter coald aire from the top of the mountaine where they remained
that night, soe cold as if they had bene in Frizland, soe that some
of thir company found themselves in the morninge, after they had
slept, soe stiffe that they were nott able to performe thir journie up;
but to prevent that, Mr. Rawdon, and one Mr. Cowlinge, a Yorkshire gentleman, would. not sleepe, but spent most of that night in
makinge great fires of Spanish brome[a] and other combustible stuffe
that grew thirabouts, with which they kept thir limbes stirringe and
plyant, soe in the morninge about fower of the clocke thir guide
calld uppon them to be marchinge; soe they went on foote, havinge
brood single soold shoes, made on purposse, accordinge to the
coustome of the country, such as the goatckeepers' that climbe up
rockes were, beinge they are nott soe subject to slip as other shoes
are.　Soe they all endeavored to follow thir guide, but some remained a quarter part of the way, some halfe the way, and could
get noe farther;[b] but Mr. Rawdon got up very well and was the
seacond person uppon the Pick, thir beinge only one German gentleman before him.　They gott to the tope of this Picke about scaven
of the clocke: the top is a brood place of about three or fower akers
of grownd,[c] hollow, like to a shallow coper kettle that people co-

and chose for his resting-place at night the "Estancia de los Ingleses," where Humboldt
and his party also passed the night. "This station," Humboldt says, "can be reached on
the backs of mules, and here has ended the expedition of numbers of travellers who, on
leaving Orotava, had hoped to have ascended to the brink of the crater."

[a] The Retama (*Cytisus Nubigenus*). "A charming shrub which grows to the height of
nine feet, and is loaded with odoriferous flowers."—Humboldt. "That unique mountain
broom, the like of which none of the other Canary Islands nor any of the African isles, and
in fact not another spot in the world, can show."—Smith. Near the place where Glas and
his party slept they found some dry withered Retamas, which was the only shrub or vegetable they saw thereabout; and with them they made a great fire to warm themselves.
"We suffered from the cold during the night," says Humboldt, "and our guides made a
large fire with the dried branches of the Retama."

[b] Glas describes the ascent of the cone from the Estancia as extremely fatiguing. When
they got to the top they were quite spent with fatigue. Humboldt says, "Of all the vol-
canoes which I have visited, that of Jorullo in Mexico is the only one that is more difficult
to climb than the Peak, because the whole mountain is covered with loose ashes."

[c] Mr. Rawdon's estimate of the dimensions of the crater is a close approximation to the

monly boile fish in; the reason is that formerly it brooke out and
was blowne up with fire, as appeares by pummice stones and other
burnt stones that yett remaine thir, and aboundance flew from thence
to severall places of the ilande.   Thir is within the earth a fire continews thir still, and thir comes out of severall cranies smooke,[a]
wher, if you hold your hand a little while, itt wilbe covered with
a sulphurous matter like brimstone,[b] and thir is a quantitie of
brimston found thir which they sell in the shops.   Itt is thought att
some time or other this greate mountaine will have a fitt of the
chollicke, and send out a blast of fire, brimstone, and stones, to the
greate prejudice of the places thir nere adjacent.   Uppon the tope
of this picke they staid about an hower, haveinge cleere sun shininge
morninge, by the benifitt of which they see six of the seven Canary
Ilands,[c] one of them beinge 150 miles distant from that place which
they see, and thosse that were twenty, thirty, and fiftie miles distant they showed closse by; but, of that Iland of Teneriffe on which
they were, though itt is threescore mile longe and fifteen miles
brood, they see nott one bitt more then part of that Picke whereon
they stood, thir beinge an interposition of clowdes betwixt them and
the earthe.   They seemed to be in the middle region, the cloudes
lyinge like fleeces of woole under them.   Whilst they staid here

truth.   According to Humboldt and other modern travellers the figure of the crater is
elliptical, the greatest breadth being about 300 feet, the smallest 200 feet.   The diameter
of a circular area of three acres is about 360 feet.

   [a] Glas says, " In many parts of the hollow we observed smoke and steams of sulphur
issuing forth in puffs."   " Vapours of sulphuric acid gas rise in abundance through crevices.
Fine crystals of sulphur are everywhere found in the crevices of the lava."—Humboldt.

   [b] "The ground in the interior of the crater was hot, moist, dissolving into white clay, and
full of apparent rat-holes.   Out of these holes acidulated vapours were every moment
breaking forth, and on the stones where they struck were producing a beautiful growth of
needle-shaped crystals of sulphur, crossing and tangling with each other in the most
brilliant confusion."—Smith, p. 305.

   [c] Humboldt was not so highly favoured.   " We prolonged in vain," he says, " our stay
on the summit of the Peak to wait the moment when we might enjoy the view of the
whole of the archipelago of the Fortunate Islands.   One of the small islands, called
the Rock of the East, cannot be seen even in fine weather from the top of the Peak."

Mr. Rawdon called thir guide, beinge a lustie proper fellow, the
tallest of all the company, gave him a pece of mony, and told him
that he would have him to taike him uppon his shoulders, and that
after that he should taike up none els, which he promised him to
doe; soe, when he was sett uppon his showlders, lookinge about
him, he said to the company, " I am now the highest man in the
world, and the nearest heaven of anie man livinge." After they
had satisfied themselves with lookinge about, and refresht themselves
with wine and provisions that was brought up for them, after an
hower or an hower and a halfe stay, they went downe to thir station
where thir horses wore, where they had a very good dinner; and,
havinge dinde, they tooke horse and returned the same way they
came to the towne of Orotava from whence they sett forthe.

Whilst he staid uppon this iland of Teneriffe he did sometimes
vizit some of the other ilands, as the iland of the Gomera, where thir
is some store of red deare;[a] the iland of the Palma, which produceth
store of sugar and some good wines;[b] and he went often to the iland
of the Grand Canaries, a pleasant iland, affordinge good store of
game for birdinge and fowlinge, as quailes, partridges of a large
sies, much bigger then the English partridge, and of a bewtifull
couller; also thir is store of turtle-doves and your ordnary wild
piggeons, stocke-doves, and ringe-doves,[c] and an infinite number of
wild rabitts all the iland over. In this exercisse of shotinge he

[a] " Here (Gomera) is plenty of deer, which were originally brought hither from Barbary."—Glas.

[b] " A great quantity of sugar is made in Palma.' The east side produces good wines,
of a different taste and flavour from those of Teneriffe. The Malvasia is not so luscious
or strong."—Ibid.

[c] Among the birds of Canaria Mr. Rawdon does not notice the pretty little warbler so
much cherished in this country, to which the island gives its name. " The mountain of
Dorada, about two leagues from the city of Palmas, is shaded by groves of different kinds
of fragrant trees, whose lofty boughs are so thickly interwoven as to exclude the rays of
the sun. The rills that water these shady groves, the whispering of the breeze among
the trees, and the melody of the canary-birds, form a most delightful concert. When a
person is in one of these enchanting solitudes he cannot fail of calling to remembrance
the fine things the ancients have written of the Fortunate Islands."—Glas, p. 231.

tooke greate delight, and did much after busnesse divert himselfe thir with.   He was a very good marksman, and did one day in the port of Santa Crux, abord Captaine John Bowden, with a musket and a single bullett, in the presence of severall English gentlemen, kill a small sea-mue that sitt on the maine top-mast yarde, the body of which was little bigger then a blacke-bird, to the admiration of them all.

He was very affable and kind to all persons that came to that place, espccially to all thosse he had formerly knowne in England, and did treate them with much civillitie were they poore or rich; and I will relate you only one passage, because thir is some thinge of varietie of fortune in itt.

Mr. Rawdon, the first yeare he came to his unckle, before he went beyond the seas, for all his unckle had allwayes a noble respect for him, yett to breed him with more humility, he causd him to waite uppon him att table, and to dine with the sarvants, in which interim thir comes up to his unckle's howse one Mr. John Cooke, a yonge gentleman, son to Dr. Cooke, Bishop of Hereford,* which bishop was a nere kinsman to Sir Marmaduke's lady; and he came up to be put forth an aprentice, soe, till a maister was provided for him, he staid thir, was bedfellow with Mr. Rawdon, but satt att table with his unckle, and soe consequently Mr. Rawdon waitinge uppon the table might give him a trencher, wine, or beere, or what he might call for; but, in conclusion, Mr. Cooke was putt forth a prentice, and Mr. Rawdon was sent beyond the seas, and, 3 or 4 yeares after, beinge uppon the Iland of Teneriffe, thir came a ship consigned to him, of which was commander Captaine John Walters, with a greate cargason of goods, more then that iland could att that time vent; soe he was resolved to goe over him selfe in the ship to the Iland of the Grand Canaries, to see if he could disposse of some of his goods thir.   As he was in the ship's boote goinge abord, he

---

* Doctor George Coke, brother of Sir John Coke, Secretary of State, succeeded Doctor Theophilus Field in the see of Hereford, and was consecrated 2nd July, 1636. He died 10th Dec. 1646.

espied one amongst the yongsters tuggin att an oare in a mariner's
habitt, a face that he thought he had formerly bene accquented with,
soe, when he came abord the ship, he called the yonge man to him
and asked him his name. He blusht, and told him his name was
Cooke; soe he presently remembred him, tooke him by the hande,
and told him he was very sorry to see him in that condition, and
askt him what had befalne him. He told him part of his hard fortune, soe Mr. Rawdon told him he was very sory for itt; but, to
make the best of his bad condition, he would recomend him to the
captaine as an accquentance of his, and that he should be putt to
noe drugery, as rowinge, or the like; and, all the while Mr. Rawdon
was abord, beinge he was nott in a condition to be brought to his
table, he orderd a bottle of Canary wine to be sent downe every
meale to his messe, that the seamen might have the better respect
for him, and, when he went away, gave him a small caske of Canary
wine for his voyage. This Mr. Cooke, I understand, now is a
worthy devine in some part of Herefordshire, where we will leave
him and Mr. Rawdon's actions, and come to thosse casuall accidents
which did happen to him duringe his abood in that iland.

Of casuall Accidents and Dangers he escapt.

One time, beinge abord a ship in the port of Santa Crux, the sea
was very high when they came ashore, brooke over them, and sunke
the boote, and with much adoe they gott on shore. He was noe
soner landed but the captaine of the castle invited him to the castle,
which was not a stone's cast from where the boote was sunke. The
captaine's lady, and hir daughter, a bewtifull yonge gentlewoman,
brought him dry linninge, and what was nesessary to shift him selfe
with, and causd him to goe to bed till his cloothes were dried,
keepinge him company all that while, and did treate him with soe
much civillitie, that he did taike that mischance rather for a happinesse then a mischance.

Another time, beinge in the country with some of his accquentance uppon a journie of pleasure by the sea-side, he had a mind to swim one afternone, which he did. After he had swame a prettie way from the shore the sea began to big, and some weedes arosse about his feete, which might have, as itt did, indanger his life; soe he made for the shore, and, beinge neare the shore and very weary, lookinge up, he see some of his accquentance sitting uppon the side of a rocke lookinge uppon him and laughinge, without stirringe in the least to helpe him; soe he fancied with him selfe that thosse would nott care much if he were drowned, which did enflame his hearte with soe much corrage, that he strove beyond his strength, not soe much for life, as to decieve the expectation of his helplesse pretended freinds, or rather accquentance. Beinge very much tird with swimminge, he was forsd to lett the sea brake over him, but, havinge his sences very well about him, he kept his mouthe closse and his handes and feete still swiminge, soe that I thinke the third wave that brooke over him heaved him uppon the sand; but he was soe weary when he came ashore, and soe blacke and blew with straininge himselfe, that he was nott able to stand without helpe.

Another time, ridinge uppon a greate horse of his owne from the cittie of Lalaguna to Garachico, goinge thorow a towne called the Realexo,[a] some curr dogs came out barkinge and bitt his horse by the heeles, at which the horse, beinge full of mettle, flew out, the way beinge a desent on all sides and dangerous; on the left hand thir was the side of a hill uppon which he did, with much adoe, turne his horse, thinkinge to have run him up the towne againe, and to have stopt him by degrees, or to have run him up against the stone steps of the church which stood att the upper end of the street; his horse run him against a greate hedge of briers a little to the right hand of the streete, and beinge uppon his full speed, the stop was soe forcible and sudden, that the horse pitcht him, with the saddle betwixt his leggs, into the hedge of briers, almost with as much force as if he had bene shott out of a gun, betwixt tow

* Realexo, or Realejo, a large place surrounded by vineyards, situated about a league or four milles beyond la Villa de Orotava.—Glas, p. 249.

greate stakes that were drove in thir to strengthen the hedge, soe if he had light against either of them they had pasht out his braines; but itt pleasd God he had no hurt at all, scarce a scratcht face. Att the noyse and clatteringe of the horse the niebours came out, and puld him out of the briers, and askt him how he did, and if he had recieved aney hurt; he answered, "none att all;" they askt him if he would have a surgeon sent for to lett him blood, a thinge much usd in thosse countries uppon aney sudden accident or affright; he told them, God be praised, he was very well, and only desird them to helpe his man to catch his horse, which they willingly did; soe, havinge fitted up the saddle, leadinge his horse to the bottome of the hill, he gott upon him againe and performed his journie.

Of casuall Accedents hapned to him.

Another time, beinge dispachinge some goods in the coustome howse of the port of Orotava, the coustomer beinge a knight of the order of St. James, this knight would have his coustomes in the same goods, but Mr. Rawdon told him, Noe, he would pay his coustomes in mony, havinge occasion for the comodities himselfe; att which the knight said, Well, lett them be counted; soe while he was lookinge uppon the men that counted the goods lest they should cheate him, the knight most treacherously drawes his dagger and gave him a small cutt att the bottome of his chinn; which he seeing, imediately drew his raper and ran att him, but puttinge his arme backe to give him the stronger thrust, one of the knight's attendants nimbly catcht hold of his elbow and hinderd the thrust, which if that had not bene he had naild my Spanish knight to the wall.

He had duringe his aboode here severall small encounters, but of noe greate importance, and was fower times in the field challanginge and challinged. The first occasion was for his freind, the seacond for his owne estimation, the third for woemen, and the fourth for wealth.

The first was with an English gentleman for some scandalous

wordes he had spooke of a deerly beloved freind of his; soe meetinge him accidently uppon the roode betwixt Lalaguna and the port of Santa Crux, he askt him if he had reported anie such thinge of his freind; he did niether confesse itt, nor alltogether denie itt, but mincd itt; soe he told him he was an unworthy person, and that he should light from his horse and he would teach him how he ought to speake of persons more worthier much then himselfe; soe after they had gon some distance from the highway they booth alighted and tied thir horses, and behind a greate cardon * or thistell, called in lattin *centum capitum*, they prepard themselves and fought; att the seacond encounter Mr. Rawdon's rapier broke about a quarter of a yard att the poynt, soe runninge on his adversary to see if he could closse with him, his adversary cried, " Hold, sir, your rapier is brooke;" he told him itt was noe matter, thir was enough left to serve his turne, he standinge still uppon his gaurd, that he should nott come to closse with him; he told Mr. Rawdon, " No, sir, I will nott fight with you uppon soe greate a disadvantage;" soe uppon better consederations they booth got on horse backe and parted.

The seacond was with a sausie Spaniard called Don Luis Villarto, an executor who came from the Court of Spaine with a comision to recover of some that owed rents to the kinge; soe this Spaniard, meetinge him in the street, presents him with a bill of exchange, payable att time to a woman which itt seemes was this Spaniard's freind; soe he told him if he would come or send when itt was dew, he should have the mony; he prest to have itt presently; he told him he would nott pay itt till itt was dew, and beinge itt was nott for him selfe he wondred he should urge itt soe much; att which the Spaniard answerd (presuminge of his comision from the kinge, and the white rod he carried in his hand), that if itt had bene for him he would have made him have paid itt presently, or he would have putt his necke in the stockes. Mr. Rawdon answerd him, he was a sausie fellow, and if he durst meete him at such a place a little

* Probably a species of the plant known in England by the name of Cardoon (*Cynara cardunculus*), a perennial of large upright leafy growth.

without the cittie, he would make him know what itt was to speake
such language to a gentleman of much better quallitie then him
selfe. He answerd he would meete him thir within an hower and
nott faile him; soe Mr. Rawdon went home to his howse to change
his raper, to taike one that was better mounted for his hand then
that he ordnaryly wore; and away he went to the place apoynted,
wher he had not staid longe, but the Spaniard apeared but with
about a dozen Spaniards alonge with him; he seeinge that, went
walkinge towards the cittie as if he had come abrood only for his
recreation, but they made up to him, and after a civill salut told him
that they see by the lookes of thir freind that he was goinge about
some desperate designe, and they thought good to follow him, and
that they were glad they did soe, beinge they concieved the quarrell
was with him, a gentleman for whom they had all a greate respect;
he thankt them for thir good will towards him, but told them he
knew of noe quarrell, but they were resolved to make a busnesse of
itt, soe they devided them selves, the one halfe caringe the Spaniard
home to his lodginge, the other halfe goinge with Mr. Rawdon to
his owne howse; soe they were made freinds, and the busnesse was
ended; and afterwards the Spaniard, for all his gravitie of carynge
his white rod in his hand, would putt of his hat to Mr. Rawdon as
far as he could see him.

The third was uppon this occasion: thir was an antient gentlewoman of good quallitie, but nott very rich, who did make all the
white worke, as bands, cuffs, shirts, handkirchers, and such like
things, for Mr. Rawdon and his famely were; people well breed, of
exclent parts in singinge, musick, and discourse; here he did use to
goe sometimes in the eavenings when he had little to doe, to recreate
and divert himselfe. Thir was a yonge gentleman, one Don Mateo
Bossa, who was afterwards a captaine in Flanders for the Kinge of
Spaine; this gentleman lived halfe a dozen howses above them on
the other side of the way in the same streete; the yonge ladies
names were, the eldest, Dona Leonora, the yonger, Dona Simona;
this gentleman pretended to be a sarvant to the eldest, but could nott

be admitted; he fancied Mr. Rawdon might be the occasion of itt, and
if he could but affright him from the howse he might speed the better
and be the better receved; soe he watcht his opertunitie and findinge
Mr. Rawdon walkinge one eaveninge alone in the fieldes, came up to
him and told him, " Sir, I have longe waited an occasion to find you
alone, for I have some busnesse of importance to comunicate with
you." Soe he desird him to declare what he had to say, and he would
heare him.   Soe he begun to this effect, " Sir, I have observed you
doe frequent much a howse of a gentlewoman's, a niebour of mine, to
whom I am nott only a niebour, but itt may be I may have some pre-
tence of marriage with one of the yonge gentlewomen, and I am, if
nott uppon that score, a little related to them, and soe consequently
concernd in anic thinge that may tuch thir reputations; uppon which
your soe often goinge thir doth cast some blemish." He answerd
him, he tooke them to be ladies of a very good fame and repute, and
if he did nott, he would nott vizit them; and beinge they were soe,
he concieved his vizitts was rather an honor to them then anie discreditt, and that his vizitts was att such lawfull houres as could nott
cause aniebody to thinke ill of them nor him; and askt him if he
had aney order from the mother or the daughters to tell him that his
comminge was aney wayes displeasinge or inconvenient for them, he
would forbeare. The Spaniard answered him, Noe, that itt was a thinge
that did appeare ill to him and some other persons. If that be all,
saith Mr. Rawdon, you may excusse to troble yourselfe aney further
in the busnesse, for soe longe as he knew noe other but they were
virtuous, he would continew his vizitts to them when he should
thinke fittinge, and that he tooke a greate deale of pleasure in thir
civill conversation. "Well then," quoth the Spaniard, "if you will
goe, be itt uppon your owne perill, stand uppon your gaurd, and say
I have given you faire warninge." Mr. Rawdon told him he would
looke to that, and soe for that time they parted.

  Mr. Rawdon continued his vizitts to the gentlewomen att his
liesure howres as formerly, and told what had past him with thir
pretended kinsman or sarvant; they answerd him, he was noe relation

of thirs, but a bold gentleman that would have intruded himselfe into thir companies, and they slighted him and would nott permitt him, and were very much displeased with him for his sausienesse to medle in aney thinge that did concern them. Soo one eaveninge, Mr. Rawdon, goinge to vizitt them, chaned to stay an houre within night, and when he was goinge home some of the howse told the gentlewoemen that Don Mateo Bosa had bene in his porch near tow houres watchinge for some body, soo they concieved he might watch for Mr. Rawdon; soe they told him of itt, and desird him to stay and nott to goe home while he stood thir, for feare some mischiefe might be don him, and if he would needs goe, to goe downe the street and soe home another way; he thankt them for thir love and care, but he was resolved, God willinge, to goe home, and to goe by his dore to see what he durst doe; soe muffelinge him selfe in his clooke, and taikinge his raper in his hande for more redinesse, he went up the middle of the streete; as he went by Don Mateo's, he askt who goeth thir, such a one? Mr. Rawdon answerd, Yes; att which the Spaniard said, " Did not I tell you that if you came aney more to this howse, itt should be att your owne perill?" " Did nott I answer you," saith Mr. Rawdon, " that I would come to this howse whensoever I thought fitt?" and with that offerd to draw his raper; but the Spaniard desird him to forbeare, that that was noe convenient place to fight in, but that if he would goe with him to such a place, nere the towne, they would thir dispute the busnesse. Mr. Rawdon told him, with all his hearte; soe they went very quietly togeather, but when they were come allmost att the place, saith the Spaniard, " Pray, sir, tell me ingeniously what doe you thinke of thosse ladies that we are goinge to fight for." He told him he thought them to be very virtuous ladies, and that he would defend thir reputation with his life against all opposers; uppon which my Don told him: " Sir, thir are tow reasons that doth much divert me from fightinge with you; the first is, my father haith a greate respect to all the gentlemen of your nation, and perticulerly to yourselfe, soe if he should know of our fightinge, as without doubt he must, I shall

encurr his displeasure very much; the other is, that I am informed
itt is quite out of fashion in the Court of Spaine for aney gentleman
to be known to quarrell about woemen, and them that did itt were
only held for fooles and cokscombes, and consequently itt could be
noe creditt for niether of them to doe itt;" to which Mr. Rawdon
answerd, that for his part he came uppon his summonds, and soe
longe as he did nott speake ill of thosse gentlewoomen, his quarrell
was att an end. "Well then," quoth he, "lett us returne;" and soe
they did, and afterwards Mr. Rawdon was noe more trobled with
this gentleman. The treweth is, the Spaniard doth not much care
for fightinge, except itt be in a street or market place, where thir
may be store of people, either to taike notice of thir vallour, or els
to part them.

The fourth and last broile, for wealth, was with one Matias de
Vexarno, a crabbed West India captaine, who had sold Mr. Rawdon
a percell of Spanish tabacco, for which he paid him according to
the agreement he had made with him; but ships comminge in from
England unexpected, his camaradas that had nott sold thir tabaccos,
sold thirs after the ships came in, att a farr greater rate then he had
done, and they jeerd him for beinge soe hastic for sellinge his soe
sonne and att soe low a price. At which which beinge madded, he
writes a letter from the cittie of Lalaguna to the towne of Garachico,[*] where Mr. Rawdon had a howse, and was then thir, beinge
thirty miles in distance, and sent itt by an expresse to give him notice
that itt was true he had sold him his tabacco and was paid for itt,
but att a low rate, and that his camaradas had all of them sold thir
tabaccos att a far greater rate, and beinge his was good, or rather
better then thirs, he did expect the same price for his as they had
for thirs, and that he should answer his letter with effect, and that
if he did nott, he might expect him in Garachico the next day, and
that he would have itt by the sworde. This letter came just as Mr.

---

[*] Garachico, or Garrachica, formerly the best port in the island of Teneriffe, was destroyed by an earthquake in the year 1704. The harbour was filled up by the rivers of
burning lava that flowed into it from a volcano.—Glas, p. 244. Since that time its commerce has been supplanted by that of Santa Cruz.

Rawdon was risinge from dinner, soe he gave order for the man to stay, went into his clossett and writ the captain to this purpose:—
"Sir, I have recieved your letter in which you give me notice that your camarados have sold thir tabaccos att a greater price then you have; to which I answer that if the English ships had nott come, they might have sold thirs for lesse then you did, or els might nott have sold itt att all. You write, you expect the same price, with which I have nothinge to doe; I have paid you accordinge to our agrement, and have your discharge; you also write, if I will nott doe itt, you will have itt by the sworde, and that I may expect you here to morrow at Garachico; to that I answer, itt is a greate journie and bad wayes, soe I wilbe soe civill with you as to meet you halfe wayes, to morrow about eight of the clocke in the morninge, behind such an old chappell nere the port of Orotava, till when I shall bid you farwell."

Mr. Rawdon the next morninge causd his horse to be sadled very carely. His cossen Marmaduke, Mr. Campion, and some other gentlemen that were in the howse, were very desierous to know what sudden occasion causd him to goe from thence soe suddenly; he told them he went about a little busnesse, and that they should know when he returnd, which he hopd would be the next day. Soe taikinge only his foote boy with him, away he went, and came thir about eight of the clocke, and leavinge his horse with his foote boy att a convenient distance, he went a foote to the place apoynted: and havinge walkt thir behind the chappell almost an hower, thir comes directly to him a sarjant, att which he was much amasd; the sarjant, alightinge from his horse, came very civilly to him, and told him that the maior of the towne of Orotava did present his respects to him and desird to speake with him; he askt if he brought anie warrant from the maior to carry him up, or if he came only uppon a private message; he told him he came only uppon a verball message, to tell him that the maior had a desire to speake with him; "Well then," quoth Mr. Rawdon, "remember my service to the maior, and tell him I stay here only to speake a worde with a freind that I apoynted to meet here, which soe sone as I have done, I will waite uppon him presently; att which the sarjant, smilinge said, " Sir, your freind is above att Orotava att the maior's howse." "What freind," said Mr. Rawdon. "Captain Vexarano," said the sarjant; att which the busnesse beinge discovered, he knew itt was to noe purpose to stay thir, soe went to his horse, and bid the sarjant goo before and tell his maister, that he would be with him presently. Soe goinge up to the maior's howse, he found his challenger; soe the maior presently made them freinds. The newes of this was spread all about the iland, every one addinge some thinge to itt, as thir fancie gave them; soo that common report caried itt to his cossen's eares before he returned home. The next day he went home him selfe, with which his Spanish Rodomontado ended. But now I am affraid I have allmost tird your patience; soe havinge now given you a perticuler of most of thosse threatninge dangers from which itt pleasd God to deliver him, I shall troble you noe more with anie relations of this nature, but will taike leave of the Canaria Ilands, and returne to find Mr. Rawdon where we left him, abord Captain Salmon's ship, plyinge his voyage for his native country, England.

His Voyage.

They set saile from the Iland of Teneriffe about the beginninge of December in company of fower ships more, all bound for England, where they continued thir voyage with indifferent good weather; and about the eighth day, they beinge then about 300 miles from ancy land, thir came an ugly blackesh foule, allmost as big as a bussard or kite, a thinge nott seene before amongst the sea-men, and flew about the ship above an hower. The sea-men lookt upon itt as some bad omen; but Mr. Rawdon remembringe a passage of Julius Ceasar's, when the Augur Preist beinge att sea told him he thought they should have bad fortune in that voyage, beinge the Augur birds would nott eate; well then, saith Jullius Ceasar, lett them

Dec 1655.

drinke, and causd them to be throwne over bord into the sea.[a] Soe Mr. Rawdon cald for a musket, thinkinge to have kild itt, but before the musket was brought and chargd, the bird flew away and left the ship.[b]

What succeded uppon this was, that within tow dayes they had a violent storme, which continued about seven dayes, most of which time they were forcet to lie adrift without a knott of saile, and for most of this time nott able to dresse anic victualls in the cook-rome, the waves still beatinge into the ship and quenchinge the fire; and one day, beinge above in the captaine's round howse att dinner, Doctor Picw sittinge att the upper end of the table, betwixt the tow Mr. Rawdons, a little shutt window beinge att his backe, a wave breake in had almost brooke his necke, threw all the victualls about,

---

[a] The classical recollections of the biographer are not to be depended upon. This was a favourite story among the Romans, but was never told of Julius Cæsar. It belongs to an earlier period and a less enlightened age. A friend has kindly referred me to several passages in which the incident is related. I will quote one :—"P. Claudius, bello Punico primo, cum prœlium navale committere vellet, auspiciaque more majorum petiisset, et pullarius non exire cavea pullos nuntiasset, abjici eos in mare jussit, dicens, Quia esse nolunt, bibant."—Valerius Max. i. 4, 3. The Consul Claudius was the son of the famous blind censor. The naval battle alluded to, is that of Drepanum, B.C. 249. See also Cicero, de Nat. Deor. ii. 3, 7; Suetonius, Vit. Tib. ii. &c.

[b] It was fortunate for Mr. Rawdon that this strange bird, which was most probably an albatross, escaped his murderous intention. The seamen on board Captain Salmon's ship might have been as capricious in their superstition as were the shipmates of the Antient Mariner :—

> " And I had done a hellish thing,
> And it would work 'em woe;
> For all averred, I had killed the bird
> That made the breeze to blow.
> Ah, wretch ! said they, the bird to slay,
> That made the breeze to blow.

> " Nor dim nor red, like God's own head,
> The glorious sun uprist:
> Then all averred, I had killed the bird
> That brought the fog and mist.
> 'Twas right, said they, such birds to slay,
> That bring the fog and mist."

and this wave brooke quite over the pupe, and raikt all the ship
over att least tow hundred tun of watter, soe that the captain was
affraid the ship would have bene founderd or brooke a peces, but,
blessed be God, thir was noe greate hurt done, not soe much as one
man washt away or hurt, for the marriners, espynge of itt before itt
came, gott such fast hold in and by the stearidge, that they all saved
themselves; the captaine opninge the round howse dore in hast to
see in what condition the ship was, the first noyce they heard from
belowe was a merry noyce of the mariners laughinge att one another
that was most wett, and dansinge and shakinge thir cloothes that
wore wett. In this greate storme they lost all the ships that were in
thir company, and were left only to the protection of the all
mercifull God, who commanded the mercilesse waves to doe them
noe hurte, which were seeminge as high as mountaines, and continually threatninge as if they would devour the ship; but this was
not all; about the last day of the storme they had like to have mett
with another danger of a different nature, and it was about fower
of the clocke in the afternone they espied a ship makinge towards
them; said the captaine, " This ship, I believe, is some rogue; letts
make up to him to see what he is before night, that we may be
prepared for him against to morrow morninge;" for the seas were
soe high then, that they could nott, if they would, lay one another
abord; soe stearinge thir course one towards another they quickly
mett; soe they haild him and askt him from whence he was, he said,
from Amsterdame; soe he askt them from whence they were, they
told him from White-Hall, which was as much as to say, one of the
Protector's ships, or a man of warr; soe he saild by them, and they
knew he lied, for he was an Ostender, full of men and new tallowed;
soe he saild about them observinge thir strength; soe they went to
supper, and after supper went to fitt up thir ship, breakinge downe
cabbins that hinderd the traversinge of the guns, stavinge all emptie
caskes, and putt the mariners' chests out of the way, fittinge cartrages,
lint, stockes, bulletts, and all thinges nescessary for the greate guns.
The gentlemen had thir places appoynted, with each halfe a dozen

men, to have the care of such and such guns, and to incourage the
seamen where thir might be most occasion; all these thinges beinge
well orderd, they went to rest themselves, to be the better able to
manage thir busnesse the next day, to offend thir enemie, and to
defend themselves.   The man of warr kept them company very
closse, observinge thir actions till midnight, but thinkinge he should
have had a hott breakfast of itt, seeinge the ship a lustie ship and
well mand, and that by thir preparations they were resolved to fight
itt out, a little before breake of day he very fairely saild away, and
left them, soe that by day-light he was quite out of sight; they were
very glad, beinge a laden ship, that they were rid of soe troblesome
a companion.   After this they mett with noe more ships, but
sailinge on directly thir course, comminge as they thought within a
day's saile or tow of England, they threw thir leade and found
grownd, and soe continued soundinge all that day and the next, but
the soundings were soe variable, that the captaine was much perplext,
nott havinge had the benifitt (by reason of foule darke weather),
niether of the sun nor starrs, to know where he was; did nott know
wheather he was uppon the coast of England or France.   But Mr.
Rawdon remembringe his old plott abord Captaine Bright in the
like casse, causd the gentlemen abord to make a purse, puttinge each
one a pece of eight into itt, and naild itt to the maine mast, givinge
notice to the seamen, that he that discoverd land first should have
that purse of mony.   Soe thir was allwayes some, with an extreordnary care, lookinge out for land night and day.   After they
had bene in this perplexitie about tow dayes, itt pleasd God the
third day that one   Gappe, a cabin boy of the ship, and the
captaine's sarvant, was got into the fore tope of the ship, and on a
sudden cryes out land—land,—soe they askt him woreabouts itt lay;
he answered soe and soe; some others went up, but could nott discover itt; this hapned about nine of the cloke in the morninge, soe
the captaine who knew the boy to have a cleere sight, and that he
had formerly espide the land before other men, causd them to stere
the ship towards that place where he said the land lay, and about an

houres saylinge, or little more, they did nott only discover itt to be
land, but the weather cleeringe up found itt to be the Lizard poynt
in the West of England, att which they wereall much joyed, and the
boy had the purse of mony for his reward.

After this they endeavourd all they could to saile up the Chanell
of England, and got as high as Portland, but the winde provinge
contrary and foule weather they were forcd to putt backe, and on a
Sunday in the afternone, the eave of Christmasse eave, they putt
into Dartmouth. Before they landed, after they were come to an
anker, thir came one Captain Webber abord them, who to welcome
the tow Mr. Rawdons into England told them that Captain Jopp, a
ship they had laden a monthe before they came from the Canaries,
in which they had three thousand powndes worthe of Canary wines,
was taiken by the French men;[a] but they remembringe Job's
sayinge, " God giveth and God taiketh, and blessed be the name of
the Lord," did beare itt with much corrage, and were very glad
that in ballance of that losse he was pleased, after all thosse greate
stormes and dangers, to bringe them into a saife harbour, where
that eaveninge they went ashore, and soe that voyage was ended.
They lodgd att one Mr. Corker's, the best inn in Dartmouth, where
we well leave them to rest this night; and to morrow I shall, God
willinge, give you a farther accompt of them.

*Of what hapned them after thir Landinge att Dartmouth, till thir
Arivall att London.*

On Sunday in the afternone, as I have allredie said, came ashore
the tow Mr. Rawdons, Dr. Picugh, Mr. William Jaques[b] thir
kinsman, Mr. John Throcmorton, Mr. William Clapham,[c] a York-

---

[a] This capture was the more unfortunate, as it must have happened at the very time
that peace was being concluded with France. The treaty was proclaimed on the 28th of
Nov. 1655.

[b] Mr. William Jaques was the fourth son of Sir Roger Jaques.

[c] Mr. William Clapham was a younger son of George Clapham, esquire, of Beamsley
in Craven, in the county of York. His eldest brother was Sir Christopher Clapham,

shire gentleman, and a little Spanish foote-boy, which Mr. Rawdon brought from the Canaria with him, called John Tosta; this was a wittie little knave, and did with his concicts make them merry sometimes, of whom I will taike the liberty a little to speake. Beinge att sea, cominge uppon the Northerne cape, beinge cold frostie weather, he came to his maister and told him, "Sir," said he, "I doe nott understand this cold, itt is gott into my fingers' endes." Soe his maister told him that the northerne frosts did use to taike peple now and then by the fingers' ends; and when they came ashore to Dartmouth, he havinge in his owne cuntry nott beinge usd to lie in a bed, but turnd with the rest of the gromes and foote boyes into the straw-loft over the stable, thought the weather was a little to cold to be served soe in England, soe goinge into the chambers where the maids were makinge the beds, he espied little trundel beds under the greate beds, which he understood were for gentlemen's men; soe fearinge he should goe to his old trade of the straw loft, he said to his maister, Sir, thir are a sorte of little beds under the greate beds in this howse, which they say are for sarvants; may nott I lie in one of thosse? Yes, saith his maister, you may, thir is one of thosse little beds provided for you; with which he was very well pleasd.   He was very forward to speake English, and one day seeinge a ladie stand, the rest beinge sett, nott knowinge the name of a chaire, he askt hir if she would nott have a sitt downe, and soe brought hir a chaire.   In the inns uppon the rood, he chansd to heare the gentlemen call the maid that waited in the chamber, Sweet-hearte; soe his maister bidinge him in Spanish call the maide, he went downe the staires, and meetinge the chamberlaine, he said to him, "Bid Sweet-harte come up to my maister," he thinkinge that had bene hir name.   Many of thosse pasages I could relate, but I hold them nott worth the while, soe now to our busnesse.

On Munday morninge, severall gentlemen, as Captain Play,[a] Governour of the towne, Captain Alford,[b] with other persons of quallitie, came to vizitt them, and bid them welcome ashore, offeringe thir service to them for anie thinge they might have occasion of; and in the afternone, some of them did come and walke abrood with them, shewinge them the porte and towne. On Tuesday morninge, Mr. William Jaques and Mr. Clapham tooke post for London; and in the afternone Captain Play, the Governour, invited them to his howse, where he made them an exelent treatment, tellinge them he knew Sir Marmaduke Rawdon very well, and though they had nott the happinesse to have him on thir side, yett he was soe noble an enemie, that he loved his memorie, and that for his sake and thir owne, would serve then in aney thinge lay in his power. Captain Alford had bene a captaine on the Kinges side, and did invite them and all thir company to dine with him the next day, beinge Christmasse day, which they did, and were nobly entertained by him and his lady with very good cheere, and exelent musick, booth soft and loud instruments and voyces, where they past very orderly all that day with much delight.

On Saint Stephen's day, Captain Alford and some other gentlemen invited them abrood into the country to a place called Tare Crosse,[c] about three miles from the towne, a place of much pleasure, thir beinge a fresh water above a mile and a halfe longe, well furnisht with fresh-water fish, on the one side, and on the other side the maine ocean, the land betwixt nott beinge above a stone's throw;

---

[a] Probably the John Plays of Dartmouth, who, after the Restoration, was accused, conjointly with Henry Hatsell of that town, of unjustly concealing from his Majesty 20,000l. remaining in their hands. Cal. State Papers, 1660-61, p. 377.

[b] Probably a younger son of Sir Lancelot Alford of Meaux Abbey in Holderness, Yorkshire, who was knighted by King James I. at York, in 1603. (Collect. Topog. et Herald. vol. iv. p. 178.) In June, 1632, the council of war recommended Captain Lancelot Alford to the King for promotion. (Cal. State Papers, 1631-33, p. 366.)

[c] Tor-Cross, by modern computation seven miles distant from Dartmouth. It is yet a pleasant watering-place. The fresh-water is a lake about 300 acres in extent, which is separated from the sea by a narrow slip of land. It still abounds in fish and wild fowl.

soe they had fresh-water fish on the one side catcht, and on the other
side, in the sea, they had a boote to drag oysters for them, and to
catch them sea fish. Here they had an exclent fish dinner, and as
they went home they were carried to the howses of thosse gentlemen's
accquentance, where they were kindly entertaind, and in this
manner they past that day.

The next day, beinge Saint John's day, they made an entertainement att thir inne for thosse gentlemen they had receved anie
civilitie from, and soe in makinge much of thir freinds they past
away that day.

The next day, they treated of thir journie, givinge order for
horses, and in the afternone tooke thir leave of some freinds; and
the next day, Fryday morninge, about nine of the clock, accompanied by Captain Play the Governour, Captain Alford, Captain
Disborow, nephew to Major Generall Disborow,[a] and severall other
gentlemen, who sett them on thir way about tow miles, they tooke
thir leaves and parted, goinge on thir journie. They lay that night
att Excester; the next day, beinge Saturday, they spent in vewinge
the cittie and cathedrall, as also in hiringe a coach with six horses
for London, for which, because they would have itt wholy to
themselves, they gave the full hire, beinge twelve powndes. Sunday
they spent fore-none and after-none in hearinge of sermons; and on
Munday morninge they prepared for thir journie.

They havinge hired, as is allredie said, the coach for themselves,
itt soe hapned that a gentlewoman,[b] upon earnest busenesse, was
very desierous to go up in the coach, and desiered the mistress of
the howse to speake to Mr. Rawdon to lett hir have a place; but
the mistress would nott, tellinge hir itt was to noe purposse, beinge
she thought that gentlemen that had paid the full hire of the coach
for thir owne pleasure, would not suffer anie to goe thir in but thir
owne company; but this would nott serve hir turne. Mr. Rawdon

[a] He was appointed Major General of the militia forces in the south-western counties
on the 28th May, 1655.

[b] "One Mrs. Fax," is a pencil interlineation in the MS.

beinge on Munday morninge betimes with some of his company in
the kitchinge drinkinge some burnt clarett before they tooke coach,
in comes this gentlewoman, beinge a proper hansome yonge woman,
and told him she had a greate suite to him. Soe he desird hir to
sitt downe and drinke a cup of burnt clarett, and that then he would
heare hir request. Soe she did, and withal told him that she came
from Plimouth thinkinge to have gon to London that weeke, but
that he hiringe the whole coach, she was disapoynted; that she had
very urgent busnesse of her husband's, soe that if she were forcd to
stay till the next weeke itt would be very prejudiciall to hir. He
askt hir what cuntry-woman she was; she answerd, Yorkshire. He
askt hir whereabouts; she said, Three miles from York. He askt hir
if she knew the Lady Jaques; she said she knew hir, and some other
of his relations he askt hir for, very well. Well, said he, mistress, I
am your countryman, and you shall nott only have a place, but you
shall have the best place in the coach, and that he would taike itt to
his care to make much of hir all the journie; and soe he did, for he
sett hir by him selfe att the brood end of the coach, and she dined
and supt constantly with them, and would nott suffer hir to pay anie
thinge.

Thus the tow Mr. Rawdons, Doctor Picugh, the Yorkshire gentlewoman, Mr. John Throcmorton, and Mr. Rawdon's foote boy,
went up in the coach togeather, and Mr. Chapman with them on
horsbacke. That night they mett with, att thir lodginge, an honest
minister, whom they invited to sup with them, who after supper
said prayers to them; the like he did in the morninge, beinge he
was goinge to London; they told him if he would please to keepe
them company he should fare no worse then they did, and itt should
cost him nothinge, which he very kindly accepted of, and did performe the office of thir chaplaine; soe then they had in thir company
a cupple of doctors, one for the soule, and the other for the body.
A merry journie they had, and with good wine and good victualls
made the best of the cold weather. On Satturday they were mett

att Branford[a] by thir kinsman Mr. Thomas Williams,[b] Mr. William
Jaques, and some other gentlemen, and att Chearinge Crosse they
parted with thir Exeter coach, and thir company, and tooke a
London coach, and went to the Vine att Bishopsgate, where thir
kinsman, Mr. William Bowyer,[c] staid for them with his owne coach
to carry them to his howse att Layton Stone. Soe they went with
thir brother and cossen Bowyer to Layton Stone, where they were
very nobly entertained by him and his lady, as also by Mr. Thomas
Williams and his lady who had likewisse thir country howse thir.
These gentlewomen were cossen germaines to Mr. Rawdon the elder,
and sisters to Mr. Rawdon the yonger. Here they staid about
three dayes, and then went to · London about thir affaires; where
they were mett in the way by one Mr. Basse, a marchant, who did
request them to dine with him that day at the Sun Taverne behind the
Exchange. ˙ Soe they, with Mr. Bowyer and Mr. Williams, who came
up with them, dined thir that day, where they had all the varieties
the season afforded. Here they staid till Saturday, att which time
they went downe to Hodsden, to pay thir dewtie to thir aunt, and
mother, the Lady Rawdon; she was very joyfull to see them, kild
the fatt calfe, and gave them as noble entertainment as in thosse
times could be expected. Here they spent the remaininge part of
the monthe of January, and the begininge of February went to
London to disposse of some Canaria wines they had remaininge.
This monthe of February, and part of March, whilst they staid in
London, they were continually feasted by one or other, and soe they
concluded the yeare of 1655.

1656   The 26 of March, the begininge of 1656, the tow cossens, who
had bene partners and companions nere twentie yeares, did now
part for a time; Mr. Marmaduke Rawdon the yonger, remaininge
with his lady mother at Hodsden, and Mr. Marmaduke Rawdon the

---

[a] Brentford.   [b] Mr. Thomas Williams of Layton-Stone in Essex married
Martha one of the daughters of Sir Marmaduke Rawdon.

[c] Mr. William Bowyer of Layton-Stone married Catharine another daughter of Sir
Marmaduke Rawdon.

elder, hiringe a coach and six horses, accompanied by his tow
nephews, Mr. Henry and Mr. John Jaques,[a] and his Spanish foote-
boy Tosta on horsebacke, went into Yorkshire to see the Lady
Jaques his sister, and the rest of his freinds and relations in that
cuntry.   He was accompanied the first dayes journey to Stevenidge
by Captain Ralfe Sidenham,[b] Mr. William Lee, Mr. Fernando Body,
Mr. Richard Hide, Mr. George Webber, and severall others, gentlemen and merchants, to the number of halfe a score.   They lodgd
att the Swan att Stevenidge, where Mr. Rawdon treated them very
nobly, and the next morninge they parted; they for London, and
Mr. Rawdon on his journie.   Itt chancd that night Sir Thomas
Ingram[c] (now Chanclour of the Dutchie and one of his Majesties
most honorable privie councill,) and his lady lay in this inn that
night; soe in the morninge he askt the host what gentlemen were
they that were soe merrie most of the night: he told him, they were
some gentlemen that were come to accompany one Mr. Rawdon, a
Yorkshire gentleman, soe far on his way.   Soe Sir Thomas desird
the host to tell Mr. Rawdon he desird to speake with him; soe Mr.
Rawdon goinge to him, Sir Thomas told him he understood he was
goinge into Yorkshire, and that he was in a hird coach, and desird
to know what company he had; he told him he had none but his
tow nephews.   " Well, then," saith Sir Thomas, " wee are goinge
into Yorkshire likewisse; soe pray lett my wife and I prevaile with
you soe much as to goe alonge with us in our coach, and we will
turne our waitinge woman into your coach to your tow nephews."
Soe he told him he was very redie to waite uppon him and his lady,
and in this manner they travaild togeather into Yorkshire, where

    [a] Sons of Sir Roger Jaques.
    [b] Probably of the family of Sydenham of Brimpton in Somersetshire. Sir Ralph
Sydenham, knight, in 1631 had the appointment in reversion of the surveyorship of the
ordnance in the Tower, after the Restoration was made Master of the Charter House, and
died in 1671.—Cal. State Papers.
    [c] Sir Thomas Ingram, knight, was the son of Sir Arthur Ingram, knight, of Temple
Newsome in Yorkshire.   His lady was Frances Belasyse, daughter of Thomas first
Viscount Fauconberg.

with good discourse they made the miles seeme very short. When they came uppon the outskirts of Yorkshire, about Bawtry, they parted; Sir Thomas and his lady goinge to see thir niece,[a] my Lord Falconbridge[b] his sister, who was lately married to the Lord Cassalton; and Mr. Rawdon went on his journie towards York, and lodgd that night, beinge Fryday, att Doncaster, where he found some of his relations that came to meet him, this place beinge 28 miles from Yorke.[c] The next day he procedded on his journie, and soo sone as he hearde them say they see the steeple of Yorke Minster, he tooke occasion to goe out of the coach to looke uppon itt, and gave hartie thankes to God Almightie, that after soe many yeares absence and dangers he had run thorrow, he was pleasd att last to bringe him in peace and happinesse within sight of the place of his nativitie.[d] Soo, proceeding on his journie, he came to a towne

[a] The niece of Sir Thomas and Lady Ingram was Grace Belasyse, granddaughter of Thomas first Viscount Fauconberg, and wife of George Saunderson fourth Viscount Castleton (of Ireland). Sandbeck near Bawtry was the seat of the Saundersons, and came from them to the Earls of Scarborough.

[b] This was Thomas second Viscount Fauconberg, who in the following year (1657) married Mary daughter of Oliver Cromwell.

[c] The computation of distances seems to have been very inaccurate in the 17th century. Upon early maps York is stated to be 150 miles distant from London, the true admeasurement being nearly 200 miles. The actual distance from Doncaster to York is 38 miles.

[d] The traveller in former days on the high road from Doncaster to the North was first greeted with the sight of the "steeple of York Minster" when he arrived at the summit of a hill that overlooks the deep valley of Barnsdale, one of the haunts of the ballad hero, Robin Hood.

> Robyn stood in Bernysdale
> And lened hym to a tree,
> And by him stode Lytell Johan,
> A good yoman was he.

From this eminence a most extensive view opens out of the great vale of York. Many a wanderer, like Mr. Rawdon, turning his face towards the place of his nativity after a long absence, has been impressed with similar feelings of delight and gratitude when his eyes once more beheld the towers of our noble minster as they rose from the midst of the plain,

> attired with golden light,
> Streamed from the west, as with a robe of power.

called Tadcaster, 8 miles from Yorke, where he founde his sister's coach to waite uppon him emptie, his sister[a] then beinge very ill, and fortie or fiftie of the chiefe gentlemen of the cittie, on horsebacke, stayinge for him; soe he causd a very good dinner to be provided for them, and treated them the best that the towne would afford. After dinner they went towards Yorke, where they accompanied him with much order, the bells of the parish church[b] where he was borne ringinge all the while he past thorrow the cittie; soe comminge to the Lady Jaques's howse[c] where he lodgd, he lighted out of his coach, and desired them to alight, and drinke a glasse of wine, but they refusinge itt, he gave them all thankes for thir respects to him, and soe they parted.

Sunday he rested him selfe; Munday, Tusday, and Weddensday, severall cittizens that had formerly knowne his father, who was very well beloved in that cittie, sent in wine and cakes to drinke with him, and bid him welcome to towne, a custome they have in that country.[d] On Thursday, after dinner, came three of the chiefe aldermen of the cittie, who had all bene Lord Maiors, vizt. Alderman Henry Thomson,[e] Alderman John

---

[a] Lady Jaques.   [b] Saint Crux in York.

[c] Sir Roger Jaques's city residence was in the street called The Pavement, near to the house in the Great Shambles in which Leonard Rawdon had lived and his son Marmaduke was born.

[d] Some of the convivial customs of the citizens of York are sarcastically described in "The Northern Heiress, or The Humours of York," a comedy produced on the York stage in the reign of Queen Anne. The scene is laid at York:—

"*Sir Jeffrey.*—Is it your custom to go to one another's houses, guzzle five or six quarts of ale, and then club round to pay for 't?

"*Lady Ample.*—Nay, Sir Jeffrey, if you find fault with our proceedings you must not be admitted into our society. I do assure you this humour prevails all the town over, and every trivial occasion brings them together.

"*Isabella.*—Aye, aye, if a friend comes to town, they come to drink with you for joy; if they go out of town, they come to help you to wash away sorrow; so that the good people are resolved to share both your pleasure and your pain, provided they may have a little victuals and drink to keep up their spirits."

[e] Alderman Henry Thomson, a wine merchant residing in High Ousegate, York, was Lord Mayor of the city in 1636 and 1653. His brother and co-partner Alderman Leonard

Gildart,[a] and Alderman Leonard Thomson, to his lodginge, to bid him welcome to the cittie, and caried him and his tow nephews to the Talbott, a taverne in Petergate,[b] kept then by one Mrs. Cornu, where they were treated very hansomely.

The weeke after, the Lord Maior[c] sent one of his squiers[d] to

[a] Thomson was Lord Mayor in 1649 and 1659. They were active and exemplary magistrates. During all the troubles of the Civil War, when many of their brethren deserted the city, they remained at the post of danger, discharging their municipal and social duties to the advantage of their fellow-citizens. They have a claim to live in the recollection of posterity for having materially contributed to the rise and prosperity of several families of the same name, who after the Restoration took rank amongst the highest and most influential of the gentry of Yorkshire. To them, three brothers, Henry Thompson, Stephen Thompson, and Edward Thompson, younger sons of Richard Thompson, esquire, of Kilham, a town situate on the Wolds of the East Riding, were indebted for their mercantile education, and no inconsiderable portion of their wealth. These three brothers settled at York, and carried on the business of wine merchants upon an extensive scale and with great success. Henry, the elder of the three, was Lord Mayor of York in 1663. He was afterwards Sir Henry Thompson, knight, of Escricke, a domain in the neighbourhood of York, previously the seat of the Knyvets and the Howards. From him descended the Thompsons of Escricke, and the Thompsons of Marston in the ainsty of York. Stephen, the second brother, an alderman of York in 1686, was afterwards knighted. He married one of the daughters and coheirs of Alderman Leonard Thomson, and from that marriage the family of Thompson of Kirby Hall near Boroughbridge trace their descent. Edward, the youngest of the three brothers, married another daughter of Alderman Leonard Thomson, was Lord Mayor of York in 1683, and represented the city in three parliaments during the reign of William III. He was the ancestor of the Thompsons of Sheriff Hutton.

[a] Alderman John Geldart, Lord Mayor in 1645 and 1654, was a draper (as cloth merchants were then denominated), and lived in High-Ousegate, an opposite neighbour of the Thomsons. He acquired wealth by his business, and purchased the manor of Askam Bryan near York, where he built a fine house. He had also estates in the North Riding, and was succeeded by his son John Geldart, esquire, of Wiganthorpe, who married a daughter of Dr. Robert Hitch, Dean of York.

[b] The great old inn called the Talbot, Mr. Drake tells us (Eborac. p. 319), was one of the most ancient timber buildings in the city. In the early part of the last century it was pulled down, and on its site Mr. John Shaw, a proctor in the court of York, built a house which was afterwards the residence of Alexander Hunter, M.D. who in 1786 published at York a new edition of Evelyn's Sylva and Terra. It is now the residence of George Shann, esquire, M.D.

[c] Stephen Watson, alderman and grocer, was Lord Mayor in 1656. He filled that office for the first time in 1646.

[d] The sword-bearer and mace-bearer of the corporation of York are styled the Lord Mayor's esquires.

invite Mr. Rawdon and his tow nephews to dinner, where severall
of the aldermen were to keepe them company; also thir were some
choyce widdowes and maides.

Severall noblemen and gentlemen did come and send to comple-
ment him, and to bid him welcome into Yorkshire, as in perticuler
my Lord Falconbridge, who lives about ten miles from Yorke,[a] sent
his chiefe gentleman, Mr. John Earneley, to bid him welcome, and
to tell him he would be glade to see him, and that his howse and
parke was att his service; my Lord Fairfax[b] the like, who likewisse.
when he came to Yorke treated him att a taverne where he had a
very noble dinner, and severall other gentlemen the like.

Whilst he staid in this cittie, some freinds did proposse a match
betwixt him and the eldest daughter of the Lord Langdall,[c] and in
order to that, Sir Roger Langley,[d] he and the said lady were
chossen to be gossips to the christninge of a child.   She was a very
discreet, virtuous yonge lady, and he had allwayes a very civill

[a] Newburgh Park, near Coxwold in the North Riding of Yorkshire, the site of an
antient priory of Augustinian canons, was then the residence of Lord Fauconberg.   It is
now the seat of Sir George Orby Wombwell, baronet, the grandson of one of the daughters
and coheirs of the last Earl Fauconberg.   "Monasterium Neuburgense prope Sylvam
Cuculinam," possesses much interest for historical students.   In the seclusion of its
cloisters was composed one of the best of our early chronicles, " Guilielmi Neubrigensis
Historia sive Chronica rerum Anglicarum."

[b] Charles Fairfax fifth Viscount Fairfax of Emley, in the peerage of Ireland.   Gilling
Castle, a fine old mansion situate in Ryedale, a few miles distant from Newburgh Park,
was the country seat of this branch of the illustrious family of Fairfax.

[c] Sir Marmaduke Langdale, knight, of Holme on Spalding Moor in the county of York,
distinguished for his loyalty in the Civil War, was created a peer, by the title of Lord
Langdale, when he was in the suite of King Charles II. at Bruges in the year 1658.   The
biographer has anticipated his elevation.   The young lady, who in 1656 was thought by
her friends to be a suitable match for Mr. Rawdon, was, most probably, Lenox the eldest
daughter of Sir Marmaduke Langdale who was at that time in exile.   A few years
afterwards she married Cuthbert Harrison, esquire, of Acaster Selby, near York, who had
been a captain of foot in the service of King Charles I.   His grandfather John Harrison,
merchant, was Lord Mayor of York in 1612.

[d] Sir Roger Langley of Sheriff Hutton Park, near York (now the seat of Leonard
Thompson, esquire), succeeded in 1651 to the baronetcy which King Charles I. had
conferred upon his father in 1641.   He was maternally descended from the Lords Lumley.

respect for hir, and did now and then vizitt hir, but nott uppon aney score of marriage. Att the same time, Sir Thomas Ingram told him he had three neces, very virtuous yonge ladies, sisters to my Lord Falconbridge, and if he would goe and see them he would goe with him when he pleasd; he gave him many thankes for the greate honor he did him, but that he thought he should have occasion to goe abrood againe, and was not as yet resolved to settle him selfe, soe did nott goe att all, and the treweth is, though he naturally loved the company of woemen, yett he was allwayes naturally averse to marriage, and some times, dreaminge he was maried, haith wept in his sleep very much.

Thosse three ladies, I heare, sence are married to three worthy knights worthely deservinge them.[a] Whilst he lived in Yorke, he did usually every other afternone ride out in his sister's coach to taike the aire, to the townes ajacent about the cittie, havinge his sister's Blacamore boy runninge on one side of the coach, and his Spanish foote-boy on the other side, and one of his sister's men, very well mounted on a good geldinge, behinde the coach. When they came to anie towne the country people would say on one side, one to another, thirs a Blacamore, and on the other side, thir goeth a Tawnie-Moore, for the Spanish boy beinge prettie well sun-burnt, they tooke him for a tawnie Moore. He seldome went abrood but he was accompanied with some ladies, amongst which thir was one Madam Ireland, a yonge bewtie, the daughter of Sir Francis Ireland,[b] of exelent parts, and sunge most incomparably well, in whosse company he tooke the most delight of aney, and seldome

[a] The worthy knights who had the good fortune to espouse the three sisters of Lord Fauconberg were Sir Henry Jones of Alston in Oxfordshire, Sir William Frankland of Thirkleby in Yorkshire, and Sir Marmaduke Dalton of Hawkswell in Yorkshire.

[b] Sir Francis Ireland, knight, sometime of Nostel Priory in the West Riding of Yorkshire, an estate which he sold in 1629 to Sir John Wolstenholme of London, one of the great contractors and monopolists of that period. Sir Francis Ireland had an only son William Ireland, esquire, of Crofton near Wakefield, who was captain of a troop of horse in the civil wars, and several daughters, one of whom married Thomas Arthur, esquire. —Hunter's South Yorkshire, vol. ii. p. 215.

went abrood but she was one, with whome he did continew a civill friendship till such time as she was married.

Some times he would goe to Elvington, five miles from Yorke, a lordship belonginge to his nephew Squier Roger Jaques, closse by which runneth the river of Derwent, of which as lord of the manner he haith the royaltie of the fishinge. Here he tooke much pleasure to see them fish; the fishermen fishinge in little square leather bootes, which, when they have done fishinge, the fishermen carry them home uppon thir backes to thir howses. Here they catch good store of salmon, the river affordinge likewisse exelent good pikes, some of an ell longe, and very good pearch; he did also, to divert himselfe this summer, goe to see Hull, and other places, as also the Spaw att Scarborow,* which lieth uppon the sea shore, where he staid above a wecke to feast himselfe with severall sortes of good sea fish, of which thir is thir good store; and havinge thus spent his time in Yorkshire, above fower monthes, about the middle of August his occasions called him up for London. He went up in a hackney coach, and chancd to goe up all alone, havinge only his foote-boy Tosta, which rid uppon a geldinge, by him. As he came allmost halfe way, within ten miles of Stamford, in the after none, beinge very hott, he bid the coachman to call att the next place he

---

* The medicinal properties of the mineral spring, called the Spa Well, at Scarborough, were first discovered in the early part of the seventeenth century. About the time of Mr. Rawdon's visit, it had acquired considerable celebrity by the commendation of the York physicians; one of whom, the learned Dr. Robert Wittie, published at York in 1667 an elaborate treatise which he entitled, "Scarbrough Spaw, or a Description of the Nature and the Vertues of the Spaw at Scarbrough, Yorkshire." In a complimentary poem prefixed to Dr. Wittie's work we have these doggrel lines:—

> "Your Scarbrough Spaw I have drunk on,
> But never drank of Helicon;
> And 'tis no matter, for I think
> Your Scarbrough Spaw far better drink."

A string of similar verses by another friend of the author concludes thus:—

> "Let Epsom, Tunbridge, Barnet, Knaresbrough be
> In what request they will,—Scarbrough for me."

came att where thir was aney good drinke. Soe he cald att a place
where thir stood a hackney coach which was come from New-Castell
with one gentleman and three gentlewoemen; soe Mr. Rawdon
goinge in, they saluted one another, and began some discourse, from
whence they came, and whither they were to goe, drinkinge one to
another; soe, the reckninge beinge paid, Mr. Rawdon helpt the
gentleman to coach the ladies, and said to the gentleman, " Sir, the
world is very uneaqually devided betwixt you and me;" " How soe,
Sir?" said the gentleman; said Mr. Rawdon, " Because you have
three gentlewoemen in your coach, and I am all alone and have
never a one." " Truly, Sir," said the gentleman, " if they please,
anie one or tow of them are att your service." Soe Mr. Rawdon
thankt him, and askt which of them would honor him with thir
good companies. Tow of them seemed to be willinge; soe he tooke
the handsomeest by the hand, and led hir into his owne coach,
tellinge the gentleman he ought in justice to leave him the biggest
share. This was a lovely yonge gentlewoman, and hapned to be
the niece to Mr. Murry,[a] the Scotchman, who was a Bed-chamber-
man to Kinge Charles the First. They lay that night att Stamford,
and orderd thir busnesse soe, that thir coaches lay att one inn, and
they dind and supt allwayes togeather, as if they had bene all one
company, and in this manner they travaild up to London.

Att Highgate, five miles from London, Mr. Rawdon was mett by
his tow kinsmen, Mr. Marmaduke Rawdon, and Mr. Bevill Rawdon,[b]
who was then new come out of Spaine, who accompanied him into
London, with which this journie was ended.

Here he staid, dispatchinge some busnesse to the Canaries, and
his cossen, Mr. Bevill Rawdon, for Mallaga. He spent some time

---

[a] " Little Will Murray," the well-known groom of the bedchamber to King Charles I.
was in 1643 raised to the dignity of Earl of Dysart and Lord Huntingtower in the peerage
of Scotland. The biographer styles him " Mr. Murry." Perhaps during the Protectorate
he had not assumed his title of nobility. I am unable to identify the lovely young gentlewoman his niece.

[b] Bevill Rawdon was the third son of Sir Marmaduke Rawdon. He was bred a merchant.

amongst his relations till the beginninge of October; att which time
he hird a hackney coach, and went downe into Yorkeshire with his
niece Mrs. Grace Jaques, a yonge gentlewoman of fiftcene yeares of
age, who had bene bred under my Lady Rawdon about twelve
monthes. She was since married to Squier Charles Alanson, whosse
godfather was Kinge Charles the First. They had that journie noe
company, only the Spanish boy on horse backe; they went out of
London on Munday morninge, and on Fryday att night they lay att
Doncaster. That night thir came into that inn where they lay, a
hackney coach from Yorke, the coachman of which Mr. Rawdon
knew; soe being att supper with his neice, he sent for him up, and
made him drinke a glasse of wine, askinge him what newes from
Yorke, and what passengers he had in his coach; the fellow told him
he had only one Mr. Swinborne, and tow ladies that he had taiken
up by the way on this side Yorke, but he did nott know thir names.
Now thir was a rich lady, cald my Lady Temple,* a Roman Cath-

* The account of Lady Temple given in the memoir leaves little doubt as to her identity.
She was a rich lady, yet either unable or unwilling to discharge the debt she had incurred
to Lady Jaques. She was a Roman Catholic, and her man of business was a Mr.
Swinburne; and at the time of her rencontre with Mr. Rawdon she was travelling from
York, or the neighbourhood. All these circumstances favour the supposition that she
was the widow of Sir Peter Temple of Stowe, and the mother of Sir Richard Temple
who is mentioned in a subsequent page of the biography.

Sir Peter Temple, baronet, of Stowe, married for his second wife Christian Leveson,
daughter of Sir John Leveson, and one of the sisters and coheirs of Sir Richard Leveson
of Trentham. This lady was, it may be presumed, a wealthy heiress, yet it is obvious
that she and her husband had been in some pecuniary difficulties. In Whitelock's
Memorials it is noticed that in May, 1649, petitions were presented to Parliament from
Sir Peter Temple and his wife and their creditors, which were referred to a committee.
About the same period Whitelock speaks of Lady Temple as a busy woman and a
great politician, and accuses her of having acted as the agent and messenger of the
infamous Lord Saville. (Memorials, pp. 157, 404.) She must have become a widow
previously to 1654, for in that year her son was returned to Parliament for Warwick
Sir Richard Temple, baronet. Lady Temple's travelling companion was, most probably
Mr. Tobie Swinburne, who, it was said, was converted to the Roman Catholic faith by the
eccentric Sir Tobie Matthews. He was the son of Dr. Henry Swinburne, the celebrated
ecclesiastical lawyer, author of the Treatise on Wills, first published in 1590, and Judge of
the Archbishop's Court at York, who, up to the time of his death in 1624, lived in that

olicke, who ought his sister the Lady Jaques six or seaven hundreth
powndes, but kept soe private that she could never gett hir. arested,
and this lady did imploy in hir busnesse one Mr. Swinborne; soe,
the coachman beinge gone, he told his niece he had a fancie that

city, in a house in Petergate, afterwards the residence of Sir Thomas Herbert, baronet.
Lady Temple's visits into Yorkshire may be readily accounted for. Her sister Frances
Leveson was the wife of Sir Thomas Gower, baronet, of Stittenham, a town in the North
Riding, ten or twelve miles distant from York. Sir Thomas Gower (lineal ancestor of the
Duke of Sutherland) was high sheriff of Yorkshire when the troubles began in 1642. He
was a zealous royalist, and several of his kinsmen were recusants.

That Lady Temple was not a very scrupulous person appears from a letter written in
August, 1660, to Sir Anthony Ashley Cooper, Chancellor of the Exchequer, in which she
is spoken of as Sir Richard Temple's mother, and charged with having stolen from the
Queen's closet one of the pictures belonging to a collection of the late King, which had
been purchased by the Earl of Sussex, and was then at Howley Hall, in Yorkshire. (Cal.
State Papers, 1600-61, p. 200.)

Another Lady Temple, living at this period, but not a widow, nor had she any connection with Yorkshire, was Elianor, the daughter of Sir Timothy Tyrrell, knight, of Oakley
in Buckinghamshire, and the wife of Sir Peter Temple, knight, of Stanton Bury, in the
same county, who was the author of "Man's Master-Piece, or the best Improvement of
the worst Condition in the Exercise of Christian Duty. By P. T., knt." 12mo., London,
1658. The little volume is dedicated by Sir Peter to his wife, the Lady Elianor
Temple, "the most perfect pattern and patronesse of vertue and piety." It is illustrated
with portraits of the author and his wife, engraved by Gaywood. A shield of arms at the
side of each portrait fixes the identity of the persons represented. Sir Peter's armorial
bearings are, Quarterly, 1st and 4th, Or, an eagle displayed sable,—the coat armour
assumed by the Temples as descendants of Leofric Earl of Leicester; 2nd and 3rd, Argent,
a fess between three crescents sable, for Lee; impaling Argent, within a bordure engrailed
gules two chevrons azure, for Tyrell. The achievement on the lady's portrait is Temple,
without a quartering, impaling Tyrell.

It is obvious that there were two Sir Peter Temples, the uncle and the nephew, living at
the same time. The uncle was Sir Peter Temple, knight and baronet, of Stowe, the ancestor of the Dukes of Buckingham of modern creation. The nephew was Sir Peter Temple,
knight, the son of the baronet's younger brother, Sir John Temple, knight, by Dorothy,
the daughter and co-heir of Edmund Lee, esq. of Stanton Bury. His widow, the Lady
Elianor Temple, became the second wife of Richard Grenville, esq. of Wotton, whose
eldest son Richard married Elianor Temple, the only issue of her first marriage. In the
next generation Richard Grenville, the grandson of Sir Peter and Lady Elianor Temple,
married Hester Temple, who was the sister and heir of Richard Temple first Lord Cobham,
and the granddaughter of the baronet of Stowe and his second wife, the Lady Temple of

one of thesse gentlewomen was my Lady Temple that ought hir
mother soe much mony; soe after supper he went downe, and
enquird of the host and hostesse if they knew who thosse ladies were.
They said they had nott heard thir names; he desiered them to
enquire of thir sarvants, which they did, but they were instructed
and would declare nothinge, which still encreasd his opinion more
that itt was she. Soe in the morninge he staid till she tooke coach,
and tooke a full view of hir face, haire, fulnesse, and shape of body.
She beinge gone, he writes presently to London by the post to his
nephew Mr. Marmaduke Jaques, then an Inns of Court gentleman
in the Temple, that he did beliove the Lady Temple was gon up in
such a hackney coach, and that he should waite hir att Stevenidge
the last dayes journie, and thir have order to arest hir, which he
accordingly did; but the busnesse was done before to his hands, for
that night, soe sone as Mr. Rawdon got to Yorke, he told his sister
what past, who by his relation did conclude itt was she; soe she
dispactht hir scacond son, Henry Jaques, with one Mr. Pickard, a
knowinge gentleman, away post for Newarke, where the coach was
to rest Sunday; soe they came thir time enough on Sunday night,
provided the under-sheriffe, and on Munday morninge before she
tooke coach, arested hir. She gave in, after some eight dayes, securitie
for appearance att London, putt hir selfe a prisner in the Kinges
Bench, but, beinge weary of that trade, within twelve monthes the
Lady Jaques, by this discovery of hir brother's, had all hir mony
paid hir, of which she run à greate danger never to have had a
groate, for if she had once gott to London thir had never bene anie
finding hir out.

Here he past the winter in Yorke very merryly, with good fires,

Mr. Rawdon's biography.   This double alliance of the Temples and the Grenvilles contributed to the vast accumulation of wealth that centred in the first Earl Temple, only to
be dissipated by his ducal descendants.

The regicides Peter Temple, esq. and James Temple, esq. were, doubtless, kinsmen of
the two Sir Peter Temples. The former was committed to the Tower at the Restoration,
and died a prisoner there on the 20th Dec. 1663. (Cal. State Papers, 1663-4, p. 383.)
For interesting notices of the Temples, see Notes and Queries, vol. xxiv.

good chere, and good company, and was soo admird amongst the
yonge ladies, that on Vallentine's day he had notice of fifteene,
whosse names I have seene, drew him for thir Vallentine, most of
which were the daughters of knights, and thosse that were nott
were yonge gentlewomen of very good quallitie.

1657.   But as thir is no happinesse in this world that continews longe,
but is interwoven, as all humane affaires are, with some troble, soe itt
hapned to this gentleman, who aboute the begininge of Aprill was
arested by a violent ague and feaver which was thought would have
brought him to his grave. The first day he was mightely trobled
att itt, nott knowinge what destemper itt might prove, fearinge he
should nott have time to settle his affaires, for though he had
allwayes his will made, yett he was desierous to alter some thinges in
itt; soo, soe sone as his destemper was abated, got into his closset,
rectified his will, and then was very well satisfied, referinge his life
or death to the pleasure of God Almightie. He had, for some
yeares before, his will allwayes redie by him, for he usd to say he
would endeavour, as much as he could, that when itt should please
God Almightie to call him, he would have nothinge els to doe but
to die.

      Very ill he was all that monthe; but the begininge of May, by
advice of his physitians, he removed to Elvington with the Lady
Jaques his sister, thinkinge the change of aire might doe him some
good; but his distemper continews still upon him, abhorringe the
smell of aney kind of meate, havinge fitts would hold him some
times eight howres, which brought him soe weake that he was nott
able to goe to bed without helpe; this continued till towards the
latter end of June, att which time his fitts began to abate, and he to
have some little relish for some sortes of meate. The first thinge he
longd for was yonge turkies and sherry sacke, which the season then
furnisht him with, and he had good store of booth provided for him,
with which he recruited himselfe, and in a shorte time gott uppon
his leggs againe. After he was perfectly well and indifferent stronge,
he thought of goinge up to London to looke after the recoveringe of

some monies was dew unto him, and soe about the begininge of October he came up in the Yorke coach with three gentlemen more, and his Spanish boy on horsbacke, towards London. In the way, the first dayes journie, they were to taike up a gentlewoman and hir maide, but knew nott in the least who itt was, but itt proved to be the gentlewoman* he mett the yeare before att Exeter. Soe this gentlewoman and he accidentally, nott knowinge of one the other, chanced to travaile 300 miles outright togeather. When she lookt into the coach, seeinge booth the ends full, she askt the coachman where she was to sitt; he told hir the ends were full, and that he could nott displace aney of the gentlemen that were thir; "Well, then," saith she, "my maide shall sitt in a boote; but if I cannott have a place att one end for my selfe, I will nott goe;" soe with that Mr. Rawdon offerd to goe out, sayinge, "Madam, rather then losse your good company you shall have my place;" which a yonge gentleman that was thir would nott permitt, but lett hir have his seate, and soe they were all accomodated. About Balduck the coach over threw, soe that Mr. Rawdon[b] straind his arme, but comminge to Hodsden his good cossen Mrs. Williams, with hir arte and care, quickly cured itt, and in ten dayes was well againe.

When he came to Hatfield, his kinsman Mr. Marmaduke Rawdon, his cossen, came in the Lady Rawdon his mother's coach to meete him, and carried him from thence to Hodsden, wher he staid most of that winter, some times divertinge him selfe with London, and Layton where his cossen Bowyer dwelt; and about the middle of May, in company of his beloved freind and fellow travelour, Mr. John Fowler, son of Squier Fowler of the Grange nere Shrewsbury,[c] he went to see the Bathe in the Bath coach, his man Tosta on

1653.

---

* "Mrs. Fax."

b "To save Mrs. Fax."

c Richard Fowler, esquire, of the Grange, near Shrewsbury, married Margaret, daughter of Richard Lord Newport, and had five sons and several daughters. Francis Leveson Fowler, the eldest son, had one child, Frances, who married Theophilus seventh Earl of Huntingdon, and was the mother of the Lady Betty Hastings, of whose well-known pious and liberal bequests Yorkshire is yet enjoying the benefits. The second son, Sir William

horsback, in which coach went one Mrs. Penelopie Wells, waitinge
gentlewoman to Sir Thomas Kemish his lady, of whom they did
enjoy very good company. When they came att Bathe, some of
Sir Thomas his sarvants came and mett hir. She told thesse gentlemen, if they would please to goe with hir into Wales, she would
for thir cevillitie towards hir in the journie, promisse them one of
the best bucks in Sir Thomas his parke. Sir Thomas was then
newly deade, and hir lady was att London att hir brother Sir
George Whitmore's.[a]

Att Bathe they staid about twentie dayes, and from thence went
to Bristoll, and soe from thence backe to Bathe, where they tooke
coach for London. In the way, att a place called Sandie-lane, halfe
way betwixt Bathe and Marlborow, they lighted to eate some thinge,
thir beinge none in the coach but Mr. Rawdon and Mr. Fowler;
soe havinge refresht them selves, they bid Tosta the Spaniard to
pay the reckning, and went out towards the coach, which was
then in the street before the inne doore, where thir was come
another coach, and a gentleman standinge by the boote drinkinge
a glasse of beere to them within the coach. Soe, Tosta stayinge
some thinge longe, when he came out Mr. Rawdon cald him
drunkard in Spanish, askinge him why he staid soe longe; att which
the gentleman, understandinge Spanish, said to Mr. Rawdon, " Sir,
how can he be drunke when thir is noe wine in the howse to make
him drunke withall?" Mr. Rawdon answerd him, thir were
severall sortes of drunkennesse; that he might be drunk in the
neglect of his dewtie in nott obeyinge his maister's comands, and the
like. " Sir," said the gentleman to Mr. Rawdon, " I never had the

Fowler, was made a baronet by Queen Anne. Mr. John Fowler, the " beloved friend
and fellow traveller " of Mr. Rawdon, must have been one of the younger sons of Squire
Fowler of the Grange.

[a] There is some inaccuracy in this account of Sir Thomas Kemish and his lady. Sir
Charles Kemyes, baronet, of Kevan-Mably in Glamorganshire, married Margaret daughter
of Sir George Whitmore of Balmes in the parish of Hackney, knight, who was Lord
Mayor of London in 1631-2. (Courthope's Ext. Baronetage, p. 112.) Sir George
Whitmore died 12 December, 1654. (R. Smith's Obituary, Camd. Soc. p. 49.)

happinesse to see you before in my life, and yet I have a stronge fancie you must be such a gentleman that lived some time in the Canary Ilands." He told him he was the same man. Saith the gentleman, " I have from Captaine Sidenham, and from some other relations and freinds of mine, herd severall times large discourses concerninge you, and I should be very glad to be better accquented with you." With that Mr. Rawdon desird to know his name, and whither he was travelinge. He told him he was eldest son of Sir Francis Dorington[a] of Dorington in Somersetshire, and that he was goinge with his wife and daughter up to London, and that that night he did intend to lie att Marlborow, att such an inne. Mr. Rawdon told him, that he should doe the like; and that if he and his lady would doe him the favour to sup with him, he would taike itt as a very good begininge to thir better accquentance; he told him he would, provided he would dine with him the next day att Newbery, which he promised to doe, and soe they supt that night togeather. The next day Squier Dorington told Mr. Rawdon, that his wife had a greate suite to him that he would goe a longe with them in thir coach; he told him he could nott well doe that, for that that gentleman, Mr. Fowler, his freind, came purposely out of London to keepe him company, soe that to leave him alone would not seeme well: he told him if he would please to goe with them, they would lett thir daughter and waitinge woman goe in thir coach to keepe Mr. Fowler company. Soe he told him he would propound itt, and give him the answer presently; soe he spooke with Mr. Fowler,

---

[a] "Aug. 31, 1644. The King sent two messengers of our troope with a letter to Sir Fr. Dorington, who hath 1,000 horse in Devon, to stop their [the enemy's] march." (Symonds's Diary, p. 62.) Sir Francis Dodington (often spelt Dorington) of Dodington in Somersetshire, was sheriff of that county in 1641. He was an active royalist, and after the destruction of his party retired to France. His eldest son and heir, John Dodington, was secretary to Thurloe, Cromwell's secretary of state. He married Hester, one of the daughters of Sir Peter Temple of Stowe, and his wife the Lady Temple previously mentioned, and died in 1663 in the lifetime of his father, who, after the Restoration, returned to England, and married the widow of John Sydenham, esquire. (Nichols's Topog. and Geneal. vol. iii. p. 570.)

who was very well pleasd with the motion; and soe Mr. Rawdon
went up in the squier's coach to London, they dininge and suppinge
allwayos togeather, and were very merry in thir journie to London.
Madam Dorington was a most bewtifull lady, and of exelent discourse, but very sicke, being very subjcct to sound away as she was
discoursinge, some thinkinge she was bewitcht.   She was sister to
Sir Richard Temple, a greate creature of Oliver's.[a]

Boinge come to London, he spent most of his time att Hodsdcn and
Layton, in buckhuntinge, and ridinge about to see his freinds, till
the 10th of August, att which time he went with his Spaniard Tosta
into Yorkshire.   He went in the stage coach, Tosta ridinge, and leadinge a spare geldinge for his maister to ride uppon when he thought
fitt.   He came to Yorke about the middle of August, where, after itt
was knowne, he was invited in one weeke to six venson pastics.[b]   He

<hr />

[a] It is not improbable that Sir Richard Temple, during the Protcctorate, was " a great
creature of Oliver's."   Ilis father, Sir Peter, it is said, was a zealous parliamentarian,
and went all lengths with his party; and in the Convention parliament, which was opened
by the Lord Protector in person, on the 4th Sept. 1654, Sir Richard was member for
the county of Warwick.   After the Restoration he became a distinguished royalist.   Ile
sat for the town of Buckingham in the first parliament summoned by Charles II., and was
selected to be one of the Knights of the Bath, specially created to attend the coronation of
the restored monarch in April, 1661.

[b] Such was the hospitality of the York citizens.   In the middle of August venison is
in high season; and venison pasty, or red deer pie, was the most attractive luxury that
could be provided for the table.   " Come, we have a hot venison pasty to dinner," was the
inducement offered by Page to his friends to cease their bickerings. (Merry Wives,
act i. sc. 1.)   When Howel was secretary to Lord Scrope, the President of the Council
of the North, and was living in his official apartmonts in the King's Manor at York, he
sent to a friend in London a present of a couple of red deer pies.   " The one (he says)
Sir Arthur Ingram gave me, the other my Lord President's cook.   In your next let me
know which is the best seasoned.   If you please to send me a barrel or two of oysters,
which we want here, I promise you they shall be well eaten with a cup of the best clarret,
and the best sherry, to which wine this town is altogether addicted, shall not be wanting.".
(Familiar Letters, ed. 1678, p. 183.)   A civic banquet was not complete without a pasty:—

> " Or if you'd fright an alderman and mayor,
> Within a pasty lodge a living hare;
> Then midst their gravest furs shall mirth arise,
> And all the guild pursue with joyful cries."

had nott bene thir one fortnight, but his kinsman, Mr. Marmaduke
Rawdon, came downe from Hodsden to see him att Yorke, where
he was very nobly feasted by severall gentlemen, particularly by my
Lord Fairfax. He was likewisse well feasted with good venson att
his cossen's lodgins; his cossen havinge att that time venson sent
him by Sir Walter Valvasour,[a] and other gentlemen.

But he had scarce staid thir a fortnight when his sister, Madam
Bowyer, sent for him, hir husband beinge very ill and lyinge a
dyinge. Soe he went up to Layton to hir, and did assist hir very
much in the ordring of his funerall, which was done with some
magnificence.

But our Mr. Rawdon, of whom we now treate, staide in Yorkshire,
setlinge some lands he had thir, till the begininge of November, att
which time he came up towards London in the Yorke coach in
company of Mr. John Brookes, son to Aldernan Brookes of Yorke,[b]
a compleate gentleman, with whom he had very good company.
He was mett att Hatfield by his kinsman, Mr. Marmaduke Rawdon,
the Lady Rawdon, his aunt, sendinge hir coach to bringe him to
Hodsden, where he spent that winter very much to his content;

Down to modern times the cooks of York have been famous for their skill in the construction of the Pasty, whether it were composed of summer venison, autumnal game, or
Christmas geese and turkeys. A contemporary receipt for making a venison pasty tells
us what were the ingredients of the dainty dish in which our ancestors delighted :—

"To bake red deer.—Parboyl it, and then sauce it in vinegar; then lard it very thick,
and season it with pepper, ginger, and nutmegs; put it into a deep pye, the coffin made
of the best paste, with good store of sweet butter, and let it bake. When it is baked take
a pint of hippocras, half a pound of sweet butter, two or three nutmegs, a little vinegar,
and poure it into the pye in the oven, and let it stand and soake an hour, then take it out,
and when it is cold stop the vent-hole."—The Queen's Closet Opened, 12mo. London,
1655; Markham's English Housewife, London, 1649.

[a] Sir Walter Vavasour, baronet, of Hazlewood near Tadcaster in Yorkshire, a zealous
royalist. His wife was a daughter of the first Viscount Fauconberg.

[b] Alderman James Brooke was Lord Mayor of York in the years 1651 and 1661. His
eldest son, "the compleate gentleman," Mr. John Brooke, was one of "the eminent and
ingenious persons of the 17th century," who were correspondents of Abraham Hill,
esquire, well known as a founder and an early treasuror and secretary of the Royal

havinge not only the good company of the lady his aunt, and cossen
Marmaduke, but also the company of Madam Forster,[a] Madam
Bowyer, Madam Crew,[b] and Madam Williams, hir daughters, in
whosse exclent company he was very much delighted. Here, and
afterwards some times att Layton, and some times att London, he
spent his time till the latter end of June, att which time for some
small distemper he founde in him selfe he went to drinke the watters
att Tunbridge, accompanied only with his Spaniard Tosta, which
waters did him much good, and he was very happy thir in meetinge
with exclent company which did much divert him, and I thinke doe
him as much good as the waters.[c] In the afternones he would ride

Society. Several of Mr. Brooke's letters to Mr. Hill, dated at York in the year 1663, are
printed in the volume of "Familiar Letters," which passed between Abraham Hill,
esquire, and his friends, published in 1767. In the year 1676, a few months after the
death of the alderman his father, Mr. John Brooke was created a baronet. In
Wotton's Baronetage (1741, vol. iii. p. 196), it is stated that this family of Brooke
descended from the Brookes of Norton in Cheshire, and that Alderman James Brooke,
before he settled at York, fined for sheriff of the City of London. However this may
be, there is no doubt that in the year 1614 James Brooke, grocer, was admitted to
the freedom of the City of York by patrimony, as the son of John Brooke, mercer, and
that seventeen years afterwards he served the office of sheriff of York, and in 1644 was
made an alderman, and that for nearly forty years of his life he was an active member of
the corporation. He had a country house at Ellinthorpe in the parish of Aldborough,
about sixteen miles from York, and died there on the 1st of December, 1675. Sir John
Brooke died in 1691. The baronetcy became extinct upon the death of his grandson
Sir Job Brooke in 1770.

[a] Elizabeth, daughter of Sir Marmaduke Rawdon, and wife of Edmund Forster,
esquire, one of the colonels of the London militia.

[b] Jane, daughter of Sir Marmaduke Rawdon, and wife of Henry Crew of Bristol,
Surveyor of the Customs.

[c] The medicinal virtues of the springs near Tunbridge, discovered in the early part of
the seventeenth century, were in great repute at this time. In 1652, Evelyn's wife, and
her mother Lady Browne, having a desire to drink the Tunbridge waters, he took them
thither, and they stayed in a very sweet place, a little cottage by the wells. (Diary, vol. i.
p. 279.) The town now called Tunbridge Wells was not built until towards the close of
the reign of Charles II. A comedy entitled "Tunbridge Wells, or a Day's Courtship,"
was published in 1678.

out with some gentlemen to see the places ajacent, as the Earle of Licester's howse att Penshurst, a gallant scate;[a] my lord of Abergany's howse;[b] also a towne where thir is a chappell where the Earles of Dorset are buried, where thir are many fine monuments worth the sceinge.[c] Some times in the after nones he would goe a fishinge, thir beinge exclent pondes well stord with fish thir abouts.

He came from thence soner then he would have done, beinge his cossen Marmaduke was to be married to a yonge gentlewoman, a

---

[a] When Mr. Rawdon visited the gallant seat of the Earl of Leicester, " celebrated by that illustrious person Sir Philip Sidney, who there composed divers of his pieces, and once famous for its gardens and excellent fruit," (Evelyn's Diary, Aug. 1652,) " the later Sidney " was living there in retirement, employed in composing his celebrated " Discourses on Government." After the death of Josceline Earl of Leicester in 1743, the princely mansion of Penshurst was allowed to fall into decay. (Amsinck's Tunbridge Wells and its Vicinity, p. 135.) Half a century ago the house was surrounded by a perfect wilderness, instead of the famous gardens admired by the author of Sylva, and so graphically described by the poet :

> " Thou hast thy orchard fruit, thy garden flowers,
> Fresh as the ayre, and new as are the hours;
> The early cherry with the later plum,
> Fig, grape, and quince, each in his time doth come;
> The blushing apricot and woolly peach
> Hang on thy walls that every child may reach."

Under the care of the late Lord De Lisle and Dudley, and his son the present noble owner, Penshurst has resumed its pristine magnificence.

[b] Eridge Castle, two miles from Tunbridge Wells, the seat of the Nevilles Lords Abergavenny. In 1659, when Mr. Rawdon was at Tunbridge, it was the same splendid mansion in which Queen Elizabeth was entertained by Lord Abergavenny for a whole week in the year 1573 ; but it was soon afterwards deserted by its owners and gradually demolished. Henry, second Earl of Abergavenny, the father of the late and present earls, rebuilt Eridge Castle, which is said to be worthy of their extensive domains and the illustrious family they represent.

[c] Buckhurst, the ancient seat of the Sackvilles Earl of Dorset, was in the parish of Withyham in Sussex, a few miles from Tunbridge. In 1659 the church of Withyham had a lady-aisle or lady-chapel, which was the accustomed place of interment of the Sackvilles. The old church was destroyed by lightning in 1663, and the fine monuments alluded to by Mr. Rawdon perished; but some drawings of them are preserved on the great pedigree at Knole, and two are engraved in Collins's English Baronage, 1727. 4to. See the Collectanea Topog. et Geneal. iii. 295.

coeheire of the fameley of the Norths, on St. James his day; soe he
came from Tunbridge the 22nd, was att Hodsden the 23rd, and the
25th, beinge the wedingday, was one of the bridemen. His kinsman
remained att Hartford, where his lady then lived; but after the
weddinge was done, Mr. Rawdon returned to Hodsden, where he
lived as formerly with the lady, his aunt, till the 17th of October
followinge, att which time his cossen Marmaduke, his yonge lady,
with thir sarvants, came to Hodsden to live in a faire new bricke
howse which his said cossen had made an end of buildinge that
summer; att which time our Mr. Rawdon, of whom we now treate,
tooke his leave of the Lady Rawdon his aunt, with whome sence his
last comminge from the Canaries he had allwayes bene very civilly
entertaind, and with hir consent came to be a guest with his old
1660. fellow traveler in his new house, and thir spent all that winter and
1661. summer, and the next winter and summer followinge, passinge his
time in country recreations abroad, and when att home, for the most
part in his closet reading or writinge, beinge naturally inclind to
studdie, and haith compild severall bookes of his owne collections.

    In this manner he spent his time without aney considerable
1662. thinge till the begininge of July, 1662, at which time his kinsman,
Mr. Marmaduke Rawdon, had a desire to travaile into France and
Flanders, and desird him to beare him company, which he was
willinge to doe; soe they sett forwards on thir journie from London
the 14th July, and soe to Dover, where the 17th att night they
embarked abord the passage boote for Callis, where the next
morninge they saifely arived. That day after dinner they tooke post
and went to Gravelinge, one of the strongest townes in Flanders, and
in possession of the French Kinge; from thence they went to Dunkirke, then belonginge to the Kinge of England, of which was then
Governour that gallant Scotch lord, the honor of his nation, the Lord
Rutterford Earle of Tiveot, who was afterwards slaine unfortunately
by the Moors att Tangier, to the greate griefe of his kinge and
country, and of all that knew him.[a]

    [a] Lord Rutherford was appointed Governor of Dunkirk in the place of Sir Edward

The next morninge they went to vizitt the Governour, my Lord
Rutterford, who was very glad to see them, and went with them to
shew them a cittadell he was makinge of sand heapes, which he had
allmost brought to perfection, and was capable of lodginge a
thousand soldiers; a place of much importance booth to command
the towne, to keepe itt in obedience, and likewisse to defend itt
against an enemie: a worke carried on with much industry, 500
men beinge att worke every day; my lord beinge the chiefe overseer,
beinge all summer longe up att five of the clocke in the morninge
amongst them.[a] This day they dind with my lord uppon the worke
in his tent, and after dinner he carried them in his coach to the
market place to see his brigade drawne up, which were all very
stoute lustie soldiers. Thir were tow of them for some misdemeaners
condemnd, the one to ride the wodden horse, the other his cloothes
stript downe to the middle, and his hands tyed to the gallows, thir
to be whipt. Some desired thesse gentlemen to beg thir pardon of
my lord; soe my lord for thir respects did pardon them, and they

Harley, in May, 1661. He was not advanced to the dignity of Earl of Tiviot until
the year 1663. "By the surrender of Dunkirk the Lord Rutherford wanting employment, his Majesty was pleased to honour him both with the government of Tangier
and the Earldom of Tiviot, and he repaired to his charge in May, 1663." He was
killed by the Moors on the 3rd of May, 1664, when marching into a wood near Tangier
with five hundred men and the principal officers of the garrison, who were all destroyed. See "An Account of Tangier. By Sir Hugh Cholmley, Bart." Privately printed,
1787.

[a] In the year 1663 the eminent naturalists, Francis Willughby and John Ray, accompanied by Mr., afterwards Sir Philip, Skippon, and Mr. Nathaniel Bacon, made a tour
through part of the Low Countries, Germany, Italy, and France, of which an account,
written by Mr. Ray, was originally published in 1673. In Holland and the Netherlands they
passed over nearly the same ground that had been traversed By Mr. Rawdon and his kinsman
in the preceding summer. Mr. Ray thus describes the citadel of Dunkirk, which a short
time after Mr. Rawdon's visit had been sold to the French king: "We went in a boat to
a fort lately built by the English; but it is on the sand, which by some winds is so driven
that you may walk over the walls. The English made two firm bulwarks which command
the sea, and under them is a broad platform, and then a thick wall (not yet finished), and
within the wall is a passage for the soldiers to stand in and shoot through; a trench round
besides; beyond the fort towards the sea, is another sand."

were imediatly, the one taiken downe from the wodden horse, the other from the gallows. After this they waited uppon my lord home to his lodginge, and soe tooke thir leaves of him for that time.

They were noe soner parted from my lord, but Captaine Delavall,* the chiefe coustomer, caried them to a garden of pleasure, wher he treated them, where they spent all that afternone.

The next morninge they went up the greate steeple of Dunkirke, beinge of a very greate hight, where they had a full view of the sea, the haven, and the country round aboute. When they came downe, my lord sent to invite them to dine with him, but they were pre-engaged by Captaine Delavall to dine with him, and soe could nott. After dinner they went to view the towne, thir religious howses and churches, and in the eaveninge went with Captaine Delavall to see what service my lord would command them where they were goinge to travaile. When they came thir, my lord was with some collonells and captaines att his usuall collation; soe thesse gentlemen, nott to disturbe my lord, would not send in worde that they were thir, but Captaine Delavall told them he must needes goe in to speake with my lord as he was eating, beinge the best time for his busnesse; soe they desird him to goe, but withall desird him nott to tell my lord they were thir till he had almost done and reddie to rise from the table; att which time he told my lord that the tow Mr. Rawdons were to goe away the next day, and were come to recieve his lordship's comands, and to give him thankes for all his favours. Said my lord, " Where are they?" He told him in the fore chamber. He askt him why he did nott tell him soner; he told him he had order from them nott to tell his lordship and the company. " Well," said my lord, " that shall nott serve thir turne." " Gen-

* Captain Delaval was most probably a member of the ancient Northumberland family of that name ; perhaps he was the Sir Ralph Delaval created a baronet by King Charles II. in 1660, " who has left a curious monument of his enterprising character at his little port of Seaton Delaval, where he built piers and sluice and flood-gates to deepen the burn which there flows into the sea." (Gibson's Historical Memoir of Northumberland, p. 82.) The engineering operations of Lord Rutherford at Dunkirk might have imbued Captain Delaval with a taste for similar works.

tlemen," saith my lord, " sitt you all downe againe every man in his
place," and commanded his sarvants to furnish the table with a new
collation, causd a cupple of chaires to be sett att the upper end of
the table, the one on the on side of him, and the other on the other;
and then said, " Now desire thosse gentlemen to walke in;" soe
causinge them to sitt downe by him, told them he was very angry
with Captaine Delavall for not tellinge him soner; which they
excusd, and soe to keepe them company did eate some thinge, and
drunke three or four healths about, beinge very cherefull and merry
with them. The drinke they dranke was exelent Canary and
exelent Renish. Soe havinge past about an hower and a halfe, they
rise from the table, they tooke thir leaves of my lord, who though
they humbly desird him to the contrary, thir beinge severall collonells and captaines and Alderman Backwell then in the rome, yet
his lordship, taikinge one of them on his right hand, and the other
on his left, went downe the staires with them to the street dore, and
thir they parted.

Havinge taiken thir leaves of my lord, collonell Alfford and some
of the captaines, with Captaine Delavall, went alonge with them to
see them saife home att thir lodginge; soe they perswaded them to
walke in, where they treated them with the best wine the howse
afforded, drinkinge severall healths, amongst which my lord's was
nott forgotten, where they spent the time allmost till midnight.
The next morninge our tow travelers went from thence to Laferne,[a]
and from thence to Newport, tow garrison townes belonginge to the
Kinge of Spaine; and from thence they went that night to the
antient cittie of Bridges,[b] where they rested Sunday. Here they
see many famous churches richly adorned, and most magnificent
cloysters, especially one called the cloyster of Dune,[c] a little out of
the towne; itt had marble walkes, blacke and white, soe longe and
spacious, that itt would dasell ones eies to looke uppon them.

[a] Furnes.   [b] Bruges.

[c] Probably the church of Damme, three miles from Bruges, remarkable for the beautifully carved tombstones that form the pavement of the nave.

Here they see a chappell, made by a nobleman of that country, who had bene twice att Jerusalem, and causd this chappell[a] to be made just of the bignesse, windows, staires, iron worke, sepulcher, and every thinge, exactly after the forme of the chappell of the Sepulcher att Jerusalem where our Saviour was buried, and thosse that have bene att Jerusalem say thir is nothinge more like then the one is to the other, a greate curiositie and much worth the seeinge. They also see a chappell wher is kept some of the blood that flowed from our Saviour's side, which is kept in a little violl,[b] believe itt who please.

This is the cittie where our Kinge Charles and his brothers, the Dukes of Yorke and Glocester, spent much of thir time, when they were out of the kingdome, and thir memories thir much esteemd.

From thence they went to the greate cittie of Gaunt, a cittie nott only greate, but exclently glorious, full of faire streets most exclently even and well paved, with statly bricke howses, and severall fine navigable rivers runninge thorrow itt; also a greate many stately churches and cloysters, of which they vizited a greate many, amongst the rest an English colledge of Jesuits, the superiour of which was a choloricke pevish fellow, who told them positively they were damnd; they also vizited an English nunnery thir, with whosse abbesse they had a greate deale of discourse, but from hir they recieved more charitable language.[c] In this cittie itt is where that

---

[a] "Built by one Merklier, who travelled thither three times about three hundred years ago, to take a true survey of all particulars." (Ray's Travels in 1663.)

[b] The precious relic, with its richly jewelled and enamelled shrine, is still exhibited in La Chapelle du Sang de Dieu. Mr. Rawdon must have been capable of appreciating the fine arts, and it is surprising that he should have left unnoticed the exquisite works of Van Eyck and Hemling, which were in his time, as they are at present, among the glories of Bruges :—

> "The spirit of antiquity—enshrined
> In sumptuous buildings, vocal in sweet song,
> In picture, speaking with heroic tongue,
> And with devout solemnities entwined—
> Strikes to the seat of grace within the mind."

[c] At the English Jesuits' College [at Gant], a mean building, we discoursed with one

greate emperour, Charles the 5th, was borne, in an old pallaice still remaininge,[a] as also the chamber where he was borne, nott much bigger then a good large clossett. Here likewisse our John of Gaunt, Duke of Lancaster, was borne.

From this cittie they went to the cittie of Brussells, where comonly the Spanish Courte is kept, and where the Governour of Flanders doth commonly reside. Here they see the kinge's pallace, the parke, and water workes in the king's garden, full of inventions; here likewisse they see a curious old armory in which were the swords, lances, coate armour, and armour for horses of Philip the Good and Charles the Hardy, Dukes of Burgundy, of Charles the 5th, and of severall other princes to whome that country did belonge;[b] they did likewisse see here severall other curiosities of importance.

From hence they went to the universitie of Lovaine, the chiefe universitie of Flanders; here they see the antient castell and famous buriall place of the Dukes of Arescott, about a mile out of the towne.[c] In the towne they see severall colleges and severall convents of English friers and nunns. This is the place where the famous Justus Lipsius[d] was professor, and they were in the howse

Green, a father; the rector's name is Bennet.—We visited the English nuns of the Benedictine order, and through a grate in their parlour freely discoursed with Madame Fortescue, the prioress. Madame Knatchbull, Sir Norton Knatchbull's sister, is the abbess." (Ray's Travels in 1663.)

[a] It has since been pulled down.

[b] Dr. Edward Brown, an English traveller, who visited the Low Countries in 1668, gives a fuller description of the curiosities of the Brussels armoury : "There remains the armour of Charles V., of Duke Albert, of the Prince of Parma, Ernestus, and of the Duke of Alva, and of the Duke Albert's horse, who, being shot, saved his master, and died the same day twelvemonth; the armour of Cardinal Infante, and of an Indian king; a Polish musket which carries six hundred paces; Charles the Fifth's sword for making Knights of the Golden Fleece, and Henry the Fourth's sword sent to declare war." (Travels in divers Parts of Europe. By Edward Brown, M.D. Folio. London, 1685, p. 110.)

[c] The palace of the Dukes of Arschot was about half a mile from Louvain. The sepulchral monuments of the Lords of Croy, Dukes of Arschot, were in the church of the adjacent convent of Celestines. Many of them were erected by Charles Duke of Croy about the years 1605 and 1606. (Ray's Travels in 1663.)

[d] This eminent critic and scholar was professor of history and eloquence in the University of Louvain, and died there in 1606.

CAMD. SOC. O

where he lived; also Cornelius Agrippa the greate[*] . . . , . . , of this universitie.

From hence they went to the cittie of Macklin, a most pleasant place, where all the greate law suites of this country are decided, and from whence, beinge once sentenced, thir is noe appeale to ancy other court.^b Here they see a famous garden belonginge to the Capuchin friers, one of the orders of St. Francis; this cittie is soe curiously neate and cleane as if only itt were to be shewne but uppon holly dayes.

From hence they went to the famous cittie of Antwerp, once the glory of the westerne world for situation, statelynesse of buildinge, and trade; and was soe rich that nott above 100 yeares agon thir marchants' daughters wore coronets of gold, as if they had bene princesses; but now Amsterdam haith suckd all the trade from them, yet as to hirselfe she may be called the mistris of the rest of the cittics of this country, and I thinke this country, in soe little a space of ground, doth shew as many and as famous cities as the sun doth see in his journie through the whole world.

The buildings of this cittie are noble and stately, her streetes large and cleane, all paved after the manner of Holborne,^c and soe are most of the citties of this country; hir churches are most stately and richly furnisht, especially the Jesuits church, which exceedes all the rest, beinge allmost all blacke and white marbel walls on the inside

^a Perhaps Mr. Rawdon hesitated to call him "the great magician," which he was reputed to be.

^b The Imperial Court of Mechlin was of such dignity and importance that Charles V. and Philip II. presided over it in person.

^c In the seventeenth century Holborn was one of the few streets in London that had the advantage of being paved. Our travellers might well be charmed with the comfort and convenience afforded by the spacious, clean, and well-paved streets of Antwerp and other towns of the Netherlands. Mr. Cunningham tells us, that down to 1762 the streets of our metropolis were obstructed with projections of various kinds, and each inhabitant paved before his own door, in such manner and with such materials as pride, poverty, or caprice might suggest. (Hand-Book, vol. i. p. xxxv.) After the Restoration Evelyn describes the road from St. James's Palace north, now St. James's Street, as being a quagmire. (Diary, vol. i. p. 365.)

and the pavinge; also the church soe richly adorned with store of
silver lamps and other curiosities, and pictures vallued att three and
fower thousand pownds sterlinge a pece.[a] Itt haith a river runs
closse by, an serves itt partly for defence, runninge in some places
closse by the walls, the walls beinge soe brood as tow coaches may
walke a brest,[b] and is planted with three roes of gallant elmes, like
Graies Inn walkes:[c] itt is a place soe curious that I am loth to part
with itt.[d] Here they staid some few dayes, and were feasted by that
gallant and valliant gentleman, Mr. Hartop, the honor of the
English nation in thosse parts.[e]

From Antwerpe they went to Amsterdam, a proud cittie, whosse

[a] The church of San Carlo Borromeo, or of the Jesuits, with many fine pictures which
adorned it, was destroyed by fire in 1718. Dr. Brown is quite as enthusiastic as Mr.
Rawdon in his admiration of the churches of Antwerp. "The Jesuits' church (he says)
goes far beyond any of that bigness that I have seen out of Italy. The front is noble, with
the statua of Ignatius Loyola on the top. A great part of the inside of the roof was painted
by Rubens, and some of it by Van Dyke. There be many excellent peices of flowers done by
Stegers, a Jesuite; the carving and gilding of all the works is exquisite.—Onser Lieven
Vrowen Kerck, or the Church of Our Blessed Lady, is the greatest in the city, and the
steeple one of the fairest in the world." (Brown's Journey from Norwich to Colen in 1668,
p. 108.) Few persons who have looked at the cathedral of Antwerp whilst crossing the
Scheldt on a bright summer's day, will be disposed to deny that "its steeple is one of the
fairest in the world."

[b] "Antwerp is a noble city, both for her cittadel and fortifications, which are so vast that
two coaches may go abrest upon the walls." (Howel's Londinopolis. Fol. London,
1657, p. 388.)

[c] Mr. Rawdon had an agreeable recollection of the beauties of Gray's Inn Walks, which
in his time were the most fashionable promenade in London. The gardens and terraces
then commanded an uninterrupted view towards Highgate and Hampstead. (Cunningham's Hand-Book.)

[d] "But there was nothing about this city [Antwerp] which more ravished me than
those delicious shades and walks of stately trees which render the fortified works of
the town one of the sweetest places in Europe." (Evelyn's Diary, Oct. 5, 1641.)

[e] The gentleman of whose hospitality Mr. Rawdon speaks so highly, was Thomas Hartopp, esquire, a younger son of George Hartopp, esquire, of Little Dalby in Leicestershire,
whose brother Sir Edward Hartopp was the first baronet of that family. He was very
remarkable for his strength and courage. It is related of him, that on one occasion at
Antwerp he distinguished himself so much by his personal bravery that a lady of quality
and fortune offered him her hand, which he accepted, and, settling at Antwerp, he served

buildings arc magnificent and costly, beinge all founded on greate
piles of wood drove into the grownd by an engin, the place beinge
of itt selfe a mere bog;[a] but thir art haith made itt a very cleanely
cittie, a place of greate trade, whosse streetes are very pleasant,
through the midest of many of which runns salt water, and are as
well furnisht with ships and bootes as ours in London are with carts
and coaches. They have built of late a famous towne house of free
stone, I thinke the like is not to be seene in christendome.[b] Thir
way of government is admirable, permittinge noc idle persons
amongst them, for rogues and vagabonds they have howses where
they saw wood, and if. they be very lasic and will nott worke, they
putt them into a place, that such a quantity of water comes in, that
if they doe nott pumpe, they will nott only be wett, but drowne, if
they doe nott worke to keep the watter downe.

For light huswives and idle woemen they have howses where
they are sett to spin; old men and old woemen have stately hospitalls
provided for them with sufficient maintenance for them as longe as
they live; yonge boyes and girles that are pore and fatherlesse the
same, where they are taught till they be fitt to putt out to trades;
also for sicke people they have a faire hospitall with good attendance;
nay the very Bedlam, where they keepe thir madd peopell, itt is soe

the King of Spain in his armies. (Burke's Commoners, vol. iii. p. 403.) When Dr. Brown
was at Antwerp he had the good fortune to receive attention from Mr. Hartopp: " One
(he says) very well known in all those parts, and of high esteem for his personal
strength and valour : a gentleman, also, so courteous that he makes it his business to oblige
strangers." (Brown's Travels, pp. 108, 191.)

[a] " Amsterdam is built, as it were, in a bog or quag; for in their fabriques they are forced to
dig so deep for a firm foundation by ramming in huge piles of wood, that the basis of a house
doth often times cost more then the superstructure." (Howel's Londinopolis, p. 389.)

[b] The Stadt-huis, or Town-house, was in progress when Evelyn visited Amsterdam, in
August, 1641. " If the design be perfected," he observes, " it will be one of the most
costly and magnificent in Europe." (Diary, vol. i. p. 22.) The burghers of Amsterdam
had no Exchange or Town-house before this was built. "The merchants in summer
meet upon the bridge, and in winter they meet in the new church in very great number,
where they walk in two rankes by couples, one ranke going up and another going
downe." (Fynes Moryson's Itinerary. Fol. London, 1617, p. 44.)

stately, that one would taike itt to be the howse of some lord;[a] and to ad to thir curiositie, they past by a butcher's shop in that cittie which was paved with blacke and white marble, and the walls lined with white and blew tiles, such as you putt in chemnies in England, soe as if they had nott seene a cupple of oxen hanginge up in itt, they should have taiken itt for a rome belonginge to some rich marchant.

From Amsterdam, havinge satisfied them selves with all that thir was to be seene of curiositie, they went to the cittie of Harlem, famous in former times for itts service in the holly warr, and now famous for makinge of linninge clooth:[b] here they went to the tope

---

[a] The burghers of Amsterdam were remarkable for their charitable institutions as early as in the reign of our Queen Elizabeth. Fynes Moryson, who travelled in Holland in 1593, tells us that "they had then two almeshouses (called Gast-hausen, that is, houses for strangers) which were of old monasteries. One of these houses built round was a cloyster for nunnes, wherein sixty beds at this time were made for poore weomen diseased; and in another chamber thereof were fifty-two beds made for the auxiliary souldiers of England, being hurt or sicke; and in the third roome were eighty-one beds made for the hurt and sicke souldiers of other nations: to which souldiers and sick weomen they give cleane sheetes, a good diet, and necessary clothes, with great cleanlinesse, and allow them physitians and surgions to cure them." (Itinerary, p. 44). At the time of the Restoration and long afterwards the only establishments in London for the relief of the impotent and diseased poor were Saint Bartholomew's Hospital, which was supported by the State, and Saint Thomas's Hospital, which the citizens of London for a while maintained, and towards the close of the seventeenth century suffered to fall into decay. A bedlam or hospital for lunatics originally stood without Bishopsgate. After the great fire of 1666 "it was magnificently built and most sweetly placed in Moorfields." (Evelyn's Diary, vol. ii. p. 119.) The Westminster Hospital, the first that was founded and supported by public contributions, was not built until 1719. (Cunningham's Hand-Book, vol. i. p. 84.) Our travellors naturally viewed with surprise and admiration the superiority of the Dutch over their own countrymen in the extent and excellence of their institutions for benevolent and useful purposes.

[b] "This citie makes great store of linnen clothes, and hath some five hundred spinsters in it." (Moryson's Itin. p. 45.) "We visited at Haarlem the weavers of holland, tiffany, camlet, damask, (at the damask weaver's we saw a very rich table-cloth, having the English arms, and many curious figures in it; it hath been three years making for the Prince of Orange,) diaper, silk damask, tape, velvet, and saw the pressing of stuffs, &c., whereby a gloss is given." (Ray's Travels in 1663.)

of the greate church, and see the greate mere or lake,[a] and the country round aboute, and the sea; a sight much worth the seinge. From this cittie of Harlem they went to the universitie of Leyden, the chiefe universitie of Holland, where they feasted thir eies with a greate many curiosities, of which I have had from them a perticuler relation, and shall acequent you with some of them; thir they see tow mummies, beinge as they said a kinge and queene of Ægipt embalmed; thir they see the skin of a Scotsman dried, and the hart, guts, and bowells of a man dried, and severall anatomies of men, women, and severall other creatures, which were in the howse where they cutt up thir anotomics; and in a longe gallery they see thesse thinges followinge, vizt. : [b]—

[a] The great water, or noted lake, called Haerlem Meere, is about twenty miles in length. (Brown, p. 95.) It is now drained and the area cultivated.

[b] Mr. Rawdon and his companion appear to have taken an especial interest in the many curious objects they saw at the University of Leyden. They were most probably acquainted with the " Museum Tradescantianum," the first collection of curiosities of nature and art that had been formed in England. In 1656 a catalogue of the rarities collected by his father was published by the younger Tradescant, and the museum at South Lambeth had then become a favourite resort of the literary and scientific world. (Evelyn's Diary, June, 1657.) The Leyden collection had probably not been formed much earlier than that of the Tradescants. Fynes Moryson, who passed some time at Leyden in 1592, does not allude to it. (Itin. p. 46.) He speaks of " the famous university in that city," and had the museum then existed it would scarcely have escaped the notice of so intelligent a traveller. Nor does Howel, who visited Leyden in 1619, appear to have been aware of any such collection. (Fam. Letters, ed. 1655, p. 13.) But when Evelyn was there in 1641, " amongst all the rarities of the place (he says), I was much pleased with a sight of the anatomy school, theatre, and repository adjoining, which is well furnished with natural curiosities." (Diary, vol. i. p. 26.) The " Museum Tradescantianum," it is well known, passed into the possession of Elias Ashmole, by whom it was given to the University of Oxford. It has recently been transferred to the splendid building which the munificence of that university has erected for the reception of an assemblage of objects which will soon become one of the finest collections in the world. To the present accomplished Professor of Geology, to whom the University has entrusted the care of its museum, I am indebted for many of the explanations given in the subsequent notes. I will venture to quote his remarks upon this part of the Rawdon MS : " The list of the Leyden *rariora* is very curious, and, if placed beside the catalogue of that noble museum as it stands at present, might fitly shadow forth an ancient Batavian's domestic discomforts, in comparison with the riches of a modern burgomaster's palace. It is not so good a

An eagle.

A walnut tree of Canada.[a]

A batt of India.[b]

A saw fish.[c]

The tow greater shell fishes.[d]

The rib of a rinocero.

The skin of a Brasillian hog.[e]

A kind of white corall composd of many particulers.

The Indian borre and the cheekes of a marine sow.[f]

The fruite of the cedar.

A bird of Brasill, much like a peacocke, havinge on his forehead a longe white horne.[g]

The yard of a white beare, also his feete, bones, and jawes.

A fish called the blasarte.

The house of a beast, which in figure, coullcr, and magnitude, carrieth the similitude of a mule.

A sportfull instrument made of straw.

The Indian Callendar.

A sea-lamprey.[h]

A bird of Paradice.

A fish whosse shell is coverd with prickles.[i]

A livinge creature called a toupan, or all-eating, and his snoute.

The skin of a Brasillian horse.

The feather of the bird called phenix.[k]

The Indian idoll.

A spider from the west part of India.

A sea batt.

The heade of a hippopotomic, beinge a water horse, livinge indifferently on land or sea.

The teeth of the same.

A bow with arrows.

The heade and the taile of Castor, a meteor appearinge to marriners.[l]

The teeth of a fish called pot.

The greater mushrome.

The fruite annanas.[m]

---

series of things on the whole as our Ashmole, following the Tradescants, placed as the foundation of the Oxford Museum in 1684; but in regard to the objects obtained from far countries it contains a good many oddities." (Professor Phillips to the Editor, Sept. 1862.)

[a] Hickory, *Carica alba*.　　　[b] Probably, *Pteropus*.　　　[c] *Pristis*.

[d] Probably *Tridacna* or clam for one, and *Triton* for the other.　　　[e] Peccary.

[f] Marsouin Porpesse, *Delphinus phocæna*.

[g] Horned screamer, *Palamedea cornuta*.　　　[h] *Petromyzon*.

[i] *Venus dione* or *Spondylus*, or probably *Echinus*.

[k] One of the chiefest rarities noticed by Evelyn in the Tradescant collection was "a feather from the phenix' wing." (Diary, vol. i. p. 322.)

[l] *Castor*, a beaver. The star of this name and his brother Pollux are like a meteor for the sailors.　　　[m] Pine-apple—*ananassa sativa*.

The fish called giob.

The horne of a rinocero.

The Indian haimaica that they sleepe in.[a]

The skin of a serpent of a vast magnitude.[b]

The stumpe of a wild fig tree in India.

The head of a jangada of Brazill.

The head of a wolvfe.

A Spanish reed.

A sugar-cane.

Divers kinds of sea-plants.

The foot of a casuary.[c]

The hog-fish.

A sea spider, or a fish called aqua viver.

The bill of a pillican.[d]

A livinge creature springin from the egg of a hen.

A crocodile.

The jaw and backe [of] a halyc.

Images from Zabba.

A stone like rock-allum, of which is made flax.[e]

The head of a stagg.

The skin of a kid of Brasill.

The skin of a luacrt.

The gourd of Brasill.

The flower of Pasion.[f]

The shape of a goose found in the liver of a oxe.

The wodden trumpett of Tappugery.

The skin of a sea maide.[g]

Tamandua peba, the greater and the lesser, castinge forth pismires.[h]

The Indian hedghog.[i]

The Indian lizard.

A sea catt.

The shell fishes of India.

The tongue of a viper.

The eggs of serpents.

An elephant that heares by his mouthe.

A serpent makinge a noise with hir skin.[k]

The skin of a beast much resemblinge the mule.

The Indian wolve.

A dragon.

A sea wolve.

The fruite of firr-tree.

The eggs of a strusi.[l]

---

[a] Whence, hammock.   [b] Boa, or *Python*.   [c] *Casuarius*.

[d] *Pelecanus*. Evelyn describes the *Onocrotalus*, or pelican, which he saw in St. James's Park in 1665, as a melancholy waterfowl, between a stork and a swan, brought from Astracan by the Russian ambassador.   [e] *Asbestos*.   [f] *Passiflora*.

[g] Fish of the genus *Raia ?*   [h] The ant-eater, *Myrmecophaga jubata*.

[i] Porcupine.   [k] Rattle-snake, *Crotalus horridus*.

[l] *Struthio*, ostrich. The eggs of crocodiles and estridges were in the Tradescant Museum.

The eggs of an eagle.

The elephant's teeth.

The egs of a crocadile.

A tiger's skin.

Cipe, a yonge tree or shrub kreepinge along the ground.

Divers kinds of the fruit of a wild gourd.

The hornes of a stagg.

An instrument of warr in Brasill.

Hose from the iland of Jappan with shoes.

A cloake of chiliarcha of Jappan.

A fish spouting water through tow holes about the nosse.[a]

The fruite of . . . .

The horne of a goate, in whosse ventrickle the besar stone is found.[b]

The portraiture of a Prusillian (Brazillian?) plowman.

A sea plant.

The mirtle berry, or graine of the mirtle.

The dolphin.

The Indian tortois.[c]

The tortosies eggs.

A kind of sleads the Norwegians goe over the snow with.

The yard of a balanæ, a fish which by some is called a whirlpole.[d]

The heade of a sea lyon.

A ducke in Scotland growinge on trees.[e]

The feathered herbe.[f]

A jackhall, beinge a beast about the bignesse of a fox, which lookes out prey for the lyon.

The scelleton of a man.

A coate of Rusia.

A paratt.

A greate skin of a dog lurkinge in the woodes.

A little boate of the Indians.

A mirtle-bery or nutt.

The coyne of Leyden.

The heade of a wolve.

Zambuaja, the greate nutt.[g]

---

[a] Dolphin, *delphinus*.

[b] *Lapis bezoardicus*. Many marvellous stories are told about the production of the bezoar-stone, and its efficacy against poison. "It is engendered in the inner part of the beast that is commonly called a goate of the mountaine. This beast is of the greatness of a harte; he hath onely twoo broade hornes, with the pointes sharpe turned, and falling much backwarde. The bezaar-stone being given to him that hath been bytten of a venomous beast and being applied to the place, he shall be healed and delivered therof, by the help of God." (Joyful Newes out of the New-found Worlde. 4to. London, 1596, p. 121.) Dr. Primrose's Treatise on Popular Errors in Physick (translated into English by Dr. Robert Wittie, London, 1651), contains a chapter, "Of the Errours about the Bezaar-Stone."

[c] *Testudo indica*. [d] Perhaps the spiral tusk of a narwhal; or the bone of a cetacean.

[e] The bernacle, or barnacle-goose of old Gesner.

[f] Feather-grass, *stipa pennata*. [g] The Zabucaya nut (*Lecythis ollaria*) of Brazil.

Havinge satisfied them selves with the curiosities of the universitie of Leyden,[a] they went from thence to the Hague, wher they see the pallace, and the best howses and gardens that were thir to be seene; they also went to kisse the Prince of Orange's hands, to see if he pleasd to comand them ancy service for England, with whom they had some discourse; a hansome hopefull yonge prince, beinge then about 15 yeares of age.[b] After that they went to vizitt some English ladies, and in perticuler the Countesse of Levistone, and hir neces, with whom they had bene formerly accquented in England. This countesse had bene, for a longe time, one of the chiefe ladies that did waite uppon the Queene of Bohemia.[c]

---

[a] Mr. Ray and his fellow-travellers were at Leyden in May 1663. " We saw (he says) the anatomy theatre, which is not so handsome as that at London, but furnished with a great many curious things." The account he gives of these curiosities is less copious and exact than might have been expected from so ardent a cultivator of natural science. Sir John Reresby, a Yorkshireman, who travelled in the Low Countries a few years earlier, is content with a still more perfunctory notice of Leyden : " This is the chief university in Holland; a handsome town, the college or schools large and well contrived, as also the anatomy room, where you see several dried dissections of most sorts of creatures— amongst others, of an entire whale, whole mummies, and other physical curiosities." (The Travels of Sir John Reresby, Bart., late Governor of York. 8vo. ed. 1813, p. 145.)

[b] William Prince of Orange, afterwards King William III. of England. He was born at the Hague, November 4th, 1650.

[c] Elizabeth Queen of Bohemia, daughter of King James I., who had passed the greater part of her life at the Hague, left Holland in May 1661, and died in England in the month of February following. The Countess of Levinstein, whom our travellers saw at the Hague in the summer of 1662, and who had been, as they inform us, for many years one of the ladies-in-waiting of the widowed queen, is a somewhat mysterious personage. Two of her letters are printed in the Fairfax Correspondence, (vol. i. p. 321, vol. ii. p. 196.) Both were written at the Hague; one in November 1637, the other in May 1641, to Ferdinando Lord Fairfax, whom she addresses as " my lord and dear father," subscribing herself " your humble and faithful daughter and servant." In each of her letters she alludes to Charles Fairfax, a younger son of Lord Fairfax, who was then an officer in the service of the States, and occasionally visited the Hague. Her styling Lord Fairfax her father, and not speaking of his son as her brother, induces the editor of the Fairfax Letters to think it " more than probable " that she was his illegitimate child.

In Bromley's Collection of Royal Letters, p. 271, is introduced an anonymous and undated document, headed " Recit fidele et véritable des faits, gestes, et prouesses de la Comtesse de Levenstein, prétendue Ambassadrice de sa Majesté, durant son séjour

After they had satisfied them selves with what curiosities this place could afford, they went from hence to the cittie of Delfe, a fine cleane towne where the English company of marchants had resided for many yeares togeather; here in one of thir churches they see a faire tombe of William of Nassau, the greate grandfather to this Prince of Orenge now livinge.[a]

Also in this towne is a faire tombe, which the States haith bestowed on thir Generall Van Trump, for the good service he did them; itt is of white marble, where in he is cutt out to the life in full proportion, restinge his heade on a pece of ordnance as a badge of his profession.[b]

From hence they went to the cittie of Rotterdam, a goodly towne and of greate trade, famous for the birth of the learned Erasmus, who stands in a statue of brasse in the market-place, in his gowne, with his colledge cap, a booke open on his left hand, and with the right, as itt were, turninge over a leafe;[c] this is the only curiositie they found in this cittie worth the seeinge.

à Breda." The narrative gives an amusing but by no means flattering account of the lady's eccentric deportment during her stay at Breda. The Court refused to treat her as an ambassadress, having discovered that the Queen, her mistress, had permitted, but not authorised, her visit. Mr. Rawdon's former acquaintance with the Countess of Levinstein increases the probability that she was connected with Yorkshire. Possibly she was the singular gentlewoman whom he encountered twice in his travels in England; once at Exeter in 1655, and again as he was on his way from York to London in October 1657. Two or three pencil notes in the MS. indicate that this lady was called "Mrs. Fax." (See notes a and b, p. 85, *supra*.) Lord Fairfax had a house at Bilbrough, a few miles from York.

[a] Fynes Moryson describes the monument of the Prince of Orange in the new church at Delft as " the poorest he ever saw for such a person, being only of rough stones and mortar, with posts of wood coloured over with black, and very little erected from the ground." (Itinerary, p. 47.) It must have been entirely renovated previously to 1641, when Evelyn visited the church. " The monument (he says) of Prince William of Nassau—the first of the Williams and saviour of their liberty—is a piece of rare art, consisting of several figures, as big as the life, in copper. There is in the same place a magnificent tomb of his son and successor Maurice." (Diary, vol. i. p. 21.)

[b] Van Tromp died in August 1653. His tomb is in the old church at Delft.

[c] " Nigh this church [St. Lawrence at Rotterdam] is a little house where Erasmus was

From Rotterdam they went to the cittie or towne of Dort, famous for a synod of protestant devins thir held in Kinge James his time; and now for the staple of English marchants thir residinge.[*]

From Dort they imbarkt themselves abord a Dutch passage boote to crosse an arme of the sea for Zeland. They went out with faire weather, but they were forc'd to come to an anker, and thir ride tow nights and tow dayes for life and death; and, though itt was about the latter end of August, with violent stormes of wind, raine, and cold, where if thir cables had faild they had all perisht; thir they lay on the bare bords without cushion, or pillow, or anie thinge to lay over them or under them, only thir portmantell, which was of a good length and sarved them for a bolster. The upper decke was ill caukt, and the raine dropt uppon them as they lay, and the rascaly Duchmen were soe basse, that, though they gave them notice of itt, would nott cause itt to be caukt, which they ought and might easely have bene done; with which they were soe extreame cold, that they shakt as if they had had an ague uppon them, and they were affraid itt would prove soe; they were nott only starved with cold but with hunger, for they could niether have meate nor drinke for thir mony, beinge a thinge very common in thosse bootes to have an ordnary or what they please to call for for thir mony; and I believe thosse that were taiken by the Turks, and caried into Barbary, might find more civillitie then thesse gentlemen did from thosse boors or rather white Moores.

But itt hapned thir was a Dutch-woman, a passenger, which for

born; the upper part of the house is a school, and a grocer's shop is underneath. In a large area or market-place stands his brass statue turning over the leaf of a book." (Ray's Travels in 1663.) In 1593 the statue of Erasmus in the market-place of Rotterdam was made of wood, "for the Spaniards brake downe that which was made of stone, and the inscription thereof witnesseth that hee was borne at Rotersdame the twenty-eight of October, in the yeere 1467, and died at Bazel the twelfth of July, in the yeere 1531." (Moryson's Itin. p. 48.)

[*] Dort "is reckoned the first and chief town of South Holland in respect of its antiquity, and also in respect of its privileges in having the mint here, and being the staple for Rhenish wine and English cloth." (Brown's Journey from Norwich to Colen, in 1668, p. 106.)

warmth lay close to them, and uppon every extreordnary motion of
the boote fartinge by them, tooke pittie of them, and lent them a
pickled heringe out of hir small store, and drest itt very hansomely
for them, with which, and a little bread, they sustented nature.
But att last itt pleased God to appease the storme, and send them a
faire wind, with which they were delivered from the violence of the
sea and the inhumanitie of thosse people, where, I have herd them
say, they sufferd more hardship then they had done in all thir lives;
and after three dayes, which in faire weather had bene but a night's
passage, they arived att Travier,[a] by some called Camphire, in Zea-
land, a small cittie, where the Scotts drive a greate trade;[b] thir they
recruited themselves with the best the towne afforded, and from
thence went to the cittie of Middleborow, a faire towne and of greate
trade, wher once the staple of the English marchants was.[c] From
thence they came to the towne of Flushinge, beinge one of the keyes
of Holland, and one of the townes which was pownd unto Queene
Elizabeth, of which for the said Queene the famous Sir Philip Sydney
was once governour, and was afterwards, with the Sluce, Ramekins,
and the Brill, delivered up by Kinge James to the Hollanders,[d]
which if they had nott bene, we should have kept thosse rebell
Hollanders in more subjection.

[a] Veere, or Ter-vfere. Evelyn calls this place De Vere, "whence (he says) the most
antient and illustrious earls of Oxford derive their name." (Diary, vol. i. p. 17.)

[b] At Ter-Vere, "where there is a good haven and harbour for ships, the Scotch have
had a factory for above 200 years." (Brown's Journey, p. 177.) Camphire in Zeeland is
mentioned by Fynes Moryson as one of the four places with which the Scots had their
chief traffic, " whither they carry salt, the skinnes of weathers, otters, badgers, and mar-
tens, and bring from thence corne." The other three places were Bordeaux, the Baltic,
and England. (Description of Scotland, Itinerary, p. 155.)

[c] Middleburg "is the chiefe place of trafficke in Zeeland. It is the staple of all merchandize excepting Rhenish wine, for which by old privilege Dorte is the staple. There-
fore French and Spanish wines are here sold much more cheap than other where."
(Moryson's Itin. p. 50.)

[d] Flushing "was one of the first towns which the Low Country-men took from the
Spaniards in 1572, and was made cautionary to Queen Elizabeth, together with Ram-
makins and the Briel, in 1585; the renowned Sir Philip Sidney being the first governor of it,
and surrendered by King James to the United States in 1616." (Brown's Journey, p. 107.)

This is a pleasant iland,[a] full of good grownd and fine orchards; itt haith four citties in itt, besides townes, and yett I believe we have some parkes in England that haith as much grownd, itt beinge nott above twenty-one miles in compasse. This towne of Flushinge is famous or infamous for sea thieves; I meane men of warr; and did more harm to marchants of England and Spaine duringe the warrs then all Holland did besides.[b] From hence they past a short arme of the sea, and soe went to Ostend, a port towne now belonginge to the Spaniard, by whom itt was besieged above 50 yeares agoe, beinge then in possesion of the Hollander, and was bravely defended by the Earle of Oxford, Sir John Norris, and thir English soldiers: the siege lasted 3 yeares, 3 weekes, and 3 dayes.[c] From whence one eavveninge they imbarked in the passage boote, and the next day, about four of the clocke in the afternone, they saifly arived att Deale; from thence they went to Dover, and from thence to Canterbury, where they spent some small time in company of thir honest nicbour Mr. William Kinge, and from thence they came to London, and soe to Hodsden, where we will leave them a little to reposse themselves after thir voyage.

After they came to Hodsden, little offerd of note; here they past **1663.** the winter for the most part, and most part of next summer, only he went to St. Albons to see the old ruines of that formerly famous cittie Verulam, from whence he brought some old coynes that were

[a] The island of Walcheren.

[b] The sea-thieves of Flushing were of the same class as the pirates of Dunkirk, of whose depredations the English merchants were incessantly complaining during the former half of the seventeenth century. (See Younge's Diary, Camd. Soc. p. 79. Court and Times of James I. and Charles I. passim.)

[c] The most memorable siege recorded in modern history. It began on the 5th July, 1601, and ended on the 22nd September, 1604.

> Small vestige there of that old siege appears,
>   And little of remembrance would be found,
> When for the space of three long painful years
>   The persevering Spaniard girt it round,
> And gallant youths of many a realm from far
> Went students to that busy seat of war.

thir digged up, which he added to a collection of coynes he had allredie gatherd up in his former travailes. He did goe to Ipsome, and to some other places not far from London, and did also spend some little time att Layton, his kinswoman Mrs. Elizabeth Bowyer beinge married to Mr. Henry Allington of the famely of the Allingtons in Lincolnshire, gentleman, the 9th of July, beinge Thursday and St. Cyrill's day.

The rest of the summer and winter followinge he spent att Hodsden and London, with out aney thinge considerable, only a strange dreame that hapned to him, which was thus: On Munday night, the seacond of November, 1663, beinge in bed in his chamber att Hodsden, about five of the clocke in the morninge, he dreamd he was in a roome where thir was an altar with a candle-sticke and a candle in itt unlighted; he kneelinge downe to pray, a grave person in a pontificall habitt, much resemblinge the pictures of Saint Ambrosse, or Saint Austin, said unto him, " If God will heare thy prayer, he will send light to lighten that candle;" and imediatly the candle lighted of itt selfe; soe the grave prelate rosse up and told him, that God had heard his prayers, and gave him a gold ringe and a greate christall ringe eight square, and said unto him, that ringe was our Saviour Christ's. This dreame, for the strangenesse of itt, I thought good to set downe, but the interpretation, or what itt may portend, only God Allmightie knoweth.

This springe he made tow journies into Norfolke, to see a place called Bromehill, within a mile or lesse of Brandon, on the other side the river, a colledge lease of about 200*l.* a yeare, a very pleasant place for fishinge and fowlinge. He had agreed with the owners for itt, provided he could agree with the maister and fellows of Christ Church in Cambridge, to whom itt did belonge. He made tow journies to Cambridge about itt; thir was 3 lives in itt, all of them alive; he offerd the maister and fellows fiftie poundes to putt in his life in stead of the yongest of the three, that he might be sure to have some thinge for his mony whilst he lived; but they denied him that reasonable demand; he then offerd them 150*l.* to make

1664.

him a new lease, and to putt in his life who was then 54 yeares of
age for one, and tow more of his freinds to whom he intended to
leave itt; but they would nott doe that neither, sayinge they were old
persons that were in the lease, that they would lett them die, and soe
taike itt into thir owne hands; he seeinge them soe unreasonable
left them, and soe disisted from treatinge anie more of that purchasse.

1664.   About this time the kinge granted that the marchants tradinge
for the Canary Ilands, for the better regulation of that trade, by his
letters pattents, that they should be a company, into which societie
he was admitted, and did underwrite in the said company fiftcene
hundreth poundes.   After this he spent his time most att Hodsden,
till the first of July, when, accompanied only with his sarvant,
William Raniel, he sett forwards from London, and went to Gobbins
in Essex to see Sir Phillip Mathews his mother,[a] and from thence he
went to Hodsden, where he staid till Thursday the 7th July, att
which time, accompanied with his kinsmen, Mr. Marmaduke Rawdon, Mr. William Rawdon, Mr. William Bowyer, and his foresaid
sarvant, they went to Royston, wher they dind that day, and from
thence went to Huntington, where they lodgd that night.   In this
towne Oliver Cromewell was borne, and plaid the brewer for some
yeares;[b] thir they see the brewhouse, which is yet standinge, but the

---

[a] Sir Philip Matthews of Gobions in Essex was created a baronet 15th June, 1662.
His mother is said to have been the heiress of a citizen with a considerable fortune.
(Burke's Extinct Baronetage.)

[b] We have here, what is of more value than an "old printed royalist lampoon," the
testimony of a contemporary that Cromwell at one period of his life carried on the business
of a brewer at Huntingdon.   Mr. Rawdon, visiting the town five or six years after the
Protector's death, saw the brewhouse, which was yet standing, in which Cromwell "played
the brewer for some years."   Much ingenuity has been exercised in attempting to dis-
prove this fact.   Mr. Carlyle intentionally leaves the question of the brewing "in a very
unilluminated state."   He is loth to soil the social rank of the Cromwells, father and
son, by acknowledging their connection with profitable trade.   He admits that the
brook of Hinchin, running through their premises at Huntingdon, offered clear convenience for malting or brewing; in regard to which, and also to the assiduous management of the same by the wife of Robert Cromwell, he is very willing to believe tradition,
but, he remarks, the essential trade of Oliver's father was that of managing his lands in

church over against, where he was made a Christian, he lett in his prosperity be puld downe, or fall downe, and thir is now nothinge but the ruines thirof to be scene.[a] In this towne they observed thir was four steepells, three churches, tow parishes, one minister, and never a preacher.

The next morninge his cosson Marmaduke Rawdon and Mr. William Rawdon tooke thir leaves of him, and returned to Hodsden, but his kinsman, Mr. William Bowyer, went with him the next dayes journie. From Huntingeton, in company of his cossen Bowyer and Will. Raniel, they went to Peterborow, where they dined, and see the cathedrall, a faire church, wher was buried tow queenes, Katherin of Spaine wife to Henry the 8th and mother to Queene Mary, and Mary Queene of Scotts mother to Kinge James. In this church they see the picture of a lustie sexton, called John Scarlet, who lived 98 yeares, buried the foresaid tow queenes, and all his parish twice over. Severall other thinges of note they see in this church; but of this and other curios observations he made, they are sett downe att

the vicinity of the town. (See Cromwell's Letters and Speeches, with Elucidations by Thomas Carlyle, vol. i. p. 36.) A later writer manifests still greater anxiety to rescue the Protector's memory from the supposition of his having been connected with the trade of a brewer. He labours to throw "very considerable doubt on the notorious story that Oliver's father or mother was engaged in the business of brewing," and he propounds his opinion "that to engage in a trade in the immediate vicinity of the seat of his family would have been by them considered, in those times, so great a blot on their honour as to have necessarily caused a rupture with Robert Cromwell, even if he, himself, had been utterly regardless of the degradation. But surely, brought up as he had been, such an idea would not easily have entered his head. The distinction between the man engaged in business, such as brewing, and the landed gentleman, was then considerable." (Studies and Illustrations of the Great Rebellion. By John L. Sanford. 8vo. Lond. 1858, p. 182.) Not a few examples may be found in the present volume of the landed gentleman of the seventeenth century having thought it no blot upon his honour to be nearly connected with persons engaged in trade.

[a] The church of St. John at Huntingdon, in which Cromwell was baptized, is said to have been pulled down in 1652 by a townsman, whose family, as a just judgment, were soon reduced to poverty. (Sanford, p. 180, note.) Probably the steeple remained when Mr. Rawdon was at Huntingdon, as he observes that there were then four steeples and three churches.

large in his manuscript called his Northerne Journie, where the reader will find much satisfaction. About a mile from hence, they see a very fine howse of Mr. Sent John's,[a] built of free stone, in which thir is a stairccasse made with much arte, and haith fine gardens, grotts, and fishponds, thir unto belonginge. In the garden were the statues of severall philosophers, and a famous statua of Livia, the daughter of Augustus Ceasar, for whome Ovid was banisht Rome; this statue, they say, was brought from Rome. Thir is a neate grote under ground, and a musicke howse over itt. I shall only give you a little tuch of the most materiall things I find in his observations, and for the rest, as I have allredie said, shall refer you to his booke, where you will find thinges discribed att large.

That afternone they went from Peterborow to Crowland, where they lay that night, a place much resemblinge Holland;[b] here was formerly a famous abbie, the church of which is yet standing. Itt is a very fenny country; the towne, seated like Venice, wher they goe in bootes, haith a triangular bridge of exelent workmanship.[c]

---

[a] Thorpe, or Longthorpe, near Peterborough, an elegant mansion, built under the direction of Webb, nephew and pupil of Inigo Jones, was the seat of Oliver St.John, appointed Solicitor-General in 1641, and Lord Chief Justice of the Common Pleas in 1648. Evelyn visited Peterborough in September 1654, "passing (he notes in his Diary) a stately palace (Thorpe) of St.John's (one deep in the blood of our good king), built out of the ruins of the bishop's palace and cloister." The statue of Livia, "of colossal proportions," and several other fine antique statues of marble which were placed in the garden at Thorpe, and suffered more from the weather than from age, are said to have originally belonged to the Arundel collection. Mr. Rawdon, or his biographer, is again at fault in his classical allusions. Livia was the wife of Augustus. It was not Livia, but Julia the daughter of Augustus, for whom Ovid was banished.

[b] Crowland, or Croyland, is an ancient town within that division of Lincolnshire which is called Holland. It is described as one of the islands in the tract of East Marshlands, which, rising from the centre of the kingdom and running about a hundred miles, fall into the sea with their weight of waters augmented by many rivers.

[c] The triangular bridge at Crowland is said to be a structure of the thirteenth century. Gough describes it as "an object of the greatest curiosity in Britain, if not in Europe." But its curiosity depends more upon the singularity of its form than upon any difficulty in its construction or beauty in its architecture. (Britton's Archit. Antiq. vol. iv.)

In former times itt is said itt was hanted with evill speritts till Saint Guthlake,[a] a holly man, conjurd them away.

Saturday, the 9th July, on horse backe uppon the tryangular bridge, he and his cossen Bowyer parted; Mr. Bowyer for Hodsden, and Mr. Rawdon and his sarvant for the North. That morninge they went to Spaldinge, a towne where formerly thir was an abey, but now only the rubbish remaines;[b] from thence they went to Swinstead, where thir was likewisse an abbey, famous, or rather infamous, for the death of Kinge John, who was poysond thir by one of the monkes.

From thence they went to Bostone, a fine towne, and a faire haven for ships, and haith a very high steeple in one of thir churches, which is a greate guide to travelours booth by land and sea; itt haith 365 stone steps up to the top.[c] Here they rested Sunday, and on Munday morninge, the 11th July, they went to Lincone, an antient old cittie with a stately cathedrall; and here a stronge castle was built by William the Conquerour. Here they dind, and from thence went to a place called Littleborow Ferry,[d] an antient towne in time of the Romans uppon the river of Trent; here they lodgd that night. Tusday, the 12th July, they went from Littleborow to Bawtry, where are store of large milstones and exclent ale.[e]

From hence they went to Doncaster, a faire towne and antient,

<hr />

[a] Guthlac, who flourished in the early part of the eighth century, was the patron saint of the abbey of Crowland.

[b] The Benedictine priory of Spalding was demolished at the Reformation, and the materials of its buildings used in the construction of private mansions. Scarcely any vestiges of the monastery and conventual church are now remaining.

[c] The height of the celebrated tower of the church of Saint Botolph at Boston is 300 foot.

[d] At Littleburgh "was a famous passage over Trent, and near it have been found some old pieces of Roman antiquities, coins, or the like, as I have heard, which I suppose determined this place to be the Agelocum, or Segelocum, of Antonine." (Thoroton's Nottinghamshire. Fol. London, 1677, p. 414.)

[e] In the seventeenth century Bawtry was one of the principal depôts or wharfs for heavy goods brought down thither from the adjacent counties, such as lead, millstones, and grindstones from Derbyshire, and wrought-iron and edged tools from Hallamshire.

beinge a collonie in the time of the Romans; itt is famous for
knittinge of stockings, wascots, and weomen's petticcoates.   In the
yeare 759 itt was burnt with fire from heaven, and lay a longe time
in itts owne ruines;[a] from hence they went to Ferry-brigs, where
they rested that night.

The next day, beinge Wednesday the 13th July, they went to
the famous cittie of Yorke, built, as is reported, by Kinge Ebrauke,
and of him in lattin called Eboracus; thorow the cittie runneth the
river Ouse, in which bridge is the fairest arch[b] in England.   Itt is
wald round about with free stone, haith in itt a most bewtifull
cathedrall and a chapter howse, booth which are famous all the
world over.   Itt haith a castell, and a tower[c] planted with ordnance,
which comands the cittie.   Here itt was where Constantine the

---

[a] Doncaster, "about the year of our Lord 759, was so burnt with fire from heaven, and
laie so buried under its owne ruines, that it could scarce breath againe." (Camden's
Britannia, by Holland; ed. 1610, p. 690.   Rog. de Hoveden, Annal. sub anno 764.)
Mr. Rawdon has obviously derived many of his early historical facts from Holland's
translation of Camden's great work.   That Doncaster was famous in the seventeenth
century for "the knitting of stockings, waistcoats, and women's petticoats," is a circumstance not noticed by Mr. Hunter in his history of the town. (South Yorkshire,
vol. i. p. 28.)   Evelyn adds another peculiarity: "Doncaster is famous for great wax
lights and good stockings." (Diary, 1654.)

[b] The central arch of the old bridge across the Ouse at York was usually compared,
for width of span and beauty of form, to that of the Rialto at Venice. The curve was
originally designed to be segmental, but by a gradual displacement of the masonry of the
piers, occasioned either by the premature removal of the temporary framework or by a fault
of the workmanship, the arch had gradually, and probably with imperceptible slowness,
assumed the catenarian form which caused it to be the object of so much admiration. Half
a century ago, this interesting and most picturesque structure was demolished to make
room for the present bridge.

[c] Clifford's Tower, an antient keep or citadel built upon a high and still more antient
mound of artificial earth, within the enceinte of the castle of York. It is a fine example
of the military architecture of the twelfth century. In the reign of Queen Elizabeth the
corporation had the good taste to resist an attempt to destroy this noble structure, and in
their memorial upon the subject, addressed to the Lord Treasurer, they described it as
"one of the fairest and highest buildings for shewe and beautifying of this city that is
within or nigh unto the same, and doth most grace, beautify, and set forth the shewe
thereof, York Minster only excepted." Clifford's Tower was garrisoned during the civil
war, and was not dismantled until long after the Restoration. Thanks to the liberality of

Great was first saluted Emperour, his father Constantine Chlorus dynge here; also the greate Emperour Severus dyed here, and his bodie was here burnt, and his ashes sent to Rome.   St. Paulinus was the first archbishop thir of; but of thesse thinges shall remitt you to Mr. Rawdon's journall, or Northern Journie, where of all thesse thinges you will find a large relation.

Wednesday, 20th July, they went to the Spaw at Knasborow;[a] thir are tow wells which they call the Sulphurus Spaw, of a most unpleasant smell and taste, and stinks like the smell of a sinke, or rotten eggs, but is very medicinable for many deseases; also halfe a mile from thence is a nother well which they call the Sweet Spaw, in tast much like the waters of Epsome and Tunbridge; of the virtue of thesse waters, one Dr. Deane haith write a small treatice.[b]

<hr>

the gentry of Yorkshire, its remains are preserved with great care, and continue to form one of the fairest ornaments of our venerable city.

[a] At the town of Knaresbrough there are no medicinal waters. Knaresbrough Spaw was the name usually given in Mr. Rawdon's time to the mineral springs on Knaresbrough Forest, which have since conferred celebrity upon the fashionable watering-place of Harrogate, then scarcely in existence as a town. Mr. Ray is one of the few writers of the seventeenth century who used the name of Harrogate. In August 1661, he notes in one of his diaries, "we went to the Spaw at Herrigate and drunk of the water. It is not unpleasant to the taste, somewhat acid and vitriolick. Then we visited the suphur well, whose water, though it be pellucid enough, yet stinks noisomely, like rotten eggs, or *sulphur auratum diaphoreticum*." (Memorials of John Ray, ed. Ray Society, 8vo. p. 142.)

[b] Dr. Deane's "small treatise" was not the earliest work in which Knaresbrough Spaw was mentioned. The medical writer by whom the mineral springs upon Knaresbrough Forest were first noticed, and who gave to them the name of the English Spaw, was Timothy Bright, Doctor of Phisicke, the author of "A Treatise of Melancholie." 12mo. London, 1586. His therapeutical essays were published between the years 1583 and 1589, and it seems probable that the "two wells called the Sulphurous Spaw" were the only springs known upon Knaresbrough Forest when Dr. Bright wrote. The discovery of the "Sweet Spaw," described by Mr. Rawdon, "in taste like the waters of Epsom and Tunbridge" (now known as the Tewit Well), is ascribed to Sir William Slingsby, an uncle of the Sir Henry Slingsby who was beheaded during the Protectorate. The little tract entitled "Spadacrene Anglica, the English Spaw Fountaine, being a brief treatise of the Fountaine in the forest of Knaresborow," by Edmund Deane, M.D. was published in London in 1626. The author was a contemporary and neighbour of Mr. Rawdon's father, and practised for many years as a physician at York. He died there in 1640, and was buried in the church of St. Crux. A 12mo. edition of his treatise issued from the

Nere the skirts of the towne is some waters which distill from the rocks, which they call the dropinge well, which turnes peces of wood into stone, and is a very pleasant place to behold.

Thir they see Saint Robart's Chappell,[a] and a little fountaine called Saint Robart's Well, and the ruines of a castell, where some times Kinge John did keepe his courte. In the church of this towne is the buriall place of the famely of the Slingsbies, where Sir Henry Slingsbie, beheaded by Oliver Cromwell, lieth buried.[b]

From Knasborow they went to Saint Mungus his well,[c] 3 miles from thence, where they found greate resort of people; itt is a well of greate virtue, doinge very greate cures uppon thosse that have weake limbs, and to children that have the ricketts to be washt thir in.

From thence they went to Rippon, a faire towne, and famous for

York press in 1654. Another chalybeate spring or sweet spa upon Knaresbrough Forest was brought into notice by Dr. Michael Stanhope, the York physician, who has been previously mentioned. (p. 2, *supra*.) His tract, "advertising the public of his discovery," was entitled "Cures without a Care, or a Summons to all such as find little or no help by the use of Physick to repair to the Northern Spa." 4to. London, 1632.

[a]   "Of Saintt Robertt, that heremytte,
          Was approved here perfytte,
          Besyde Knaresburgh in a skerre [scar,]
          In a creves [crevasse] closed hym ferre,
          And full devoutely he lay
          In contemplacion nyght and day."

(The Metrical Life of Saint Robert of Knaresbrough, Roxburghe Club book, 1824.) St. Robert's Chapel has since become famous as the spot where the murderer Eugene Aram buried the body of his victim Daniel Clarke in 1745.

[b] Sir Henry Slingsby was attainted of high treason, and beheaded on Tower Hill on the 8th June, 1658. Lord Fauconberg, who married the Protector's daughter Mary Cromwell, was Sir Henry Slingsby's nephew.

[c] This well was at Copgrove, a village near the road from Knaresbrough to Boroughbridge. In 1661 Mr. Ray went to "St. Mongus his well at Copgrave;" "whither (he tells us) a great number of poor people resort to bathe themselves; they put on their shirts wetted in the water and let them dry on their backs." (Memorials, p. 142.) Dr. Wittie describes "St. Mugnus' Well" as a quick spring, "of great repute for curing the rickets in children, whom they dip into it naked, and hold them in a little while, but they must observe to dip five, seven, or nine times, more or less, according to custom,

spurrs and steele bowes, or stone bowes.[a] Itt haith a very large market place, where thir is twice a yeare a greate horse faire;[b] here is a faire cathedrall church, and a vault under the ground, where thir is a hole like the mouth of an oven, where they say none can passe thorrow but maids, and is called St. Winifrids nedle.[c]

Fryday, 22th July, they went from thence to Borrowbrigs, where, about a quarter of a mile from the towne, they see three stones of a yard and a halfe square, and about ten yards high, maid some thinge after the manner of a pyramid; the cuntry people call them the devill's arrows, but how they came thir noe man knowes.[d] From

or some think it will not do." (Scarbrough Spaw, by Robert Wittie, Dr. in Physick. 12mo. York, 1667.) At the time of Mr. Rawdon's visit, Copgrave was the seat of Sir Thomas Harrison, knight, who was the owner of the spring. His father, Robert Harrison, was an alderman of York, and Lord Mayor in 1607.

[a] Ripon "is remarkable for affording the best and most curious spurs in England, whose rowels might afford a passage through a piece of silver, and sooner break than bend. Whence came that proverbial saying, to express a man of intrepidity, honesty, and fidelity, *That such a person is as true as Rippon Spurs.*" (Gent's History of the Loyal Town of Rippon. York, 1733.)

[b]   Ad forensem Rippon tendo,
                        Equi si sint cari, vendo,
                        Si minore pretio dempti,
                        Equi à me erunt empti.
                                    Barnabæ Itinerarium.

[c] This is a slight and inaccurate notice of the crypt beneath the nave of Ripon minster, called "Saint Wilfrid's needle," which is said to be "one of the most undoubted and singular specimens of Anglo-Saxon architecture in the kingdom." (See "Observations on the Saxon Crypt under the cathedral church of Ripon, commonly called St. Wilfrid's Needle." By J. R. Walbran, esq. Proceedings of the Arch. Inst. at York, 1846.)

[d] The great monoliths at Boroughbridge, called the Devil's Arrows, have been a puzzle for antiquaries from Leland's time to the present. The dimensions of them given by Mr. Rawdon are tolerably accurate. It may be truly said that how or why such rude blocks of stone were placed where they are no one knows. Leland took them "to be *trophæa à Romanis posita* on the side of Watheling Street, as in a place most occupied in journeying, and so most in sighte." (Itin. vol. i. fol. 102.) Camden did not venture upon any different hypothesis, but he observes that many learned men thought they were not made of natural stone, but compounded of pure sand, lime, vitriol, and some unctuous matter. (Britannia, ed. Holland, p. 701.) Even to Ray and his scientific friends they seemed to be factitious stones, but yet (he remarks) they endured the weather exceeding well, and might in probability stand there till domesday. (Memorials, p. 143.) There is no doubt,

hence they returned to Yorke, where they staid till Wednesday the
third of August that they went to Tadcaster, which haith a faire
bridge, beinge 8 miles from Yorke. In the middle of the bridge are
the armes of the cittie of Yorke to shew how fare the previledges of
that cittie reacheth.[a]

From thence they went to Leedes, a rich towne of clothinge,
where are many very rich men; here one Mr. John Harison, a
clothier, built one parish church,[b] a very faire one, of free stone, and
a faire steple with four bells; itt haith in itt six rankes of pewes of
exelent wrought wainscott, the roffe of the church all freet worke.
He founded an hospitall of twentie almes howses; he built likewisse
a chapell to itt, and a howse for a vicar to live and say prayers to
them; he built a free schoole all of free stone; he built a wholle
street with faire howses on booth sides, the howse next the church
beinge for the parson of the parish; and att his owne proper cost and
charge did all this, and left large revenews to maintaine thesse
thinges, which were all finisht about 30 yeares agoe.

however, that the stones were extracted from the great rocks of Brimham or Plumpton,
two ancient quarries in that district of Yorkshire. (Prof. Phillips's Rivers, Mountains, and
Sea-coast of Yorkshire. 8vo. Lond. 1855, p. 65.)

[a] For many centuries the municipal authorities of the city of York had jurisdiction
over the wapentake of the Ainsty, a rural district that extended from the suburbs of the
city in a southerly direction as far as the middle of the river Wharfe at Tadcaster. Modern reform has incorporated the wapentake of the Ainsty with the West Riding of the
county of York.

[b] The church of St. John the Evangelist, in Upper-Head Row, was the earliest of the
now numerous places of worship provided for the religious wants of the populous town of
Leeds, in addition to the old parish church. It was begun in 1631, and consecrated in
1634. The building of a church by an individual, at his sole cost, was an unusual occurrence in those days. Ray and his friend Willughby were at Leeds in 1661, and saw
the new church. He says of the pious and benevolent founder, that "from a poor boy he
came to great estate, the most whereof he bestowed in building this church, and alms-
houses for thirty poor persons which are near the church." (Memorials, p. 140.) The
historian of Leeds, proud of his fellow-townsman, speaks of him as "the chief glory" of
the populous town of which he was a native, whose inhabitants, when he founded, finished,
and liberally endowed this noble and stately structure, were grown so numerous that the
old church, though very great, could not contain them. (Thoresby's Duc. Leodiensis, p. 27.)
Mr. Harrison died on the 29th October, 1656, in the 77th year of his age, and was

Thursday, the 4th August, they went from hence to Kirstall
Abbey, tow miles from Rawdon, a towne where the fameley of the
Rawdons haith continued ever sence the Conquest, and in this monastery had thir place of buriall, and were to itt greate benefactors;
a stately abey itt was, and some part of itt yett standinge.[a]

From thence they went to Bradforth, a greate towne and wealthy,
they havinge a greate trade of makinge Turkie-worke stooles, chaires,
and carpitts.[b]

From thence they went to Hallifax, a rich towne of clothinge,
and have a law to behead men within themselves.[c]

buried in the church his munificence had raised. In his epitaph, written by Dr. Lake,
then vicar of Leeds, afterwards Bishop of Chichester, and one of the famous seven, he is
called "The wonder of his own, and pattern of succeeding ages."

[a] The part of Kirkstall Abbey which is now standing forms one of the finest monastic
ruins in Yorkshire. By a charter without date Michael de Rawdon gave to God and the
monks of St. Mary of Kirkstall all the land which Hugo de Franceis held of him in the town
of Rawdon. I do not find upon record any other benefaction to Kirkstall by a Rawdon.

[b] The biographer speaks of Leeds, Halifax, and Wakefield, as "rich towns of clothing,"
and there is no doubt that all these places were the prosperous seats of manufacturing industry long before Mr. Rawdon visited them. But the rise and early progress of the important manufacture for which Bradford is now eminent are involved in some obscurity.
The author of "The History of the Worsted Manufacture in England," (8vo. London,
1857), states that, "Singularly enough, the parish of Bradford, afterwards destined to be
the chief, the supreme centre of this mighty manufacture, is the first place in Yorkshire
in which traces of it have been found. There are extant documents in the latter portion of
the seventeenth century in which persons residing in the parish are described as shalloon
manufacturers." (p. 200.) The writer was not aware that at York we had shalloon-
makers, then called chaloners, as early as in the fourteenth century. Mr. Rawdon's
notice of Bradford as "a great town and wealthy," soon after the Restoration, and then
"having a great trade in making of Turkie-worke stooles, chaires, and carpitts," may
throw some light upon the history of its manufactures in the seventeenth century.

[c] Throughout the forest of Hardwick, an extensive district or liberty of the West
Riding of Yorkshire which includes the town of Halifax, a remarkable custom had im-
memorially existed, known as the Halifax Gibbet Law. It is upon record in this form:
If a felon be taken within the liberty, with goods stolen without or within the precincts
of the forest, either *hand-habend*, *back-berand*, or *confessand*, being cloth or any other
commodity of the value of 13½d., and after three markets or meeting days within the
town of Halifax next after such apprehension being condemned, he shall be taken to the
gibbet and there have his head cut off from his body. "The engine wherewith the execution is done is a square blocke of wood of the length of foure foote and an halfe,

This towne is famous for the birth of Johanes Sacro Bosco, who was the authour of the Sphere.[a]

From hence they went to Wakefield, a greate towne and rich of clothinge; here they lodgd that night.

From hence they went to Sandall Castell, built by John Earle of Warren and Surrey, afterwards belonged to Richard Duke of Yorke (father of Edward the 4th), who, with his yonge son, the Earle of Rutland, were booth slaine in the battaile betwixt him and Queene Margaret, wife to Henry the sixt.[b]

From thence they went to Pumfrett, where once stood a faire castell, but booth itt and Sandall Castell were booth blowne up with powder by the late rebells. In this castell itt was where Richard the

which doeth ryde up and downe in a slot, rabet, or regall, betweene two peeces of timber that were framed and set upright of five yardes in height. In the nether ende of the slyding blocke is an axe keyed or fastened wyth iron into the wood, which being drawno up to the top of the frame is there fastened with a woodden pinne (the one ende set on a piece of woodde which goeth crosse over the two rabets, and the other ende being let into the blocke, holding the axe with a notche made into the same after the manner of a Sampson's post), unto the middle of which pinne there is a long rope fastened that commeth downe among the people, so that, when the offendour hath made his confession and hath layde his neck over the neathermost blocke, every man there present doth eyther take hold of the rope (or putteth foorth his arme, so neere to the same as he can get, in token that he is willing to see true justice executed), and, pulling out the pinne in this maner, the head blocke wherin the axe is fastened doth fall downe wyth such a violence, that, yf the necke of the transgressour were so bigge as that of a bull, it should be cut in sunder at a strocke, and roll from the bodie by an huge distaunce." (Harrison's Description of Britaine, p. 107. Holinshed's Chron. fol. Lond. 1571.) This was the famous Halifax Maiden, the prototype of the not less famous guillotine. The last execution by the maiden at Halifax took place in the year 1650. (Watson's History and Antiq. of Halifax. 4to. London, 1775, p. 231.)

[a] Thoresby alludes to "the hill at Halifax, upon which the famous Johannes de Sacro Bosco lay on his back to observe the motion of the stars, when he writ his celebrated book de Sphæra." (Duc. Leod. p. 194.) Dr. Watson, the historian of Halifax, doubts the nativity of the astronomer at that town. It is said that he took his surname from the abbey of Holywood in Dumfries-shire, where he was probably educated, and that he ultimately became a professor of mathematics in the university of Paris, and died there in 1256. An edition of his Sphæra was printed at Venice in 1478.

[b] The battle of Wakefield was fought on "the plains near Sandal Castle" on the 31st December, 1460.

Seacond was murderd by comand of Henry the 4th,[a] and Anthony Earle Rivers and Sir Richard Grey, knight, booth inocent persons, wore beheaded by the comand of Kinge Richard the 3d. A mile from hence they see a faire howse of the Lord Peerpoynt's,[b] and from thence they went to Yorke, att which time Mr. William Bowyer came to Yorke to see his cossen Rawdon, and to beare him company, in whosse company, Wednesday the 10th August, they went to Hemsly Parke, 15 miles from Yorke, where they had a warrant from the Duke of. Buckingham for a fat bucke, which they hunted, and had very good sport, and, havinge kild him, the next day they went from thence. In this towne thir is a faire castell, but much of itt ruinated, called Hemsley Castell. The castle and parke did belonge formerly to the Earles of Rutland, but by marriage came to the Duke of Buckingham, his mother beinge the Earle of Rutland's daughter.[c]

[a] When the three military gentlemen of Norwich (whose MS. account of their travels in the year 1634 is preserved in the Lansdowne collection, Brit. Mus. No. 213) visited Pontefract Castle, they were shown the very post round which King Richard II. was enforced to flee till his barbarous butchers inhumanly deprived him of life. "Upon that poste the cruell hackings and fierce blowes doe still remaine." (Brayley's Graphic and Historical Illustrator, p. 94.) Notwithstanding these evidences, the result of modern investigation goes far to prove that the deposed king died at the castle of Stirling in the year 1419. (See "Chronicque de la Traison et Mort de Richart Deux, Roy d'Engleterre." By Benjamin Williams, F.S.A. p. liii.)

[b] New-Hall, the once fair seat of the Pierrepoints, is now dilapidated, and occupied as a farm-house. During the civil war it was the residence of Francis Pierrepoint, esquire, an active parliamentarian. He was associated with Wilfred Lawson, esquire, and Sir Henry Cholmley, as one of the parliamentary commissioners to whom Pontefract Castle was surrendered by the royalists, after the second siege, in July 1645. In 1648, when Colonel Morice and his little band of royalists had regained possession of the castle, and it was besieged, for the third time, by Sir Edward Rhodes and Sir Henry Cholmley with 5000 men of regular troops, the besieged "kept a gate open on the south side of the castle, which was covered by a small garrison they placed in an house called New-Hall, belonging to the family of Pierrepoint, being about a musket-shot or two from the castle." (Account of the Sieges of Pontefract Castle, Miscell. Vol. Surtees Soc. pp. 82, 92.)

[c] It is a well-known incident of family history that in the reign of King James I., by the marriage of the royal favourite Buckingham to Katherine, sole daughter and heiress of the Earl of Rutland, one of the finest domains in Yorkshire passed from the ancient

Friday the 12th August they came from thence to Gillinge Castle,
a faire howse and parke belonginge to my Lord Fairfax, Vicount

baronial house of Roos of Hamlake (now called Helmsley) to the then recently ennobled
name of Villiers. In the year 1664, when Mr. Rawdon had a warrant to kill a fat buck
in Helmsley Park, the vast estates which had descended to his mother were in the possession of the second George Villiers, Duke of Buckingham; but Helmsley Castle, where
his maternal ancestors had for many centuries lived in princely state, had been ruined and
dismantled by the siege it sustained during the civil war, and was wholly unfit for the
permanent residence of its gay and voluptuous owner. His marriage, a few years before
the Restoration, to Mary Fairfax, the only surviving child of Thomas Lord Fairfax, brought
him frequently into Yorkshire. The nuptials were performed at Nun-Appleton, the country
seat of Lord Fairfax, eight or nine miles distant from York. The family mansion of the
Fairfaxes in York appears to have been part of the fortune which the young lady brought
to her husband, for not long after the Restoration the Duke speaks of it as his own. This
mansion was a stately edifice built by the first Lord Fairfax in the early part of the reign
of Queen Elizabeth, in a secluded district of the city called Bishophill. It was placed in
the midst of gardens and pleasure-grounds, occupying a large area, extending from the
street of Skeldergate near the river Ouse to the south-western rampart of the city walls.

About the time of Mr. Rawdon's visit, the duke was desirous of adding to the convenience of his York mansion, by the purchase of a piece of ground adjoining to it which
belonged to the corporation. In the year 1663 he was in friendly correspondence upon
this subject with Sir Henry Thompson (afterwards of Escricke), who was at that time
Lord Mayor. Two or three of the duke's letters to Sir Henry are, oddly enough, introduced into the collection of his works published in 1715. (London, 2 vols. 8vo.) The
negotiation was concluded and the ground conveyed by the corporation to the duke in
1665. In the month of January following the duke addressed to the Lord Mayor the
following letter :—

"Newmarket, Jan. 2.

"My Lorde.—Though I have received too many testimonies of kindnesse from your
Lordship and the citty of Yorke to bee surprisd at your continuing mee still in your
esteeme and good opinion, yett I doe assure you that you could not have fownd out any
way of giving mee a more agreeable evidence of it then by the order you have made in
my behalfe which I received in your last letter, since it will be a meanes of accomodating
mee to live amongst you, which is a thing I am very desirous of, both in order to my owne
satisfaction and the giving me frequent oportunities of letting you see how entirely and
cordially I am the cittles and

"Your Lordships
"Most affectionat friend and servant,
"BUCKINGHAM.

"For the Lorde Maior of the citty of Yorke."

I transcribe the duke's holograph, *verbatim et literatim*, to show that some of the

Emely,[a] and from thence that night they went to Crake Castle to see his nece, the yongest daughter of Sir Roger Jaques, maried to Charles Allanson of Crake Castle, esquier;[b] here they staid till Munday, and then they went to Yorke, where the staid till

peculiarities of the uncouth orthography of the Rawdon MS. were in use by contemporaries of the highest rank and literary distinction.

When sated with the pleasures of the Court, or driven from it by party strife, this versatile nobleman often during the subsequent twenty years of his life sought a change of scene and occupation at York, where in the luxurious saloons of his mansion upon Bishophill he dispensed his hospitalities to the citizens and aristocracy of the northern metropolis, and presided at many a gay and festive scene. It was one of the splendid entertainments given by the duke during the season of Christmas 167$\frac{1}{2}$, at which the young lady was a guest who was the cause of that fatal duel between Mr. George Aislaby and Mr. Jonathan Jennings, which "created a greater sensation in Yorkshire than any other affray in the seventeenth century." The true history of this lamentable occurrence has been given to the world by my esteemed friend the Rev. James Raine, in the highly interesting volume he has recently edited for the Surtees Society: "Depositions from the Castle of York relating to Offences committed in the Northern Counties in the Seventeenth Century."

The skeleton only of the Fairfax mansion was standing in Drake's time. (Eborac. p. 269.) That has since been demolished, and within the last three or four years a street of small houses, dignified by the name of Buckingham Street, has been built upon its site. Drake speaks of an outshot from the mansion, which, he was told, was built for the duke's laboratory; and tradition yet points out a small house of Elizabethan aspect, now standing in Skeldergate, as that in which chymical experiments were carried on by him

> Who, in the course of one revolving moon,
> Was chymist, fiddler, statesman, and buffoon.

Of the lines which are said to have conferred immortality upon "the great Villiers," it is not easy to determine whether the delineation of his character by one poet, or the description of his death by the other, is the more inaccurate.

[a] See note b. p. 77, *supra.*

[b] Charles Allanson, esquire, of Crake Castle, married to Mr. Rawdon's niece, Grace, the youngest daughter of Sir Roger Jaques, was the eldest surviving son of Sir William Allanson, knight, a citizen and alderman of York, who acquired some notoriety in the time of the Commonwealth. As he was nearly connected with several persons whose names appear in Mr. Rawdon's biography, a brief sketch of his career may not be inappropriate.

Sir William Allanson was the second son of Christopher Allanson, a respectable yeoman at Ampleforth in the North Riding of Yorkshire, who died in 1612, leaving a widow and a numerous family. A short time before his father's death he had settled in

Thursday, the 25th August, att which time his cossen Bowyer and he resolved upon a journie for Scotland. Soe he, his cossen

York as a draper or cloth-merchant. His first introduction into the corporation was in 1617, when he was made one of the city chamberlains. On the 12th June, 1621, at the parish church of Saint Crux at York, he married his first wife, Lucy, the daughter of Alexander Orracke, by whom he had several daughters and one son, who died in infancy. Being now a thriving tradesman, he was deemed a proper person to fill the higher municipal offices, and in September, 1622, he was elected one of the sheriffs of the city, having for his colleague Leonard Weddell, a merchant then residing at York, who was the ancestor of the Weddells of Earswick, from whom the late Thomas Philip Weddell Robinson, Earl de Grey, derived one of his names, and a considerable part of his estates. In April, 1632, upon the death of Mr. Leonard Weddell, the future Sir William Allanson was elected to succeed him in the office of alderman. Having become a widower in September, 1631, he took for his second wife Anne the daughter of Charles Tankard, esquire, of Whixley in the West Riding, by Barbara daughter of William Wyvill of Osgodby in the East Riding of Yorkshire. By this marriage he became connected with several of the oldest families in the county. His elevation to the civic chair quickly followed his second marriage. In February, 1633, he was sworn into the office of Lord Mayor, and a few weeks afterwards the Lady Mayoress presented him with a son and heir, the future Charles Allanson, esquire, of Crake Castle. On Friday, the 24th of May in the same year, King Charles I. visited York on his way to Scotland to be crowned, and on the Sunday following the Lord Mayor had the honour of entertaining his Majesty at dinner. A sumptuous repast was prepared at the Lord Mayor's house in the Pavement, where the King dined alone. After dinner, the King ordered the attendance of the noblemen and others of his suite, who had dined at the house of Sir Roger Jaques on the opposite side of the street, and in their presence called for the city sword, and with it conferred the honour of knighthood upon the Lord Mayor, and William Bolt, esquire, the Recorder. We learn from Mr. Rawdon's biography, that whilst the King was in York his Majesty condescended to be the sponsor of Sir William Allanson's infant son, who was baptized by the royal name of Charles.

In the reception of Charles I. at York upon this occasion, and during a similar visit a few years later, there was no lack of the outward demonstrations of loyalty on the part of the citizens; yet a strong undercurrent of discontent was rapidly gaining ground among the higher class of the inhabitants. This feeling was aggravated by the arbitrary proceedings of the great Court of the Council of the North, of which Lord Wentworth (the future Earl of Strafford) was president. Previously to his being appointed to the vice-regal government of Ireland, he passed much of his time at York in the discharge of his duties as Lord President, and by many acts of petty tyranny, in matters both civil and religious, and especially by attempts to interfere with the citizens in the exercise of their municipal privileges, he excited great public dissatisfaction and created many personal enemies. The principles of Puritanism, or Presbyterianism, were favoured to a considerable extent

Bowyer, one Captain William Baker, and Will. Raniel, Mr. Rawdon's sarvant, they sett forwards on thir journie, and that

among the commercial classes, as well as by many of higher rank resident in the city and the neighbourhood. Of those who held the chief offices in the corporation a large proportion were zealous Puritans, and of that party Sir William Allanson was one of the leaders. Another prominent man on the same side was Alderman Thomas Hoyle, whom Sir William Allanson succeeded in the mayoralty, and who was afterwards his colleague in the House of Commons. In the short parliament which 'sat in the spring of 1640, York was represented by Sir Edward Osborne, a nominee of Strafford, and Sir Roger Jaques, a Royalist alderman. But at the election in the following autumn the citizens threw off the trammels of the court, and returned their two Puritan aldermen, Sir William Allanson and Thomas Hoyle, both, as Mr. Drake styles them, "stiff fanatics." They were thus launched at once upon the stormy sea of politics, and became distinguished as active and zealous Parliamentarians. They did not, however, belong to the Andrew Marvel school of patriots. They were not unwilling to share the benefits reaped by some of those who took the popular side. Sir William Allanson was made Clerk of the Hanaper, a place said to be worth 1,000l. a year. Hoyle succeeded Sir Peter Osburn in the office of Treasurer's Remembrancer in the Exchequer, valued at 1,200l. a year. The unhappy fate of Alderman Hoyle is well known. On the first anniversary of the King's execution, he was found dead, by his own hand, in his lodgings at Westminster. Drake has reprinted the doggrel lines in which the royalist versifiers displayed their exultation upon this event, and he dilates upon it with all the bitterness of party spirit. · (See Eborac. p. 172. Rump Songs, ed. 1662, p. 288.) It is not imputed to the members for York that either of them took any part in the King's trial, although Sir William Allanson's name appears in the Act constituting the High Court of Commission.

After the establishment of the Commonwealth, the profits of his place enabled Sir William Allanson to be a purchaser of church estates. He became the proprietor of the castle and rich manor of Crake, part of the vast possessions of the see of Durham. In the account of the sale of bishops' lands between the years 1647 and 1651 (see Collectanea Topographica, vol. i. pp. 3, &c.) Crake is stated to have been sold for 1,163l. 8s. 2½d., and to have been conveyed on the 7th March, 164⅔, to Sir Thomas Widdrington and Thomas Coghill. There is no doubt that these persons were merely trustees, and that Sir William Allanson was the actual purchaser. And thus Crake, "which had regularly belonged to the see of Saint Cuthbert from his time to the present day" (Raine's St. Cuthbert, p. 27, note), passed to a draper and a city knight. Sir William Allanson was also the purchaser of the manor of Ouseflete in Howdenshire, another part of the possessions of the bishops of Durham. Besides these acquisitions, we find him to have been at the time of his death, not only the owner, but the actual occupier, of the ancient mansion of the Deans of York within the close of the cathedral, usually called the Deanery. At what time or upon what terms he made this purchase I am unable to discover.

Happily for Sir William Allanson, he did not live to witness the Restoration. His death

night lodged att a faire market towne called North Allerton,
24 miles from Yorke. This hapned to be a faire day for oxen, kine,
and sheepe, the greatest in England.[a] This towne affords most
exclent ale[b] and beere, and very good entertainement; here are

took place in 1656, the year after he had served, for the second time, the office of Lord
Mayor of York. By his will, dated the 11th June, 1656, he bequeathed to his wife the
manor of Ouseflete and his house called the Deanery, in the Minster-yard of York, wherein
he then dwelt, and other houses in Peter-gate and Grape-lane. The manor of Crake,
which he purchased of the Commonwealth, and the mansion-house of Crake Castle, he
bequeathed to his son Charles. He remembered the poor of Ampleford, where he was
born, with a legacy of ten pounds. He was buried in the church of Saint Michael le
Belfrey in York on the 7th December, 1656. Lady Allanson survived her husband
nearly twenty years. A few years after his death she became the second wife of Sir
Solomon Swale of Stainley, who for his distinguished loyalty was rewarded with a baronetcy immediately after the Restoration.

As Mr. Allanson retained possession of Crake so late as the year 1665, he must have
made some arrangement with the commissioners who were appointed in October, 1660,
"to inquire into the pretended sales and purchases of crown and church lands."

The last of the elder branch of the lineal male descendants of Sir William Allanson
was Charles Allanson, esquire, of Sion, in the county of Middlesex, who died without
issue in 1775. His estates passed to his sister's grandson, George Winn, esquire (whose
father was a younger son of Sir Rowland Winn, baronet, of Nostel Priory), and he then
took the surname of Allanson, in addition to that of Winn. In 1776 he was made a
baronet, and in 1797 he was raised to the Irish peerage with the title of Lord Headley,
Baron Allanson and Winn, of Aghadoe, county Kerry. By his great-nephew, Charles
Allanson Winn, the present Lord Headley, the name and blood of the Puritan York
alderman of the seventeenth century are now represented.

The arms now borne by his descendants were granted to Sir William Allanson by William Le Neve, Norroy, soon after the honour of knighthood was conferred upon him: Paly
wavy of six or and azure, on a chief gules a lion passant gardant of the first. Crest: Upon
a mount proper a demi-lion rampant gardant or, holding a cross gules.

[a]   "Veni Allerton, ubi oves,
           Tauri, vaccæ, vituli, boves,
           Aliaque campi pecora
           Oppidana erant decora:
           Forum fuit jumentorum."
                           Barnabæ Itin. 1648-50.

[b]   "Where may we find this nectar, I thee pray?
           The boon good fellow answer'd, I can tell;
           North Allerton in Yorkshire doth excell

the ruines of a stronge old castle built by one of the bishops of Durham.[a]

From North Allerton they went towards Durham. In thir journey the day before, they past the river of Swale twice; this river is famous for that uppon a Christmasse day thir was (some say by Saint Austin the monke, others say by Paulinus the first Archbishop of Yorke) baptized ten thousand soules; the archbishop hallowed the river, and by the voyce of a crier comanded them to goe confidently into the river tow by tow, and soe in the name of the Father, Son, and Holy Ghost, to baptize one another; and itt soe pleased God that who soe ever went into that river that day of anie ach or lamenesse, came out perfectly sound; a greate and wonderfull cure booth of bodie and soule.[b] As they went this dayes journie they dind att a greate market towne called Darnton,[c] and lodgd thatt night att the cittie of Durham.

This cittie of Durham is built uppon a hill, and the river of Weere doth compasse itt allmost round aboute. Dr. Besier, a Frenchman,[d]

> All England, nay all Europe, for strong ale.
> If thither we adjourn, we shall not fail
> To taste such humming stuff, as, I dare say,
> Your highness never tasted to this day."
>
> *The Praise of Yorkshire Ale; a poem by George Meriton.*   York, 1685.

[a] A traveller in 1658 saw the Bishop's palace "demolished with age and the ruins of time, and serving as a receptacle for bats and buzzards, owls and jackdaws." (Northern Memoirs. By Richard Franck. London. 8vo. 1694, p. 223.) Not one stone upon another is now remaining of either the feudal castle of Northallerton or of that which Leland describes as "the strong and well moted" palace of the Bishops of Durham.

[b] Drayton thus sings of the river Swale :

> "A wondrous holy flood (which name she ever hath),
> For, when the Saxons first receav'd the Christian faith,
> Paulinus, of old Yorke the zealous bishop then,
> In Swale's abundant streame christned ten thousand men,
> With women and their babes, a number more beside,
> Upon one happy day, whereof shee boasts with pride."
>
> *Poly-Olbion*, 28th *Song*, p. 144, ed. 1613.

[c] Darlington.

[d] Isaac Basire, D.D. archdeacon of Northumberland and a prebendary of Durham in the reigns of Charles I. and Charles II. He was born at Rouen in 1607, the son of a

and one of the prebens thir, haith been att Jerusalem, and saith this
cittie is an absolute epitomie of Jerusalem, nott only for the temple
or cathedrall, which is a very faire one, standinge uppon the highest
hill in the towne, like mount Sion, but the skirts of the towne resemble Jerusalem, and nott only that, but the country about resembles the country about Jerusalem, beinge, as the scripture saith,
a hilly country.

In this church lieth the body of Saint Cuthbert, the first founder.
Itt is vastly stronge, the pillars beinge of six and seaven fathum
about; in the body of the church lyeth in a tombe the Earle of
Westmerland, who was in rebellion with Henry Hotspur, Earle of
Northumberland, against Henry the 4th.[a]

From hence, Satturday the 27th August, they went from Durham
towards New-Castell; they went a little out of the way to see Lumley Castle, a seate belonginge to the Lord Lumley; itt is a very
faire buildinge all of free stone, and in itt are gallant princely
roomes where the pictures att length of most of that famely, which
have bene before the Conquest, are extant; also thir is in the said
castell a faire gallery well furnisht with exclent pictures, this castle
havinge had the happinesse to escape the rude hands and harts of
thesse late unhappie times.[b] From thence they went to New-Castle,

Protestant of the lowest order of French noblesse; educated at the university of Leyden,
and ordained in 1629 by Thomas Morton, then Bishop of Coventry and Lichfield. When
Morton became Bishop of Durham he made Basire his domestic chaplain.   In the civil
war Dr. Basire was deprived of all his preferments, and, having no means of subsistence
for himself and his family, he went abroad. From 1647 to 1661 he was travelling in
various parts of Europe and Asia. Evelyn, in his Diary, speaks of Dr. Basire, "the great
traveller, or rather French apostle, who had been planting the Church of England in divers
parts of the Levant and Asia," and whom he heard preach at the Abbey in July 1661. Dr.
Basire's correspondence, with a memoir by W. N. Darnell, B.D. was published in 1831.

   [a] Ralph Neville, the first Earl of Westmoreland, was of the King's party in the rebellion
of the Percies against Henry IV. The chapel o the Nevilles in Durham Cathedral does
not contain his remains. He had contemplated Durham as the place of his sepulture, but
was eventually buried at Staindrop. See "A brief account of Durham Cathedral. 12mo.
Newcastle, 1833." The late Dr. James Raine was the author of this little work, which
is a guide-book of a very superior class.

   [b] Lumley Castle in the county of Durham is one of the finest of the baronial strong-

where they dined that day; this is a towne of good trade, and thorow the middle runneth the river of Tine, of a good depth, soe that ships of 150 and 200 ton come and deliver thir goods up att the towne key, which key is very brood, longe, and comodious. They have of late built a famous towne-howse,[a] where they have thir courts of judicature, and underneath itt is thir exchange, a very faire place for marchants to walke in, supported with very faire pillers of free stone. Itt haith in that towne four churches; the fonts thirin are made with more then ordnary curiositie.

From Newcastle they went that night to a towne 16 mile of, called Morpith, a large towne, where they rested that night, and the next day, Sunday. Itt haith a church, a prison, the ruines of a castle belonginge to my Lord of Carlile, which the Scotch ruind in thesse warrs, and a free scoole with a chimney in itt, where the boyes have a fire all the winter longe, each boy bringinge a horse loode of coales, which thir costs 3 pence.[b] Closse by itt runns the river Wentsbecke.

Munday, the 29th August, they went from hence to an antient towne called Anwick, were they dined; itt haith tow faire gates of free stone, which shewes itt haith bene some thinge in former times,

---

holds of the North. It yet stands, almost as perfect in outward form as when it was re-built and castellated by Ralph Lord Lumley in the reign of Richard II. The Lumleys are among the very few English families who can boast of a well-authenticated genealogy from a period antecedent to the Conquest. The Earls of Scarborough, the lineal male representatives of this ancient race, have had the good taste to maintain Lumley Castle, although it is no longer their residence, in the same state of preservation as when it was seen and admired by Mr. Rawdon. (See Surtees' Hist. of Durham, vol. ii. p. 156.)

[a] The present exchange and town-court, of beautiful architecture, were built between the years 1655 and 1658. Robert Trollop of York, mason, was the architect. (Brand's Hist. of Newcastle-upon-Tyne. 4to. 1789, vol. i. p. 29.)

[b] Perhaps Mr. Rawdon remembered that St. Peter's school at York had no chimney, and was surprised to find the luxury of a fire-place at Morpeth. The free grammar-school of that town was founded by King Edward VI. Not many years after Mr. Rawdon saw the school-house, Charles Howard, third Earl of Carlisle, and William, fourth Lord Widdrington, were upon the roll of its scholars, and doubtless would have to contribute their annual horse-loads of coals like the rest.

but now the howses are all thactht, and soe contemtible little, that,
like the cittie of Mindus,[a] the towne may easely run thorrow the
gates; here is a faire stronge castle, which makes a greate shew to
the cuntry, but ill contrived within for lodgins.[b] Itt belonges to my
Lord of Northumberland, whosse auditor comes thir twice a yeare,
sitts to order busnesses, and to recieve his rents.

In this place our forefathers shewed much vallor against the
Scotts. They tooke, in the yeare 1176,[c] William Kinge of Scotts,
and presented him to Kinge Henry the Seacond; and when Mal-
come the Third, Kinge of Scotts, came, and besieged this castell,
beinge brought to such extremitie as they were redie to yield,
seemingly offerd uppon the poynt of a lance to deliver the kinge the
keyes, run the kinge thorow the body and kild him; and, his son
Edward cominge to revenge his father's death, they wounded him
soe that he shortly after died.

After dinner they went to a towne called Belford, where they
had but meane lodginge, but exelent fresh cod and very good whitt-
ings, booth fresh and dried, reasonable good beare, and very good
French wine, with which they past that night very well;[d] but thir

---

[a] Myndus, a city of Caria in Asia Minor, near to Halicarnassus; a small town with
large gates.

[b] Alnwick Castle had long ceased to be the residence of the Earls of Northumberland.
The contemporaries of Mr. Rawdon were Algernon Percy, the tenth earl, and his son
Josceline, who succeeded him in 1668 and died in 1670. These were the last of the
Percys of the male line. Preferring the more genial climate of the South of England,
they lived chiefly at Petworth. In the seventeenth century Alnwick was neglected and
had fallen into decay.

[c] The chroniclers place this event two years earlier. The story is told by William of
Newburgh (lib. ii. cap. 33). "Our forefathers" were Robert de Stuteville, Ranulph
de Glanvilla, Bernard de Baliol, William de Vesci then Lord of Alnwick, and their
retainers.

[d] The mean lodging which Mr. Rawdon had at Belford was much superior to that
described by a traveller in 1639 when Charles I. was in the North with his army.
"Belfort, nothing like the name either in strength or beauty, is the most miserable
beggarly sodden town, or town of sods, that ever was made in an afternoon of loam and
sticks." "In all the town not a loaf of bread, nor a quart of beer, nor a lock of hay, nor a peck
of oats, and little shelter for horse or man." (Court and Times of Cha. I. vol. ii. p. 285.)

horses but reasonable for want of grasse, the church-yard beinge
the best pasture, by which they percieved they drew nigh Scotland.

Tuesday, 30th August, they went from thence to the stronge
towne of Berwick uppon Tweed, which divides England and Scotland, where they baited, and of which shall give you an account att
thir returne out of Scotland; and from thence they went that night
to Dunbarr, beinge twenty miles from Barwick. This is the place
where Cromewell, Generall Monke, and Lambert beate the Scotts
and totally routed them. Itt is a pore beggerly towne, nothinge
worth seeinge, only in the church thir is a faire tombe of the Earle
of Barwicke, Lord of Dunbar, who died about 50 yeares agoe.[a] This
is a sea towne, where they had good fresh cod, which they causd to
be boild in sea watter, which made it eate hard and savory; they
had likewisse good French wine thir. But thir horses where forcd
to eate fresh straw and oates, thir beinge niether grasse nor hay thir.
They lodgd in the chamber where the Duke of Monmouth's lady and
hir mother lay;[b] but there are few pettie ale howses in England but
afford a better lodginge.

From Dunbarr, Wednesday the 31th, they went towards thir
much talkt of cittie of Edenborow; they travaild 15 miles, where
in the way they found but one blinde ale howse, which had a wispe
of straw for a signe. Here they dranke some of thir blincht ale, which
had a sowrish tast, which gave some of them the chollick;[c] but att

- [a] The fair tomb mentioned by Mr. Rawdon was a splendid marble monument to the
memory of Sir George Hume, Lord High Treasurer of Scotland, whom James I., soon
after his accession to the throne of England, created Lord Hume of Berwick and Earl of
Dunbar. He died in 1611.

[b] Anne, Duchess of Monmouth, and her mother the Countess Dowager of Buccleuch.
The young duchess, esteemed the greatest fortune and the finest lady in the three king-
doms, was married to the Duke of Monmouth in the preceding year, but was not more
than thirteen years of age at the time of Mr. Rawdon's visit to Dunbar, her husband
being two or three years older.

[c] "I did never see or heare that they have any publike innes with signes hanging out;
but the better sort of citizens brew ale, their usuall drinke, which will distemper a strangers
bodie, and the same citizens will entertaine passengers upon acquaintance or entreaty."
(Moryson's Description of Scotland, p. 156.)

last they came to a towne which is nere the sea side, and of a bed of
mussells which comonly arc thir tooke the name of Musselborow; itt
is partly wald about. Here they gott some French wine, which did
a little helpe the distemper the ale had causd; and from hence they
went that night to Edenborow.

Here they staid, in Edenborow, till Fryday att none, to see the
cittie; where thay had very good oysters, but as big as Kentish
oysters.[a]

This Edenborow is cittuated uppon a ridge of a hill or rocke, and
haith in itt only one faire streete, allmost a mile longe, beinge all
the length of the towne; itt reacheth from Hallowrood howse, the
king's pallace, att the boottome, to the Maiden Castell which is att the
very tope of the hill; standinge uppon the extent of the said ridge.
The king's pallace is a darke mallancholly buildinge, and the roomes
within noe wayes pleasant; the iron grates makinge itt rather looke
like a prison then a pallace; the orchard and garden that belongs to
itt very meane. Itt haith a place wald about itt, neare of about tow
miles compasse, which they call the parke; but thir is never a tree or
deere in itt,[b] only I thinke in some of the rockes thir is some rabitts.
Uppon the highest rocke is a place called Kinge Arthur's Chaire; a
little below that, a chappell and a springe called Saint Anthonie's
chappell and well. Besides the great street, thir is about tow streets
more, and severall crosse lanes on booth sides, booth which streets

---

[a] In old times the people of Edinburgh were great lovers of oysters:

> When big as burns the gutters rin,
> If ye hae catched a drowkit skin,
> To Luckie Middlemist's loup in,
>   And sit fu' snug,
> Owre oysters and a dram o' gin,
>   Or haddock lug.

> *Chambers's Traditions of Edinburgh*, vol. ii. p. 270.

[b] It was not so in the preceding century, when the court was at Holyrood. Camden
describes it as "a park stored with game." (Scotia, p. 24.) "Over the king's palace,
in a parke of hares, conies, and deare, an high mountain hangs, called the chair of Arthur."
(Moryson's Account of Edinburgh in 1598, p. 273.)

and lanes stink soe, that they are able to chooke anie that are nott usd to them. Thir buildings in the greate street haith nothinge of comelinesse, thir frontispice beinge most of boords havinge ovall holes cutt out of them to looke out att, in stead of windows, which seeme as if they were lookinge out of a pillory. They are in thir howses and persons naturally sluttish booth men and woemen; and to cover that sluttishnesse the woemen have a thinn chequerd stuffe, much like the chequerd howsinge clooth we use for our horses, which covers them all downe to thir anckles, which thinges they call plads.[a] They have four churches in this towne, but mean buildinge without, and worse furnisht within, the seates beinge oppen, and most of deale bords, almost like thosse scaffolds we make in the streets to see anie greate show;[b] one of the churches is built

---

[a] Mr. Rawdon's description of the streets of Edinburgh and the sluttish habits of the people is not exaggerated. In the preamble of an Act of their own privy council made in 1619, the condition of the town is set forth with amusing ingenuousness :

"Forasmickle as the burgh of Edinburgh, quhilk is the chief and principall burgh of the kingdome, quhair the soverane and heich courtes of parliament, his Majesties Previe Counsall and Colledge of Justice, and the Courtis of Justiciarie and Admiralitie ar ordinarlie haldin and keipt, and quhairunto the best pairt of the subiectis of this kingdome, of all degreis, rankis, and qualities, hes a commoun and frequent resorte and repair,—is now become so filthie and uncleine, and the streittis, venallis, wyndis, and cloissis thairoff so overlayd and coverit with middingis, as the noblemen, counsellouris, servitouris, and uthers his Majesties subiectis, quha ar ludjeit within the said burgh, can not have ane cleine and frie passage and entrie to thair ludjeingis; quhairthrow thair ludgeingis ar becum so lothsume unto thame, as they ar resolved rather to mak choice of ludgeingis in the Cannongate and Leyth, or some utheris pairtis about the towne, nor to abyde the sycht of this schamefull uncleanes and filthiness; quhilk is so universall and in such abundance throuch all the pairtis of this burgh, as in the heitt of somer it corruptis the air, and gives greit occasioun of seiknes : and forder, this schamefull and beistlie filthines is most detestable and odious in the sicht of strangeris, quho, beholding the same, are constrayned with reassonn to gif oute mony disgracefull speiches againis this burgh, calling it a most filthie pudle of filth and vncleannes, the lyk quhairof is not to be seine in no pairt of the world."

[b] The cathedral church " is large and lightsome, but little stately for the building, and nothing at all for the beauty and ornament. The king's seat is built some few staires high of wood, and leaning upon the pillar next to the pulpit; and opposite to the same is another seat very like it, in which the incontinent use to stand and doe pennance." (Moryson's Account of Edinburgh, p. 273.)

north and south, contrary to the coustome of all other churches.
They have a reasonable good buildinge of stone, which they call the
Parlement Howse;[a] serves for that, and for the judges att terme
times. They have also a very faire outside of an hospitall,[b] built by
one Mr. Herick, Kinge James his jeweler, who died before he could
perfectly finish itt. But now thir once maiden castell, the top of
. the towne, and the top of thir glory, where nature and art haith
booth indifferently done thir parts to make hir strong, yet for all hir
strength, she was deflowrd by Olliver Cromewell, who violently
enterd hir, tooke away hir best adornments, hir greate guns, and
sent them for England. The place is very much worth the seeinge,
beinge well contrived booth for fortification and pleasure, consistinge
of about sixteen roomes, large stables, and accomodation for horses;
here, they say, when the kinges feard aney falce play from the Scotts,
they would retire themselves as to a sanctuary; and a place of
greate strength itt is.

Fryday, the seacond of September, after dinner, they went to a
place called Lithgoe, an antient towne, in time of the Romanes
called Lindum; itt is partly walled about and bewtified with a noble
howse of the king's, built with free stone, but goeth much to decay,
which is greate pittie.[c] On the one side of the king's howse is a
faire lake, very pleasant to behold, in the middle of which is a little
iland, in the middle of which groweth a tree, the which iland and
tree are the armes of the towne. This lake, they say, abounds with
pike, pearch, and elles. The waites of this towne, as likewisse of
most greate townes in Scottland, is a drume and bagpipe.[d]

. [a] Begun in 1632 and completed in 1640.

[b] Mr. Rawdon saw the " very faire outside " of the noble hospital founded by " Jingling
Geordie " in all the freshness of its beauty. The building was commenced in 1628, but,
its progress being interrupted by the civil wars, it was not completed till 1660. George
Heriot died in 1624.

[c] It is a still greater pity that this, the fairest of the palaces " built for the royal
dwelling," should have been reduced to an empty and blackened ruin by the English
dragoons after the rebellion of '45.

[d] The drum and bagpipe of the waites of Linlithgow would bring to our traveller's recollection the superior minstrelsy of his native city. The corporation of York had five or

Saturday, the 3d September, they went from thence to the cittie of Glascow, an archbishop's seate, haith under itt Galloway, Argile, and the Iles; the archbishop then was Doctor Burnett,[a] a grave wisse prelate; they went to vizitt him, and were invited by him the next day, beinge Sunday, wher in the cathedrall they herd him preach an excellent sermon. This archbishoprick is nott worth, as the archbishop told them, above 1500*l.* per annum. This is the best cathedrall in Scotland, but very meane in comparison of our cathedralls of England;[b] here is nothinge of organs, singinge men, nor surplice: they bury all thir deade in the church yard. This church yarde may be about tow akers of grownd or more, is all wald about by the townes men with free stone about tow yeards ½ high; each fameley havenge about tow yeardes length of wall, where his armes, if he have anie, are ingraven; if nott, some other devise; as, if he be a taylor, a paire of sissers with an inscription,—This is the buriall place of such a one, taylor, and his fameley: which is very pleasant to behold. Thir are likewisse severall tombes in other places of the church-yard. This towne is one of the universities of Scotland, and att thir beinge thir was a very faire colledge of free stone a buildinge. The towne haith tow crosse streets very longe and very brood, allmost as brood as Holborne, and paved after that new way; a pleasant place itt is, and of greate trade; but for the further perticulers thirof I shall refer you to Mr. Rawdon's journall.

six waits, skilful musicians, who, clad in scarlet liveries and adorned with silver chains and badges, patrolled the streets at Christmas, and roused the midnight echoes with the enlivening strains of the sackbut, the shalm, the trumpet, and other kinds of music.

[a] Dr. Alexander Burnett was translated from the see of Aberdeen to the archiepiscopate of Glasgow in 1663. The archbishop would recognise in Mr. Rawdon a former acquaintance, as they had most probably met at Dunkirk in July, 1662, when Dr. Burnett was chaplain to Lord Rutherford, the governor of that town, and had an English congregation there. He was advanced from Glasgow to St. Andrew's in 1679, and died in 1684. (Keith's Scottish Bishops, by Russell. London, 1824, pp. 42, 265.)

[b] Mr. Rawdon's English prejudices are here apparent. There are few nobler ecclesiastical structures than the cathedral of Glasgow. "The pile is of a gloomy and massive, rather than elegant, style of Gothic architecture; but its peculiar character is so strongly preserved and so well suited with the accompaniments that surround it, that the impression

Munday, the 5th September, they went from hence to a towne
called Dumbarton, ten miles from thence, where, uppon a high
rock in the sea, is situate a stronge castle, which commands the
mouthe of the River Cluid that runs up to Glascow, a thinge, if
victualed, impregnable; itt is much higher then Paul's steple, and
yet haith a very large springe of fresh water one the tope of itt, and
tow springs more a little lower.[a]

From this castle they see the greate lake Lommond, which spreads
itt selfe under the mountaines, about 24 miles in length, and about
8 in breadth; itt haith store of fish, and one fish called a pollac,
which is found noe where ells. The country people told them that
in this lake were three thinges observable: waves without winde,
fishes without fins, and a flotinge iland; the fishes without finns are
good for woemen in child bed.[b]

This castle was a stronge hold in time of the Romanes, and the
Earles of Lenox are by birth and right governours of this castle.

Uppon the top of this castle they sett up thir Hirculas Pillars,
with *non plus ultra*, resolvinge to travaile noe further northward,
havinge scene enough of Scottland; soe on Tuesday, the 6th September, they turned faces about to the southe, and went to that
antient towne of Sterlinge, situated in a cleere aire uppon the side

of the first view was awful and solemn in the extreme." This was the feeling of him whose
genius has illumined the low-browed vaults of the church of Saint Mungo.

  [a] The rock upon which Dumbarton Castle stands springs suddenly from the point of
junction of the Leven and Clyde to the height of 560 feet. The extreme altitude of the
steeple of Old Saint Paul's was 520 feet. (Howel's Londinopolis. Fol. 1657, p. 313.)

  [b] Loch Lomond "is well stored with variety of fish; but most especially with a peculiar
fish that is to be found no where else (they call it pollac), as also with islands concerning
which many fables have been forged and those rife among the common people." (Camden,
Scotia, p. 24.) A later traveller says, "The lake abounds with fish of several sorts, particularly a sort called poans, and by some pollacks, peculiar to it, a kind of eel, very
delicious to eat. This gave occasion to the mistake of authors who said this lake had fish
without fins." (Defoe's Tour through Scotland, 8vo, 1714.) Neither the finless fish
nor the floating island is mentioned in modern accounts of Loch Lomond. Several
species of a fish, called pollack in Scotland, are described by Yarrell in his history of
British Fishes, but none resemble the eel, nor is the Scotch lake their habitat.

of a hill, 28 miles from Dumbarton, strongly wald aboute. Uppon
the top is a magnificent castle belonginge to the kinge, where Prince
Henry was borne, and baptized in a faire chappell built by Kinge
James in this castle for the same purposse.

In this castle is a very faire hall, nere 35 yardes in length, and
about 12 in breadth, besides the breadth of the bay windowes. In
this hall the kinge used to dine; in itt att the bottome is a faire
gallery above, full the breadth of the hall, for musick and trumpeters;
thir is in this castell a springe of good water, a faire garden with
hansome walkes, trees, and flowers, well kept; here they were presented with nosegayes of very faire gilleflowers and other sweet
herbes, which they caried in thir coate pocketts to sweeten the Scotch
wash of thir hand kirchirs. Itt haith within itt a conie-warren and
a small padoc where in are some deere kept. They were told that
out of the hall window in a cleere day one might see three score
miles, and, which is a very pleasant thinge to looke uppon out of
the hall, is the river's windings, which, though itt is not above four
miles from the sea, yet the meanders are such, that thosse that come
up itt must come twentie-foure miles.[a]

Fouertene miles from hence or little more, att Dumfermlinge, the
Kinge haith a howse, where Kinge Charles the First of glorious
memory was borne. Wedensday, the 6th [7th] September, they
went backe to Edenborow, and the 7th [8th] they went to Lieth,
beinge the port towne of Edenborow; itt is a reasonable good towne,
and haith a convenient haven for a greate many ships. Itt is a
place affords very good oysters. Here they see one of the four

---

[a] "From a pretty little flower-garden upon one of the bastions on the north side of the
castle we had a most agreeable prospect over the valley and of the meanders, turnings, or
reaches of the river Forth, which are extremely beautiful. Here are three double reaches,
which make six returns together, and each of them above three Scots miles in length,
and, as the bows are almost equal for breadth as the reaches are for length, it makes the
figure complete. The form of this winding may be conceived by the length of the way,
for it is twenty-four miles from Stirling to Alloa by water, and hardly four miles by land."
(Defoe's Tour.)

greate forts the English made in Cromwell's time to subject the
Scotts; a thinge soe well done, that itt speakes much to the honor
of the English nation, that in soe short a time they could finish soe
greate a worke.

From Lieth they went to Dunbar, of which we have allredie
spooken, where they lodged that night.

The next day, beinge Fryday the 8th, they went to Berwick,
beinge thirtie-tow miles from thence, where they lodged that night,
and were made happie in the company of Captain Ralfe Siddenham,
one of the captaines of that garrison, who treated them that after
none, and shewed them some sport with his hawke, and lastly was
pleasd to afford them his good company att supper.

This towne stands uppon the mouth of the river Tweed, which
devides the kingdome of England and Scotland. Itt is a place very
stronge, well fortefied, with good ordnance, where the Kinge keepes
a constant garrison, and haith remained in the possession of the
English ever since the time of Kinge Edward the 4th.

Satturday the 9th they went from Berwicke to Belford, ridinge
a longe in sight of the Holly Iland; they staid att Belford that after
none, and the next day, Sunday, where was a greate concourse of
people, itt beinge the day of thir anuall feast; a greate deale of
mirth thir was after the manner of that country.

Sunday morninge, the 10th, they haveinge heard that Saint Cuthbert, who lived uppon the Holly Iland, to the end that the inhabitants of Northumberland might come over from the maine every
Sunday to be instructed in the Christian faith, did by his prayers
prevaile with God Allmighty that every Sunday the tyde should
alter his course, and that itt should be low water from eight of the
clocke in the morning till tow in the after none, and that itt continued soe ever sence; soe they went to try this miraculous trewth
and found itt to be soe, and by the inhabitants were informed that
itt is constantly soe every Sunday;[a] a very strange thinge, and as

* This adds one more to the numerous miracles ascribed to the great Northumbrian
saint. None of his biographers mention the supposed Sunday tide at Lindisfarne. In

much to be wonderd att as the passage of the Isralites over the Red
Sea. Itt is from the maine land about a mile and a halfe over the
sands, and where they went over dry on Sunday, on Saturday they
see it coverd over with the sea, and bootes a fishinge thir. Here
they see the abbey church founded by St. Cuthbert; this church
speakes much antiquitie, the pillars beinge all of a carvd worke nott
usuall;[a] the lead of this church not longe agoe was plunderd, and
shipt for London; but what was very remarkable was that the ship,
with severall passengers, in a faire season of wind and wether, sunke
in the sea, and they all perist.

Hard by this abbey, within a stone's cast, is the ruines of a faire
castell. The iland is about three miles longe and one mile over; thir
is booth pasture and corne grownd sufficient for the inhabitants, and

Dr. Raine's comprehensive account of the medieval traditions relating to Saint Cuthbert,
I find no allusion to this exercise of his supernatural power. The only incident having
any resemblance to it is said to have happened in 1069 as the priests of Durham were
removing his body to Lindisfarne. When they reached the strand opposite the island, "as
it happened to be full tide, they found the passage across hid under the waves, and, in
addition to this sad mishap, the night was dark and stormy, and no shelter was at hand.
Those who were advanced in years began to tremble at the prospect before them, when
on a sudden the sea opened its breast and laid bare the track upon which they were anxious
to tread." (Saint Cuthbert. By James Raine, M.A. 4to. Durham, 1828, p. 63.) We
should hardly have expected our shrewd and intelligent travellers to have accepted with
so much complacency from the rude inhabitants of Lindisfarne so gross a delusion as the
marvellous story of the Sunday tide.

[a] Upon Holy Island stood the first Christian church that was erected between the Tees
and the Frith of Forth. Of this church not a vestige now remains, and a second structure
reared upon its foundations is now level with the ground. The church of the Priory of
Holy Island, which Mr. Rawdon calls the Abbey Church of Saint Cuthbert, was built
towards the close of the eleventh century under the auspices of Carileph and Lambard
successively Bishops of Durham. Considerable remains of this church are yet standing,
and are of a highly interesting character. The carved work of the pillars and arches,
noticed by Mr. Rawdon, presents the peculiar variety of decoration that distinguishes the
ecclesiastical architecture of that early period. The parish church of Lindisfarne, which
stands half a stone's throw from the church of the priory, was erected half a century
later, and is of the early-English style. It is now undergoing the process of restoration.
(See Hist. and Antiq. of North Durham. By the Rev. James Raine. Folio. Lond. 1852,
p. 137.)

the best and most juiciest rabitts that England affords.[a] ·In this iland, uppon the sea shore, are found severall little round stones which in the midst haith a little starr or mullet, which they call Saint Cuthbert's beades;[b] and without doubt they made rosaryies of them in former times.

Here they staid from eight in the morninge till one in the after none, att which time they see people goe over, some on foote and some on horsebacke, and soe they went to Belford againe, where they lodged that night; this iland affords store of greate lobsters and severall sortes of fresh fish.

This constant course of the sea on Sundayes may be compared and is no lesse wonderfull then the sabatticall river soe much spoken of in histories that every Sunday stands still.

To this iland were thosse tow saints of thesse latter times, Harry Martin and Alderman Tichborne, confind.[c]

[a] There was at Holy Island a valuable rabbit warren belonging to the see of Durham, which was under the superintendence of a keeper specially appointed by the bishop. In 1528, Wolsey, then Bishop of Durham, granted a lease of the warren at the yearly rent of 4*l.* (Raine's Hist. and Antiq. of North Durham, p. 156.)

[b]   On a rock by Lindisfarne
                        Saint Cuthbert sits, and toils to frame
                        The sea-born beads that bear his name.

Saint Cuthbert's beads (entrochites, or encrinites), are single joints of the stem of the fossil lily. They are round, and have always a marginal milling, and sometimes a radiation over the face. (See Phillips's Geology of Yorkshire, vol. ii.) They still occur in abundance at Lindisfarne, and are found in other localities. In Scotland they are known as " Witch Beads," and on the shores of Germany as "the Beads of Saint Boniface." (Hist. Mem. of Northumberland. By W. S. Gibson, Esq. London, 1862, p. 6.)

[c] The fact of either of these regicides having being imprisoned in Holy Island is not mentioned by Noble. He states, that, after three or four removes, Martin was confined in Chepstow Castle, where he died in great destitution and misery in the year 1681. (Mem. of the Regicides, vol. ii. p. 58.) A more cruel punishment cannot be imagined for the gay and witty and somewhat dissolute Harry Martin, than to be immured in the desolate fortress of Lindisfarne, a tall circular tower perched upon the lofty summit of a rocky pinnacle at the most remote extremity of the island, exposed on every side to the bitter winds and storms of the Northern sea.

Of the fate of Alderman Tichborne a touching story is disclosed by the State Papers. Two years' confinement in the wretched castle of Holy Island had ruined his health. In

Munday, the 11th, they went from Belford to Morpieth, beinge 24 miles, of which we have allredie spooken.

Tuesday, the 12th, they went to New-Castle, and on Wednesday they went downe the river to the Shields, a towne att the bottome of the river, about 7 miles from Newcastle, where the ships most of them ride to lade thir coales; here they boile salt water, and make greate quantities of white salt,* but itt causeth such a smooke that one would thinke the towne were on fire. This towne affords good store of exclent sea fish, of which they had severall sortes boild in salt water.

From hence they went to Tinmouth Castell, beinge about halfe a mile of, a large and stronge place itt is, situated uppon a rock over the sea, att the very mouth of the river Tine; itt is well for-tefied, haith very good guns, and a good guard of soldiers that doe constantly keepe itt, of which was then captain a worthy gentleman,

January, 1663, he was so lame and infirm that his wife petitioned the king for leave to send a servant to him, and her request was complied with. In March following she again petitioned the King. Her husband was weak and ill, and she not able to administer the help necessary for the preservation of his life. She prayed that he might be removed to some other place. More than six months passed and nothing was done. The anxious wife, dreading the approach of winter, wrote to Bennet, Secretary of State, to propitiate his favour, and to urge that her petition might be granted. Her husband was weak and ill, and another winter would endanger his life. Her pleading prevailed. In the fol-lowing March we find Tichborne a prisoner in Dover Castle, and his wife again a suitor to the King. In her petition she expresses her thanks for her husband's removal from Holy Island, whereby his condition was much bettered, and asks permission for herself, two children, and a maid-servant to remain with him in the castle. In May the royal clemency was extended to her, a warrant was issued to Captain John Strode, Lieutenant of Dover Castle, "to permit Ann Tichborne with her two children and maid-servant to see her husband, Robert Tichborne, and, if she pleased, remain shut up with him in prison." (Cal. State Papers, 1662-3-4.)

* The first source of any great emolument to South Shields seems to have been the manufacture of salt. *Salinæ de ferro pro sale bulliend.* are mentioned in documents of the fifteenth century. In the reign of Charles I. the salt-pans attracted settlers to South Shields. In 1667 there were 121 salt-pans in use, and in 1696, when the salt trade had reached its height, the number of pans amounted to 143. The trade has since gradually decreased, and half a century ago only five salt-pans remained. (Surtees' Hist. of Durham, vol. ii. p. 94.) The salt-pans used at Shields were the largest used anywhere in Great Britain. (Dr. Brownrigg on the Art of making Common Salt. 8vo. London, 1748, p. 52.)

Captain Guillims, who was of thosse that killed Ascham, Oliver's ambassador in Madrid.[a]   Thir is within itt a prettie faire church gon much to decay, but since, I heare, repaired; itt haith a bowlinge greene, and convenient howses for thosse that live thirin; itt haith a faire watch tower lately built, where every night all the yeare longe thir is a greate coale fire made to be a guide to ships that saile into that port.   One Collonell Moyer,[b] a greate sticler in Oliver's time, was here prisner.   Here they were very courteously entertaind by Capt. Guillims' lady, he beinge then absent.

Thursday, the 14th, they went from thence to Durham, of which we have allredie spoken; here they see the bishop, Dr. Cossens, a gallant old gentleman, who carries him selfe with the grandeur of a prince.[c]

Fryday, the 15th, they went from Durham to North Allarton, of which we have allredy spoken.

[a] A more cruel and atrocious murder was never committed. Anthony Ascham was the author of a treatise published in 1648, entitled "Of the Confusions and Revolutions of Government," which gave offence to the King's party. In 1650 he was sent by the Parliament to be the English envoy at the Court of Spain. Soon after his arrival at Madrid, he and his interpretor John Baptista Riva were assassinated, in the house where they lodged, by six exiled royalists. Captain John Guillim, whom Mr. Rawdon coolly designates a worthy gentleman, was at the head of the murderers. His confederates were William Spark, Valentine Progers, John Halsall, William Arnett, and Henry Progers. They were tried at Madrid and condemned to die; but after a short imprisonment had an opportunity given them to make their escape, which was successfully accomplished by all except one, who happened to be a Protestant, and he was sent back to prison and beheaded. (See Clarendon, vol. iii. p. 564. Harl. Miscell. vol. iv. p. 280.)

[b] The person whom Mr. Rawdon calls "one Colonel Moyer" was Captain Lawrence Moyer of Low Leighton in Essex, Warden of the Trinity House. Soon after the Restoration he was charged with disaffection to the government, and his house was searched for concealed arms. In February, 1661, information was given to the Secretary of State that Captain Moyer, three years before, had declared the murder of the late King to be a piece of heroic justice, and Bradshaw the best patriot that ever lived. (Cal. State Papers, 1660-61, p. 517.) In January, 1664, we find him a prisoner in the Tower, and ordered to be sent to Tynemouth. (Ib. 1663-4, p. 461.)

[c] Dr. John Cosin, Bishop of Durham, 1660 to 1671. "Among the many liberal and high-minded prelates who had held the see of Durham, the name of Cosin stands eminently distinguished for munificence and public spirit." (Surtees, vol. i. p. cix.)

Saturday, the 16th, they went from North Allarton to Yorke, vizt. Mr. Rawdon, Mr. Bowyer, Captain Baker, and Mr. Rawdon's sarvant, with which they gave a conclusion to thir Scotch journie, which was very pleasant to them, they nott havinge the least disaster, niether to them selves nor horses, havinge all the way exclent weather. Here they rested them selves att Yorke till Thursday the 29th September, beinge Michaelmasse day, att which time they went to a towne called Malton, 14 miles from Yorke, where thir is kept the greatest horse faire in England;[a] also itt is a greate faire for cattle, and other comodities which booth English and Scotch sell thir. Here they see the ruines of a castle and monastery,[b] likewisse a faire howse built of free stone by my Lord Euers.[c] This towne now belongeth to tow daughters, coheires of the Lord Euers.

Fryday, the 30th September, they went to Scarborow, a sea towne of which we have allredy spooke some thinge; itt haith a reasonable good port for shippinge, and a large castle in which is a garison of soldiers; itt is seated uppon a high rock, and compast all about with the sea, save only towards the towne, where itt haith a narrow steepe comminge up to itt; itt haith within itt, uppon the top of a rocke, a springe of fresh water, and a well likewisse, from whence they draw fresh water, and haith within the walls above 25 akers of pasture ground; itt was built in the time of Kinge Stephen. Att the bottome of the towne, as I have formerly said, is a spaw,

[a]
> Veni Malton, artem laudo,
> Vendens equum sine cauda,
> Morbidum, mancum, claudum, cæcum,
> Forte si maneret mecum,
> Probo, vendo, pretium datur;
> Quid si statim moriatur?
> *Barnabæ Itiner.*

[b] The Gilbertine Priory at Old Malton, founded in the twelfth century.

[c] This house was built upon the site of the ancient castle of Malton by Ralph third Lord Eure, who succeeded to the title upon the death of his father in 1594. The two coheirs who were in possession when Mr. Rawdon was at Malton in 1664 shortly afterwards quarrelled respecting the partition of the estates, and in 1674 the house was pulled down, and the materials divided between them. The lodge still remains to attest the magnificence of the mansion that thus fell a sacrifice to a family feud.

very medicinable and much frequented by ladies that have a desire to be gott with child. Uppon the sea shore are gathered little pible stones very transparent and of severall coullers, as white, red, blew, and yeallow,[a] of which they gatherd some, and brought with them.

Saturday, the 1th October, they went from thence to a sea towne called Whitbie, 12 miles from thence, passinge by the sea side alonge Robin Hood's Bay; here att Whitbie is a reasonable good port and harbour for shippinge, and a place of prettie good trade. Uppon the top of the hill ajoyninge to this towne was a famous abbey for nuns, a great part of which church is yet standinge, by which one may guesse the magnificence of itt when itt was in itts perfection; this abbey was founded by Santa Hilda, a virtuous lady, desended of the blood royall of the kinges of the Northumbers; she was, about the yeare 680, the first abbesse thirof, on whom the cuntry people have this story: the country beinge full of woodes was much infested with snakes and hag wormes, which did much anoy the people, soo Santa Hilda, armed with faith and prayer, went out with a white rod in hir hand, strucke of one of thir heades, and chargd them, in the name of the livinge God, to depart from thence into the sea; which, they say, they did, and were turned into stone,[b] where they lie amongst the rockes, and are found, quantities of them, uppon the rockes, where thesse gentlemen, Mr. Rawdon and Mr. Bowyer, gatherd some and brought with them; they are very much like snakes, but all without heades.

[a] Ray notices the clear white pebbles found on the shores about Scarborough, "which (he says) by jewellers are polished and cut in the manner of diamonds and placed in rings." (Diary, August, 1661.) Beautiful agates, heliotropes, and jaspers are yet to be gathered on the sands at Scarborough after the wintry storms have caused the fall of some portions of the diluvial cliffs.

[b] The miracle performed by Saint Hilda was a favourite medieval legend. It is one of the stories that "Whitby's nuns exulting told" to while away the night they passed at Lindisfarne:

And how, of thousand snakes, each one
Was changed into a coil of stone
When holy Hilda prayed;
Themselves, within their holy bonnd,
Their stony folds had often found.

This abbey was formerly a place of much devotion, but now is turnd into a den of wild beasts; for, as they went in to see the church, thir bouncd out uppon them a brasse of fatt buckes, this place now servinge as a padocke to Sir Hugh Cholmley, to whome the place doth belonge.[a] Here uppon the sea shore they did much please them selves to see the sports of nature, producinge severall sortes of stones, some painted of severall coullers, others rounde and sharp poynted, about the length of ones finger, which the country people call thunderbolts; other stones like wormes and snakes, &c.[b]

Munday, the 3d of October, they went from thence to Malton, 20 miles of, where they past a barren moore above ten miles over every way, with soe much wind as they could hardly sitt thir horses; thir they lodgd that night, and on

Tuesday the 4th they went from Malton to Yorke, where they rested them selves till Satturday the 15th of October, att which time they went to Hull, where they staid the next day, Sunday, where in the eaveninge, after sermon, they went to see the Lady Thomson[c]

---

[a] In the year 1664, when Mr. Rawdon visited Whitby Abbey, the title and estates of this branch of the family of Cholmley had devolved upon a minor, Sir Hugh Cholmley, baronet, who died in his infancy shortly afterwards. He was the grandson of Sir Hugh Cholmley of civil war notoriety, whose autobiography was privately printed in 1787. A correspondent of Thomas Gent, the old York printer, thus describes the ruin as it stood in the early part of the last century: "Forlorn and roofless appears the edifice, which is so far demolished that it is very perilous for any person to enter therein. To prevent which danger the lord of the manor, Hugh Cholmley, esquire, has inclosed it with a high wall adorned with a pair of iron gates." (Gent's Hist. of Hull—Addenda.) The Cholmleys have been for more than three centuries negligent guardians of the fine remains of the church of the Benedictine Abbey of Whitby, a church that was hardly surpassed in architectural magnificence by that of any other English monastery. " It is a matter of deep regret that the great tower and other conspicuous parts should have fallen within our own memory." (Phillips's Yorkshire, p. 140.)

[b] "All along in the cliffs and on the shore [at Whitby] are found in great plenty the serpent-stones, called by naturalists in Latin cornua ammonis. We found also plenty of the lapides belemnites, or thunder-stones." (Ray's Itin. August, 1661. Memorials, p. 147.) A friend informs me that the name of "thunderbolts" is given in Shetland to the early stone knives. The lightning, as the people think, cannot strike the house in which one of them is kept.

[c] Lady Thompson was the wife of Sir Henry Thompson, knight, of Middlethorpe near York, an alderman of that city and Lord Mayor in 1672. She was one of the daughters

and hir daughters, as also Alderman Dobson and his lady, where
they were very nobly treated, and Mr. Bowyer and he they next day
invited to dinner, where some of the chiefe ladies of the towne were
invited to keepe them company.   On Munday in the morninge they
tooke a view of the towne, which was founded by Edward the First,
and called King's towne uppon Hull, to which he granted severall
privilidges: itt is a place of greate trade, and walled about and
moted; they can, when they please, drowne allmost three miles
about them.   Itt haith severall block houses well furnist with ordnance towards the sea, and haith a convenient haven for ships.
Kinge Henry the Sixt granted them a maior and sherife, and
William de la Pole, knight, father to Michael de la Pole, Earle of
Suffolke, was the first maior thir of.   They have tow churches, a
towne-howse, and a Trinitie howse for orderinge of sea affaires,
where thir is an hospitall for pore seamen's wives.   Thir they see the
statue of a Groinland man, which was taiken att sea, sittinge in a
little boat of about tow yards longe, and about halfe a yarde or more
brood; in the midle of the boote thir is a hole just to hold his body,
wher he sitts with his oares in his hand, and a dart to throw att fish;
the boote beinge all coverd, save that hole which he fills, soe that
noe water can gett in to sinke itt.   If one of his oares had not brooke,
he had nott bene taiken.   He had a blacke leather coate over him,
and a thin pece of boord over his face like a boon grace.   It is a
curiositie much worth the seeinge.[a]

of William Dobson, merchant and alderman of Hull, and twice mayor of that town. This
Sir Henry Thompson founded an hospital for old men in his native parish of Saint Mary
Castlegate at York. He died in 1692. He was of a different family from the Thompsons
mentioned in note [c], p. 75, *ante*.

　[a] Ray, who saw this curiosity in 1661, says, "The Groenlander has on his forehead a
thing like a trencher which serves as a *bonne-grâce* to fence his eyes from the sun, and it
may be too from the dashing of the water." (Memorials, p. 135.) Gent tells us that
Captain Andrew Barker took the Groenlander upon the sea (in his boat, with all these
implements still preserved, except the natural body, for which the effigy is substituted) in
the year 1613. But so ill did this seeming son of Neptune brook his captivity, that, re-
fusing to eat what was offered him, he died in three days' time. (Annales Regioduni
Hullini. By Thomas Gent. 8vo. York, 1735, p. 38.)

From Hull, in the eveninge, they went to a towne called Beverly, six miles of; this is a faire market towne, haith a faire cathedrall, where St. John of Beverly archbishop of Yorke, a man of greate pietie and learninge, was buried.   Our English kings held the memory of this John to be sacred, espesially Kinge Athelstane, who for his sake granted greate previlidges to this towne.   In the church, betwixt the picture of the kinge and the saint, is writt, as spooke from the kinge:

> " As free make I thee
> As hearte may thinke or eie may see."

Also itt had granted the priviledges of a sanctuary, soe that bank-rupts and men suspected of aney capitull crime, worthy of death, might be free and saife thir from the danger of the law, if they got but to sitt in the free stoole which they see thir in the cathedrall, beinge a greate marble chaire, whole and entier to this day, about which was writt in lattin to this purposse: "This seate of stone is called freedstoole, that is, the chaire of peace, unto which what of-fender soe-ever flieth and cometh, haith all manner of securitie."[a]

Much more is to be said of this towne; but, nott to make this booke to big, I will remitt you to Mr. Rawdon's journall, who haith writt very largely of itt.

From thence they came to Yorke, Tuesday the 18th October, where they rested till Munday the 24th, att which time they went to Stearsbie, 9 miles from Yorke, where they lodged that night att his cossen Hebden's.   The next day they dind att that worthy gentleman's Mr. Marmaduke Cholmeley,[b] lord of the manner of

---

[a] Mr. Rawdon, in his account of Beverley, closely follows Camden.   (See Britannia. Holland's transl. p. 711.)

[b] The founder of the Yorkshire families of Cholmley was Sir Roger Cholmley, knight of the body to King Henry VIII., who sprang from a younger branch of the antient house of the Cholmondeleys of Cheshire.   Having married a daughter of Sir Marmaduke Constable, knight, of Flamborough, Sir Roger settled himself at Roxby near Pickering in the North Riding.   He died in 1538, and was succeeded by his eldest son Sir Richard Cholmley, knight, of Roxby, who was the purchaser of Whitby and other estates in that neighbourhood.   Sir Richard made two illustrious marriages.   His first wife was a

Bransbie and Stearsbie. That eavéninge my Lord Fairfax came to thir lodginge to vizitt them, and invited thom to his castle att Guillinge the next day, but Mr. Bowyer and he were preingaged to dine with his nephew Squier Alanson att Crake Castell; but they promised to waite uppon his lordship before they went out of the country; soe Squier Cholmely, Mr. Rawdon, and Mr. Bowyer went the next day to Crake Castell to dinner, where they staid till Fryday, att which time Squier Alanson, Mr. Rawdon, and Mr. Bowyer had an invitation from Sir Salomon Swale, Mr. Rawdon's schoolfellow, to his howse att Stancley,[a] a gallant seate about 14 miles from thence, were they went, and staid thire till the 2th of November, all which time they were very nobly entertaind by Sir Salomond and his lady, into whosse chamber after supper they were severall times invited to banquetts of sweet meats,[b] she beinge of a longe

daughter of William Lord Conyers ; his second was a daughter of Henry Clifford, first Earl of Cumberland. The Cholmeleys of Brandsby, of whom, in Mr. Rawdon's time, Marmaduke Cholmeley, esquire, was the head, descended from the first marriage. The Roxby and Whitby estates passed to the descendants of Sir Richard by his second wife.

Brandsby and Stearsby (the birth-place of Lawrence Rawdon and his brothers) were held as one manor by Mr. Marmaduke Cholmeley, as they had been by Cnut before the Conquest. The Christian name of Marmaduke was, doubtless, adopted by the Rawdons of Stearsby as a mark of respect for their chief feudal lord.

[a] South Stainley Hall, the residence of Sir Solomon Swale, baronet, stood in a picturesque and fertile part of Yorkshire, near the valley of the Nidd, half way between Ripon and Harrogate. The house was demolished in the early part of the last century, but some indications still remain of its having been " a gallant seat." In 1717, or 1718, the materials of the hall were purchased by " Chancellor Aislabie," the owner of Studley, and used in building a tower which now crowns a conspicuous eminence called How-hill, above the ruins of Fountains Abbey. The baronetcy became extinct upon the death, without male issue, of the fourth possessor of the title, Sir Sebastian Fabian Enrique Swale, whose father had settled as a merchant at Malaga.

[b] In the seventeenth century, " when the party rose from the dinner-table, they proceeded to what was then called the banquet, which was held in another apartment, and often in the garden-house. At the banquet the choice wines were brought forth, and the table was covered with pastry and sweetmeats, of which our forefathers were extremely fond." (Wright's Domestic Manners and Sentiments in England during the Middle Ages, p. 467.) At an earlier period the rere-supper *(arrière souper)* was called the banquet in France. (Ibid. p. 387.)

accquentance with Mr. Rawdon; and hir sister married to a cossen germane of his, Squier Barton of Cauton Hall. Whilst they staid here, Squier Swale, Sir Sallomon's son, went with them to shew them the ruines of that once famous abbey of Fountaines, by whosse ruines one may see itt haith bene a goodly thinge; thir they see the biggest seller that ever they see in thir lives, beinge above 100 yards in length, and haith in itt tow rowes of stone pillers strongly archt over, havinge a faire walke above them; itt haith a brooke of water runninge thorow itt, and thir is yet remaininge a faire large round stone in which they did wash thir glasses, canns, and potts.[a] Mr. Rawdon, in his journall, haith made a large relation of what he observed of this abbey, to which I refer you.

Wedensday, the 2th November, they went from Stainely[*] with Squier Alanson to Crake Castell, where the staid till Fryday the 4th November, att which time they went to Thursk, a greate markett towne where was formerly a stronge castell; here Robart Mowbray displaid his banner of rebellion, callinge in the Kinge of Scotts against his naturall soveraigne Kinge Henry the 2d, who in reward of his treason distroyed his castle, and gave the towne to one more deservinge then him selfe. From thence they went to Carlton Miniot, a small lordship of Mr. Rawdon, and from thence to Rascalfe,[b] to his nephew Mr. Henry Jaques, where they were very nobly entertained, and staid thir till

---

[a] Fresh from the convivialities of Stainley Hall, the admiration of Mr. Rawdon and his friends was more excited by what they supposed to have been a stupendous wine-cellar than by any other part of the magnificent remains of the abbey of Fountains, which was one of the noblest monastic foundations in the kingdom. The greater portion of that which they mistook for the cellar was the great cloister or ambulatory, vaulted, and divided into two aisles by pillars. A large octagonal stone basin standing in the east aisle had originally been a lavatory.

[b] Raskelfe, a village near Easingwold, where Sir Roger Jaques held a mansion-house and land under a lease for lives granted by the Bishop of Chester in 1640. (Gill's Vallis Eboracensis, p. 119.) In the "Catalogue of the Lords, Knights, and Gentlemen that have compounded for their Estates (London, 1655,)" this entry appears :—" Sir Roger Jaques of York, knight, with 8l. p. an. settled, 258l." Mr. Henry Jaques was Sir Roger's second son.

Munday the 7th of November, they went to Coxwould, by some called Cuckcold, a towne belonginge to my lord Falconbridge; here is a faire free schoole founded by one Sir John Harte,[a] of which more att large in Mr. Rawdon's journall. From hence they rid closse by Biland Abey built by Robart Mowbray in William Rufus his time; the walls are yet standinge, which sheweth the bignesse thir of. A mile from hence they past by a towne called Wasse, famous for bleachinge of lin clooth, where they see above a thousand webbs a whiteinge, the waters thir beinge very convenient for that purposse.[b]

From thence they went to a place called Kirbiemooreside, a towne of no small consideration, and now belongs to my lord Duke of Buckingham.

From hence they went to a pore towne called Lessengham, where they lodgd in a poore ale howse, and had a very stout bed that would not yield an inch to no man; and the trueth is, by reason of the meane accomodation they had thir, they were affraid they were gott againe into Scotland; and itt is nott much unlike itt, beinge in the mores of Yorkshire. Here in this towne is a very antient fashiond church, and in the churchyard tombe stones of much antiquitie, some beinge about the length and bignesse of a man, carved, others plaine, others with stone croses croslett att heade and feete, others made in forme of a pyrimid. Ten miles from this place they herd thir was a church sunke in this towne, but examininge the busnesse they found itt was this church, which was built uppon a faire vault and arches, haith tow rowes of stronge pillars, and resembles much St.

[a] The grammar-school at Coxwold was founded in 1603 by Sir John Harte, knight, citizen and grocer, Sheriff of London 1579, and Lord Mayor 1589.

[b] Wasse is a small village in the upper part of the secluded valley which is now adorned by the magnificent ruins of the Cistercian monastery and church of Byland, planted there by the Mowbrays in the twelfth century. It is a curious fact that the process of bleaching webs of linen cloth should have been carried on in this obscure spot to so great an extent two centuries ago. Probably at that period the manufacture of linen still flourished in the neighbouring towns of Thirsk, Kirbymoorside, and Malton. As early as in the reign of Henry II. the weavers of those towns were of sufficient importance to be specially named in a charter by which that monarch confirmed the privileges of the weavers' guild of York.

Faith's under Paul's, and I believe in former times did serve them to say masse in on some sollemne dayes; within a stone's cast of this church, on the side of a hill, was an abey.[a] This towne belonged to the Blundevills, and is the parish where Ralph Trattle,[b] Mr. Rawdon's cossen german, was borne, and the church where he was baptized.

Tusday, the 8th November, they went from thence; and 9 miles of, they past by Slingbie Castle, a place built by the Mowbrayes, Earles of Northumberland, and now belonges to the Duke of New-castle,[c] who haith lately re-edified the same.

From thence they went to Sherriffe Hutton, where they lodgd that night; here is the walls of an antient large castle, called Sheriffe Hutton Castle, was built by one Sir Bertram Bulmer, and repaired by Ralph Nevill, the first Earle of Westmerland, and when Kinge James came into England itt belonged to the Crowne, and was begd of him by one Lumbsdell, a Scott, who puld of the leade and sold itt with the iron and timber that was about itt, and left only the bare walls standinge.[d] Itt is most gallantly seated, and to

[a] In the seventh century, Lestingham, situated in a remote part of the wild and desolate moors of the North Riding, was chosen for the site of a Benedictine monastery by Cedde, a monk of Lindisfarne, afterwards bishop of the East Saxons. The "very antient fashioned church" admired by Mr. Rawdon is yet standing. The crypt or underchurch, which he compares to Saint Faith's under Paul's (see Stow's Survey of London, by Thoms, p. 123) exhibits manifest proofs of the most early antiquity. The large square pedestal, the short circular column, the rudely-sculptured capital, and the absence of ribbed groining, indicate that the church of Lestingham, if not the original building of Cedde, is at least the most antient ecclesiastical structure in the kingdom. (Raine's Hist. and Antiq. of North Durham, p. 55.)

[b] Ralph Trattle, esquire, of Greenwich, married Jane Rawdon, one of the daughters of Sir Marmaduke. In the earlier half of the seventeenth century a family of this name was living at Appleton-le-Street, in Rydale, not far distant from Lestingham. (Dugd. Visit. Surtees Vol. p. 368.)

[c] William Cavendish, first Marquis and Duke of Newcastle, distinguished for his loyalty in the civil war. Slingsby Castle, now in ruins, was re-edified by his brother Sir Charles Cavendish who died in 1653.

[d] The massive fragments that still remain of this antient stronghold of the great baronial families of Bulmer and Neville indicate its former extent and magnificence. In

be seene from all parts of the cuntry; they see itt att Fountaine
Abbey 20 miles from thence.

Wedensday, 9th November, after they had well viewd the ruines
of this castle, they went to Yorke, where they staid till Munday, the
5th December, att which time they went to Leedes, of. which we
have allredie spooken; from thence they went to Rawdon, where is
the antient howse from whence this familie descends; here they
founde in the mannor howse, which is an antient howse built of
free stone, thir kinsman Mr. Francis Rawdon,[a] an antient gentleman
of about fower score yeares of age, and then lord of the mannor, and
father to Sir George Rawdon who lives now in Ireland.   Here they
were very much made of, and the next day they went to Yorke,
where they staid till Saturday the 10th of December, att which time
they were invited to Crake Castle, Mr. Rawdon neice, Madam
Allanson, beinge brought to bed of a boy; soe Mr. Rawdon and
Mr. Bowyer were godfathers, and the child was called Marmaduke.
Here they were highly feasted, and staid till Satturday the 17th, att
which time they went to see thir kinsman Mr. Barton of Cawton
Hall; this hall belonged to Mr. Rawdon's grandfather, who was lord
of the towne, and in this howse Mr. Rawdon's mother was borne.
Here they were civilly entertaind, and on Munday they were invited

the year 1624 a survey of the manor of Sheriff Hutton, which then belonged to the
Prince of Wales, afterwards King Charles I., was made by John Norden the elder and
John Norden the younger, by virtue of a royal commission. It contains this statement:—
"The bowels of this worthy pyle and defensive house are rent and torn, and the naked
carcase lately, as is affirmed, by his Majesty aliened in fee, among other things, to one
Lumsden, or Lindsdon." (See Speculi Britanniæ Pars. By John Norden, 1594, Camden
Soc. Vol. p. xxix. Castellum Huttonicum. By George Todd. 8vo. York, 1824, p. 36.)

  [a] In the diary of the eminent Puritan minister, Oliver Heywood, it is noted that in
May, 1666, he visited Rawden, where a very old Mr. Rawden resided, at whose house
he preached to a large auditory; and in the spring of the following year he spent a
Sunday at Mr. Rawden's at Rawden, and conducted a service, which he concluded the
earlier because Dr. Hitch, the Dean of York and Rector of Guiseley, in which parish
Mr. Rawdon lived, was "to pay that antient gentleman a visit that day, which he did."
Mr. Rawdon died on the 25th April, 1668, nearly 86 years of age. (The Life of Oliver
Heywood. By the Rev. Joseph Hunter, F.S.A. London, 1842, pp. 176, 191, 209.)

by my Lord Fairfax to his castell of Gillinge, where they were very nobly entertaind.   On Tusday the 20th they went to his nephew Jaqueses, to Rascalfe, and from thence the next day to Yorke, beinge St. Thomas his day, where they staid till

Tuesday, the 10th January, in which time they, all that Christmasse, were highly feasted by the Lord Maior and Aldermen, the chiefe of the clergie, and gentry; after which, the 10th of January, Mr. Rawdon, Mr. Bowyer, Mr. Akeroid,[a] and Mr. Rawdon's man, and his foote boy, itt beinge a hard cleere frost, came from Yorke to Tadcaster, through which runs the river Wharfe, wher all the free stone was shipt that built Yorke Minster.[b]   From thence they went to Shirborne, a place famous for makinge of pins, and abondance of cherries;[c] in the way they past a small river, called Cock, which when the greate battaile was fought on Palme Sunday betwixt Kinge Henry the Sixt and Edward the Fourth, the slaughter of men was soe greate that itt changd the water into a bloodie couller.[d]

[a] Mr. Henry Akeroyd, a York merchant, younger son of Henry Akeroyd, esquire, of Foggathorpe, in the East Riding. The family became connected with York by the marriage of a sister of the elder Henry Akeroyd to Christopher Herbert, the father of Sir Thomas Herbert, baronet.

[b] Great part of the stone used in the building of York minster was got from a quarry originally belonging to the Percys, in a place called Thevesdale, a few miles south of Tadcaster. It was brought from thence to the river Wharfe at Tadcaster and there shipped for York. "Anno 1400. In cariagio xxxiiij damlad lapidum a quarera de Thevedale per carectas usque Tadcastre per Ricardum de Stutton 6*l*. 6*s*. 8*d*. In cariagio xliij damlad corumdem lapidum per navem de Tadcastre usque Ebor. per eundem Ricardum, 8*l*. 12*s*." (The Fabric Rolls of York Minster. By the Rev. James Raine. Surtees Soc. Vol. p. 29.) Similar entries are of frequent occurrence in the Rolls.

[c] In the topographical dictionaries of the latter part of the seventeenth century Sherburne is said to be noted for its pins and cherries, and Aberford, a neighbouring town, to be famous only for making of pins. No pins are now made at either place, and, instead of cherries, Sherburne has long been famous for producing in great abundance a species of plum called winesour. This delicious fruit is peculiar to Yorkshire, and attains the highest perfection where magnesian limestone is the substratum of the soil.

[d]   Small Cock, a sullen brook, comes to her succour then,
   Whose banks received the blood of many thousand men,
   On sad Palme Sunday slaine, that Towton field we call,
   Whose channel quite was chok'd with those that there did fall.—*Poly-olbion* p. 141.

From thence they went to Doncaster, of which we have allredie
spooke, where they lodgd that night.

Wedensday, 11th January, they went from Doncaster to Newarke,
a maior towne, haith a faire church, a faire quadrangle for the
market place, and a stately castle built by Alexander, a Norman,
Bishop of Lincolne; closse by which runneth the river of Trent;
here they lodged that night.

Thursday, the 12th January, they went from Newarke to Grantham; the church of this towne haith a spire which is held to be the .
highest in England. From thence they went to Stamford, a maior
towne, haith four parish churches, in one of which they see a faire
tombe of the Lord Burliegh, Earle of Exeter; itt had a castle and
small universitie or some colleges, but all distroyed, as also was
the towne, by the civill warrs of Yorke and Lancaster, and haith
hardly recovered itt selfe; itt is walld about. Here they lodgd
that night.

Fryday, the 13th January, they went from Stamford to Huntington, of which we have allredie spooken, and from thence to
Kaxton, where they lodgd that night. Nere Stamford is to be scene
part of the Roman high way which went from London into Scotland.[a]

Satturday, the 14th January, the frost continuinge hard and
cleere, they from Kaxston went to Royston, from thence to Pucaridge,
and from Puccaridge to Warre, a greate towne belonginge to my
Lord Fanshaw.[b] This towne tooke the name from a ware or dam

---

[a] The Roman way from London to the north, called the Ermyne Street, passed through
Brig-Casterton, near Stamford.

[b] In the reign of Queen Elizabeth, Ware was purchased by Thomas Fanshawe, esquire,
whose grandson, Henry Fanshawe, was made a Knight of the Bath at the coronation of
Charles I. In 1641 he took the King's side, to the great prejudice of his fortune, and at
the Restoration he was rewarded with an Irish peerage. Lady Fanshawe, the wife of Sir
Richard Fanshawe, baronet, of Ware Park, a younger brother of Lord Fanshawe, relates
in her memoirs an incident which shows that the Rawdons of Hoddesdon were upon
friendly terms with her family. In May, 1645, she was on her way from Oxford to join
her husband at Bristol. "We were to ride all night," she says, "for fear of the enemy

that was made to catch fish, and did formerly belonge to the Baron
Wake, who turned the London highway into the north, from
Heartford thether, beinge then a very small poore towne; but by
this meanes came to enrich itt selfe, and haith many good inns in itt,
and much talkt on for a greate bed which is in the St. George
Inne, called the greate bed of Ware.

From thence they went 3 miles farther to Hodsden,[a] the place of
Mr. Rawdon's aboode, a faire market towne which formerly did
belonge to Henry Bourchier, Earle of Essex,[b] who had nere unto itt
a faire howse. Itt haith bene much adorned of late by the famely
of the Rawdons, who have built here tow faire bricke howses, and
Sir Marmaduke Rawdon did, att his owne proper cost and charges,
much beawtifie itt with a conduit of water, which in the shape of the
Samaritan woman, of free stone, with a pitcher in hir hand, doth fill
water to the service of the whole towne.[c] Here they concluded thir

surprising us as we passed, they quartering in the way. About nightfall, having travelled
about twenty miles, we discovered a troop of horse coming towards us, which proved to
be Sir Marmaduke Rawdon, a worthy commander, and my countryman; he told me, that,
hearing I was to pass by his garrison, he was come out to conduct me, he hoped as far as
was danger, which was about twelve miles; with many thanks we parted, and, having re-
freshed ourselves and horses, we set forth for Bristol." (Memoirs of Lady Fanshawe.
8vo. Lond. 1830, p. 66.)

[a] Hoddesdon, a town in Hertfordshire about seventeen miles distant from London, on
the road to Ware. The Thatched-house at Hoddesdon is immortalised by "honest Izaak"
in the opening dialogue of his "Complete Angler." *Piscator.*—"I have stretch'd my
legs up Totnam-hill to övertake you, hoping your business may occasion you towards
Ware, whither I am going this fine fresh May morning." *Venator.*—"Sir, I shall
almost answer your hopes; for my purpose is to drink my morning's draught at the
Thatched-house in Hodsden."

[b] The possessor of Hoddesdon in Henry VII's time was Sir William Say, who had
only two daughters, Elizabeth married to William Lord Montjoy, and Mary to Henry
Bourchier, Earl of Essex, and upon them he settled the manor of Hoddesdon and
other estates. King Henry VIII. by charter granted to the Earl of Essex and his lady
a market on Thursdays at Hoddesdon. (Salmon's Hist. of Hertfordshire. Fol. 1728,
p. 22.)

[c] "Hoddesdon having no convenience of good water very near it, one of the ancestors
of Mr. Rawdon laid pipes from a spring at some distance to serve his house where Mr.

six monthes travailes, in all which journie they had but one day of
rainie weather, though many times itt did raine in the night sufficient
to lay the dust, niether had they the lest mischance hapned to them,
thir sarvants, or horses, which was a great blessinge, for which I
hope they gave hartie thankes to God Allmightie, who doubtlesse
sent his good angell alonge with them; and soe I will conclude this
journie.

They were no soner come to Hodsden, but, as to give a pleasant
conclusion to thir pleasant journie, thir was an accidentall feastinge
prepared for them, and was that the next day, Sunday, they knowinge nothinge of itt till they came to Hodsden; thir nere kinswoman
Mrs. Martha Forster, daughter to one of Sir Marmaduke Rawdon's
daughters, was to be married, soe they were invited to waite uppon
the bride and bridgrome, where they spent most of that weeke in
mirth and feastinge.

I forgott to give you notice, that, whilst Mr. Rawdon was in Yorke
this winter, he was by the aldermen and gentry (who were wondrous
desicrous that he might stay and settle thir amongst them) desiered
to marry, and had tow very gentlewoemen booth for parts and fortune, booth widdows, the one was the Lady Key, sister to Sir
Henry St. Quintin, who had 400 pownds a yeare joynter, besides redie
monies and a howse well furnisht with plate and other nescesaries, a
sober discreet gentlewoman; the other was the widdow Stanhop,
who had 500 pownds per anum to give away to whome she should
please, and 400 pownds a yeare more duringe the minoritie of hir
yonge son; thesse were booth gentlewomen without exception, att
whosse howses he was severall times highly entertaind, had the
aprobation and well wishes of all thir freinds and the whole cittie;
but this pill of marriage seemd soe bitter to him, that he durst nott
venter to swallow itt; but sence his comminge away they have made

Rawdon now dwells. The waste water is of great use to the inhabitants hereabouts,
being brought from his house into the middle of the street, and running all day from a
conduit erected by that family." (Ibid.)

tow gentlemen very hapie, to whom they are married and live very well.[a]

After Mr. Rawdon's comminge to Hodsden, his kinsman and fellow travelor, Mr. Bowyer, went to his mother's howse att Layton, Mr. Rawdon remaininge for the most part att Hodsden, some times divertinge him selfe att London and Layton, and some times att Greenwich att the howse of his cossen germaine Mr. Ralph Trattle, till itt was the beginninge of July, att which time he thought his tow geldings might doe somethinge for thir meate; soe he resolved uppon a Westerne journie, att which time he assisted in puttinge his former sarvant Will. Raniel prentice to a furrier, and with his other sarvant Will. Coates, the 6th July, beinge a Thursday, the same day twelve monthes he sett forwards on his Northerne journie, soe holdinge itt to be a fortunate day, he sett forwards from Hodsden in company of his kinsman Mr. Marmaduke Rawdon and his sarvant William Coates, about six of the clocke in the morninge, and went from thence to Hartford, a shire towne where the assises for the countie are kept. Itt haith a castle built by one Ralph Limsey[b] in time of William the Conquerour; which afterwards fell into the King's hands, and was given by Kinge Edward the 3d to his son John of Gaunt, then Earle of Richmond, afterwards Duke of Lancaster, and father to Kinge Henry the 4th, and now belongs to the Earle of Salisbury. From hence they went to Hitchinge, a greate market towne, where they dind; from hence they went to Bedford, the shire towne, governd by a maior; itt haith 3 parish churches and formerly an hospitall for lepers; itt had a faire castle, built by

[a] Catherine, sister of Sir Henry St. Quintin, baronet, of Harpham in the East Riding, was first the wife of Michael, son of Sir George Wentworth, knight, of Woolley in the West Riding, and afterwards of Sir John Kaye, baronet, of Woodsome in the same Riding. Her third husband was Henry Sandes, esquire, of Downe in Kent. This sober discreet gentlewoman had, moreover, a fourth husband, Hugh, Earl of Eglinton. (Wotton's Baronetage, vol. ii. p. 276.) I am unable to identify the widow Stanhope.

[b] According to Camden, Ralph Limsey, a nobleman, built at Hertford, in William the Conqueror's time, a cell for Saint Alban's monks. "The castle it hath upon the river Lea was built, as men think, by Edward the elder." (Britannia, p. 407.)

Paine de Beauchamp, and afterwards taiken by King Stephen, and now converted into a curious bowlinge green, the chiefe thinge to be scene in the towne, from whence you have the prospect of the whole country.　Here Offa, Kinge of the Mercians, was buried. Through this towne runs the river Ouse.　When they came here, they found the judges att the assises, soe, good lodgings beinge scarse, they went from thence to Turvie, where they lodgd that night, where they had exelent fresh fish, pike, pearch, and clls, which thir landlord catcht after thir arivall thir; here they had most exclent beere and ale, and good French wine.　This towne is famous for a joviall tinker which they call the tinker of Turvey, and one of the inns of the towne haith him for a signe.

　Fryday, the 7th July, they went from Turvy to Northampton, the shire towne, where they dind; this is a goodly towne, bravely situated uppon a hill; itt haith very faire streets, faire howses, and a very faire market place; on the south side runneth the river Nen. This towne was formerly built of stone and walled about, is governd by a maior, and tow bailifs; here was a large castle built uppon a hill by Simon de Santo Lizio, comonly called Senlis, the first Earle of Northampton of that name, in the time of Kinge William Rufus,[a] but is now gon to decay.　From Northampton they went to see the ruines of Holdenbies howse, built by Sir Christopher Hatton in Queene Elizabeth's dayes, and did afterwards belong to the Kinge. Here the rebells kept our good Kinge Charles prisner, and afterwards distroyed the howse; itt haith only soe much of the walls and gates standinge as shewes that itt was a noble buildinge, and moves compasion in the beholders to see its ruines.[b]

　From thence they went to Daintry, where they lodged that night;

---

　[a] Simon de Saint Liz succeeded to the earldom of Northampton in 1153.　(The Descent of the Earldom of Lincoln.　By J. G. Nichols.　Lincoln Vol. Arch. Inst. p. 267.)

　[b] "Near Northampton is the ancient royal house of Holmeby, which was formerly in great esteem, and by its situation is capable of being made a truly royal palace.　But the melancholy reflection of the imprisonment of King Charles I. in this house, and his being violently taken hence again by the rebels, has cast a kind of disgrace upon the place, so that it has been forsaken."　(Defoe's Tour.)

here, within a mile of the towne, they see a famous fortification uppon a high hill, nere three miles in compasse, made by the Danes, where is often digd up old coynes of the Danes; a yeare agoe a laborer, digginge a dich here, found a man's scull with the iron head of a pike in itt.[a] Thir they see the ruines of an abbey which belonged to the Austin Friers: the armes of this towne is the picture of a Dane and a tree, so is called Danctric.

From hence, Saturday the 8th July, they went to Coventry, a pleasant cittie and of importance;[b] itt was walled about with free stone, but since the comminge in of Kinge Charles the 2d itt was commanded to be puld downe, partly for thir former rebellions, and partly to prevent the like. Thir buildinges are faire, and in the market place is a crosse of much workmanship, full of statues and rich worke;[c] haith tow faire churches, the one havinge a spire 300 foote high. Here they have a convenient towne howse with a faire kitchinge and larders thirto belonginge, where they have greate feastinge every yeare; but for this, and thir Lady Godiva, who rid naked thorrow the towne, whosse picture they have in thir towne

---

[a] "From Daventry we went a little out of the road to see a great camp called Burrow [Borough] Hill. They say this was a Danish camp, and everything hereabouts is attributed to the Danes, because of the neighbouring Daventry, which they suppose to have been built by them. The road hereabouts too being overgrown with Daneweed, they fancy it sprung from the blood of the Danes slain in battle, and that, if upon a certain day in the year you cut it, it bleeds. Originally it seems to have been Roman, but perhaps new modelled by the Danes." (Defoe's Tour.) Camden ascribes the construction of this remarkable fortification to Ostorius. "Much deceived are they who will needs have it to be a work of the Danes, and that of them the town under it was named Dantrey." (Britannia, p. 508.) Dane-weed, (*Eryngium campestre*.) Watling-Street thistle is the more common local name of this rare plant, whose only known habitat is the old Roman road. (Baker's Northamptonshire Glossary, vol. i. p. 172.)

[b] "Coventry, a large, fair, and walled city, and at this day it is the fairest city within land, whereof the chiefe trade of old was making round caps of wooll, but, the same being now very little used, the trade is decaied." (Moryson's Itinerary. Folio. 1617. Part III. p. 141.)

[c] The Coventry cross was erected in 1544 and wholly taken away in 1771. (Britton's Arch. Antiq. vol. i.)

CAMD. SOC. Y

hall on horsbacke, I shall refer you to Mr. Rawdon's journall of his
Westerne journie, where he haith sett downe the story at large.

From Coventry, after dinner, they went to Kenelworth Castell,
which Queene Elizabeth bestowed of my Lord of Licester, who
spared noe cost in the repairinge of itt; a goodly large thinge itt was,
pleasantly seated amongst woodes and parkes, but was distroyed by
the rebells in thesse late warrs. Thir is little standinge but the gate
howse, the walls, and some peces of towers, by which you may guesse
what itt was, and bewaile the destruction of itt.[a]

From thence they went to Warwick, where they lodgd that night
and the next day, Sunday; this towne is most pleasantly seated
uppon a hill or rocke risinge from the river Avon, over which is a
faire and stronge bridge, nere which standeth the castell, which was
much repaired by Sir Fulke Grevill, and by my Lord Brookes the
now lord thir of. Thir is in itt very faire and noble roumes, a bowlinge grene, gardens, orchards, and walkes of much curiositie, soe
that for strength and pleasantnesse thir is noe castle in England will
out doe itt, except itt be Windsor Castle.

Some say this towne was built by Gurguntus, the son of Beline,
375 yeares before the cominge of Christ; itt was formerly walled
about, as appeares by the pasages of the tow gates, which are hewne
out of the rock; itt haith tow churches, in one of which are stately
tombes of the Earles of Warwick, particularly one hardly to be

---

[a] The Norwich tourists in 1634 had the good fortune to visit the princely castle of Kenil-
worth before it lay "crushed under its own ruins, the monument of its owner's ambition."
" We were detayned one hour at that famous castle of Killingworth, where we were ushered
up a fayre ascent into a large and stately hall, the roofe whereof is all of Irish wood neatly
and handsomely fram'd. In it are five spacious chimneys answerable to so great a roome.
We next viewed the great chamber for the guard, the chamber of presence, the privy
chamber, fretted above richly with coats of arms, and all adorned with fayre and rich
chimney peeces of alabaster and black marble, and of joyner's worke in curious carv'd
wood; and all those fayre and rich roomes and lodgings in that spacious tower, not long
since built and repayr'd at a great cost by that great favourite of late dayes, Robert Dudley,
Earle of Leicester; the private plain retiring chamber wherein our renowned queen, of
ever famous memory, alwayes made choise to repose her selfe."

matcht in England; itt haith 37 statues of brasse about itt of his owne relations as mourners, besides an intermixture of angells.[a] But for the curiositie of thesse tombes, Guy of Warwick's sword, his helmet, his cliffe where after his adventures he turned hermit, where is his chappell and picture cutt in stone, beinge to much for our small treatis, I shall refer you to Mr. Rawdon's journall, who haith made a large discription of itt. This towne is about the center or middle of England.[b]

Munday, the 10th July, they went to a towne called Limington, three miles from Warwicke, where they see a well, out of which springeth salt water, which they tasted, and found as salt as sea water, for all itt is soe farr from the sea.[c] Att this towne the tow Mr. Rawdon's parted, the one for his howse att Hodsden, and the other, with his sarvant, backe for Warwicke in prosecution of his entended journie, where he staied till

Tusday, the 11th July; he went from thence to a merket towne called Aulter[d] wher they baited, and from thence to the cittie of Worster where they lodged that night. Worster is an antient cittie, close to which runneth the river Severne, by which itt is served with all comodities from Bristoll; itt was walled about, but the rebells puld them downe for thir loyallitie to thir kinge. Thir buildings are hansome, soe are thir streets, the people courteous and affable; itt haith a very faire cathedrall of greate length, built by

---

[a] For an admirable account of this "most sumptuous work of art," see Description of the Church of St. Mary, Warwick, and of the Beauchamp Chapel. By John Gough Nichols, F.S.A. 4to. London, p. 14.

[b] Camden thought that Warwick was the Præsidium of the Romans, "as the site itself, in the very navel and mids almost of the whole province, doth imply." (Britannia. p. 563.)

[c] Nearly a century later this now fashionable watering-place was but little noted for the medicinal properties of its spring. "Leamington rises up about a stone throw from the river Leam in Warwickshire. It's very clear, purges and vomits strongly, being drunk by rustics from two quarts to three. It's noted for curing sore legs, breakings out, and mangey dogs. It tastes brackish. Dr. Guidot put abundance of nitre in it formerly, but, by some malevolent aspect of the planets, it's now all turned to marine salt, or a common weak brine spring." (History of Mineral Waters. By Thomas Short, M.D. 4to. Sheffield, 1740, p. 87.)   [d] Alcester.

Sexwulph, Bishop of the Mercians, in the yeare 680,[a] and in the yeare 1041 the cittic was sett on fire by Harde Canutus, the Dane, who slew the cittizens, every mother's son, except some few that saved them selves in a little iland compasd about with the river; the church was likewisse set on fire, but repaired by Wolstan bishop thirof anno 1090. In this church licth entombed Kinge John in his princely robes, in whitt marble cut out to the life; and the monument of Arthur Prince of Wales, son to Kinge Henry the 8th, in a tombe of blacke jett,[b] in a little chappell which is called Prince Arthur's chappell. Nere to this church was a castell, which by fire, none knowinge from whence, was consumed in the yeare 1113. This cittic in the civill broiles of Kinge Stephen was twice fired and re-paired againe.

Thursday, the 13th July, they went from Worster to a towne called Kedermaister, a greate merket towne where are store of stuffes made;[c] here they baited, and from thence went to Bridgnorth where they lodged that night; this was a stronge towne, and att the Norman Conquest posessed by Welshmen. Itt was first built by Æthelfleda, a lady of the Mercians, and afterwards Robart de Belesme walled itt about, who was then Earle of Shrewsbury; itt was fortefied with this wall, a ditch, a stately castle, and the river Severne, to which this carle, to much trustinge, rebelled against his soveraigne Kinge Henry the First, as did likewisse Roger Mortimer against Kinge Henry the Seacond, which the said kinge besieging, an arrow was leveld att him, and had bene shot thirwith quite thorow the

[a] "But the fame and reputation that it [Worcester] now hath, ariseth from the in-habitants, who are many in number, courteous, and wealthy by the trade of clothing, but most of all from the bishop's see which Sexwulph, bishop of the Mercians, erected there in the yere of Christ 680." (Britannia, p. 576.)

[b] "In a chapell is a monument of that noble Prince Arthur, eldest son to K. Hen. VIII., of blacke marble and jet." (Norwich Tourists in 1634.)

[c] A traveller in the former half of the eighteenth century says of Kidderminster, "it is very considerable for its woollen trade, particularly the weaving of what they call lindsey-woolsey, in which the inhabitants are almost wholly employed." The manufacture of carpets was of later introduction.

bodie, had not one Sir Hubert Syncler, a trustie sarvant of the king's, percievinge itt, stept betwixt the kinge and itt, soe receved his death's wound and saved the king's life. This towne was fired by thesse late unhappie warrs, and the castell demolisht downe to the grownde.[a]

Fryday, the 14th July, they went from thence to the Grange to see his freind and fellow traveler, Mr. John Fowler; but, beinge nott att home, he went from thence to Shrewsbury, a pleasant place, situated uppon a hill about which runneth the river Severne in manner of a horse shoe, and if itt were nott for one bitt of land itt might be accounted for an iland. As itt is naturally fortefied, soe is itt likewisse by art, beinge strongly walled about, and on that bit of land afore mentioned is a stronge castell built by Roger of Mountgomery, to whome Kinge William the Conquerour gave itt; here they see then 13 peces of ordnance mounted, the then governour beinge my Lord Newport.[b] The buildings of this towne are very good, the streets large and comely, a place of greate trade with the Welsh,[c] and a greate collonie in time of the Romanes; itt haith a faire free schoole of which thir are fowr maisters, and thir are some times six hundred schollers, and a hansome library thirunto belonginge;[d] itt haith fowr parish churches within the walls, and one

---

[a] Bridgenorth was almost destroyed by fire in its defence against Sir Lewis Kirke, an officer in the Parliamentarian army. (Defoe's Tour.)

[b] Francis, Viscount Newport, appointed governor of Shrewsbury Castle soon after the Restoration.

[c] "About 700,000 yards of Welsh webhs, a coarse kind of woollen cloth, are brought here annually to the Thursday market, and bought up and dressed, that is, the wool is raised on one side by a set of people called Shearmen. At this time only forty are employed, but in the time of Queen Elizabeth the trade was so great that not fewer than 600 maintained themselves by this occupation." (Pennant's Tour in Wales, 1778.)

[d] Camden speaks of Shrewsbury "as a faire and goodly citie well frequented and traded, full of good merchandize, and, by reason of the citizens' painful diligence with cloth making and traffic with Welshmen, rich and wealthy." He remarks that "in the school at Shrewsbury, there were more scholars than in any one school throughout all England." (Britannia, p. 596.)

without the walls, and a faire stone buildinge which they call thir corne merket.

Saturday, the 15th, they went to a towne about 5 miles from thence, called Pitchford, of a well in a private man's yarde thir, out of which commeth perfect pitch. Thir is in this well fowr little hooles about halfe a yard diep, out of which comes little lumps of pitch, but that which is att the tope of the well is softish and swimes uppon the water like tarr, but beinge skimd togeather, itt incorporates and is kneed togeather like soft wax, and becomes hard. Of this pitch they brought some home with them, which the inhabitants say is more medcinall then other pitch. In the Holy land there are some springes that cast up a bitumus stuffe like this.[a] From hence they returned backe to Shrewsbury, where they staid till

Munday, the 17th July, att which time they went for West Chester, and by the way, in Denbieshire, they baited att a place called Rixsome, a goodly merket towne[b] where they speake booth English and Welsh; itt haith a faire church of free stone, and a faire steeple neatly wrought with curious workmanship.[c]

From hence they went to West Chester, where they lodged that night; this is an old fashiond cittie built with sheds, that you may

---

[a] "Pitchford, a little village which our ancestors (for that they knew not pitch from bitumen) so called of a fountaine of bitumen there in a private man's yard, upon which riseth and swimmeth a kind of liquid bitumen daily, skumme it off never so diligently, even as it doth in the lake Asphaltites in Jewrie, in a standing water about Samosata, and in a spring by Agrigentum in Sicilie." (Britannia, p. 592.)

[b] "Trim Wricksam towne, a pearle of Denbighshiere." (Churchyard's Worthines of Wales, 1587.)

[c]
But speake of church and steeple as I ought,
    My pen too base so fayre a worke to touch:
Within and out, they are so finely wrought,
    I cannot praise the workmanship too much.
But buylt of late not eight score yeeres agoe,
Not of long tyme, the date thereof doth shoe;
No common worke, but sure a worke most fine,
As thongh they had bin wrought by power divine.
                                        Ibid.

goe most part of the cittie without beinge wett;[a] but itt hides the
beautie of the howses and shops, soe, except you goe into thosse
walkes, you hardly see aney shops, and thosse soe darke and dull,
that they are nott worth the seeinge. The river Dee runs closse by
the walls, under a faire stone bridge of eight arches; a little below
itt is a castle, rounde in forme, but much gon to decay, yet is kept
by soldiers; and some roumes thir are where the courts pallatine and
the assises are kept, and the sword of Hugh Lupus, the first Earle
of Chester, or rather the sword of William the Conquerour given to
the said Earle when he made him Earle of Chester, is kept. This
Chester was a garrison or collonie of the Romanes, and in time of
Vespasian the Emperour, Jullius Agricola was governour thirof; itt
haith 4 gates opninge to the 4 winds,[b] and 3 posternes. From the
castell to St. John's church, which standeth likewisse uppon the
river, was Kinge Edgar rowed in a barge by seven kinges, he holdinge the helme him selfe as thir supreame and governour.

On the north side of the cittie is the minster built by Earle
Leofricke and didicated to Saint Werburga the virgin, and afterwards
sumptuously repaired by Hugh Lupus. Itt is but an ordnary
cathedrall; itt is said Henry the 4th, Emperour of Germany, lieth
buried here. This cittie haith bene counted the key into Ireland, but
now the enterance is almost chookt up with sand;[c] itt haith 8 parish
churches, and is governed by a maior and aldermen.

Tusday, the 18th July, they went to Flint, the shire towne of
Flintshire, but as pore a one as may be, the most of the howses
beinge thatcht; nere to itt is the castle decayed, the walls to the sea
only standinge; here itt was where Richard the Seacond was be-

---

[a] "The houses are very faire built, and along the chiefe streets are galleries or walking
places; they call them rowes, having shops on both sides, through which a man may walke
dry from one end unto the other." (Britannia, p. 605.)

[b] The east gate (Pennant says) continued till of late years; it was of Roman architecture,
and consisted of two arches formed of vast stones. (Tour in Wales, 1778.)

[c] In 1732 the river Dee was so choked up that vessels of burden could not come within
some miles of it, and an Act of Parliament was passed to render it navigable.

trayed [a] and delivered into the hands of Henry, Duke of Hereford, afterwards Kinge Henry the 4th; from thence he was carried to London and deposed, and from thence sent to Pumfrait Castle and thir murdered.

From thence they went to Saint Winifrid's well, or holly well, as many call itt; a place much frequented in former times by pilgrims in devotion to Saint Winifrid virgin, who was thir ravished by a tyrant, and severall mirackles done by hir after hir head was cutt of.[b] Out of this well cometh a forcible springe of water with soe much violence, like the boilinge of a greate chaldron of water, and is of that force that itt drives a mill closse by, and makes a small rivelett as itt goeth a longe; in the bottome are white stones speckled with red spotts,[c] which they say was the blood of Saint Winifred. About the well groweth a mosse of a very sweet smell, of which they gathered some and brought with them.[d] Itt is a place very convenient for bathinge, haveing iron barrs to hold by, which otherwayes the force of the streame would throw some downe. Over the well thir standeth a chappell of free stone curiously wrought, to which ajoyneth a little church, which now serveth for people to undresse themselves, and to putt on a shifte when they goe into the

[a]
> Go to Flint Castle; there I'll pine away;
> A king, woe's slave, shall kingly woe obey.
>
> Richard II. act 3, s. 2.

[b] The legend is, that Gwen-vrewi, or Winifred, a female saint of the seventh century, had her head struck off by a chieftain named Caradog, whilst she was escaping from his unchaste embraces; and that on the spot where the head fell a spring of water immediately gushed forth.

[c]
> "But stained red
> Still are the stones, where ravisht was her bed
> From off her bodye, in a fountaine cleere,
> Which at this cruell deede did first apeere."

Iter Lancastrense. A poem written A.D. 1636, by the Rev. Richard James, B.D.

[d] Camden mentions "the moss there growing of a most sweet and pleasant smell." (Brit. p. 680.) But Pennant remarks that some eminent botanists of his acquaintance have reduced the sweet moss and the bloody stains to mere vegetable productions, far from being peculiar to this fountain. The first is *jungermannia asplenioides*. The second is *byssus jolithus* (Linn.), likewise odoriferous, which adheres to stones in form of fine velvet.

well;[a] and to have a fire and to be rubd when they come out againe.
Here they found store of ladies, whosse good company oblidged Mr.
Rawdon to goe in and bathe him selfe, though the water was as cold
as ice. Thir they found a greate number of beggers, men, woemen,
and children, some lame, some blind, which saide they came to be
cured, though itt was thought thir chiefe designe was to beg, beinge
thir is abundance of gentry that doth resort thether every summer.
The towne haith good accomodation of good victualls and good ,
wine, with good ale and beere.

From thence, after dinner, they went to Hardinge Castell,[b] the
only castle in repaire standinge in this country; itt belongd to the
Earle of Derbie, but Sarjant Glin[c] begd itt of the Parloment and
preserved itt, in time of the warrs, he beinge then Lord Chiefe
Justice. From thence they went to Chester that night, where they
supt with Mr. Barington and his lady, in whosse company, Wedensday the 19th July, they went to Holt Castell in Denbieshire,
which belonged to Sir William Stanley, Chamberlaine to Kinge
Henry the 7th, to whom he did good service att the battaile att
Bosworth against Kinge Richard the Third, but, presuminge to much

[a]   "They builde a structure, chappell, cloysters, rounde
Aboute the well; to put off clothes they founde
A joining roome: in seventh Harrye's time,
And in Queen Mary's, with such toys they chime
Much people in with coyne to buye no health,
But to encrease their Greenfield Abbye's wealth;
The smocks which now for bathing we doe hire,
Were then belike theis monks' rent and desire."
                              Iter Lancastrense.
The monks of the neighbouring abbey of Greenfield, or Basingwerke, had the charge of
Saint Winifred's well.

[b] Hawarden, commonly called Harden Castle, originally the seat of the Barons de
Mount-hault. It was afterwards transferred to the Stauleys, Earls of Derby, and continued
in that family till the execution of the gallant James, Earl of Derby, in 1651.

[c] Serjeant Glynne was made Chief Justice of England in 1655, and died in 1666.
His son, Sir William Glynne, who was created a baronet in 1661, completed the dis-
mantling of the castle which had been ordered by the parliament, but this was not done
until after his father's death. (Pennant's Tour.)

CAMD. SOC.   Z

uppon his services, incenced the Kinge, and soe lost his heade,[a] and
of this castell thir is only the walls standinge.[b]

From thence they went to one Mr. Wright's, where they lodgd
that night and were very nobly entertaind. Thursday, Mr. Rawdon
and his man went from thence backe againe to Shrewsbury, where
they lodgd that night.

Fryday, the 21th, they went from thence to Ludlow, where they
rested that night. This Ludlow is a small towne wald about, standinge uppon a hill, uppon the upper part of which standeth a faire
castell built by Roger of Montgomery; afterwards itt belonged to
the Mortimers, and now to the Kinge: from hence you have a gallant prospect, vewinge all the country about.[c] This castell escaped

---

[a] " Forgetting that sovereignes must not be beholding to subjects, howsoever subjects
fancy their owne good services." (Brit. p. 677.)

[b] In December, 1646, the parliament ordered that Holt, Flint, Harding, Rotheland,
and Ruthen Castles should be slighted. (Whitelock. p. 231.)

[c]

        The town doth stand most part upon a hill,
           Built well and fayre, with streates both large and wide;
        The houses such, where straungers lodge at will,
           As long as there the counsell lists abide.
        Both fine and cleane the streates are all throughout,
           With condits cleere and wholesome water springs:
        And who that lists to walk the towne about,
           Shall find therein some rare and pleasant things:
        But chiefly there the ayre so sweete you have,
        As in no place ye can no better crave.

        The castle now I mynd here to set out,
           It stands right well and pleasant to the vewe,
        With sweete prospect, yea all the field about,
           An aunciente seate, yet many buildings newe
        Lord Presdent made, to give it greater fame:
           But, if I must discourse of things as true,
       There are great works, that now doth beare no name,
           Which were of old, and yet may pleasure you
        To see the same; for, loe, in elders' daies
        Was much bestow'd, that now is much to praise.
                    Churchyard's Worthines of Wales.

the fury of the late times; itt is of a greate circumpherance, haith a faire hall, and a greate dininge rome over itt, and many convenient lodgins where the Lord President of the Marches of Walles and his lady and children were lodgd. Within this castell are kept the courtes of justice for the said Marches, establisht by Henry the 7th, who sent his eldest son, Prince Arthur, to keepe his court thir, who died thir in a small roome called to this day Prince Arthur's chamber; also the 4 judges of the councill have thir lodgings here, and they and the president dine togeether, thir charges beinge borne by the kinge; they have thir thir cooke, and all thir nescesary attendants,[a] and keepe 4 termes every yeare, where all law suites are determined; they have within the said castell a prison, a bowlinge greene, a tenis court, and stable roome for above 100 horses, and quantitie of armes. This is a very pleasant towne, and by itt, close under the castell, runs the river Corve.

From hence, Saturday the 22th, they went to the cittie of Hereford: this is a fine towne, built in the Saxon's time, as itt is thought, by Kinge Edward the elder; by itt runneth the river Wie. This place came to be in greate creditt by the buriall of Saint Etheldred,[b] Kinge of the East Angles, murdred att Sutton by the treachery of Queen Edred, wife to Offa, Kinge of the Mercians, he comminge a suter to hir daughter. In honor of him was built the cathedrall by Milfrid, a pettie kinge of that cuntry. The towne is walled about, haith 6 gates, and 15 watch towers: the Normans built here a very stronge castell, which was distroyed in thesse last warrs.

Munday, the 24th July, they went from hence to the cittie of Gloscester; in this cittie, the Welshmen say, Kinge Aviragus was buried, who raigned about the time our Saviour suffered; also that Lucius the first Christian kinge was here buried. Here is a faire cathedrall in which lieth, in a faire tombe, Kinge Edward the Sea-

---

[a] The Lord President of the Marches had an allowance to live in great state and grandeur and had a numerous household to attend him and the rest of his officers of the court. (Hist. of Ludlow and the Lords Marchers. 8vo. London, 1841, p. 16.)

[b] Ethelbert.

cond in his kingly robes; he was murderd att Barkly Castle about
16 miles from thence; also Robart Curthose, sonne to William the
Conquerour, who haith his figure cut out to the life in Irish oke,
which lieth within an iron grate in the middle of the chancell; this
man was Duke of Normandy and heire to the Crowne of England
after William Rufus, but by his yonger brother, Henry the First, he
had his eies putt out, and was kept prisner in Cardiffe Castle in
Wales 26 yeares till he died. In this cathedrall are severall monuments of greate personages; in this cathedrall are 12 chappells dedicated to the 12 Apostles, and one fairer then the rest which they
call our Ladies Chappell; in itt is a wisperinge place made in an arch
with curious art, where att a little hole you may heare what is said
to you 24 yeards of, though spooke never soe softly.[a] This cittie is
thought to have bene built by the Romans and was a Roman collony,
and here was a faire castle built in the Conquerour's time, but is now
gon to ruine; here was founded by Osorick, Kinge of Northumberland, a nunnery of which Keneburge, Eadburge, and Eve, queenes,
were abbesses succesively. Itt haith faire streets, and standes soe that
itt is dry almost all winter.

From hence, July the 25th, they went to Barkly, a market towne,
famous for a stronge castle thir, and the lordes thirof, who have
bene persons of eminent note by the name of Lord Barklies. Itt is
now made a convenient dwellinge howse by the now Lord Barkley;[b]
in a tower of this castle they see tow little roomes where Kinge
Edward the Seacond was kept prisner and murderd.

From hence, Wedensday the 26th, they went to Thornebury,
where is to be seene the ruine of a stately castle which Edward Duke
of Buckingham was a buildinge about the yeare 1511,[c] when by the

---

[a] "But a thing most admirable is that strange and unparalleled whispering place of
24 yards circular passage above the high altar, next to the Lady-chappell, the relation
whereof I leave to such as have beene (like us) both spectators and auditors of that miraculous worke and artificiall devise." (Norwich Tourists at Gloucester in 1634.)

[b] George Lord Berkley, advanced to the dignity of Earl of Berkley by King Charles II.

[c] "There we saw a ruinated stately large old castle, where, over the gate-house, now the
chiefe habitable place thereof, is engraven in free-stone letters thus:—The Castle Gate at

instigation of Cardinall Wolsie he was, by command of Kinge Henry
the 8th, beheaded,[a] which made the Emperour Charles the 5th, when
he hearde of itt, to say that a butcher's dog had kild the fairest
bucke in England. Thir is a greate part of the walls and some
chimnie peces of the castle standinge, which shewes the noblenesse
of the fabricke. From hence they went for Bristow. Of Barkley
Castle and this castle thir is a large discription in Mr. Rawdon's
journall, as also of an ungodly trick put uppon the poore nuns thir,
by Godwine, Earle of Kent, whom God punisht by an unfortunate
end accordinge to his deserts.[b] He haith likewisse made a large
discription of Bristoll, of which I shall only give you a tuch. This
is a cittie well populated, of greate trade, haith a cathedrall, but I
thinke the meanest in England;[c] they have convenient havens for
ships; they imitate London very much in thir hospitall boyes in blew
coates, which waites uppon the maior to church, thir leveries in thir
companies, and severall other thinges; itt haith itts exchange, where
are severall brasse pillars about an elle high for peopell to leane
uppon, and to talke, tell mony, signe anie writinges, or the like. In
this cittie are many proper men, but very few handsome woemen,
and most of them ill breed, beinge generally men and woemen very
proud, nott affable to strangers, but rather much admiringe them
selves, soe that an ordnary fellow that is but a freeman of Bristoll,
he concicts himselfe to be as grave as a senator of Rome, and very
sparinge of his hatt, in soe much that thir preachers haith told them
of itt in the pulpitt. They use in the cittie most sleds to cary thir
goods, and the drivers such rude people, that they will have thir
horses uppon a strangers backe before they be awarr.[d] Here was

Thornberry was begun 5th Hen. 7 by Edward, Duke of Buckingham, Earl of Hereford,
Stafford, and Northampton." (Norwich Tourists in 1634)

[a] The Duke of Buckingham was beheaded on Tower Hill on the 17th May, 1521.

[b] The story is told at length by Camden. (Brit. p. 362.)

[c] Bristol cathedral is among the smallest in England, but it has a certain singularity in
its interior construction that produces considerable beauty and picturesque effect.

[d] Mr. Rawdon's account of the people of Bristol in 1665 accords with the experience
of a tourist half a century later :—" The greatest inconveniences of Bristol are its situation,

a castle built large and stronge by Robert Earle of Gloscester, basse
son of Kinge Henry the First, but in thesse late warrs demolisht [a]
and made dwellinge howses of. As you goe downe the river Avon,
a mile from the towne is a well coverd every tyde with salt water,
yett the water is very fresh; itt is called the hott well, and is constantly as warme as bloode; itt haith severall medcinall virtues.
Above itt are some rockes of redish earth and stones which they call
St. Vincent's rocke, where within the earth, about 8 inches deepe,
are found thosse stones they call Bristoll diamonds, which are very
bright, and naturally poynted with squares, as if they were cutt on
purposse.[b] On the other side of the river is an extreordnary cold
springe, where the ships water for thir voyages; three miles below
the river, att a small towne called the Pill, rideth the greate ships.
The river is very windinge, havinge high hills with trees of each side,
very pleasant to behold, and a man would wonder how the river
found his passage amongst soe many high rockes.[c] They have uppon
one of thir gates the pictur of Brenus and Belinus who they would
fancie to be founders of thir cittie,[d] but by the best writers itt began

its narrow streets, and the narrowness of its river: and we might mention also another
narrow, that is, the minds of the generality of its people, for the merchants of Bristol,
though very rich, are not like the merchants of London. The latter may be said to vie
with the princes of the earth; whereas the former, being raised by good fortune and prizes
taken in the wars, from masters of ships and blunt tars, have imbibed the manners of
these rough gentlemen so strongly that they transmit it to their descendants, only with a
little more of the sordid than is generally to be found among British sailors." (Defoe's
Tour.)

[a] The castle was demolished in 1656 by order of the parliament, and now scarcely a
vestige remains.

[b] Saint Vincent's rock "is so full of diamants that a man may fill whole strikes or
bushels of them. These are not so much set by, because they be so plenteous. For in
bright and transparent colour they match the Indian, if they pass them not." (Brit.
p. 239.)

[c] "But what appeared most stupendous to me was the rock of Saint Vincent, the
precipice whereof is equal to anything of that nature I have seen in the most confragose
cataracts of the Alps, the river gliding between them at an extraordinary depth."
(Evelyn's Diary in 1654.)

[d] "It has always been the common tradition of Bristol, that it was built by Brennus

to pecpe out a little before William the Conquerour. They have one church, called Ratliffe Church, of neat worke, which excells the cathedrall, and was built by one William Cannings, a rich marchant, who was five times maior of Bristoll; he built another church at Westbury, tow miles from thence, did furnish itt with cannons, and taikinge orders was dean thirof him selfe.[a] He maintaind for the space of 8 yeares 800 handicraft men, besides carpinters and masons, and maintaind 2470 ton of shippinge for Kinge Edward the 4th:[b] with which I will taike leave of Bristoll. But here, by reason of the greate sicknesse in London,[c] Mr. Rawdon staid in this country nere five monthes, travelinge from one place to another; and Thursday, the 15th August, he went to the cittie of Wells, which is a prettie towne, haith a fine cathedrall,[d] the frontispiece of which is the best in England, boinge bewtified with many statues of kings and saints

and Belinus, the two kings whose figures sit in state on the south front of Saint John's Tower." (Seyer's Hist. of Bristol, vol. i. p. 55.)

[a] " Dominus Wilelmus Canynges, ditissimus et sapientissimus mercator villæ Bristolliæ, decanus ecclesiæ Westbery, obiit 17 die Novembris anno Christi 1474, et exaltus fuit in ordine presbiteratus 7 annis, et quinquies major dictæ villæ fuit electus pro republica dictæ villæ." (Itiner. Willelmi de Worcestre, ed. 1778 p. 83.)

[b] " Per octo annos exhibuit 800 homines in navibus occupatos, et habuit operarios et carpentarios, masons, &c. omni die 100 homines."——" Item ultra ista Edwardus rex quartus habuit de dicto Wilelmo iij. milia marcarum pro pace sua habenda." (Ibid. p. 99.)

[c] " In 1664, 65, 66, London was most grievously visited with the pestilence, the contagion whereof spread as far as Bristol." (Seyer, vol. ii. p. 513.)

[d] Camden's discriminating taste and just appreciation of the works of medieval art are nowhere more conspicuous than when he speaks of the magnificent church of Saint Mary Redcliffe and the exquisite statuary of the cathedral of Wells. Of the former he says: " But the most beautiful of all the parish churches is S. Maries of Radcliffe without the walls; so large withall—so finely and curiously wrought, with an arched roofe over head of stone, artificially embowed,—that all the parish churches in England which hitherto I have seen, in my judgment, it surpasseth many degrees." (Britannia, p. 237.) He thus expresses his admiration of Wells:—" The church itself all thorowout is verie beautifull, but the frontispiece thereof, in the west end, is a most excellent and goodly peece of worke indeede, for it ariseth up still from the foot to the top, all of imagerie in curious and antike wise, wrought of stone carved and embowed right artificially; and the cloisters adjoyning very faire and spacious." (Ibid. p. 255.)

in full proportion, intermixt here and thir with lesse imagery; and
in the midst of all, the statue of our Saviour and his 12 apostles. Itt
haith a convenient chapter howse, and a place where all the singinge
men dewell togeather called the vicars closse, with a private way
into the church; thir is likewisse a howse for the singinge boyes and
thir maister, and a faire pallace for the bishop, inclosed about with
the river, which lookes like a stronge castle, and very pleasant itt is
to behold; and within the said pallace are convenient gardens and
orchards. Thir is faire howses nere the church for the dean and
prebends, with thir gardens, and all thinges convenient, of all which
Mr. Rawdon haith in his journall given a large discription.

Wednesday, 16th August, they went from thence to Glastenbury,
formerly an iland compasd about with the sea, called Avilon.
Josephe of Aramathea, that buried our Saviour, was by the malice
of the Jewes put into a boote (with Lazarus whom our Saviour
raised from death, Mary Magdelen, Martha, and some others) without
ruther, saile, oares, or anie other tacklinge, and soe left to the
mercie of the mercilesse waves, but, beinge by God's providence
protected, they saifly arived att Marcellias in France, where Martha
founded the first religious howse of nuns, and Josephe with eleven
more came here into England, landed att Avilon, now Glastenbury,
about the 31th yeare after our Saviour's pashion. They have a
tradition that Joseph, havinge a thorne-sticke in his hand, stucke itt
thir in the earth, which grew to be a tree which budded, leaved, and
blosomd, every Christmasse day in the morninge, till thesse late times
that the ungodly soldiers cutt itt downe; the place was wald about,
but now nothinge to be scene but the stumpe. Here Joseph
founded a chappell the walls of which is yet standinge, a curious
pece of worke; also the walls of the abey and abey church are yett
standinge, which moves compasion in the beholders to see soe gallant
a fabricke distroyed; the abott's kitchinge, beinge built 8 square all
of free-stone, and coverd with slate stones, is yet entire, havinge in
itt 4 large chimnies, from whence the bowells of the poore were
every day refresht. This was the first seminary of the Christian

religion in England, called by some the fountaine, the mother, the nursery, and buriall place of saints; here Josephe, havinge lived 45 yeares, was buried, and afterwards Kinge Arthur was here buried. This abbey, by the charitie of severall princes and well disposed people, sweld soe big that itt lookt more like a cittie then an abbey, beinge a mile in compasse, wald about with free stone, the walls beinge nere 8 yards high, part of which is yett standinge. Saint Patrick, the apostle of the Irish, was bred here:[a] but for this, and other curiosities thirunto belonginge, I shall refer you to Mr. Rawdon's journal, who haith writ att large thirof.

Thursday, 17th August, they went to see one of the wonders of England called Ouky hole, a vast caverne in the earth, the entrance beinge about a yard square; each carried a candle in thir hands, and for feare of damps Mr. Rawdon causd the guide to cary a candle lighted in a lanthorne.[b] In this journie of Wells, Glastenbury, and Ouky hole, Mr. Rawdon was accompanied with his cossens Mr. Henry Crew and his lady, one of Sir Marmaduke Rawdon's daughters, and by Mrs. Katherin Bowyer the yonger, one of Sir Marmaduke's grandaughters. The first place they came to, thir was a rocke shind like diamonds; from thence they went to a place, some times asendinge, some times desendinge, as high as a church, which they called the hall;[c] then by slippery watry wayes they went to another roome full of dry sand which they called the dancinge roome, where

---

[a] Mr. Rawdon repeats without scruple the fabulous and romantic stories connected with Glastonbury, which were invented by some of the early monkish chroniclers. He probably derived them from Fuller's Church History, which was published in 1655. But the quaint historian betrays less credulity. "We dare not (he says) wholly deny the substance of the story, though the leaven of monkery hath much swoln and puff'd up the circumstance thereof."

[b] This remarkable cavern of the Mendips was explored by William of Worcestre, the eminent topographer of the fifteenth century. His description varies little from that of Mr. Rawdon. "Woky-hole per dimidium milliaria a Wellys infra parochiam est quidam introitus strictus; populi portant, anglice, *shevys de reede segge* ad luminandam aulam." (Itin. p. 288.)

[c] "Est ita largus sicut Westminstre-halle, et ibi pendent pinnacula in *le voult* archuata mirabiliter de petris; et *le enterclose* per quam vadit a porta ad aulam est longitudinis

a dozen cupple might well dance; from thence they went to another greate cave called the kitchin;[a] here was a table of a rocke and scates to sitt downe, which they called the gyant's table, and a faire cesterne of cleere rocke water, above tow yardes longe, and about a yard brood; here they dranke a health in a good bottle of old sherry to all thir freinds in the other world. From thence they went to a place called the seller; soe farr they went up and downe, some times in dry, some times in slipery places, that the ladies were almost weary and desird to see the light and sun againe. This cave is 168 yardes within' the earth; over itt growes a grove of trees, and under itt runs a greate springe of water, which when they came out, havinge bene soe longe in darknesse, was very pleasant to behold; the springe of water is soe greate that itt drives a cupple of mills.[b] A thinge of greate admiration itt is, and soe I leave itt.

Fryday, the 18th August, they went to Mendip hills to see the lead mines thir; they see them wind up thir ore out of the pitts, wash itt, breake itt, melt itt in a furnasse, and after in sand cast itt into barrs or pigs. From thence they went to Bristoll to Mr. Crewe's, where Mr. Rawdon kept his head quarters till

Thursday, the 31th August, he went to a towne called Alderley, 16 miles from Bristoll, uppon whosse hills are found cockles, oysters, and periwinkles, petrieficd;[c] whether they were ever cockles and oysters, or only the sports of nature, none knowes.

---

secundum estimacionem dimidium furlong : Et est quædam lata aqua inter *le tresance* et aulam per spacium v. *steppys* lapidum, et quod *steppys* est latitudinis circa iv. pedes, et si homo vadit extra *lez steppys* cadit in aquam circumquaque per profunditatem circa quinque vel sex pedum." (Ibid. p. 288.)

[a] The kitchen described by Mr. Rawdon was, in the fifteenth century, called a parlour : "Et tunc officium *de le parlour* sequitur, et est rotunda domus de magnis rupibus constructa latitudinis circa xx. gressuum. Et in boriali parte dictæ parluræ est quoddam anglice dictum unus *kolie hole*, et in dicto puteo bene desuper archuata plena aquæ pulcherrimæ, et nemo sit dicere quam profundius fuerit'dicta aqua." (Ibid. p. 289.)

[b] " Item de dicto Wokynghole fluit magnum gurgitum, et currit usque *le meere* juxta Glasconiam per spacium duorum miliariorum; et octo molendina in . . . . . . villa." (Ibid.)

[c] In the upper lias shale and marlstone at Alderley the fossil *conchifera* are numerous and of many genera, as Ostrea, Pecten, Lima, Cardium, &c.

From hence they went 15 miles from thence to Bathe, a prettie
little cittie, wald about with free stone very neatly, and haith
severall carved images in the walls and inscriptions of much antiquitie; itt is seated in a bottome environed with hills round about
itt.   Whithin the cittie springeth the hott bathes, waters very
medcinable for curinge of people that are num, stiffe, or lame in thir
joynts; itt haith the King's Bathe, the Queene's Bathe, the Crosse
Bathe now called Queene Katherin's Bathe;[a] thir is also the Lepers'
Bathe, where none but lepers and ulsurous people wash them selves,
and closse by itt is an hospitall for lepers built by one Reginald, a
Lumbard, the 19th Bishop of Bathe.   Itts cathedrall church is none
of the bigest; where itt stands was formerly a temple dedicated to
the goddesse Minerva, and she, as they say, was patronesse of thesse
waters; others say that Bleydon, the Magisian Kinge of the Brittons,
found them out; others say that the hott quallitie they have was
given them by Saint David about the yeare 620.   This cittie defended itt selfe bravely against the Saxons.   By itt runs the river
Avon downe to Bristoll.   Mr. Rawdon, in his journall, haith given
a large discription of itt, to which I shall refer you.

Saturday, 2th September, they went from Bathe to Bristoll, where
they staid till Tusday the 19th September, att which time they
went to a place called Alst, ten miles from Bristoll, where they
staid till sun sett before they could passe the Severne, which is about
tow miles from shore to shore, and some times very rough; but the
bootes are stout bold bootes, and soe seldome miscarry.[b]   The towne

---

[a] The Norwich travellers give an amusing account of what they saw here in 1634.
"Upon our arrival we took a preparative to fit our jumbled weary corps to enter and take
refreshment in those admired, unparralelled, medicinable, sulphurous hot bathes.   There
met wee all kinde of persons, of all shapes and formes, of all degrees, of all countryes, and
of all diseases, of both sexes: for to see young and old, rich and poor, blind and lame,
diseased and sound, English and French, men and women, boyes and girles, one with
another peepe up in their caps and appeare so nakedly and fearfully in their uncouth
naked postures, would a little astonish and put one in mind of the Resurrection."

[b] The old passage across the Severn from Aust to Beachley, near the mouth of the Wye,
is said to have been ugly, dangerous, and very inconvenient.   "When we came to Aust,

on the other side the river is called Beatsla,[a] or rather beate and slay, being the place where the Danes were totally beate and routed out of thesse countries; here they lodgd that night, and were very well treated with all thinges nescesary. From hence they went to another towne called Buttington,[b] where the Danes made a stop or stay, fortefyinge themselves till they were beate out from thence and kild att Beatsla; the trenches of thir fortifications are yet to be seene.[c] This is part of the forest of Dane, and in this little village is made 3000 ton of syder and perry every yeare. From hence they rid alonge the forest till they came to a place called the Chace, where the Danes were first chasd before they fortified them selves att Buttington; from hence they went downe a very steepe hill and narow stony way worse then the stonie pasages of the mountaines of Teneriffe, which they call Croud stone hill, which stone is in the middle of the desent, and is growne a proverbe in that country; if they will expresse to make a man feele sorrow, they will say they will make them see Croud stone hill.[d] Att the bottome of this hill runs the river Wie, which parts England and Wales, over which they ferried into Monmouthshire, where they see the ruins of

the hither side of the passage, the sea was so broad, the fame of the bore of the tide so formidable, the wind also made the water so rough, and, which was worse, the boats to carry over man and horse appeared so very mean, so that, in short, none of us cared to venture; but came back, and resolved to keep on the road to Gloucester." (Defoe's Tour.)

[a] Beachley, antiently Betteslegh.

[b] Buttington, antiently Buttingdune on Severn, is the disputed site of the settlement of Danish pirates, which received Hastings in his flight from Alfred in 894-5. (Archæ-ologia, vol. xxix. p. 18.)

[c] The lines supposed by some persons to be Offa's Dyke are by others thought to be merely an entrenchment thrown up in the civil war of the seventeenth century. (Ibid. p. 17.)

[d] "Hard by Buttington, Corndon Hill mounted up to a very great height, in the top whereof are placed certain stones in a round circle like a coronet, whence it taketh that name, in memorial, it should seem, of some victory." (Britannia, p. 650.) The stone in the middle of the descent, spoken of by Mr. Rawdon, was probably the detached mass of Offa's Dyke which is called Buttington Tump.

Tenterne Abbey, a famous place in former times, as by the walls
and some arches yet standinge appeares. Itt had severall lordships
belonginge to itt, and is exclently well wooded, but now the Marques
of Worster and the Earle of Pembrooke enjoy thosse lordships. Here
they see the iron mills and the iron furnases, where the iron is first
melted before itt is beate by the mills into barrs, which mills worke
by the force of water. About halfe a mile higher up on the side of
the hill are severall mills driven by water, wher they draw wire
from little iron barrs into severall sieses, a curiositie worth the seeinge.

The fire of the furnace where they melt the iron is soe greate,
that, lookinge into the hole where the nosell of the bellowes are, itt
lookes like the sun in a hott day att noone.[a]

From hence they went to Monmouth, the chiefe towne of that
shire, famous for the birth of that Mars of England and scourge of
France, Kinge Henry the 5th, who was borne in the midle tower
of that castle. This castle and towne is scated twixt the tow rivers
of Munnow and Wie; the castle is gone to decay, thir beinge only
the gate howse, the hall, and part of the middle tower where Kinge
Henry was borne, with the walls, standinge; all the rest time haith
consumed. This towne is likewisse famous for Jefery ap Arthur,[b]

---

[a] The seclusion of the lovely valley of the Wye at Tintern is yet disturbed by the iron
foundries mentioned in the journal. Their appearance is thus described by a modern
tourist:—" Immediately opposite to the room in which we were lodged stands a large iron
forge, one amongst the many that are constantly worked night and day in the valley of
Tintern. The wide folding doors were thrown open, and the interior part of the edifice,
with its huge apparatus and the operations carried on in it, were displayed to our view.
Here the dingy beings who melt the ore and prepare it for the bar-hammer were seen
busied in their horrible employment, all the detail of which we clearly discovered by the
assistance of the strong illumination cast on them from the flaming furnaces." (Warner's
Walk through Wales. 8vo. 1798, p. 232.)

[b] " Monmouth glorieth also that Geffrey ap Arthur or Arthurius, Bishop of Asaph, the
compiler of the British history, was borne and bred there; a man, to say the truth, well
skilled in antiquities, but, as it seemeth, not of antique credit, so many toies and tales hee
everywhere enterlaceth out of his owne braine, as hee was charged while hee lived, in so
much as now hee is ranged among those writers whom the Roman church hath censured
to be forbidden." (Britannia, p. 632.)

commonly called Jefery of Munmouth, the greate antiquary, who writ the History of Greate Brittaine, and was a fryer in a monastery of this towne. Here one Mr. Joanes,[a] a haberdasher of London, built a faire hospitall of bricke for 10 pore men and ten pore woemen, allowinge them every Christmasse a new gowne and halfe a crowne every Saturday, which is thir market day, to buy victualls with; he founded a free schoole, allowinge the chiefe maister 100 markes a yeare, the usher 30 powndes per anum, with faire howses and gardens: in the market place he founded a towne house, and left meanes for the repairinge of itt. Here they lodgd that night, and were well entertained att the signe of the King's Armes.

Thursday, the 21th, they went from thence to Ragland, where they see the ruines of that noble howse and castle belonginge to the Marquese of Worster, called Ragland Castell,[b] famous for its loyaltie to the kinge in the late warrs. Itt had a stately parke about itt, but they have hardly left one tree standinge; itt would move compasion to see soe stately a thinge, which was the ornament of the whole

---

[a] William Jones, born at Monmouth, was forced to quit his country for not being able to pay ten groats. Coming to London he became first a porter and then a factor; and, going over to Hamburgh, had such a vent for Welsh cottons that he gained a very considerable estate in a short time. He founded a fair school at Monmouth, besides a stately almshouse for twenty poor people, each of them having two rooms and a garden and half a crown a week; all which he left to the oversight of the company of haberdashers of London. (Williams's Hist. of Monmouthshire. App. p. 79.) This munificent citizen died about the year 1614, having left for these and other charitable uses 18,000l. (Herbert's Hist. of the London Livery Companies, vol. ii. p. 543.)

[b] The brave and loyal Marquess of Worcester was one of the last to yield to the power of the parliamentary forces. In a letter from General Fairfax to his father, dated Ragland, August 10, 1646, he says, "I am now before Ragland. It is very strong, well manned, and victualled. I have offered the soldiers honourable conditions, and that the Earl should remain quiet in his house till the parliament be pleased to dispose otherwise of him." (Memorials of the Civil War, vol. i. p. 316.) A week afterwards the garrison surrendered, and Fairfax took possession of the castle. Ragland Castle had three parks of considerable extent, and the fertility of the surrounding estate enabled its possessor to support in hospitable security a garrison of 800 men. Soon after its surrender the castle was demolished and the timber in the three parks cut down. (Williams's Monmouthshire, p. 311.)

country, should be distroyed by thosse of itts owne nation.   Here they see that greate Welsh hill called Skerry vaur.[a]

From Ragland they went to a towne called Usk, uppon the river Usk, where is an old castle belonginge to my Lord of Pembroke, an antient towne knowne by the Romanes; here they dind, and after dinner went by another old castell, called Langippe, where one Sir Trevour Williams lives.[b]

From thence they went to Carrlegion, now commonly called Carlin, formerly a greate cittie, by report 7 miles longe, where Kinge Arthur kept his court;[c] here was a collonie of Romanes, as by severall coynes, inscriptions, and alters, dayly found, doth appeare; here lay the seacond Romane Legion, called Augusta, and by the Romans was wald about with bricke, and had in itt, built by the Romans, goodly pallaces after the magnificence of Rome, with theaters, hott bathes, and temples wald about; here vaults and water pipes are dayly found under ground.[d]   Here Amphibolus, the in-

---

[a]   Skyrryd-vawr, the highest and most picturesque hill in Monmouthshire.

[b]   "Upon a mighty hill
                    Langibby stands, a castle once of state."

Sir Trevor Williams, a zealous supporter of Charles I., was made a baronet in 1642. He afterwards professed to change his politics, and in 1646 was appointed commander-in-chief of the parliament's forces in Monmouthshire.   The sincerity of his conversion to the popular cause is questionable.   Cromwell, when besieging Pembroke in June, 1648, writes, "Wee have plaine discoveries that Sir Trevor Williams of Langebie, about two miles from Usko, was very deepe in the plott of betrayinge Chepstowe Castle, soe that wee are out of doubt of his guiltynesse thereof.   I doe hereby authorize you to seize him. Hee is a man (as I am informed) full of craft and subtiltye, very bold and resolute; hath a house at Langebie well stored with armes and very strong."   He subsequently compounded as a delinquent.   (Cromwell's Letters and Speeches, by Carlyle, vol. ii. p. 8.)

[c]   King Arthur sure was crowned there,
                    It was his royall seate;
                    And in this town did sceptre beare
                          With pompe and honor greate.
                                        Worthines of Wales.

[d]   There are such vautes and hollow caves,
                    Such walls and condits deepe;
                    Made all like pypes of earthen pots,
                          Wherein a child may creepe.
                                        Ibid.

structor of our protomartir Saint Albon, was borne, and here thosse
tow famous Christian Brittains, Julius and Aaron, suffred martir-
dome and were buried here; here lived 200 phylosophers a little
before the comminge of the Saxons, who, beinge skilfull in astronomie
and all other arts, did dilligently observe the course and motion of
the starrs; to this place itt was where in Kinge Arthur's time the
Romanes sent thir ambasadors to him.[a] This cittie was of good
strength in Kinge Henry the 2d time; but of this goodly cittie,
temples, pallaces, and theaters, thir is scarce aney thinge to be seene
but peces of walls and rubish, and is now a verie pore market towne.

From hence they to a towne uppon Usk which rose out of the
ruines of Carlin,[b] where to passe into the towne over the river Usk
is a longe wodden bridge of a vast hight, and betwixt the bridge and
the towne is a castell which belonges to the Earle of Pembrooke,
over against which, with a kind of shove netts, they catch greate
store of salmon: here they might have had a salmon of a yarde longe
for three shillinges.[c]

Over against this towne comes downe, noe man knowes from
whence, quantitie of coales which the pore people att a low water
gather and make a livelyhood thir on, some famelies getting twentie
powndes a yeare by itt. In thesse late warrs one Plumley, one of
Cromewell's sequestrators, put an imposition that the pore people

---

[a] Britannia, p. 636. For a copious and highly interesting description of the numerous
remains of Roman art and luxury discovered at Caerleon, see Isca Silurum, or An
Illustrated Catalogue of the Museum of Antiquities at Caerleon: by John Edward
Lee, F.S.A. 1842.

[b] Out of the ruins of Caerleon, a little beneath, at the mouth of the Uske, grew up
Newport.

[c]   A thing to note when sammon failes in Wye,
   And season there goes out, as order is,
Then still of course in Oske doth sammons lye,
   And of good fish in Oske you shall not miss.
And this seems straunge, as doth through Wales appeare,
In some one place are sammons all the yeere;
So fresh, so sweete, so red, so crimp with all,
That man might say, loe, sammon here at call.
                       Worthines of Wales.

that gatherd them should pay soo much a load; soc itt pleasd God that in three yeares togeather none came downe, till they tooke of that imposition.[a]

This towne haith bene formerly wald about, as appeares by the gates and some part of the walls yet standinge, and would make a fine towne for trade, boinge ships of a thousand ton may ride closse to the towne; here they lodgd that night, att the signe of the Ship, and were well entertaind with good beere, good wine, and all thinges nescessary. This river of Newport runs downe and dischargeth itt selfe in the Severne.

Fryday, the 22th September, they went from Newport, which is uppon Usk in Monmouthshire, and went towards Cardigan[b] in Glamorganshire. In the way they past by Tredegar, a seate belonginge to Squier Morgan, which they were told was the chiefe Morgan in Wales: he haith thir a stately parke throw which runns the river Ebwith, soe that in his parke he haith salmon trouts and what fish that river doth afford; he haith likewisse severall fish ponds with what fish will live in pondes; he haith a warren nere his parke, and in his parke a thousand head of deere, besides wild goates and other cattle about his grownds; soe that I thinke he is prettie well provided towards house keepinge.[c]

---

[a] "As marvellous circumstances are blended with all British blessings, depositions of coal, by the tide, in the mud and sands of the shore, are here ascribed to a faculty bestowed on the river by Providence; and the people generally testify, that, while the lord of the manor imposed a duty, the river ceased to deposit coal, and when the duty was withdrawn it exercised its usual bounty. The poor collect the coal and apply it to their use, and the probable opinion is that a vein of it hath been laid open by the river." (Williams's Monmouthshire, p. 147.)

[b] Cardiff is evidently meant.

[c] "Tredegar, among the present residences of Monmouthshire, is an object of the first consideration. Everything within and around it has an air of magnificence that pervades the house, the parks, the river, the woods, and even the vast level moor on the edge of which it is placed.—The parks are of great extent." (Williams's Monmouthshire, p. 280.) Tredegar is now a title in the British peerage, worthily conferred upon the present representative of the house of Morgan, one of the most antient and important in the principality.

From hence they past to Cardiffe, which is the chiefest towne in all South Wales; itt was taken from Rhese the prince thir of, by Robert Fitz Hamon, a Norman lord, who fortefied this towne with a stronge wall and castle, in which castle, as we have allredie said, Robart Curthose, Duke of Normandie and heire to the crowne of England, had his eies burnt out by command of Kinge Henry the First, his yonger brother.

From Cardiffe they went to Landaffe, a pore towne, but a bishop's see, of which was then Bishop Dr. Hugh Floyd;[a] itt haith a cathedrall, but a pore one, and the revenews as poore, beinge not much above 400lb. per anum; but, Mr. Rawdon saith in his journall, if itt had but the tenth part of the revenews which he haith seene by a catalogue of landes that did belonge unto itt, itt would be the richest church in Europe. Some thinke this church was first built by Kinge Lucius about the yeare of Christ 180, and one Dubritius the first bishop thirof; the seacond was Saint Tellian, to whom itt is consecrated;[b] they have an antient record called Saint Tellian's booke,[c] which gives a large accompt of thesse thinges. In the church are severall monuments of the Mathiews, who have, nere the church, an old castle which in former times haith bene of good strength, as appeares by the walls and some part of itt yet standinge; from hence runs a small river called Taffe to Cardiffe Castle. Cardiffe Castle now belongs to the Earle of Pembroke, who was then repairinge of itt to make a dwellinge howse thirof. From Landaffe they returned backe to Newport, where they lodged that night.

Saturday, the 23th September, they went from Newport to a place called Caerwent in Monmouth shire; this was a very antient cittie, and in time of the Romans was called Venta Sylurum, or the chiefe

---

[a] Dr. Hugh Lloyd, elected Bishop of Llandaff 17th Oct. 1660, died 7th June, 1667.

[b] "The present fabric was built by Bishop Urban in 1120, and dedicated to St. Peter, St. Dubricius, St. Teileian, and St. Oudoceus. It hath of late fallen into great decay." (Tanner's Notitia, ed. 1744, p. 712.)

[c] Liber Landavensis—Llyfr Teilo—or the Antient Register of the Cathedral Church of Llandaff. (See Hardy's Catalogue. British History, vol. i. part ii. p. 830.) In this MS. all the lands that were given to the church of Llandaff were registered.

cittie of the Sylures; here Kinge Caradoc, a Welsh prince, sent
Saint Tachaius, from a desert where he lived a hermit, to governe
this place, beinge then an academie of learninge, and a place of
devine worship. Either warrs, or the devouringe sithe of time, haith
soe mowed itt downe, that thir is only some part of the wall and
some peces of gates remaininge.[a]

As they rid alonge, they past by an old castle belonginge to that
old soldier Collonell Morgan, who lived in the time of Kinge James
and the late Kinge Charles, and from thence they went to a towne
called Chepstow, where they dind.

This Chepstow is a market towne, partly wald about, haith a
stronge castell situated uppon a rocke, much like the maiden castle
att Edenborow; this towne rise out of the ruines of Caerwent. They
came thir on thir market day, where they had abundance of hogs
and sowes with thir litters of pigs, to be sold in pens, as they sell
sheepe in Smithfield. The castle belongs now to the Marques of
Worster, and haith in itt about 50 pece of ordnance; itt is thought
this castle haith remaind ever since Julius Ceasar's time.[b] Here is a
woden bridge suported with manie greate timbers 12 fathomes high,
for thus high, some springe tydes, doth the river Wie, which runs
under itt, flow, which is held to be the greatest flood in England.[c]
This bridge, the halfe of itt is in Monmouthshire, the other Gloster-
shire. From hence they went to Beatsly, where they past the Severne,

[a] Caradoc ap Ynyr, King of Gwent, in the early part of the sixth century gave certain
lands at Caerwent to his wife's nephew Saint Tathay, who here founded a school and
monastery. The identity of Caerwent, or Caergwent, with the Venta Silurum of Antonine,
has been uniformly admitted. See the interesting account of the Excavations within the
Walls of Caerwent in the summer of 1855. By Octavius Morgan, Esq. M.P. F.S.A.
Archæologia, vol. xxxvi. p. 418.

[b] A stratum of Roman bricks may be observed in the walls, which is probably the
authority for attributing the structure to Julius Cæsar. A better opinion is that these
bricks were brought from the ruins of Caerwent. (Williams's Monmouthshire, p. 141.)

[c] The bridge over the Usk at Newport and that over the Wye at Chepstow rested on
wooden piles, and were floored with loose boards; the tides, rising sometimes to the height
of sixty feet, would otherwise have blown up the bridges. (Ibid. p. 147.) In 1826 the
old bridge at Chepstow gave place to a substantial iron one.

beinge about tow miles over, and soe went that night to Bristoll, where they staid till

Munday, the 2th October, att which time, in company of Mr. Henry Crew, his lady, Mrs. Katherin Bowyer the yonger, Madam Vaughan, and some other ladies, they went in the king's wherry, up the river of Avon, to a greate towne called Cansham,[a] of Keyna, a holly British lady that lived thir; here they dind, and viewinge the towne, Mr. Rawdon see a snakes stone, which was formd in some stone quaries thir about, of 21 inches over,[b] which knowinge to be a greate rarietie and the like nott to be seene in England or scarce in the world, he bought itt, and sent itt up into the south for a present to his kinsman Mr. Marmaduke Rawdon, who haith itt in his garden att Hodsden, and haith bene seene by some virtuosi and greate travelours, with much admiration. After dinner, towards the eveninge, they returned to Bristoll, where they staid till Thursday the 30th November.

Duringe his stay att Bristoll he was feasted by the sheriffe, the colector of the coustome howse, and by severall gentlemen and marchants of quallitie, and att his goinge away invited them all to the Starr taverne, and gave them his farwell; and, as I have said, Thursday, the 30th November, accompanied with his kinsman Mr. Henry Crew, who was then survayour of his majesties coustome howse, and his sarvant Will. Coates, he came from Bristoll to Tedbury,[c] where they dind, and from thence to Cerencister, where they lodgd that night. This is a very antient towne, and was called by the Romans Durocornovium,[d] of the river runninge by itt, then called Corinus, now Churne; here are many times Roman coyns,

　[a] Keynsham, halfway between Bristol and Bath.

　[b] The blue lias at Keynsham was quarried in Leland's time. He says, "there be stones figured like serpents wound into circles found in the quarries of stone about Cainsham." (Itin. vol. viii. fo. 76.) The ammonites are numerous, and some are of vast size, but few so large as twenty-one inches across. (Phillips's Guide to Geology, p. 150.)

　[c] Tetbury.

　[d] Corinium Dobunorum. See Illustrations of the Remains of Roman Art in Cirencester, the site of Antient Corinium. By Buckman and Newmarch. London, 1850.

chequerd pavement, and engraven marble stones, found. This cittie, as by the walls apeares, was about tow miles about, and is that cittie which histories mention beinge besieged, and not to be taiken, the enemie caught some of the towne sparows, and tyinge fire to thir legs att midnight, let them fly, soe they flyinge to the thatcht howses where they usd to roust, sett the towne on fire, and soe itt was forced to yield, and of this itt was called Passerum urbem.[a] Itt had an abbey and a castle, but booth distroyed.

Fryday, the 1th December, Mr. Rawdon and his kinsman Mr. Henry Crow (whosse guest he had bene, and very civilly entertaind duringe his stay att Bristoll) parted, the one for Bristoll, and Mr. Rawdon and his man for the south; and from thence he went to Faringdon, where he dined and went to the church to see the chappell and vault where the pretious reliques of his ever honored unckle, Sir Marmaduke Rawdon, were interd;[b] here that brave soul spent his last breath in the service of his prince Kinge Charles the First, beinge governour of that towne when he died, as appeares more att large in the history of his life which is writ in the history of his fameley. Here he mett with an old woman, who had bene nurse to Sir Marmaduke in his sicknesse, to know some perticulers concerninge his end, by whom he was informd that itt was soe full of pious ejaculations to God, with penitent prayers for the pardon of his sins, with honest and earnest exortations to his soldiers to continew thir loyaltie in the defence of the place, and things of this nature such as might be expected from soe good a christian towards God, and from soe loyall a subject to his kinge.

Here he dind, and after dinner went to Abington that night, where he sent for one John Provote, a Frenchman, who had bene an old sarvant and caterar to Sir Marmaduke for many yeares: that

[a] Britannia, p. 366.

[b] The only memorial of Sir Marmaduke Rawdon now remaining in the church of Faringdon is a large blue slab placed on the floor of the middle aisle near the pulpit, half covered by one of the pews, which conceals great part of the inscription. The parish-register is imperfect at this period, and contains no entry of his burial.

night he invited the said John Provote, his wife, and all his sons
and daughters, maried and unmaried, to sup with him, in whose
company he was much pleasd that night.

In this towne was a famous abbey built by Cissa, Kinge of the
West Saxons, from which itt is thought itt tooke itts name, and soe
called Abbeys towne.[a] Itt haith in times past, and att present, much
enricht itt selfe by maultinge, which with the convenience of the
river Isis that runs by the towne they send to London in barges.

Saturday, the 2th December, they went from Abington to a
market towne called Tame, a place affordinge exclent ale, where
they dind, and from thence they went to Alsbury, where they lodgd
that night. This Alsbury is an antient towne, and was wonne from
the Brittans by Cuthwolfe, the Saxon, in the yeare 572, and was
famous for Saint Edith's taikinge the veile of a nun here, who was
much renowned for hir holy life and mirackles; this towne is the
place where the assises are kept for Buckingham shire. In William
the Conquerour's time itt was a manner belongd to the kinge, and
certaine lands were given by the kinge, with this condition, that the
possessor thirof should find litter for the king's bed when he came
thether;[b] soe itt seemes in thosse dayes kings did not scorne to have
fresh straw put under thir beds.

Munday, the 4th December, they went from Alsbury to Bark-
hamsteed; this is a longe market towne and antient. Here some noble
men, by perswasion of the abbat of Saint Albans, were resolved to
shake of the yoake of William the Conquerour; but he appeared
amongst them, and tooke an oath to maintaine all the English lawes,
and soe they parted; which oath he never kept, but turnd most of
the nobles thir met out of thir possessions, and gave this towne to
his halfe brother Robart, Earle of Cornewall, who fortefied the
castle in which Richard, Earle of Cornewell and Kinge of the

---

[a] Abbandune, i.e. Abbatis oppidum. (Lel. Itin. vol. vii. fo. 64.)

[b] "And certaine yard-lands were heere given by the king, with this condition, that the
possesor or holder thereof (marke yee nice and dainty ones) should find litter for the king's
bed when the king came thither." (Britannia, p. 395.)

Romans, died; afterwards Kinge Edward the Third gave itt to his eldest son Edward the Blacke Prince.[a] Thir is little in this towne worth the seeinge, only the free schoole and the ruines of the castle.

From hence they went to Saint Alban's, where they dind; this is a greate towne which rose out of the ruins of old Verulam about a mile from thence; the grownd worke of walls are yet in some parts to be seene, and seeme to have bene about 2 miles in compasse. Here itt was where our protomartir Saint Alban lived, and in the persecution of Dioclesian, for beinge a Christian, was beheaded nere the place where the greate church of Saint Alban's stands; and he that beheaded him, his eies imediatly fell out of his heade, and he likewisse became a Christian, and, I thinke, was likewisse martired. This cittie of Verulam, beinge by warrs sore wasted and distroyed, Offa, the greate Kinge of the Mercians, built over against itt a goodly large church and monastery in the memory of Saint Alban, and the said Offa and other succedinge kings endowed itt with large possesions, and got large previlidges from the Pope for itt, that itt should be subject to no bishop nor archbishop, and that the abbatt should have jurisdiction over all the priests that lived uppon thir possesions; and Pope Hadrian, our countryman, who was borne in Hartfordshire nott far from Saint Alban's, ordered that, as Saint Alban was the first martir of England, soe the abbat thirof should have the superioritie of place of all the other abatts of England.[b]

This towne by the devotion of pilgrims grew greate and rich, and the church, now remaininge the parish church, is a faire church, as longe as most of our cathedralls, but goeth to decay, the townes men, to whom now itt belongeth, beinge soe pore they are hardly able to keepe itt in repaire. 1665.

This eaveninge they went from Saint Alban's to Hatfield, where

---

[a] Britannia, p. 414. For an excellent contribution to county history, see Two Lectures on the History and Antiquities of Berkhamsted. By John Wolstenholme Cobb, M.A. 8vo. London. Nichols and Sons, 1855.

[b] Britannia, pp. 410—419.

they lodged that night; this place is called Bishops Hatfield, and thir was given by Kinge Edgar here certaine landes to the Bishop of Ely, and formerly itt did belonge to the said bishop;[a] John Morton, Bishop of Ely, reedified itt. Here the kinge had a faire howse, but now the howse and lands thir about belongs to my Lord of Salisbury, whosse father repaired, or rather new built, the howse in a most sumptuous manner.

The 5th of December, beinge Tusday, they came before dinner to Hodsden, where, though the towne had bene greatly vizited with the plague, they found all thir relations, God be praised, in good health. Beinge within a stones cast of home, Mr. Rawdon's curious nag, on which he had made all this journie, fell stark-lame, but was afterwards recovered, and was all the mischance they had in all this journie, which hapned in a good place, beinge here Mr. Rawdon gave a conclusion, and, I concieve, harty thankes to God Allmightie, who in soo dangerous a time, the sicknesse beinge spred allmost over all the kingdome, had brought him saife home. Here at Hodsden he staid for the most part, some times divertinge him selfe att London, till the monthe of June, 1666, att which time his kinsman and quondam fellow travelor Mr. William Bowyer was recomended to a younge gentlewoman for a wife, of the fameley of the Wingates of Harlington in Bedfordshire;[b] soe he desiered Mr. Rawdon to accompany him to give him his advice and opinion thirin, which he was very willinge to doe, and did assist him till the busnesse was concluded, to the satisfaction of him and all his relations, and shortly after they were maried. After this he staid most part att Hodsden till the yeare 1667, duringe which time he compild a briefe history of the foundations of all the cathedrall churches in England and Wales, and some other peces of antiquitie.

1666.

---

[a] Britannia, p. 407.

[b] The Wingates had a seat at Harlington, now belonging to their representative John Wingate Jennings, esquire. Edmund Wingate, the arithmetician, who was sent to France to teach the Princess Henrietta Maria (afterwards queen of Charles I.) English, was of this family. It is said that he resided at Harlington during the Protectorate, and died in 1656. (Lysons's Bedfordshire, p. 90.)

Beinge att London, he had thesse English and Lattin verses presented to him by a yonge scholler to whome he had done some small civillities: vizt.

Sir,—As the bright sun's rayes all eies invite,
   Soe haith your virtue drawne my muse to write.
   Your fame cann't be exprest, that spacious field
   Requiers more store then my pore barne can yield.
   If I had Ovid, Virgil, Homer's straine,
   Then would I not your fame to speake disdaine.
   If all my wit I exercisse, my verse
   Is to too meane your praises to rehearse.
   Itt is for happie witts to sound thy facts,
   Whosse loftie straine can reach your glorious acts.
   This I attempted once but sone recoild,
   Seeinge thy fame was by my scriblinge spoild.
   For though perhaps I find my lighter veine
   To smaler toyes and triffles may attaine,
   And though a sculler on the Theames may enter,
   Yet he may not on the maine sea adventure;
   Soe dare not I, because I cannot tell
   Enough, your worth, your fame, who all excell.
   Late, Sir, may you unto the heavens assend,
   Much time on earth with your deere freinds to spend.
   Not that we envy heaven you, but wee
   Are loth to part with your good company.
   Into your virtues, Sir, when I doe dive,
   What doe I els but for to number strive
   The drops of water in the sea, yea, more,
   To tell the sands that lie uppon the shore.
   Verses, 'tis true, make not your fame the greater,
   To which naught can be ad, to make itt better.
   Pray now, most worthy Sir, be not offended,
   Though in a low stile your facts are comended;
   And seeinge your worth my verse cannot aspire,
   I will continew still itt to admire.—Yours, R. T.

The Lattin verses are thesse:

O reverende vir, insignis tua fama manebit
   Dum tenerum pennis aera pulsat avis,

Splendida dum rutilo fulgebunt sydera cœlo
  Aut rigidam terram dum premit acer hiems
Dum folia arbor habet, dum latas littus arenas,
  Dumque fretum pisces, ovaque piscis habet,
Dumque cadunt altis majores montibus umbræ,
  Fertilis æquoreas dum vehit amnis aquas,
Agricola obliquo terram dum findit aratro,
  Aut dum frugiferos sol recreabit agros,
Præbet odoriferos flores dum fertilis hortus,
  Sedula dum ex violis mellificabit apis,
Præbet ovis pavidus dum mollia vellera tergo,
  Dum Nereus placat murmura sæva maris,
Œolides saxum dum volvit Sysiphus ingens,
  Dum Phœbus mundo lumina clara dabit,
Tantalus a labris dum poma fugacia captat,
  Dum nova crescendo cornua luna geret,
Dum quoque sævus hiems crudelia frigora habebit,
  Et dum præterient æquora magna rates.
O decus et patriæ per te florentis imago!
  O vir! non ipso ævi patet orbe minor,
Nunc precor ut possis cœlos ascendere tarde,
  Et Lachesis vitæ fila beata dabit
Nestoris innumeros utinam transcenderis annos
  Succedant animo prospera cuncta tuo
Nunquam Lœtheis candentur facta sub undis,
  Nec Stigias unquam nomen adibit aquas.
Virtutes mentis magnas si dicere conor,
  Icariæ numerum dicere conor aquæ.
Sed donec spiro, aut lumen vitale videbo
  Serviet officio spiritus iste tuo.—R. T.

Translated by Mr. D. Williams.

Sir,—Your renowne and fame shall never die
  Soe longe as through the aire the bird doth fly.
  Itt shall remaine as longe as starrs doe shine,
  Whilst that the earth for winter doth repine,
  Whilst sands the shoares and leaves the trees array,
  Whilst seas breed fish, and fishes eggs doe lay,
  Whilst higher mountaines shade the field soe wide,
  And pleasant rivers to the sea doe glide;

Whilst th'husbandman doth plow the firtile field,
And Phebus to this earth his light doth yield ;
Whilst that from gardens pleasant flowers springe,
And to thir hive pure hony bees doe bringe ;
Whilst sheepe soft woole doe yield, and of the seas
Whilst Nereus doth the raginge noise appease ;
Whilst Sysiphus that stone doth rowle in vaine,
And whilst the world doth the sun's light obtaine ;
Whilst raginge stormes the winter fierce doth blow,
And crosse the seas the nimble ships doe goe.
May you transend in yeares old Nestor's age,
May all thinges happie to your wish engage ;
Your deedes shall not be buried in the waves
Of Stix, or goe to the Lethean graves.
If all the virtues I should strive to place
Within this paper, which your mind doth grace,
I may as well to number strive in vaine
Each severall drop which the sea doth containe.
But, whilst I breathe and here doe dwell on earth,
I allwayes will admire and praise your worthe.

Aboutt the month of Aprill, 1668, ridinge outt to take the ayre one morninge with his cossen Marmaduke Rawdon, some doggs, unhappily, came outt of a howse uppon his horse which was schittish, and causd his horse to fly outt with him, insomuch that hee could nott hold him in, butt hittinge against a post, tumbled downe of his horse, and unfortunately broke his left arme betwixt the elbow and the wrist; which was nott so very well sett as might have bene, and is imadgined that might cause afterwards a greate paine in his stomach, which, a little before hee dyed, hee was much trubled with, by fitts that held him aboutt ¼ of an houre very violently, with cold sweats; in one of which fitts, sittinge in a chaire att his aunt's howse in Hodsden the Lady Rawdon (whome hee dined withall that day, and was very merry att dinner), hee fell in a small slumber and dyed away immediately, beinge the 6th day of February, on Saturday in the eveninge aboutt 5 of the clocke, anno 1668, and was afterwards embalmed in his cossen Rawdon's howse, and buried a fortnight

after in Broxbourne Church, with a blacke marble stone over him,
with his coates of armes and inscription on the stone. Hee left his
cossen Marmaduke Rawdon his executor, and the bulke of his
estate gave away in legasies. The chiefest was 400lb. to inlarge the
markett plase att Yorke, where he was borne: 100lb. to bee employed every Sunday in bread for the pore of Crux Church in Yorke:
100lb. for a pure gold cupp for the Lord Mayor there and his successors to drincke in; 60lb. for a gold chaine for the Lady Mayoresse
and her successors; and the best part of his estate in other legasies
to freinds and poore kindred: and so God have mercy on his soule.

Amen.

Of his Personage and Character.

He was in
hight 5 foot
4 inches.

He was of a meane stature, beinge some thinge lower then the
middle sort of men, but straite and well proportiond to his height;
his visage was rather longe then rownde, his eies gray, his nose
somethinge thicke and bigg, his haire browne and curlinge, his
countenance manly but somethinge sterne, yet sufficiently and full
of pleasant discourse amongst his freinds and relations, to whom he
allwayes had a tender love and fatherly care; his lownesse of stature
was recompenced with extreordnary naturall guifts, his little body
beinge full of vigour and valour and endued to his elder yeares with
the blessinge of a perpetuall health, and greate memorie. In his
affaires, which for severall yeares were many and greate, he was extreordnary active and dilligent, beinge one that did seldome trust to
the benefitt of a latter gaine, but did allwayes endeavour to taike
time by the fore top; and for the greatest part of his life did commonly risse with or before the sunne, booth in England and forraine
parts, which was noe small advantage to his health, and the dispatch
of his affaires; and for the most part in what he undertooke he was
very successfull, and did seldome miscarry in his designes. His
nature was eaqually composd, booth for action abrood and his
studdies att home, and itt is hard to say in which he tooke most
delight, he followinge booth with some earnestnesse.

INDEX.

ERRATA.

Page 75, note c, *for* Leonard *read* Laurence.
Page 126, note, line 7, *for* who *read* whose uncle.

Westminster: Printed by J. B. Nichols and Sons, 25, Parliament Street.

www.ingramcontent.com/pod-product-compliance
Lightning Source LLC
Chambersburg PA
CBHW030815020726
47499CB00006B/1922